Anthony Gilbert and The Murder Room

⟩⟩⟩ This title is part of The Murder Room, our series dedicated to making available out-of-print or hard-to-find titles by classic crime writers.

Crime fiction has always held up a mirror to society. The Victorians were fascinated by sensational murder and the emerging science of detection; now we are obsessed with the forensic detail of violent death. And no other genre has so captivated and enthralled readers.

Vast troves of classic crime writing have for a long time been unavailable to all but the most dedicated frequenters of second-hand bookshops. The advent of digital publishing means that we are now able to bring you the backlists of a huge range of titles by classic and contemporary crime writers, some of which have been out of print for decades.

From the genteel amateur private eyes of the Golden Age and the femmes fatales of pulp fiction, to the morally ambiguous hard-boiled detectives of mid twentieth-century America and their descendants who walk our twenty-first century streets, The Murder Room has it all. **⟩⟩⟩**

The Murder Room
Where Criminal Minds Meet

themurderroom.com

Anthony Gilbert (1899–1973)

Anthony Gilbert was the pen name of Lucy Beatrice Malleson. Born in London, she spent all her life there, and her affection for the city is clear from the strong sense of character and place in evidence in her work. She published 69 crime novels, 51 of which featured her best known character, Arthur Crook, a vulgar London lawyer totally (and deliberately) unlike the aristocratic detectives, such as Lord Peter Wimsey, who dominated the mystery field at the time. She also wrote more than 25 radio plays, which were broadcast in Great Britain and overseas. Her thriller *The Woman in Red* (1941) was broadcast in the United States by CBS and made into a film in 1945 under the title *My Name is Julia Ross*. She was an early member of the British Detection Club, which, along with Dorothy L. Sayers, she prevented from disintegrating during World War II. Malleson published her autobiography, *Three-a-Penny*, in 1940, and wrote numerous short stories, which were published in several anthologies and in such periodicals as *Ellery Queen's Mystery Magazine* and *The Saint*. The short story 'You Can't Hang Twice' received a Queens award in 1946. She never married, and evidence of her feminism is elegantly expressed in much of her work.

By Anthony Gilbert

Scott Egerton series
Tragedy at Freyne (1927)
The Murder of Mrs
  Davenport (1928)
Death at Four Corners (1929)
The Mystery of the Open
  Window (1929)
The Night of the Fog (1930)
The Body on the Beam (1932)
The Long Shadow (1932)
The Musical Comedy
  Crime (1933)
An Old Lady Dies (1934)
The Man Who Was Too
  Clever (1935)

**Mr Crook Murder
  Mystery series**
Murder by Experts (1936)
The Man Who Wasn't
  There (1937)
Murder Has No Tongue (1937)
Treason in My Breast (1938)
The Bell of Death (1939)
Dear Dead Woman (1940)
  aka *Death Takes a Redhead*
The Vanishing Corpse (1941)
  aka *She Vanished in the Dawn*
The Woman in Red (1941)
  aka *The Mystery of the
  Woman in Red*

Death in the Blackout (1942)
  aka *The Case of the Tea-
  Cosy's Aunt*
Something Nasty in the
  Woodshed (1942)
  aka *Mystery in the Woodshed*
The Mouse Who Wouldn't
  Play Ball (1943)
  aka *30 Days to Live*
He Came by Night (1944)
  aka *Death at the Door*
The Scarlet Button (1944)
  aka *Murder Is Cheap*
A Spy for Mr Crook (1944)
The Black Stage (1945)
  aka *Murder Cheats the Bride*
Don't Open the Door (1945)
  aka *Death Lifts the Latch*
Lift Up the Lid (1945)
  aka *The Innocent Bottle*
The Spinster's Secret (1946)
  aka *By Hook or by Crook*
Death in the Wrong Room
  (1947)
Die in the Dark (1947)
  aka *The Missing Widow*
Death Knocks Three Times
  (1949)
Murder Comes Home (1950)
A Nice Cup of Tea (1950)
  aka *The Wrong Body*

Lady-Killer (1951)

Miss Pinnegar Disappears (1952)
aka *A Case for Mr Crook*

Footsteps Behind Me (1953)
aka *Black Death*

Snake in the Grass (1954)
aka *Death Won't Wait*

Is She Dead Too? (1955)
aka *A Question of Murder*

And Death Came Too (1956)

Riddle of a Lady (1956)

Give Death a Name (1957)

Death Against the Clock (1958)

Death Takes a Wife (1959)
aka *Death Casts a Long Shadow*

Third Crime Lucky (1959)
aka *Prelude to Murder*

Out for the Kill (1960)

She Shall Die (1961)
aka *After the Verdict*

Uncertain Death (1961)

No Dust in the Attic (1962)

Ring for a Noose (1963)

The Fingerprint (1964)

The Voice (1964)
aka *Knock, Knock! Who's There?*

Passenger to Nowhere (1965)

The Looking Glass Murder (1966)

The Visitor (1967)

Night Encounter (1968)
aka *Murder Anonymous*

Missing from Her Home (1969)

Death Wears a Mask (1970)
aka *Mr Crook Lifts the Mask*

Murder is a Waiting Game (1972)

Tenant for the Tomb (1971)

A Nice Little Killing (1974)

Standalone Novels

The Case Against Andrew Fane (1931)

Death in Fancy Dress (1933)

The Man in Button Boots (1934)

Courtier to Death (1936)
aka *The Dover Train Mystery*

The Clock in the Hatbox (1939)

Death Wears a Mask

Anthony Gilbert

An Orion book

Copyright © Lucy Beatrice Malleson 1970

The right of Lucy Beatrice Malleson to be identified as the author of this work has been asserted in accordance with the Copyright, Designs and Patents Act 1988.

This edition published by
The Orion Publishing Group Ltd
Orion House
5 Upper St Martin's Lane
London WC2H 9EA

An Hachette UK company
A CIP catalogue record for this book is available from the British Library

ISBN 978 1 4719 1036 4

www.orionbooks.co.uk

CHAPTER I

THE WEATHER that Thursday night was as temperamental
as a prima donna. At one instant the moon shone brilliantly, painting houses and trees with a silver brush, the
next it vanished behind a cloud and passers-by on the far
distant earth were obscured in shadow. There was no wind,
but the forecast said rain to come.

May Forbes, 49, unwed and envying no man, came down
the sixty-two steps from her apartment, a small covered
basket in her hand and two sixpences concealed in her fabric
glove. She turned away from the town and headed in the
direction of a wild piece of land known as Broomstick Common. Rumour said there had once been a coven of witches
there, and even if they'd gone they'd left their cats behind.
Cats of every sort and colour, wild as young tigers, thin as
the proverbial rail. May might have paraphrased Captain
Cuttle—Cats are my passion. One day, when she retired,
she'd have a tiny place of her own, with a handkerchief of
garden. You couldn't keep a cat in a bed-sitter, cooker on
the landing and all sanitary facilities shared with the tenants
on the floor below.

But until that time she was contented with her job at the
Misses Robinsons' Drapery Store in Wells Street, and life
was full of interest. How full it was going to be within
four-and-twenty hours she couldn't guess.

Across the street old Mrs. Politi, the immensely stout,
self-styled widow of a Soho restaurateur, pulled back her
curtain to watch her neighbour go. After Signor Politi
disappeared after the war—the ribald said she'd overlaid
him and he'd got swept away with the rest of the rubbish—
the Council put a compulsory purchase order on the premises, so Mrs. Politi, undeterred by presumed widowhood,

1

adopted an anglicised form of address—she'd been Signora in Soho—took over the lease of an old rag-shop that wasn't much more than a showroom, open to the street with a counter at the back, and filled it with crockery, glass, ornaments, mostly picked up at sales and street markets. Aladdin's cave it was derisively called, but May, defending her friend, reminded detractors that that cave had contained the Magic Lamp.

She and Mrs. Politi met when May bought half-a-dozen cracked saucers at a penny apiece—for her cats, she explained.

"You have cats—here?" Mrs. Politi was horrified.

"On the Common. They live quite wild and of course no one feeds them. They have to scavenge for themselves and there can't be much that would appeal to a cat. They're much more delicate feeders than dogs, so they're mostly half-starved."

"So you feed them?" Mrs. Politi repeated scornfully. "You think they grateful?"

"I don't expect them to be grateful," retorted May, surprised at the suggestion. "And if you think they're fierce, ask yourself what sort of an example the human race has been giving the animal world for the past thirty years."

"So now cats eat off plates, like Christians," jeered the fat old woman, wisely relinquishing the point to May, who was too polite to enquire who else would be likely to want cracked penny saucers and odd ones at that. She was amazed that there should be a market for such trash. Half the goods on show were labelled Cracked or Damaged, even the simpering china shepherdesses were minus hands, and there was a great funeral urn that looked as though a giant had bitten a piece out of the rim.

Mrs. Politi followed her train of thought and was in no whit offended by it.

"Nothing you can't sell if it's cheap enough," she declared. "Like those women pay a pound for a hat started at six pounds, they don't stop to ask when can they wear such a hat, it is a bargain. So—they see a nice bowl—real class—ten shillings. They don't stop to ask, What use to me? A bargain, see?"

"I suppose there are a lot of fools going about," May conceded.

"You one of them," Mrs. Politi retorted. "Toil and moil for those old maids when any of the big shops in the High Street pay you half as much again."

"I'm an old maid myself," said May. "And I couldn't bear to work at one of the big shops, all branches of something bigger still, no—no individuality. With the Miss Robinsons . . ." She paused.

"You someone? Ho, yes. Someone to be trampled on, taken advantage of."

"Miss Alice and Miss Phyllis don't trample. It's like— it's almost like having a family of my own. I haven't anyone, you know, except a niece married in America, and she only sends a card at Christmas. I don't suppose she tells anyone her aunt works in a shop."

"And when the shop close down?" Mrs. Politi had asked that question only to-night, when May looked in on her way back from work in case there were any scraps to go in her cat basket. A frugally-run household of one didn't leave much over, though Miss Phyllis was very good about giving her bits now and again, anything her precious pigeons wouldn't eat. And every evening she stopped at Mr. Liverseed, the fishmonger, to exchange a few coppers for offal, bones and fish-heads and sometimes fish even he wouldn't dare try to sell.

"All this fuss about a lot of blasted cats!" said Mr. Liverseed reprovingly. "And half the people in the world not having enough to eat."

"You convince me that these scraps will go to Biafra if my pussies don't get them," retorted May spiritedly, "and of course I'll waive their claim. But you and I both know they won't. They go into the offal-bucket . . ."

It was no wonder she was an old maid, thought Mr. Liverseed sourly. No man likes a woman who knows all the answers. But, since he liked his coppers as much as Mrs. Politi did, he wrapped up the rather smelly parcel and took his payment.

It was after calling at his shop that May rang Mrs.

3

Politi's bell. To-night Mrs. Politi surprised her by giving her a quite sizeable piece of rabbit. True, the rabbit was a bit "high," but cats who live on commons and haunt rubbish tips can't be choosers, and even human beings sometimes liked their food, game for instance, in a state that May, down to earth as always, frankly considered rotten.

Mrs. Politi asked after Miss Alice, the older of the two sisters, who had recently had a stroke.

"She's getting along quite well," declared May, undaunted. "It was only a little stroke."

"One little stroke followed by one bigger stroke," nodded Mrs. Politi. (When Arthur Crook met her a little later on he said, "There's one won't give even the Angel Gabriel best, and if he knows his onions he won't waste time trying." But at that stage May had never heard of Mr. Crook, and if anyone had told her she was going to meet him that very night she would hardly have believed him.)

"She doesn't step out quite the way she did," May began, and Mrs. Politi said, "That one don't step no further than her coffin one fine day and that soon."

"Miss Phyllis and I manage quite well." May refused to admit that trade was on the decrease, they were still covering expenses, and it's nature for tides to ebb and flow. "And that nephew . . ."

"That nephew!" Mrs. Politi nodded sagely. "He never come in twenty years, why he come now?"

"Because Miss Phyllis wrote to him and told him about her sister. He must have the right family feeling, because he came over from Canada straight away. He'd gone out there about three years ago, after his father died, to make his fortune, he said."

"Maybe he don't find no fortune in Canada." There was no hushing Mrs. Politi's scepticism.

"He must be crazy if he thinks he's going to find it here," retorted candid May. "I don't mean that we don't get on quite comfortably, but then we're three old maids, and what would be sufficient for us would probably seem very short commons to an enterprising young man."

"Why he *never* come *before* he go to Canada?"

"I'm not perfectly sure," May acknowledged, "and naturally I can't ask Miss Phyllis about her family affairs, but I don't think her father approved of Mr. Hardy. I remember her telling me once that she never saw her sister after the marriage—Mr. Hardy had some sort of business in the North . . ."

"The North Pole?" enquired Lilli sarcastically. "Trains run from the North—no?"

"If there'd been trouble at the outset—never darken my doors again, and between you and me, Lilli, old Mr. Robinson sounds exactly the sort of person who would say such a thing—well, there might be some delicacy . . ."

Lilli snorted. It was like hearing a whale turn over in its sleep.

"And I don't think the business can have been very successful," continued May, steadily. "Perhaps that was why Mr. Robinson didn't approve of the match—because why should Jack go out to Canada as soon as his father died? He met another Englishman *en voyage* and they were going to try their luck together. You mustn't think he ignored his aunts," she added, quickly. "He wrote, not very frequently, of course, but birthdays and Christmas, and sometimes picture postcards. Miss Alice loved those, and she's kept them all. After her sight began to get weaker she liked to have the letters read over to her, I'm sure I almost know them by heart, and Linda Myers used to read them to her too, though it can't have been very exciting for a young girl, but though she wasn't very much good in the shop, she was very kind to Miss Alice."

"Ho!" sniffed Mrs. Politi. "Miss Alice make it worth her while."

"You know what they say," declared May, who for all her gentle appearance wasn't easily discouraged, "nothing is for free. And then," she hurried on, "when Miss Alice had her stroke Miss Phyllis wrote to tell Jack, and he came over at once, he said he could leave the business in his friend's hands for a little while. I don't think he meant to be away so long, but Miss Phyllis has come to depend on him—the man of the family—you understand."

"Men!" snorted Lilli.

"And he's given his aunts so much pleasure, he helps with the accounts and sits with Miss Alice, she doesn't come into the shop much any more, and he's taken her out in his jalopy, as he calls it, which is a great treat for her. She always loved her little walks . . ."

Mrs. Politi threw up her hands. "Oh, May, you too simple to live. Young men don't come half over the world because an old lady they wouldn't recognise have a stroke. You think him an eagle, soaring (she rolled her r's in a way that aroused May's admiration) in the blue, so close to Heaven. I tell you, he a vulture. One day soon you find the boards up and you out of work."

"Then Miss Phyllis and I will have to put up a little stall on the pavement, won't we?" said May. "Or we might get a corner in the Market."

Mrs. Politi would have shrugged her shoulders if her neck hadn't been so short her head was sunk between them.

"You go to your cats!" she cried. "They fit company for you. And when they tear you limb from limb, maybe you remember what I say."

May bustled off, a little cottage-loaf of a woman, rosy as an apple—must have been pretty as a girl, Mrs. Politi thought, but May had calmly accepted a difficult, not to say curmudgeonly, male parent as her duty and thought how fortunate she was to have her own home. And after he died and left her with nothing she had fallen on her feet once more and got this job with the Misses Robinson. Like a new home, and in a small shop you soon got acquainted with the regulars. And then she'd always been clever with her hands, she did repairs, lining, lengthening and shortening skirts, according to the fashion, replacing zips, taking in coats when their owners shrank with the years and, where possible, letting them out when the reverse process happened. A full, pleasant life, with Wednesday half-day closing. On Wednesdays she and Mrs. Politi generally went to the local cinema, and afterwards to The Pilgrim's Progress for a drink and so to a trattoria where Mrs. P. talked to the proprietor in his native tongue, and they got special service. Saturday was choir practice for the chapel, and Sunday nights, of course, it was chapel itself. But the other four evenings she trotted along to the Common bringing whatever she'd been able to salvage for her beloved cats.

She stopped at the top of the main road to get the carton of milk—she always brought two sixpences in case the first proved to be a rejected coin, or the machine was out of order and took the money but didn't yield the milk—then she crossed the main street, walked down beyond the library, the chemist, the tobacconist, crossed another road and it was like finding yourself in a different world. For some years now local Councillors had been suggesting the site should be drained and used for building, to be opposed by other Councillors who pointed out that such a course would involve considerable expense, that there was no other place to dispose of moribund cars, that there was a rubbish tip extensively used, and, most of all, that the far end of the site overlooked the canal, which was as neglected as the rest of it. Even lovers and tramps didn't come here much, it was too uncomfortable. The dumped cars had been stripped of everything usable, and no one cared about them any more except some of the local children, and they were never in evidence after dark. Even romantic May didn't pretend she could recognise individual cats. Mostly they were streaks of darkness flying from shadow to shadow. "Probably the rats eat your food," Mrs. Politi had suggested, but May said she'd never seen any rats there. Of course there might be water-rats in the canal, but they were rather pretty things, with blunt noses and rounded furry ears. "You!" cried her friend once, stung to annoyance. "You argue with the Lord God Himself and you see where that get you."

But one cat in particular she had come to know, a little white creature, light as a snowflake and so small she seemed scarcely larger than a kitten, yet this same cat had recently littered and there were five little bunches of fur who would one day, if they were enabled to grow up, join the population on the Common. May was certain that that thin form couldn't possibly provide adequate sustenance for the family, and she had started to bring an extra allowance of milk for the mother, and put down twice as much fish and meat as before. She came very carefully through the bushes, slipped out and set her saucers and vanished again like a shadow. The moon that had hitherto been very bright now moved languidly behind a cloud, but she thought that all to the good. She knew no wild cat would emerge so long as she was in sight, and for her own comfort she must be assured that the provender did go to the little white cat, and not to some fabulous monster envisaged by Mrs. Politi. Scarcely daring to breathe, she waited. And, sure enough, after a minute or two one slender white paw appeared as the little cat fastidiously made her way towards the milk. How gracefully animals move, May reflected. Perhaps it's having four legs all more or less the same length. The cat ate some of the meat, then carefully collected what was left and retreated with it to her lair. May backed cautiously away and round the edge of the tip.

That tip was the source of one of Mrs. Politi's grimmer jokes. Come the Last Trump, it won't be just the sea that gives up its dead, she prophesied. The tips will give some big shocks, too. May tried to forget that as she scurried past, depositing her saucers in accustomed places, but to-night she had, as Crook would have put it, her eyes on sticks looking for a particular cat seen only twice previously, but instantly winning her heart. His appearance—she took for granted it was a male—was undeniably striking. He was black with patches of deep amber; she had gone to the Public Library the following day to consult a book on cats and decided he was a Burmese with just a touch of the tarbrush, which, of course, set him beyond the pale. All the same, his smallness and solitariness haunted her. He might be hunted away by the resident cats or even, if Mrs. Politi were right, be attacked by a rat. Looking for him by the light of the tiny torch she always carried, she progressed farther into the wasteland than she had hitherto done, and was reluctantly about to abandon the search when suddenly, coinciding with the return of the moon, he shot out from a clump of plant known to botanists as Fat Hen and went charging towards the canal. Fencing this canal from the Common was a paling marked in large insolent words— KEEP OUT THIS MEANS YOU. Rumour said there was an unexploded bomb on the tow-path, others that the paling was simply to prevent a large mortality rate among the children who played there. May saw the little cat streak into the bushes, then emerge and vanish through a weak place in the paling. Her first thought was, he probably doesn't know there's a canal there, he could fall in, probably he can't swim, even if he could he might be attacked by water-rats for trespass.

While these crazy thoughts blew like cobwebs through her brain she was herself hurrying along the side of the paling looking for a weak spot. It was asking too much of human nature to expect the children wouldn't have broken through somewhere, and, sure enough, there was a place where the fencing was so dilapidated that even her plump form could squeeze through. The canal looked sinister and deserted in the fading light. It saddened May, who remembered that once canals were part of the lifeline of England, loud with traffic and gay with flags. This canal was more like a graveyard, with nettles growing along the edge. May imagined all kinds of rubbish being shot there, possibly even dead animals. She shivered and turned back towards the gap. It was hopeless to try and catch the kitten. She would put down the saucer and hope it would find it on its return.

She had just squeezed cautiously through the paling when she heard a sound that brought her to an abrupt halt. Someone or something was coming through the wasteland from the direction of the road. She was so accustomed to the notion that no one but herself used this place after dark that she was instantly apprehensive. All Mrs. Politi's warnings rushed through her mind.

"One of these dark nights, May, you wake and find your throat cut and no one more surprised than you," was a familiar one.

The newcomer clearly was not on foot. It was a car that

was nosing its way over the rough ground, bumping from one uneven surface to another. At first she thought it was some owner come to discard a useless model, but a moment later she knew that wasn't so. No driver herself, she yet could tell that this was no wreck approaching her direction in the darkness. Fortunately there was a good deal of wild growth and bushes where she stood and she concealed herself, crouching down, in the hope that she would escape notice. Why should anyone come here on such a night, if it wasn't to discard an aged car? But the site for old cars was some distance away. She knew, of course, that various amorous activities take place in the backs of cars, though it had always seemed to her a most uncomfortable arrangement, but again—why come so far when there was virtually no likelihood of interruption much nearer the road? There was, of course, the possibility that the car's owner had brought rubbish to dispose of in the tip, but her earlier objections held here, too. Nobody bringing something bulky would want to carry it so far when the tip was readily available farther along the upper road.

While she thought all this, her heart racing and pounding, the car came to a standstill a little distance away. The door opened and someone alighted. She dared not put on her little torch for fear of revealing her whereabouts, and common sense told her that no man with honest intentions would be skulking down here at such a time. She found that by parting some of the twigs of her concealing bush she could just make out a shape, a man undoubtedly. She saw him walk round the side of the car and open the boot. Perhaps, she thought in her romantic way, he is a bank robber. Banks were being robbed nearly every day and surely the spoils must be concealed somewhere. She believed that a large part of the train robbery notes were still hidden in some place whose whereabouts the police had not been able to uncover. Or if not bank-notes then jewellery, or rather massive silverware, even crates of furs. It was improbable the police would think of looking here and the children who played on the site didn't come to this part, they frolicked over the skeleton cars and ventured, illeg-

ally, through the palings and along the canal bank. May
was of a law-abiding temperament, she knew it is every
citizen's duty to assist the police in every possible way. All
the same, like most people, she had an illogical disinclina-
tion to tangle with them, even on the right side of the law,
if it could be avoided. She wondered if, while X was digging
a pit to conceal his treasure, she could edge out unheard
and unperceived.

While she was still considering these possibilities the
unknown had extracted a spade from the boot and had
turned on the headlights. It was fortunate for her that she
was outside their aura. The ground under these shrubs and
stunted trees was sandy, which she supposed was why
this place had been chosen. Very cautiously she moved a
few steps. These brought her close to the rear of the car, so
that she caught a glimpse of the contents of the boot.
Something large, ungainly and rolled in a rug had been
thrust therein. Her heart almost stopped beating, then
began again with such violence it seemed to her it must be
audible through the length and breadth of the Common.
Because surely if you were hiding stolen treasure you would
wrap it in a macintosh sheet to preserve it from damage
from damp. A rug suggested hideous possibilities. She
moved away more quickly, and her speed was her un-
doing. She liked to say of herself that she had been born
under a lucky star, but now her luck deserted her. Her
foot caught in a trailing bramble, she slipped, the torch
fell from her hand and as it did so its minute beam
streamed out—like a fallen shooting star, she reflected,
scrabbling quickly, finding it and pressing the button so
that once more darkness reigned. But it was too much even
for an optimist to hope that it had not been noticed. The
sound of the spade delving and flinging the sandy earth
came to a dead stop.

"Who's there?" called a voice. She lay still as death—
an unfortunate comparison really. The man moved a step
or so in her direction.

"Who are you?" the voice demanded.

May remembered a favourite saying of her platitudinous

old dad. *"L'audace, l'audace et toujours l'audace."* Which,
translated into English, meant roughly, "Grasp your nettle
boldly and then you'll rarely find it stings." May thought
that might be true but she had never made the experiment.
Arthur Crook's more down-to-earth version was—Be
bloody, bold and resolute. May could dispense with the
blood, but boldness and resolution were clearly called for
here. She straightened herself, pushed aside the undergrowth and said, "Oh, have you seen a little cat, a Burmese,
at least mostly a Burmese? It came this way and I'm so
afraid it may be lost. But I don't suppose you have seen
it, have you? It's so young and all these wild cats about,
and then the canal . . ."

She caught a fleeting glimpse of the man, he had a black
mask, resembling those worn in harlequinades in her far,
far distant youth, and a balaclava helmet over that.

"You mean you're here on account of a blasted cat?"
The man's voice, which had a muffled quality, was incredulous.

"I didn't mean to come so far," acknowledged May,
boldly standing her ground. "But it ran off, I think it must
have got frightened. There are some wild cats here . . ."
Just in time she bit off a reference to the mother and her
brood, thinking this might be just the kind of man who'd
think it fun to stamp on the heads of a family of new-born
kits. "Well, if you haven't got a garden it's dull for any
animal, kept indoors most of the day." ("The situation
provides the man," had been another of her father's plati-
tudes, and how right dear Father was, as always, May
reflected.) "So whenever it's fine we come down here, it's
the nearest open space and usually I don't let him out of
my sight. But he ran off suddenly and squeezed through
the palings, and I don't like the idea of him so near the
canal, cats can't swim, you know. And the fact is," she
wound up, breathlessly, "I've rather lost my way. We've
never come this far before."

"What way's that?" the man asked.

"Do you know St. Leonard's Road?" It was more than

a mile from her own flat but it isn't only the lady lapwing that can practise deception in the interests of its young.

"You've come a long way," said the man, suspiciously.

"The worst of it is you can't put a cat—a kitten, really —on a lead as you can a dog. Of course, they say they're wonderful at finding their way back—cats, I mean." (Oh Father, help me, she prayed, and she wasn't addressing her Heavenly Father at that.)

"If I do see him," said the man slowly, "I might bring him back for you. What's your number in St. Leonard's Road?"

"Oh, you'd never be able to catch him," said May, quickly. "He's very timid, half-wild really."

"You're not supposed to go through those palings," the man said. There was a thoughtful, even a leisurely note in his voice that froze her blood. (Like Arthur Crook, she found clichés very satisfying.) He seemed to be considering what was the best thing to do with her.

"Naturally I know that," she said quickly, answering his rebuke, "but you can't expect Tom Jones—that's my kitten —to realise that. And he's so young . . ."

"You take my tip," said the man, "you go back to St. Leonard's Road, toot sweet. If the authorities knew you'd been trespassing you could find yourself in a lot of trouble."

"I'm sure you're right," she acknowledged meekly. "I'm sure it's going to pelt and I haven't brought an umbrella."

"What's your name, in case the kitten does surface?" the man demanded.

She made herself sound surprised. "Miss Jones, of course. That's why he's Tom Jones. I live at No. 4. Mind you, I have to be very discreet. My landlady doesn't really allow animals, but with him being so small, and I'm very careful he doesn't harm the furniture or carpets . . ." (If Father had heard her prayer he was playing up like a trump.) "I can't understand that, can you? Not liking animals, I mean, when so often they're nicer than human beings."

"The proper place for animals is a zoo," said the man,

roughly, and she got his underlying meaning at once: The proper place for old gits is the bin. "Now then, missus, you get off home . . ."

"It's Miss Jones," she corrected him. "I work in the Post Office . . ." The lies came falling out of her mouth like water spilling from a tap. And the odd thing was she'd always regarded herself as a very truthful person.

"Can't expect to be very popular then, can you?"

"Oh, people enjoy grumbling, it's called the law of compensation," she said wildly. "Oh dear, this is the strangest conversation I've ever held. It's like talking to a ghost. I can't even see you. I suppose if I keep going I shall eventually come to the road, and of course from there I know my way."

"Luckier than some of us if you do," the man said. He suddenly switched on his torch, keeping the light low, and she stumbled away, hardly able to believe her good fortune. To-morrow would be time enough to wonder if she should say anything to the police. But I don't even know where the place is, she reminded herself. And there was a text in the Bible, "Sufficient unto the day is the evil thereof."

It had been, on the whole, the sort of day you wouldn't want to live through again. It wasn't only this last terrifying encounter. Although she had stood up so bravely to Mrs. Politi, she had known her first real stab of fear long before she set out for the Common. That morning young Mr. Hardy—he was the old ladies' nephew, son of the only Robinson sister who had married—had approached her while Miss Phyllis was searching for a particular kind of vest in the little stockroom to say, "I'm glad to have a chance of a word with you, Miss Forbes. It's my Aunt Alice, I'm very much concerned about her."

She had looked surprised. "You don't have to worry, Mr. Hardy. Miss Phyllis and I . . ."

"That's not quite what I meant. But it must be obvious to you both that she isn't going to be able to carry on here much longer, and when she breaks down—I'm sorry to seem brutal but it's best to be plain—she's going to be a

wholetime job for someone. And that someone will be my
Aunt Phyllis. So—what's going to happen to the shop?
You couldn't carry on single-handed, you know, even if
there wasn't an economic factor."

"I believe in crossing bridges when you come to them,"
May had said.

"I've had a word with my aunt's doctor, and in his
opinion she should give up work immediately, and husband
her strength."

"Then she'd better change her doctor," was May's
spirited reply. It was fantastic as well as impertinent,
twenty years of virtual silence and then this sudden appearance and attempt to change all their lives overnight.
"What value will Miss Alice's life have if she can't work?
It seems to me you need a training for being idle just as
much as for a profession. And being alive means more
than just not being dead."

"So you'd have her run herself into the ground," the
young man suggested.

"It's where we shall all end," May pointed out. And he
groaned :

"You're as bad as my mother. She never sat if she could
stand, and she never walked if she could run. You've missed
your vocation, I used to tell her. You should have been a
marathon contestant, probably got a gold medal."

May didn't think this was quite the way to talk of your
dead mother, but she passed it over.

"I think at her age Miss Alice should be allowed to
choose what she wants. Retirement may be all right for
rich, healthy people, who can travel and play golf, or
whatever it is rich retired people do to ameliorate their
boredom, but my father's doctor used to say that more men
broke up during the first five years of retirement than at
any other age. Miss Alice wouldn't thank you for tying
her into a chair and putting it in the window and telling
her to watch the world go by. She's been a part of that
world too long."

"There's your own future to consider," young Mr.
Hardy urged.

"If they gave up the shop what would they live on?" May demanded intelligently.

"If they strike while the iron's hot they'd get a good price for the site. If they invested that, with Aunt Alice's retirement pension, and Aunt Phyllis will be due for hers in a couple of years, they'd have enough to live on in some quiet hotel or boarding-house."

"They may not like the idea of living in a boarding-house after they've had their own home for so long." They lived very cosily in rooms above the shop and despite her stroke Miss Alice could still manage the stairs, if she took them slowly. Being a shop, there were what house agents call sanitary facilities on the same floor behind the stockroom, so she only had to do the stairs once a day.

"They'd get used to it," urged the young man.

"I daresay you can get used to a coffin," May agreed. "But that doesn't mean you want to settle down in one until you must."

"I was talking to a chap in the Golden Fleece last night," Mr. Hardy went on. "He tells me the Council are probably going to requisition that site and the sites of a number of other shops around it for their building programme."

"They can't do that," exclaimed May. "It's people's living."

"They'd make just the same reply if you asked them. And the place is spreading rapidly. You'll find it won't be possible to meet increased rates and rising costs of living out of a few pairs of stockings and papers of pins. The fact is people nowadays don't want to go to the village shop, they like the big stores where there's more choice and you find all the novelties. You must face facts, Miss Forbes. My aunts' contemporaries are a dying race . . ."

"We're all a dying race," declared May.

"But some of us die sooner than others. Oh, don't misunderstand me, I know you have their interests at heart, but I feel some responsibility for them, too. I can't stay over here much longer, I've got my own interests in Canada, I'd like to know their future was assured. If they wait till they get a compulsory purchase order the price will drop considerably, they'd do much better for themselves to bow out gracefully now. And from what they say about you," he added more kindly, "I'm sure you'd have no difficulty getting employment."

"I shall be all right," May assured him. "The Lord looks after His Own."

"Plenty of people have said that, and look where they are now. I had hoped you'd support me when I put the project to my Aunt Phyllis . . ."

"You're talking as if Miss Alice was a moron. She's as sharp as ever. It's not that I don't appreciate what you're trying to do," May had added more graciously, "but change is difficult when you get older."

But though she had defended the sisters both to this young man and to Mrs. Politi, she knew there was good sense in his arguments. She also had heard rumours of the Council's plans but she had chosen to discount them. But supposing they were genuine . . . Maybe I should urge them to take the best possible price, May reflected. It would be a blow to her, of course. It wasn't that she doubted her ability to earn a living, if the worse came to the worst you could always take a pail and brush and go round charging goodness knows how much an hour doing the jobs more delicate-minded people didn't want to do for themselves. And she liked doing housework. But that rather dark, cluttered shop had become a second home to her.

Am I letting myself be prejudiced in my own interest? she wondered.

So concerned had she been, turning over these facts in her mind, that she found she had reached the main road before she expected. Her knowledge of the neighbourhood where she had lived for so many years was limited to a mile or so from her home, and this part of the road was completely strange to her. She looked hopefully for a bus stop but there was none in sight. She had taken so many turns and twists, avoiding bad places, declivities, and solid obstacles of shrubs, that her bump of locality, never very large, now betrayed her completely, and she set off resolutely in the wrong direction. The road seemed very quiet, no one was about. The moon seemed to have decided to pack up for the night, an ominous wind had arisen, bringing with it the promise of rain. When she had walked a little farther she found a bus stop, but it was only a request sign carrying no timetable, so she couldn't tell when the next bus might arrive. At this hour of the evening they probably only ran at long intervals. There was no one standing about here, which seemed to indicate that no bus could be expected at present. And while she hesitated the first lances of rain began to fall. She decided to walk on to a compulsory stop, where there might be a bus shelter, in which case there would also be a time-table, but before she reached this she heard a sound on the road behind her, the sound of a car being driven fast and, she thought, erratically. At the cinema shows she saw on Wednesdays, both she and Mrs. Politi preferred thriller films, and she recalled one they had seen only a week or two previously where an inconvenient witness had been run down by a car that hadn't stopped. And there were other cases of cars running amok by accident, a woman had been pinned against a wall in a case recently where a bus skidded on a damp road, and when she came round she was in hospital minus a leg. May had very little doubt that the driver of the car was the creature she had partly seen on Broomstick Common. She looked wildly up and down, but there was nowhere to hide. She hurried round a corner and found herself face to face with a gaily-lighted public house called the Mettlesome Horse, with a swinging inn-sign of a horse prancing on its hind legs, though what that had to do with beer and spirits she couldn't imagine. The car came steadily up the road behind her, and without pausing for more reflection she darted forward and pushed open the swinging door.

Mr. Forbes had been a teetotaller—"Wine is a mocker, strong drink is raging," he would declaim from nonconformist pulpits—and May had never entered a publichouse until after his death and then only in the company of stronger characters like Mrs. Politi, in whose shadow she thankfully concealed herself.

There seemed to be a good many cars standing in the

inn's forecourt—a large dark one, a low blue number, an aged but dignified yellow Rolls—it was one of the few makes of car she could recognise—only a duke or a pop star would dare drive anything so conspicuous—and the usual gaggle of minis and small cars with 1000 or 1100 scrawled on the boot. Obviously quite a popular place, she reflected, and one where a woman on her own should be able to hide for a short time. Another cliché popped into her mind—there's safety in numbers. All she had to do was wait here, if necessary till closing-time though one hoped it wouldn't come to that, and then spill out with all the rest. There were bound to be a few people going home by bus, particularly in these days of breathalysers, and of these a proportion would be going in the same direction. But no sooner was she inside than she began to wish herself back in the anonymous dark. For some inexplicable reason she felt as conspicuous as if she were wearing no clothes. The bar was pretty full. All the seats at the counter were occupied and so far as she could see all the tables. There wasn't a single other woman by herself, there weren't even any female doubles. All the women present were with husbands or what were nowadays called boy-friends, and they came in every conceivable shape and size.

Out of the crowd a voice said, not violently but very definitely, "For Pete's sake, shut the bleeding door." She hadn't realised she was still holding it open, but she dropped it like a hot brick. The diversion had caused several people to look in her direction who wouldn't otherwise have noticed her. She tried to appear calm, searching the crowd with her gaze as if she expected to recognise someone, but naturally she didn't. It wasn't even her manor, assuming she was a regular pub-crawler, which she wasn't. She saw one woman lean over to her husband and murmur something with a knowledgeable grin, and she felt the blood pouring into her cheeks. Just when she felt ready to drop dead with embarrassment she noticed a small table in a darkish corner that no one seemed to want, and she made for it, as though it were the Rock of Ages sticking up out of a boiling sea. She had abandoned her notion of staying here, unnoticed, until she could leave in a crowd. She'd just wait a little to get her bearings. If she was right, and the driver of the car was after her blood, he'd come in, and he'd be bound to order something to drink, and while it was being brought she could make herself scarce. Her ears were strained for the sound of wheels and after a minute she heard a car draw up, a door slammed and the pub door opened. A man and a girl came in together. They were quite young and she knew at once had nothing to do with the mystery man from the Common. For one thing *he* was much too short. The two threaded their way over to the bar, the man hadn't even looked round the room. She drew a deep breath. Another five minutes, she thought, and then she'd make her bid for escape. Suddenly she became aware of someone standing beside her table and looked up to see a young man with more hair on his face than a Dandie Dinmont, wearing a dubious white coat.

"Want to order?" he asked, insolently.

She stiffened her spine. "I'm—waiting for someone," she explained. Well, so she was, waiting for the driver of the bus.

"P'raps he's got held up," suggested the young man in the same tone. "Better have something to while away the time."

"I'd prefer to wait," said May.

"This isn't a railway station," the youth pointed out. "We only provide seats for patrons."

"I'll wait another five minutes," May said, firmly. "The truth is, I'm feeling a little faint."

The young man breathed exasperation. "It's not a hospital either. That's about a mile up the road. If you ring them they might send an ambulance. Or there's a hire car firm . . . phone's on the stairs." He nodded his hairy head in its direction.

"I shall be quite all right if I can wait a few minutes," May insisted. Oh, go away, go away and leave me in peace, screamed her heart, but they couldn't have been on the same wave-length because the young man didn't seem to hear a thing.

"If you're feeling faint you should take a drop of brandy."

For the first time since her entry she realised that her sole capital was the spare sixpence she had brought for an emergency in case the milk-vending machine let her down. You couldn't even get a cup of coffee with that. Come to think of it, it very likely wasn't enough to get her home, now that all the fares had been raised.

"I don't care for brandy."

Oh help me, help me, she prayed, though this time she couldn't have told you whom she was addressing. Certainly not Father, who would have turned in his grave if there'd been enough left of him for any action so energetic, to think of his daughter sitting on her lonesome in a public-house. But someone must have heard, because her desperate prayer was answered immediately in the most unexpected fashion.

CHAPTER II

MR. ARTHUR CROOK, a legal beagle from the Smoke, and owner of the yellow car that had attracted May's attention, had been sitting at the bar for some time, reflecting that if he were Prime Minister he'd make it a capital offence to serve hog-wash under the glorious name of beer. He noticed May the instant she entered, and his heart had warmed to her on sight. Just my cup of tea, he thought. These no-longer-young biddies, looking as though butter wouldn't melt in their mouths, had, in the past, furnished him with some of his most satisfying cases. He saw at a glance that she was frightened to death, and not only by the company in which she now found herself, though he wouldn't have blamed her if that had been the sole reason. A rumty-too lot he called them, in his sturdy Edwardian way. The voice of the young barman that he didn't attempt to lower —playing for laughs, thought the outraged Mr. Crook, well, I'll soon have him laughing the wrong side of his face

—swept through the bar. Mr. Crook set down his glass and marched across the room.

"Well, fancy seeing you here, Rosie," he said, dumping himself in the spare chair. "A bit off your normal beat, aren't you?"

The young man sniggered.

"And you can wipe that smile off what you call a face," Mr. Crook went on, raising his voice slightly, "unless you want to find yourself plastered against the wall like a blowfly." He turned to May. "What'll it be, Rosie?"

"Lady doesn't like brandy," smirked the young man.

"Then you shouldn't be trying to sell it to her. On paper at least, this is still a free country." About half the crowd in the bar were looking at them now. Mr. Crook didn't mind; he was more surprised when people didn't stare. "O.K., Sugar, you leave it to me," he added blithely.

He gave an order that May couldn't comprehend. When she went out with Mrs. Politi she generally had a glass of sweet sherry or on occasion a small port.

"And I'll have a double Scotch," Mr. Crook continued. "And any water that's needed I'll add myself."

"You can't talk to me like that, chum," said the young man, suddenly recovering his spirit.

"You must have got cloth ears," was Mr. Crook's imperturbable if discourteous retort. "Didn't you hear me say just now it's a free country? And we'd like those drinks before the bar closes."

The young man hesitated, then decided that discretion was the better part of valour and beetled off in the direction of the bar.

"Sometimes I think we've jumped into 1984 when the pig is king," Mr. Crook continued affably to his companion. "Though why we should insult the pigs I couldn't tell you. Had a shock, have you, Sugar? Well, that shows you ain't dead yet, and that's more than can be said for some of the folk I've met hereabouts."

May looked at him, wholly fascinated. It wasn't simply gratitude that he'd got her out of a very nasty situation, it didn't even occur to her it might be a case of jumping out of the frying-pan into the fire, she didn't think that angels came in strange disguises—another of dear Father's clichés —she was simply fascinated, there was no other word for it. If he'd been Sir Lancelot and St. George for Merrie England rolled into one, she couldn't have been more enchanted. And yet all she saw was a round brown barrel of a man with popping bright eyes and red hair and brows that wouldn't have shamed a fox.

"I'm very grateful," she panted. "The fact is—I'd forgotten I hadn't any money except my bus fare—and I lost the road . . ."

"I'd be glad to lose practically any road I've been on in these parts," agreed Mr. Crook, buoyantly. "You should have called the boss. No inn-keeper wants trouble in his bar, he's got his licence to consider. Must be hard up for help if that's the best he can muster, but maybe it's his brother's son and . . . Well, well, look who's here."

The landlord himself brought the drinks. "I'm sorry about that, Mr. Crook," he said, and May wasn't the only person present who was startled to realise her companion had been recognised. "My lad didn't understand the lady was with you."

"All this free education," grumbled Mr. Crook, putting some coins on the extended tray, "and that's all there is to show for it."

"And we have to pay S.E.T. just as much as if it was someone who was some actual use," the landlord complained, his voice unexpectedly fierce.

"Where did we meet?" Crook asked affably. "It's not often I forget a face."

"Well, one of my patrons recognised your car, Mr. Crook. Quite a landmark, I understand."

"At this rate," suggested Mr. Crook agreeably, "I'll find myself getting buried—no, interred, you don't get buried in abbeys, do you—in Westminster Abbey, and then there'll be a rattling of bones to wake the dead."

The landlord grinned and went away. May was watching with an admiration that bordered on soppiness. And this is happening to me, she thought, forgetting for the moment the other things that had happened that evening that were responsible for her being here at all.

"See how it is, Rosie?" said Mr. Crook. "More people know Tom Fool than Tom Fool knows. You can drink that stuff with confidence," he added. "It'll be what they serve to the family, not the swill they consider's good enough for customers."

"I don't know what came over me," May confessed. "Only—there was no sign of a bus, and there was this car . . ."

"Like I said, you've had a shock." He felt in his pocket and produced an over-size business card. "Do as a marker for your prayer-book if you don't need it for any other purpose," he offered encouragingly. "Who was that chap who was always waiting for someone or something to turn up?"

"Mr. Micawber," said May. "And my name's Forbes, May Forbes." She looked at the card he'd given her. It said Arthur G. Crook and bore two addresses and "Trouble is our Business" and "Round the Clock Service." It didn't occur to her at the moment that he might be a lawyer, she put him down as a music-hall comedian, a busker, or perhaps someone who went out to entertain parties, though there was no mention of conjuring on his card.

"Angels come in strange disguises—what's the matter?"

"My father used to say that."

"In my case, it was my mum. And, of course, the converse is equally true. According to her, my dad looked like Sir Galahad and your own particular guardian angel rolled into one, but if ever there was a case of appearances being deceptive . . ." He shook his big red head. "I've been wondering all evening what in tarnation I was doing in this dump, and now I know. You're my answer to prayer."

"I was just thinking the same about you," said May.

"What was it?" Crook enquired curiously. "You came in as though all the bears in the Himalayas were after you."

May picked up her glass. "What is this?"

"Called black velvet," said Crook. "Good for the nerves."

"What a lovely name for a drink! I do feel such a fool," she confided. "I think I just panicked. I was feeding the cats on the Common, and usually there's no one there, but to-night there was this man . . ."

"Which man?"

"The one who frightened me." Suddenly she felt more foolish than before. One was constantly hearing of middle-aged spinsters suspecting quite innocent strangers of raping intentions or some sadistic treatment, the local paper had had just such a case only a week or two before, and it had turned out to be a case of sex frustration. Apparently the poor creature had secretly wanted to be raped, at least that was what the doctors said. She had a vision of herself in court, faced by a contemptuous jury who would doubtless write her off as an hysteric, if they didn't use even more direct language. And probably it was a dog, she decided, the idea having just come to her. A big dog. If people don't have gardens and the dog doesn't actually die at the vet, it's a problem to know what to do with the body. You can't treat it just as rubbish, not someone who's been your friend. She couldn't imagine why she hadn't thought of that before. It didn't precisely explain the mask and the balaclava, but she was a slow-witted creature, she reminded herself, the right explanation for that would probably strike her when she was going to bed or even making her early morning cup of tea. She felt she'd made herself quite ridiculous enough for one evening. "It was so startling," she added, quickly. "I didn't expect a voice then."

"Like I said," Mr. Crook pointed out, "it's a free country. Any reason why you shouldn't have been there? Or, come to that, why he should?"

"Well, I don't know. I went for the cats." She explained about the cats. "And I was afraid of the kitten getting drowned." She explained about the kitten.

"And this chap was on his owney-oh?"

"Well, I don't know, do I? He just asked what I was doing there."

"Any business of his?"

"I didn't think of that."

"Ask him what he was doing there?"

"That wasn't any business of mine."

"Sauce for the goose," suggested Mr. Crook, wondering what she was concealing and why. She didn't look the sort that hung about hoping to collect insults and thereby win a little publicity. Anyway, in that case she wouldn't have made a bee-line for the Mettlesome Horse. Still, let patience have her perfect work, and usually she achieved a bonanza. He didn't say as much to May, who wouldn't have understood what he was talking about if he had.

"So you behaved like Little Miss Muffett, who was frightened away?"

"It's not a very nice neighbourhood," May pointed out apologetically. "And it was quite dark—and Mrs. Politi always says there may be rats there. I always say of course not, but she could be right."

"Rats with human faces," Mr. Crook acknowledged. "Now, you hold on to that card and if ever you find a use for it don't hesitate to ring. You can even reverse the charges, if it's more convenient. You're what I've been waiting for all evening."

"But you didn't know I was coming," May protested.

"The wicked didn't know the flood was coming, but it caught them just the same," Mr. Crook reminded her. "I wouldn't mind betting my Sunday morning titfer that chap wasn't there for any good reason, and I hope I'm a good citizen . . ."

His guardian angel might have taken this unwinking, but the authorities would have seen it as a rather considerable poke in the bread-basket. "And remember, if I was drinking slops because you were on the way, you came in, whether you know it or not, because I was here. And I never did hold with this ships-that-pass-in-the-night malarkey. There's something round the corner, and the odds are you and me are going to trail it together. And if your suspicions should be aroused, remember, before you go into your Joan of Arc act, it's always as well to get a legal opinion. It's my experience that most people who've lived blameless lives don't know their own rights, and it's not every rozzer thinks it's his job to explain them."

Recalling this conversation later, it surprised him a little to realise how certain he was that this was going to turn into a matter for the police.

Mrs. Politi had closed her shop a long time ago; for a while she had sat in her doorway on an upright wooden chair, an ordinary enough proceeding in her native land but one looked at askance by her prim suburban neighbours. "I don' go to the world no more," Mrs. Politi would explain. "The world, she come to me."

Pulling back the curtain of her bedroom, she saw that there was no light across the road in the top-floor room where May lived. "I always warn her she get eaten by those hungry cats," she muttered, "and no one but herself to thank." Presently, however, she saw a big yellow car roll majestically down the street and stop a few doors away. The door opened and May got out. Mrs. Politi couldn't believe her eyes. Mind you, she didn't suspect the worst. The car itself was of a vintage that commanded respect. Crook's enemies, who were legion, said it dated back to the time when a man walked in front of these new-fangled monsters waving a red flag, and the maximum speed was five miles an hour. "You try it," Mr. Crook told one of them once, "you won't have to pull out your stop-watch before you're under the wheels." Mrs. Politi gasped with delight. Who'd have thought it of her, the demure little spinster, always yapping about her cats and collecting bits of offal, and all the time . . . She a deep one, thought Mrs. Politi. Like a well. But no well had ever been dug that she couldn't plumb in due course. She looked forward to getting the whole story out of her friend—and I will do it or I am a Dutchman, she assured herself, utilising a phrase from the country of her adoption. And everyone knew her parents had come from Turin and she had never set foot in Holland in her life.

The next evening she waited impatiently for May's ring

27

at the bell. May always rang, though often there was nothing for her. It was a warm, even a sultry evening, and Mrs. Politi brought out her chair and eagerly watched the street. Later, she thought, there might be rain. When half-past seven, May's normal time of call, had gone by and there was no sign of her, Mrs. Politi began to feel a little anxious. You could set your clock by May. At a quarter to eight she hadn't arrived, then the Protestant Church clock sounded the hour. Mrs. Politi lifted her eyes, not to the hills, but to the top window almost opposite and saw through a crack in the curtain that a light was burning. She heaved herself out of her chair and waddled over the street. When May heard the bell she peered cautiously out of her window. Mrs. Politi's bulk was unmistakable, May could no more have suspected her of being last night's mystery man in disguise than she could have suspected a circus elephant. She came hastening down the stairs.

"Come in, Lilli, come in," she said warmly, almost pulling her friend across the threshold. "What's wrong?"

"You should tell me," retorted Mrs. Politi, staring with dismay at the steep flight of steps facing her. "Why, you not ill? You went to work this morning as usual. That I see with my own eyes. So—to-night I collect food for your worthless cats . . ."

"Oh don't, Lilli. Call them worthless, I mean. The fact is, I'm not going to the Common to-night."

"Then you *are* ill?"

"No, not exactly. I do feel rather tired, though."

"Too tired to feed your adored cats? That I cannot believe. May, you are concealing something."

By this time they were in May's neat bed-sitter. This was furnished in a quite unexceptional manner, the only striking features being a large photograph of an uncommonly dogmatic old man, Papa Forbes, deceased, and regretted by no one except his daughter, and a plethora of cats. A chowder of cats. Lilli couldn't recall where she had heard the expression. Wherever the eye turned it lighted on a cat —in china, bronze, plaster—old birthday cards, even the drying-up cloths bore representations of cats.

"You will turn into a cat yourself one of these days," Lilli warned her.

"If you must know," acknowledged May reluctantly—she had spent all her defiance keeping the truth from Mr. Crook, who, she suspected, might be a good deal more ardent if she had so much as mentioned her suspicions—"a man spoke to me."

Lilli Politi put back her head and laughed. It was a lovely laugh, girlish and gay and very surprising to come from that stout old woman.

"So—a man spoke to you? He was perhaps the one who brought you home?"

May didn't stop to wonder how her friend knew about Mr. Crook, any more than she would wonder on the Last Day how the Recording Angel knew so much about activities of which she'd never spoken to anyone. She answered with complete candour.

"Oh no, Lilli. He—he came to my assistance, there wasn't a bus and of course I hadn't any money, only sixpence, you know I never take any money with me—and it was just starting to rain and he offered me a lift. I had gone further across the Common than I meant and took the wrong road."

Lilli raised her thick brows. "The girl who took the wrong turning," she intoned. "May, you a slyboots. Did you ask this man who he was?"

"He wasn't going to abduct me," cried May, with a sudden return of her old spirit. "It was—it was his good deed for the day. I was a bit shaken, I admit it."

"And that is all you have to say?"

"Everything," said May firmly. If she hadn't confided in Mr. Crook she certainly wasn't going to give any details to Lilli Politi. She was a good neighbour, and she really did care for May, which was surprising, seeing she thought her a fool and declared that fools were anathema, but once she mounted the steed of her imagination, Pegasus wasn't in it with her.

Lilli, however, was not disposed to let her off so easily. "What did he say to you, this man on the Common?"

29

"I don't think he was alone," cried May. "He just wanted me out of the picture. He didn't try and assault me, if that's what you're thinking. I told him I'd lost a kitten and he said if he found it he'd bring it back."

"You told him your address?"

"Yes, but not the right one. Oh Lilli, it was such a sweet little cat, mostly Burmese, I think."

"Burmese, Chinese, Celanese, they are all one to me," Lilli declared. "Have you told the police?"

"The police? I've got nothing to tell them. I told you, he didn't try and attack me in any way. And if I did tell them they'd say I had only myself to blame wandering about on the Common after dark. You don't seem to be able to make people understand about dumb animals."

"I have heard," said Lilli, "that the giraffe can make no sound. If that is true, it is the only dumb animal I know. But I see you do not wish to confide in your old friend."

"I've told you," May insisted. "I had a bit of a shock and I decided to give it a rest for a few days. After all, the scraps I take can't really make a lot of difference. It's just that one likes to feel one's doing what one can."

Lilli didn't pursue the subject any further, she could see she would learn no more to-night. But one day, probably quite soon, May would feel the need for a confidante. She could not, however, forbear to put one final question.

"What were they doing, these two—trespassers?"

She watched, eyes alight with mischief, to see how May would cope with that one. But May flummoxed her completely when she said, "If you really must know, Lilli, they were burying a pet dog."

She had told herself this so often that eventually she might have come to believe it, only before that happened, the balloon went up. In fact, while she tried to fend off Lilli's enquiries, it was already on its perilous flight.

Reuben Gold (Ben for short) was the son of a local jeweller and pawnbroker, Solly Gold, who had a corner shop in Dorset Street. From the front he looked like any other jeweller and watchmaker, but round the corner the notorious three brass balls flaunted themselves. He did a good pawnbroking business, though he seldom spoke of it, for he was known to give a fair price, and his reputation with the police was high enough for them to know that if he were offered stolen goods he would report it at once. He was a short, hard-working man, who kept his nose clean, co-operated with authority, made a fair but not an exorbitant profit on all his transactions, and thanked his stars that he was now a citizen of a country where he need not conceal either his religious or his natural origins. Ben was nine years old, the child of his father's middle age and the only son. Two daughters had already made advantageous marriages and quitted the home roof. On the Friday following May's perilous adventure, Ben and two school-friends were playing on Broomstick Common among the wrecked cars, giving themselves the names of famous racing drivers and making all the appropriate noises for a Monte Carlo rally. A few other lads were doing much the same. Of the wild cats there was no sign, they never came out till after dark, and in any case Ben had brought his family dog with him. This dog's name was Who, not after the famous doctor, but because even an expert might be forgiven for not being sure about his parentage.

"Who did your mother meet after dark?" someone had demanded, when Solly brought him back from the dogs' home, he being then about a year old.

"A dog is a dog, no?" Solly enquired. Ben had wanted a dog. Solly thought Who would be a companion for his wife, Leah, while he was at the shop and the boy at school. Leah, who had no particular feelings either way, wanted whatever her menfolk wanted. Who was certainly no beauty, but Solly declared that a dog of such fearsome and unusual aspect would frighten off any child-stealer. (There had been one or two cases of children being approached by a nameless man during the past year or two, and one child had actually been criminally assaulted.)

"He's got a heart like butter," Ben scoffed. "He wouldn't only let the burglar in, he'd show him where everything was hidden."

"You talk too much, my son," Solly reproved him. "Do I want a dog that will bite strangers, bring the police about my ears? So long as he looks that he would attack, that is all I ask."

Even Ben couldn't argue that Who didn't look like a real villain, with his cropped ears and huge teeth. He had some Alsatian blood in him, everyone agreed about that. Solly, who had heard of pure-bred dogs becoming hysterical and attacking even their owners, had no fault to find with his appearance, and he paid no attention to Ben's witticism that he was a sheep in wolf's clothing. On this evening he snuffed about contentedly enough while the boys played, then suddenly, to their dismay, he began to move towards the palings through which venturesome May Forbes had squeezed herself.

"Who, come back. Come back, sir," Ben ordered. Solly had extracted a promise from his son that, come what might, he would never go into that forbidden area. But for once the normally obedient Who paid no attention. Nose to ground, looking remarkably like a wolf, he followed a trail the boys couldn't detect.

"Oh, look," cried Frank Vines, one of the three, "he's gone over the fence."

"He can't," cried Ben. "He's such a fool he'll probably fall into the canal."

"He can swim, you idiot."

"That won't help him if he comes back stinking of canal water, and shaking it all over Mum's carpet."

He began to run alongside the fence calling to the dog. To his relief after a minute or so he saw Who had stopped, then he sailed back over the fence and went into the wood.

"Perhaps he'll find buried treasure for you," suggested the third boy.

Who, when they came up to him, had his nose to the ground and was pawing among stones and clods of earth. Ben caught his collar, but he might as well have tried to shift the Rock of Gibraltar.

"Oh come on," Ben adjured him. It was Friday night, when the family kept the Jewish family feast and there would be trouble indeed if he were back late. Leah would light the candles in a ceremony that had been enacted for centuries, even Ben, accustomed as he was to heathen companions to whom God was an expletive rather than a Divine Being, would have felt the bottom had dropped out of his world if his parents had abandoned the practice.

"Come and help me to pull him," he yelled.

Frank, whose father had a butcher's shop in the High Street, said, "He's probably a police dog in disguise. Perhaps some of the train robbers' loot is hidden here."

"How would Who smell that? Dogs don't understand about money."

The third boy, Jim, a small pale creature who looked as if he'd grown up in a dark cupboard, said acutely, "Well, he's found something, I suppose you could call it treasure, though it's not exactly buried."

Stooping, he picked up a small gleaming object that the dog must have unearthed in his frantic pawing.

The other two clustered round him. "What is it?"

"It's a ring, any fool can see that."

"Probably came from Woollies," said Frank scornfully. "No one would leave a real ring here."

Ben took the ring gently from his friend's palm. "No," he said after a moment. "This didn't come from Woollies. It's what they call an antique. I know, my father's told me."

"Then perhaps it comes from Woollies' antique department." Both boys yelped with laughter. Only Ben remained grave.

The ring was quite charming, an antique gold setting with three minute flowers whose petals were made of coloured stones.

"They're only chips," said Ben knowledgeably, "but they aren't glass. I'd like to show this to my father."

"Perhaps he'll be able to tell you what it's doing here," jeered Frank.

"Perhaps it's part of a hoard," contributed Jim. "I say, Who is excited, isn't he?"

"I expect he wants his share of the treasure." Frank

looked at the eager dog, the great excavating paws. "He looks ready to dig his way through to Australia."

"Give him a chance," Jim urged.

"I can't. I've got to go back. Come *on*." Ben lugged furiously at the big dog's collar.

"We might get some spades," Frank began, but to the surprise of both boys Ben exclaimed, "No. Leave it. If there is anything there it's nothing to do with us."

"How about the ring? We found that."

"I found it," insisted Jim.

"No, you didn't. Who found it. Anyway, if it's valuable it doesn't belong to any of us. Only—he doesn't dig for nothing. My father stopped him doing that when he started digging in our yard."

"It's probably only a dead cat," said Frank earnestly.

"Since when did cats wear rings?" Jim riposted.

"Then some chap and his girl were walking here and she dropped the ring . . ."

"Without noticing?"

"Perhaps it was loose."

"It ought to have a guard on it," said Ben. He didn't subscribe to the idea that it had been thrown away. He was too much his father's son to believe that anyone wilfully discarded something worth real money.

"We ought to mark the place," Frank suggested. "There must be a stick or something."

Ben stepped backwards on to something that cracked under his tread. "It's a saucer," he discovered. "What on earth's that doing here?"

"It'll do to mark the spot. There can't be many saucers lying about."

"Perhaps the witches had a tea-party," suggested Frank, who considered himself the wit of the party.

Ben had managed to prise the dog away from the mysterious spot. Now he began to make his way back as speedily as possible.

"Perhaps someone's offered a reward," Jim put in resourcefully.

"If there was a reward there'd be a notice outside the copper shop."

"Perhaps there is. Have you looked?" But of course they hadn't.

Solly Gold had a glass screwed into his eye and was examining a watch when the three boys and the dog came bursting in. He flapped a hand at them to enjoin silence. After a minute he removed the glass and enquired formally, "And what can I do for you, gentlemen?"

Jim giggled and exchanged glances with Frank. Ben said, "It's this ring, Dad. We found it near the canal, at least Who unearthed it. They think it's Woollies, but it isn't, is it?"

Mr. Gold took the ring and let it lie for an instant in the palm of his hand. "The canal, you say? I thought that was Council property."

"This side of the fence, Dad. Who went over the paling and we had to get him back, and then he started digging and Jim saw this ring. And we thought it queer because nobody really goes down that way."

"Because of the bomb," Frank explained.

"I daresay there never was a bomb there," said Jim.

"So you know better than the police. So clever boys are nowadays. When I was your age I knew nothing, we believed what our elders told us. But you were right to bring me the ring. I know it well. It was an unredeemed pledge. But in such a place—why? why?"

"We could hardly drag Who away," Ben assured him, eagerly. "He was digging like mad."

"As if he thought there was buried treasure," added Jim.

"A dog has not enough sense to be interested in buried treasure," Solly assured him soberly. He turned to his son. "My son, could you find this place again if you should be asked?"

"There was a saucer there, I don't know what it was doing."

"A saucer. Then perhaps—there is a little lady who goes to feed the cats—perhaps she . . . but why down by the canal? No, that is very strange."

"Is it really valuable, Mr. Gold?" demanded Frank.

"Valuable!" Solly shrugged. "A relative word. I know what the young man who bought it paid for it. I made him a reduction because then he may return for the other ring, the ring for the wedding." He could never resist an opportunity to instruct the boy he regarded as his heir. "It is good business to come down a little on your price with an eye to the future. Remember that, my son. Make an exorbitant charge and you have money in the bank, but next time your customer goes elsewhere."

"It's a gamble really, isn't it?" suggested Frank intelligently.

"It is a knowledge of human nature." Solly always answered questions courteously, even when they were put to him by young hobbledehoys like Frank Vines. One day Frank might be a man of substance, then he might give some of his custom to Ben. Look ahead, that was Solly's motto. Life is the present and the future. The past is over and done with, so waste no time on that.

"Do you think we ought to take it to the station, Dad?" Ben enquired.

Solly could never quite accustom himself to the title of Dad. He had called his own father Papa all his life, but he felt that being a Jew by birth and British only by adoption meant that Ben would have enough to differentiate him without his insisting on the old-style title.

"You forget what day it is, my son? It is Friday night." And Ben nodded. He would no more have questioned his duty to be present in the family circle than he would have questioned his own legitimacy.

"Go back, now. Explain to your Mama that I may be a few minutes late. Leave the ring with me. If there should be a reward you will be told, rest assured of that."

"Coo, what do you bet there is buried treasure there?" Frank cried as the three of them turned away. "I don't know about you chaps but I'm going back to have a dekko."

"Me too," agreed Jim enthusiastically. "Too bad Ben can't come. Ben's got to go back to his Mumma."

Ben shrugged his shoulders in a very good imitation of

his father. "You couldn't be expected to understand," he said. "What do goys know? And anyway had you thought that perhaps the one that left the ring there may have thought of looking for it, and he might be—well, might be a bit annoyed if he knew you'd taken it? My father will give it to the police, well, report it, anyhow."

"You're only saying that because you can't come with us," jeered Frank, but when Ben and the dog had gone their ways Jim murmured uncertainly, "Suppose there really is a bomb down there and we step on it?"

"The bomb's the other side of the palings—remember?" But Frank's step had also slowed a little. If Solly really intended to talk to the police they might come haring down and be none too pleased to find their job had been taken over by the public. Mr. Vines was always on at his son about the importance of staying on the right side of the boys in blue.

"We could go to the Common anyway, there's no law against that." So off they went, thanking their stars that Friday night was the same as every other night of the week in their households, except that, being pay-night, their dads had an extra session at the Case is Altered.

CHAPTER III

MR. GOLD put up his shutters promptly on the stroke of six and went along to the police station. The first officer he saw took the matter pretty lightly. Some girl had lost a ring, he conceded. What of it?

"I think," said Mr. Gold, "if I wore your uniform I would ask if anyone had lost a girl."

After that the station sergeant surfaced. They all knew Solly by reputation at least; he was a reliable member of the community, he wouldn't be trying to make monkeys out of them and the sergeant thought he wouldn't be much pleased if someone reversed the process and tried to make a monkey out of him.

"I am telling you what my son told me. Ben is a truthful boy. And he had witnesses, two of them. One is the son of Mr. Vines, the other I do not know. Moreover, they all agreed that the dog wished to continue digging and must be pulled away by force. Now, the dog was not interested in the ring—you would agree there?"

"If you say so, Mr. Gold."

"I say more," Solly continued. "I have seen that ring before to-day. I sold it to a young man . . ."

"You can't give his name."

"A young man who paid cash? With cash you do not ask for a name."

"You'd know him again?"

"There are some faces a man does not forget."

"This lad of yours, will he be able to find the place again?"

"There is a broken saucer near by. In any case, the dog would know." He looked through the station window. Clouds were coming up fast. "There is no hurry," he suggested softly. "If there is treasure underground it can wait till the morning. If you are afraid of trespassers, you can set a man to watch."

"I can't turn out a squad of men to dig a bit of deserted ground because a tuppenny-ha'penny ring was picked up there," Spence exploded, when Solly was gone. "Most likely the girl was larking and dropped it out of her pocket or something. We'll be the laughing-stock of the force if we start digging and all we find's a dead dog."

"News to me, Sarge, that dogs wear rings."

The sergeant scowled. The young rookies these days didn't know where to draw the line.

"A lady's ring, isn't it? You know, Solly Gold might have something . . ."

"Mr. Gold to you," the sergeant snapped.

"He said he might start asking about a missing girl."

"Get cracking on the records," Spence said. "Anyone local been reported missing?"

"Well, not that I remember. All the same . . ." But no one had reported a missing girl.

Nor had there been any enquiry for a lost ring answering this description.

"You can't do much about missing persons, not if they're over eighteen," said Spence rather gloomily. "Unless there are particular circumstances, sickness, lunacy or of course some suggestions of a criminal record. The Sally Army's the best bet for that."

"We don't know any girl is missing yet."

"The ring could belong to whoever put that saucer there. It's hardly the kind of place where you'd look for one."

"Funny no one's enquired about it, then."

A police constable, one of those hard-working men who always seem to be behind the door when promotion's handed round, murmured, "I might ask Nance."

"Who's she?"

"My wife, Sarge. I don't know how it is—I always tell her she's a loss to the force. I don't know if it's a sixth sense or what, but there are occasions when she seems to know about a crime before it's been committed."

"You want to watch your tongue, Hunter," the sergeant advised him. "You mean, she might have heard about a missing girl before we did?"

"That's what I'm saying. It's like the bush telegraph. Don't ask me how she does it, but if there is a local girl missing and her family don't choose to come to us, you could do worse than talk to Nance. There's the ring, too."

"You think she'll be able to tell us who that belonged to?"

"I don't know about that, but she'll recognise it all right. It used to be in Solly Gold's side-window. We were walking past one evening not so long ago when it caught her eye. Now that's a good-class thing, she told me. You'd never think of buying me anything like that. I ask you, Sarge, on a police constable's pay! He was asking something like fifty quid for it, though I daresay he came down a bit when it came to the crunch. And here's something else I remember. About a week ago she came back and said, You've missed the boat, George. You won't be able to buy me that ring, after all, because it's sold. Someone's pipped you on the post. Well, I said it didn't mean, because it had gone out of the window, Solly still hadn't got it. He's always changing his stock. But she said no she'd gone in and asked him."

"You've taken your time remembering all this, haven't you?" suggested Sergeant Spence ungraciously. "Anyway, we know it was sold and to a young man Solly thinks he'd know again. But it stands to reason he wouldn't be buying it for himself. Have a word with your wife, Hunter, by all means, but make it clear to her that we've no knowledge that anyone's missing, and we haven't been asked to make enquiries."

Nancy Hunter sniffed when she heard her husband's story. "Some girls don't know their luck," she said. "If all she was going to do was lose it down by the canal it might as well have stayed in the window. Canal." She thought. "That's a funny place to go courting."

"Haven't heard of anyone doing a flit, I suppose?" her husband suggested.

"I thought you were supposed to be the policeman, not me." She considered for a minute. Then she said, "That Linda Myers walked out of the house a day or two ago, at least that's what Brenda Myers says."

"Linda Myers? That's Tom Myers's girl."

"Mind you," continued Nance, paying about as much attention to her husband as she usually did. "I reckon Tom was crazy expecting a girl like Linda to settle down with a new wife barely ten years older than her. And since Peter was born it's been a regular Fifth of November in that household, fireworks day and night. At least, that's what I hear."

"Linda's never been in trouble," reflected George Hunter thoughtfully.

"She may not have been in trouble, but she's the kind that makes it all her days. If you ask me, Brenda Myers doesn't want to know."

"Doesn't want to know what?"

"What's happened to her. She's always fancied herself, you know. Lolita No. 2, that's Miss Linda. And always on with the new love before she's off with the old."

"What you mean is the two didn't get on."

"And that's the understatement of the year. It's no wonder you haven't got your stripes yet, George. If you ask me, Linda hoped she'd drive Brenda round the bend or make her get out or something. She's been Number One in Tom Myers's house ever since her mother died when the kid was thirteen, and then suddenly she finds herself sitting at the side of the table and expected to baby-sit. If it was my kid I'd sooner have a gorilla for a sitter."

"When did she light out?" George was accustomed to winnowing the chaff from grain where Nance was concerned. A less patient man wouldn't have bothered, but he knew that when you'd sifted the chaff, you often got quite a nice little harvest.

"I told you, about a couple of days ago. Walked out in just what she stood up in, from what Brenda says. Mind you, there was some talk a while back about her going with a married man, but you can't believe all you hear."

"You hear such a lot," suggested George, "maybe you know who she is going with just now."

"I'd need to be a computer to keep tabs on all her conquests." Nance sniffed again. "Mind you, I'm not bringing any accusations. Let's say she gets bored a bit quicker than most or needs more attention. I did hear she was going around with a foreigner." Meaning, as George readily understood, a stranger to the district.

"How did you hear about Linda going AWOL?" he asked.

"I was in the Post Office, and Brenda was sounding off about it. She'd arranged to go to a Bingo session or something with a friend and asked Linda if she'd look after the kid."

"More likely told than asked," George Hunter murmured.

"Anyway the girl said, He's not my kid, and there was a

41

real up-and-a-downer. Linda said if Brenda wanted a baby-sitter she could do what everyone else did and get one in, but you know that's not so easy and some of these girls . . . Bessie Bates did that and she said something made her come back early and there was this girl shacked up with her boyfriend on the sofa and the poor kid yelling its head off. Anyhow, Linda said she'd had enough, she had her own life, and thank-you and goodbye. And that was the last Brenda saw of her."

George Hunter looked considerably more troubled than his wife. "When was this?"

"Bingo clubs are Thursdays, and Brenda didn't mention it till that morning, so I suppose that was the day Linda walked out."

"But—doesn't Mrs. Myers know where she's gone?"

"I shouldn't think Linda was much of a hand with a pen. And she is eighteen, there's not much Brenda can do about it. In fact, she said it was something to have peace in the house, and she was going to make the most of it while it lasted."

"But Tom Myers?"

"He's a traveller, as if you didn't know. Only gets back at week-ends. That's one of the reasons he wanted Linda to stay at home, company for his wife—that's what he thought. It's a funny thing how some men never learn. Two wives and a daughter and he knows no more about women than the day he was born."

"The overstatement of the year," suggested her husband. "I suppose you don't happen to know if it was Linda wearing that ring you fancied?"

"Well, but you said it was found by the canal. Linda 'ud never go there. We know the type of girl who goes down to the canal with a fellow, and the type of fellow. Linda may be a bit wild, but she's not that daft. She may be young," added Nance shrewdly, "but she knows how many beans make five."

"That's where the ring was found," said her husband, "and no one's put in an enquiry for it, and it wasn't bought at any five-and-ten store, as we both know. And to date no one's been reported missing. You know such a lot, Nance, you don't happen to know who she was going around with just lately. Besides this foreigner no one else seems to know about," he added, quickly.

"That girl changes her boy-friends more often than you change your shirts," Nance told him. "Had it occurred to you to ask Brenda Myers? She may not know where the girl is, but she'd recognise the ring. It's not the sort you'd easily forget."

"We don't want to alarm her unnecessarily," said George. He looked disturbed.

"I wouldn't say Brenda Myers scares easy," was Nance's cool retort.

"There's nothing more we can do to-night," decided Sergeant Spence, when he had received his subordinate's report. "We'll get on to Mrs. Myers in the morning and see if she recognises the ring. We can't put out a search for the girl officially without a bit more evidence that someone could have harmed her. She's a right to change her address without informing her stepmother, but I'll tell you this." He paused weightily. "I wouldn't care to be in Brenda Myers's shoes when Tom comes home, not if anything has gone wrong. Tom Myers will do his nut, and we've trouble enough in the manor without that."

Brenda Myers, interviewed next morning, proved unco-operative. It was clear she was not unduly worried by her stepdaughter's absence.

"I don't know why you wanted to get me up here, Saturday and all," she scolded. "Tom 'ull be back after dinner and he likes to find everything just so. It's not as though it was the first time Her Ladyship's gone off in a huff, and for the same reason, because I suggested she might give a hand in the house. Well, it's her home too, isn't it?"

"What happened the last time?"

"She stayed away a couple of nights, then walked in as cool as you please. I've been staying with Sophie, she said. Didn't she mind you using her tooth-brush? I asked, because she hadn't taken a stitch with her. And fancy a friend of yours not having a phone! Oh, she said, I phoned but there wasn't any answer. You don't have to believe her, but what authority have I got? The girl's eighteen, she earns her living, even if her father doesn't let her pay a penny into the house, money doesn't go far these days, he says. The fact is, that girl's done nothing but make trouble ever since I was married, always nestling up to her father and saying, Do you remember, Daddy, when Mummy was alive we did this and that, making out she misses her so. As if Tom wants to keep on being reminded. She only does it to spite me, of course."

Sergeant Spence sighed. Another one-eyed witness, he reflected, the sort that can never see more than one point of view and that her own.

"So you're not worried, Mrs. Myers? Even though you recognise the ring? And you know where we found it?"

"I don't know that it is hers," declared Brenda defiantly. "Oh, it's like at a glance, but then I never saw hers really close to. Anyway, you can take my word, she'll be back by three o'clock. Tom gets back then and she won't let him find her gone. And she'll have the same story as before, she tried to phone but there was no reply."

"You can't think of any place where she might have gone, where you could contact her? This Sophie . . ."

"Sophie's in London. Come to think of it, she might have gone there, I suppose."

"Without any luggage?"

"She probably wouldn't think about luggage till she was in the train. The only thing is—who paid her fare? She's always skint by Thursday. The chap you want to get hold of is Mr. Polly, find out if she asked for her salary in advance. She seems able to do just what she likes in that place."

"You're sure she didn't tell you who gave her the ring, Mrs. Myers?"

"According to her, she earned it. I was surprised in a way, I mean you'd have expected her to choose something a bit more showy. As to who gave it to her—how should I know?"

"We know it was bought by a young man who wanted it for a girl. Mr. Gold remembers him, but doesn't know his name, and didn't know it was for Linda. He got an idea it might be an engagement ring."

"Linda 'ud expect something with a diamond in it for that. Though she has been going around with a chap from London, according to her. Not that she ever brings any of her fellows home, doesn't stick to most of them long enough to know their second names."

"Did she ever mention the first name?"

Mrs. Myers considered. "Come to think of it, she did talk about someone called Chris. Funny, I thought it was a girl. Where did you say you found it, the ring, I mean?"

When she heard she paled, she seemed to think, for the first time, that the situation might really be serious.

"If anything's happened to that girl Tom 'ull kill me," she said. "Are you sure, Mr. Spence, the boys weren't having you on—about finding it down by the canal, I mean? You know what kids are."

"I don't think Ben Gold would try and pull anything like that over his father."

"What were they doing down by the canal?"

"Walking Mr. Gold's dog. It was the dog really that dug up the ring."

Her breath whistled in her throat. "You didn't say it was dug up."

"Well, the dog scratched about a bit, and then one of the boys noticed the ring, and Ben took it back to show his father, and he recognised it and brought it to us."

"Perhaps Linda gave it back to this fellow and he was so riled he threw it out," Brenda suggested, but there was no conviction in her voice, and the sergeant didn't even pretend to consider the possibility. During this past minute her composure, which had been stiffened by a sort of scornful rage, left her, she was white as paper. Hurriedly the sergeant despatched one of the constables for a cup of tea.

"And don't forget the sugar," he added. "Sit down, Mrs. Myers." For she had come to her feet. "It's been a bit of a shock, but we don't know that anything's happened to the girl."

"You try telling Tom that," Brenda said in a wraith of a voice. "I've always been afraid of that girl getting herself into trouble in the back of a car, say, but the canal!"

The tea came and she sat stirring it absently, round and round until it began to slop into the saucer.

"This Mr. Polly," Spence urged. "He has the hair-dresser's at Crisps Corner?"

"They don't call them that any more. Beautician, Linda says. She did work for a bit for old Miss Robinson, though what use she was to them don't ask me. I could have told them she wouldn't stick that long. A lot of old pussies going in for packets of hairpins and cheap lines of handkerchiefs. Still, Miss Alice seemed to take to her. She must do quite well at Polly's, she always seems to have enough to buy a new dress or a handbag. I don't doubt she could wind him round her little finger, as she does her father. Oh, I don't deny," continued Brenda grudgingly, "she's got a taking way with her. She did want to go in for modelling, have a London flat, you know, but her father put his foot down there." She sighed. "The truth is he knows nothing about her. You'd have thought a man who'd been married twice would have learned something about women, but not Tom."

When pressed to amplify that, however, she simply shook her head. The police went off on another tack.

"Wouldn't Mr. Polly wonder if she didn't turn up on Friday? It's usually a pretty busy day."

"She'll have covered herself somehow, you may be sure of that. Anyway, these young girls, no sense of responsibility, change their jobs as often as they change their hair-do's. What happens now?"

"We can't do much until she's been reported missing, and even then only if there's some suspicion of foul play. It's not a crime to walk out on your job or leave home."

"You just wait till her father gets back," said Brenda

46

grimly. "He won't thank me for sticking the police on to her if she's simply gone off for a lark, and like I said, I wouldn't be surprised to find her on the doorstep when I get home. She knows which side her bread's buttered, and she'll have a story as pat as you please."

"What do you make of that?" the sergeant asked a colleague when Brenda had departed.

"Frightened to death of Tom Myers, couldn't care less about Linda. Wouldn't really surprise me if the girl had planted the ring . . ."

"Don't know how you ever got taken on the Force," commented the sergeant brutally. "One thing, you'll never make it for the Brains Department. Plant the ring indeed! It could have stayed there a month without anyone finding it. All the same," he brooded, "I'm sorry for Mrs. Myers when Tom gets back, if the girl's still missing."

The constable, quite unmoved by his superior's remarks, commented brusquely, "Wouldn't surprise me if we were a bit sorry, too."

Tom Myers came storming up to the station within twenty minutes of his return to Churchford. He demanded to see the ring, which he instantly identified.

"I couldn't be mistaken, my daughter showed it to me. She got it from a young chap called Chris. No, I don't know his other name, but according to her he should be coming over to-morrow to meet the family."

"Did you assume it was an engagement ring, Mr. Myers?"

"Don't ask me. The present generation doesn't seem interested in engagements. But from what my girl said it did sound serious. Mind you, she's had small presents before, like all girls—a charm bracelet, a brooch, but nothing like this. The young chap didn't get that for half a dollar. Well, what have you done—about finding her, I mean? My wife says she walked out on Thursday."

When he heard they were waiting for him, he blew up.

"Your daughter's not been notified as a missing person, Mr. Myers, she's over eighteen, and the ring was only

47

brought in last night. We don't even know she was wearing it at the time she left Churchford."

"You don't know my daughter. If she didn't want to go on wearing it she wouldn't throw it away. You could raise a few pounds on that. And what's it doing down by the canal? Let me tell you this. My girl wouldn't let me come back and find her gone, not without a note or a phone call or something, and there's been nothing. She didn't take any luggage with her, all her muck's on her dressing-table, even her wig, though they call 'em hair-pieces nowadays. All the girls seem to have 'em, don't ask me why. Even that's in its box. How many more suspicious circumstances do you want before you can get to work? And let me tell you this, if they're not enough for you, they're a damn' sight too many for me. If you won't get on with the job, I'll call in a couple of pals and we'll take some spades and go down and dig on the canal bank ourselves."

He means it, too, the sergeant thought. He was a man who'd confronted plenty of violent no-gooders, but not many had chilled his blood like this pale desperate father facing him across a table—like a hand-grenade when the pin's loose, he described him later. They didn't like the situation themselves, and if it should prove they were barking up the wrong tree, at least that should calm Tom. At all events they could see for themselves if there'd been more digging there than the dog would account for. It was odd what a difference Tom's visit had made. There wasn't one man setting out on that Saturday afternoon who didn't feel his blood chill a bit at the prospect before him.

They borrowed Solly's dog, Who. Tom suggested that. "He knows where he found the ring," he insisted. "There's been enough mucking time wasted as it is."

"The boys said they could identify the place by a cracked saucer," one of the policemen said.

Tom turned on him like the wrath of God. "I said get Solly's dog. This is my girl we're talking about. What do I care if your faces are red?"

So they agreed. After all, there could be more than one saucer and they didn't want to spend half the afternoon trailing through the muck and brambles of Broomstick Common looking for the right one.

"And keep the crowds away," added Tom Myers fiercely. "This isn't a peepshow."

They piled into the police van, the officers with their spades, Tom Myers, the dog and last of all Solly, because the dog wouldn't go without him. One of the policemen muttered that he wasn't a police dog, wasn't even trained. Solly, overhearing this, said, "He made it possible for the boy to find the ring. And I tell you this. We buy him a ball and presently the ball is lost. So he must have a piece of wood instead. Then we find him sitting by a cupboard in the hall, hour after hour sitting—like a cat watching a mouse-hole. At last we look, and there is the ball in the pocket of an old coat. I had forgotten. That dog is no fool."

The bush telegraph had been busy already with Linda's name and when the van drew up as near the canal as was possible a small crowd was standing about, muttering, speculating. Tom Myers turned, his face white and clenched.

"Haven't any of you people got homes to go to?" he demanded. And to the police, "Get those ghouls out."

"Stand back, please," said the senior sergeant. But they didn't move until Who suddenly turned and showed his tremendous fangs and, throwing up his head, let out a roar that made someone exclaim indignantly, "That dog's a menace."

"Too true he's a menace," Tom agreed. "Say the word and we'll let him off the leash. Well, you've come here for sport, haven't you?"

"We'll deal with them, sir," the sergeant promised, but though they withdrew they didn't go far. The Common was public property, wasn't it?

When they reached the palings Who was shown something belonging to the missing girl and taken off the leash. As he had done two nights before, he leaped forward like a great black cloud, with the men in pursuit.

"There's the saucer," exclaimed one of them. It was a

large pale blue affair, cracked across the middle. There was no time to stop and speculate as to how *that* got there, for the dog was digging furiously. Solly had some difficulty in prising him away, but once he had got the leash on his collar he beat a quick retreat. They'd done what was demanded of them, and Solly believed in keeping his nose clean and out of other men's affairs. Besides, he was a father himself; and he knew Who would never have made that furious assault on the earth for nothing.

The presence of Tom embarrassed all the others, but they could hardly ask him to go, and in any case he wouldn't have listened.

So the hideous job began.

She hadn't been buried very deep. If whoever was responsible had dug the regulation six feet the dog mightn't have found her. No one, seeing her for the first time, would have guessed she'd passed for a real beauty, so light, so vivid, great violet eyes and shining, shining hair. The youngest of the constables turned aside, retching. One of his superiors caught his arm.

"None of that, my lad. You're a copper, and don't you forget it. This may be the first time you've ever seen anything like this, but it's not likely it'll be the last." But he spoke without rancour, remembering his own first experience, when he'd been one of a party to find the body of a small boy, assaulted, strangled and concealed in a ditch. The young policeman was sheet-white, but he stood his ground after that. Tom Myers stared at the body with the awful expression of a man who has learned that what seemed too bad to contemplate is after all the truth.

"You identify her, sir?" the sergeant said.

"Do you have to ask that?" Tom muttered between clenched teeth.

"Yes, sir. We have to ask."

"That's my daughter. Was my daughter, rather." He still seemed unable to accept the appalling truth. This—this Thing, with blackened face and staring eyes, nothing here of the reputed peace or beauty of death—he couldn't yet equate it with his reckless darling.

"We'll get the chap responsible," the sergeant promised.

"And notch up another victory for the Force? I daresay. It'll be too late to help her—or me."

Two of the men had gone back to the van for the stretcher they had brought with them against just this emergency. They lifted her out of the unhallowed grave and covered her quickly.

"Get ahead, Bevan," the sergeant said to one of his men, "clear that lot off from round the van. We don't want another murder on our hands."

"Now get back," said the policeman to a crowd that seemed mysteriously to have doubled. News that the stretcher had been sent for had brought their interest to boiling-point. "You've had your fun, haven't you? Just think—we've got the father here—suppose it was one of your kids?"

"If she was mine she wouldn't be in this situation," declared one hardy soul.

"That's what you think." Bevan's voice was suddenly so fierce they all recoiled. "You don't know. That's one of the Creator's jokes. You just don't know."

They retreated then, though he suspected they were only watching from behind clumps of shrubs and trees. But when the dreadful little procession came crashing through the undergrowth he decided it wouldn't have mattered either way. Tom walked like a man in catalepsy, seeing nothing but that swollen unknown face.

"Where are you taking her?" he asked presently.

"It'll have to be the mortuary, Mr. Myers."

"For all the ghouls to come and gape?"

"No one'll be allowed in who can't show he's got a good reason. And we'd like you to come along with us now, we shan't keep you long. We must just have your formal evidence of identification. Better than you having to come back later . . ."

P.C. Hunter was on duty when they got back. "Nip round to Mrs. Myers and let her know what's happened," the sergeant said. "It's not going to break her heart, but she'd better be warned. Tom Myers has had as much as he can take, she's going to have a lot of responsibility during the next twenty-four hours."

"You would have to pick on me," Hunter muttered.

"You're a married man, aren't you? I can't send one of the lads. The best thing would be for him to get as drunk as an owl to-night, only he's not that sort. And if ever you say I told you that I'll call you a liar on the Book."

They brought Tom a cup of tea that he said he didn't want, but was surprised to find he had drunk almost before he'd finished speaking. Superintendent Boscombe of the local C.I.D. had a word with him—he began to think they'd never be done. These official reassurances that they'd get the chap, never fear, ran off him like water from a duck's back. At present he was wholly possessed by grief. There would be a time for vengeance but that would be later. Even the thought of his wife and baby son was no comfort to him now. He had some ado to absolve Brenda from blame. If she had won the girl's confidence—he wrenched his mind away from that tack. It wasn't that simple. He answered questions like an automaton, said that if he heard from Chris he'd be in touch, agreed to attend the inquest, and refused the offer of a car home.

"Better keep an eye on him when he starts coming round," said Boscombe sagely. "Still waters run deep—no one ever said a truer word."

CHAPTER IV

THE ENQUIRY shifted to the Polly household. Two police officers went round—the job had passed out of the jurisdiction of the uniform branch—and rang the bell. But though there was a light burning in what Mrs. Polly called the lounge no one answered the door.

Detective-Sergeant Bailey tried to peer through the curtains, but these had been cunningly drawn to show just a crack of light. There wasn't any sound from within and though Bailey stepped back nobody was peeping through curtains on the upper floor. From the gate a voice called unexpectedly, surprising them both.

"If you want Mrs. Polly," it said, "she's gone to the pictures. Saturday, see?"

"The light," murmured Inspector Crowthorne, who was in charge of the enquiry. The anonymous voice laughed.

"She always leaves that on. Thinks it gives the impression there's somebody in the house. Of course, to make a proper job of it you should leave the telly on, too." The neighbour draped herself conversationally over the gate. "A friend of mine has had a record made of a little dog barking," she confided. "If she has to leave her house on its lonesome she puts the record on, it's the sort that keeps repeating itself. Me, I leave the telly on. Well, these days you never know, do you? Such a lot of cheeky monkeys about and—you know how it is—when you look for a policeman there never seems to be one."

"You might put that on a record, too," suggested Bailey.

"You the police? I wondered. I mean, anyone else would know they go to the cinema every Saturday."

"Any idea when they'll be back?" Crowthorne enquired.

"They generally go to the second house. Starts about 4.30, programme's over about 7. Sometimes they come home right away, sometimes they have a snack."

"You know a good deal about their affairs, missis," Bailey ejaculated.

"I'm interested in humanity. You know that poem—the proper study of mankind is man, and that includes woman, wouldn't you say?"

It wasn't quite the phraseology Mrs. Polly herself would have employed. She put it more shortly. Nosey, she declared. "One of these days she'll get that long nose of hers caught in a trap, and may I be there to see."

"Are you sure there's no one at home?" Crowthorne persisted. "How about a baby-sitter?"

The neighbour let out a second screech of laughter. "I reckon Mr. Polly's the only baby he'll ever give his wife. Shame really, seeing how he likes kids. When Mrs. P.'s daughter by her first marriage—she's older than him, you know—had her little girl you could hardly keep Mr. P. away."

"If the programme's over about 7 and they drop in for a drink somewhere . . ."

"You try telling Mrs. P. that and she'll faint right off into your arms," she promised him, "and she's no light weight. Queen of the Temperance Club, that's her. You'd wonder a man could stand it. It's no wonder you hear of chaps keeping bottles in their bedrooms, only it wouldn't help much, Mrs. P.'s like the saints, more of a nose for sin than any sinner would dare to have." She looked casually up and down the road. "Well," she cried, "if you aren't in luck. Here they come. That's a nice car Mr. P. has, has it washed at Warren's twice a week, and if there's a screw loose round it goes. Better be safe than sorry, that's what Mr. P. says." She grinned. In the light of the street-lamp she showed a gay, skinny face, with two front teeth missing. "I'm off to get something warm inside me," she confided. "Don't tell Mrs. P. She'd probably put me on the black list, and the next time I went to have my hair done I'd find there wasn't a vacant date all week."

She vanished like a witch. Mr. Polly's sedate blue car drew up and the pair alighted. Mrs. Polly made strangers think of the Statue of Liberty, large and commanding and virtually indestructible. Like a wall she was, she'd never collapse, but on the other hand she'd never let you through, and if you tried to surmount it as like as not you'd find broken glass all along the top.

While Mr. Polly put the car away in the garage Mrs. Polly came marching up the path to say, "Are you sure you've come to the right address? We weren't expecting anyone—were we, Fred?" This last to her husband who came hurrying out of the garage.

"Speaking for myself, no," agreed Fred Polly. "Still, they say surprise . . ." He stopped. Something about the stance of the visitors seemed to halt his ready tongue. "You didn't mention who you were?"

He was a trim figure of a man, well-set-up in a slightly old-fashioned way, neat as a new pin.

The detective-inspector produced his warrant. "We're enquiring about Miss Linda Myers," he explained.

"That girl!" cried Mrs. Polly scornfully. "Well, open the door, Fred. We don't want to be seen standing about on the doorstep talking to the police. The neighbours . . ." she shrugged expressively and swept into a hall where no particle of dust would dare to settle. Mr. Polly politely ushered in the callers.

"I don't quite understand why you should come here," he said. "I'm the girl's employer, she doesn't lodge with us."

"When did you last see her, sir?"

Mr. Polly, hanging up his hat on its familiar peg, answered, "Actually, not since Thursday. She asked if she could get off a little early, she had some appointment . . ."

"And I suppose you let her go," interrupted Mrs. Polly, scornfully. "Weak as water, that's you, Fred."

"I thought you approved of water, my dear," said Fred in a meek voice. "Well, it was only half an hour to closing time, and she had no appointments booked, and, well, as I'm always telling Mrs. Polly, you have to give the young a bit of leeway these days, they have the power and well they know it."

"The power, sir?"

"You must think us very inhospitable," improvised Mr. Polly swiftly. "I'm afraid we don't keep any spirits in the house, but I'm sure Mrs. Polly could rustle you up a cup of coffee."

"Very acceptable," agreed Crowthorne promptly. It was the only way he could think of of getting Mrs. Polly out of the room for a couple of minutes. Mrs. Polly glared, but she went.

"About the power, sir," insinuated Crowthorne.

"Yes. Mrs. Polly may call it being irresponsible, but if you can't be that at Linda's age, it's a poor look-out. You can't expect old heads on young shoulders. Take your fun while you can get it, that's her gospel, and between you and me I think she gets quite a lot—of fun, I mean. And in a sense she has me over a barrel."

"What sense would that be, sir?"

"Oh, she could get herself a job at Agnew's any day of the week and we both know it. We're a very conservative establishment, running with a small staff, and nowadays the bulk of the money's in the hands of the young people. Since Agnew started up in the High Street a couple of years ago the competition's been fierce, very fierce indeed. My wife says it's all young men with beards wanting permanent waves and girls in mini-skirts, but that's where the money is. My chief assistants, Miss Reith and Miss Buxton, have been with me for some years, but what I wanted was someone contemporary. And Linda's certainly that. She's got the makings of a very good little hairdresser if only she can stay the course."

The door was pushed open and Mrs. Polly came back, carrying a tray with two cups on it.

"None for you, Fred," she said, briskly. "You know it keeps you awake. Now, Inspector, seeing my husband can't tell you anything I don't know, I take it there's no objection to my remaining."

"Did you know the girl?" asked Crowthorne.

"I suppose I'd recognise her in the street, if that's what you mean. A regular little flibberty-gibbet, a here-to-day-and-gone-to-morrow sort of girl. Oh, I daresay she can wind my husband round her finger and not only my husband. Never you count on that one, I tell him."

"You say you saw her Thursday evening and that's the last time?" This was to Mr. Polly, who answered, "Yes. Mind you, I expected her yesterday morning, but her father telephoned to say she had a chill."

Before the inspector could speak Mrs. Polly burst out, "You never told me that. And surely you didn't believe it?"

"Why shouldn't I believe it?" demanded Mr. Polly, turning red.

"Because her father's a commercial traveller, who doesn't get back till Saturday. I should have thought even you would have known that. No," she turned to the police officers, "it's perfectly obvious what happened. She felt like taking a day off and got one of her friends to send a message—why are you here, anyway?" she added, suspiciously. "What's Linda Myers done?"

"You haven't heard, madam? But the whole place is buzzing with it. Of course, if you've been at the cinema . . . ."

"Who told you that?"

"I don't know the lady's name."

"That Mary Hampton, I daresay. Knows more about your own business than you know yourself."

"The inspector's going to tell us why he's here," interjected Mr. Polly in an agitated voice.

So Crowthorne told them about the find on Broomstick Common.

Mrs. Polly was the first to speak. "I can't pretend to be surprised. No, Fred, it's the truth. That girl was asking for trouble, and now she's got it."

"I can't take it in," said Mr. Polly in dazed tones. "She was like—oh, like a beam of sunlight. Even some of our older customers couldn't resist her. She had such coaxing ways. She'd make them try out new styles they'd never dreamed of. If you don't like it I'll take it all down and do it again for free, she'd say. You couldn't help being attracted by her. You'd hardly think anyone would dare—put out a light like that, I mean."

"I never knew you were such a poet, Fred," said Mrs. Polly dryly. "Oh, I admit the girl was a good little actress, but then she had plenty of practice."

Mr. Polly turned a pale outraged face upon her. "Don't talk about her like that," he said hoarsely. "She's dead, isn't she? But why, Inspector?"

"We don't know that yet, sir. It could even have been a sort of accident, only that's not the way a court's going to look at it."

"Murder under extreme provocation," suggested Mrs. Polly.

"It's a funny thing," said Inspector Crowthorne reflectively. "The public's going to think worse of this chap for burying her than for strangling her. Murder can be a matter of impulse or, as the lady says, of accident, it's even possible to get it reduced to manslaughter if you can show there's no premeditation. But burying the body, that's something you do deliberately."

"If she was stupid enough to go down to the canal," Mrs. Polly began, but her husband said, "We don't know she did go down there, do we, Inspector? You only know you found the body there. And she wasn't a wicked girl, she liked to feel she could—well, you said it yourself, Laura— she liked to think she could wind people round her little finger. I don't think she got much change out of that step-mother of hers . . ."

"If any sympathy's going, mine's with Brenda Myers," said Mrs. Polly frankly. "I always told Fred, that girl will play her games once too often."

"What did you mean by that, Mrs. Polly?"

"The way she used to play one man off against another. She didn't even bother to get off with the old love before she was on with the new."

"Then you might be able to tell us the names of some of her admirers. That would be of great assistance."

Mrs. Polly shrugged her expensively-covered shoulders. "I wouldn't even know their names. I only know that she always seemed to be around with a new man—there was that chap said to have come from London, she was running around with him for a while . . ."

"You don't know his name?"

"Tall, fair fellow. I'd have thought he was a cut above Linda. Not that Tom Myers isn't a very respectable sort of man. I daresay it's not his fault the girl ran so wild."

"Laura, can't you take it in you're talking about a girl who's been murdered?" Mr. Polly's voice sounded anguished. "I daresay she made trouble for herself, but no one deserves that sort of come-back."

"She never mentioned anyone called Chris, I suppose?"

Mr. Polly frowned. "I don't recall—but then I didn't see such a lot of her. Why don't you have a word with Miss Reith or Miss Buxton?" He hesitated. "Perhaps I should say that Miss Buxton isn't altogether unprejudiced. She and Linda never really got on. Miss Reith was different. She was more tolerant. She's only young, she'd say, and she'll have responsibilities soon enough." He supplied the addresses of both his assistants. There was a girl who helped with the shampoo-ing, and he gave her name too, but he didn't think she and Linda saw much of each other. This girl had only been with them for a fortnight. "Agnew snaps up the young ones, it's better money for them there," he explained.

"Friday's the day she draws her salary, isn't it, Mr. Polly?"

"That's right."

"You didn't think it odd her not coming in to collect?"

"I told you, I had this telephone call."

"Oh yes. From someone calling himself Mr. Myers. Can you remember if it was long-distance?"

"Now I come to think of it, it was a call-box. It didn't strike me at the time."

"No question of your sending her salary round?"

Mr. Polly looked a little sheepish. "As a matter of fact, she'd subbed most of it during the week. She'd wanted to buy something and she'd put down a deposit and she wanted it specially, she said, for a date she had on Thursday."

"Do you generally allow your assistants to sub on their wages?"

"Miss Buxton and Miss Reith wouldn't dream of asking. Well, they're middle-aged women, they budget. I did think it was some proof of the relations between her and her stepmother that she couldn't ask Brenda Myers to lend her the cash."

"Probably asked her once too often," suggested Mrs. Polly waspishly. "I know the type, take, take all the way."

"It's the way she was born," said Mr. Polly. "Some people are like that. It's second nature to them to put out their hands and expect whatever they want to be put into them. Just as there's the other sort that do the giving automatically. Why, even clients who'd never have tipped Miss Buxton or Miss Reith more than a shilling or eighteenpence at most would part with half-a-crown to Linda."

"I don't want to speak evil of the dead," said Mrs. Polly,

"but she was a little gold-digger. I'm sorry, of course, that she's come to this terrible end, and I hope you find the man who did it. I suppose she wasn't in trouble?" she added abruptly.

"Isn't getting yourself murdered trouble enough?" her husband demanded, his voice as harsh as the north wind. "And she simply lived for the day. Yesterday's gone and we don't know about to-morrow, she used to say." He stopped there, as though it was being borne in on him more finally than ever that to-morrow would no longer be her concern.

"He protested a lot, didn't he?" said Crowthorne to Sergeant Bailey who had accompanied him. "In his favour in a way. He wouldn't have dared to be so partisan if there'd been anything between them."

"I don't think Linda Myers would ever have looked at a man like that," said the sergeant simply. "Polly's forty if he's a day, and if he even looked across the road at another woman Mrs. Polly would have his head on a charger for breakfast. The whole place knows that."

"I shall have to get up a bit earlier in the morning and learn what everyone else seems to know," the inspector murmured. "Let's see Miss Buxton and Miss Reith and get their reactions. Women are always the best witnesses where another woman's concerned, I mean, they see things a man wouldn't even notice or understand if he did."

The bush telegraph had been at work, all right. Miss Buxton had heard the news and had immediately telephoned Miss Reith. Crowthorne found them together in Miss Buxton's flat, which reminded him of the Polly establishment, a place for everything and everything in its place (particularly Mr. Polly). Miss Buxton expressed genteel shock, but the inspector saw that, to her illogical female mind, justice had in some way been done. (Crook, who saw her later, said, "The girl might have been a jackdaw strung up by a farmer as an awful warning, for all the feeling she showed.")

"I can't tell you anything," said Miss Buxton firmly, taking the lead as Mrs. Polly had done. "Neither of us knows anything, do we, Margaret? No, of course we don't, all we know is rumour and rumour isn't proof, and proof is what the police want, isn't that right, Inspector?"

"I couldn't have put it better myself," Crowthorne agreed.

"Still, you might know the name of someone she'd been going around with," put in Sergeant Bailey. "She could have confided in you—I mean, her and her stepmother . . ."

Miss Buxton laughed harshly. "I don't see Linda confiding in Brenda Myers. Why, it was war to the knife between them. Brenda was as jealous as could be of that girl—well, we all know she was the apple of Tom Myers's eye. Yes, we do, Margaret, you know how startled we all were when he got married again, and only a man would have been crazy enough to suppose those two would settle down together. Why, I believe Linda would have made a play for the boss himself, if she hadn't known it was a waste of time. Poor Mr. Polly, he's like one of those birds with a label tied on its leg . . ."

"Oh, Audrey, don't," Miss Reith besought her. "I know you didn't always approve of Linda, but she's dead, and in this dreadful way. I do hope you find out who did it, Inspector, and if I could help you in any way I would, but Linda hardly spoke to us. I suppose to her we were as old as the hills . . ."

"Speak for yourself, Margaret," Miss Buxton snapped. "And she stayed because she knew she could do just what she liked here. Don't tell me Agnew's would have let her keep her own hours, well, more or less, ten minutes late in the morning, an extra quarter of an hour for lunch, and did you ever know her stay five minutes after we closed to help to clear things up or take a late appointment? And we all know how she favoured her friends, saying she'd just trimmed a neck when you and I know she had given a full cut, and not charging for a shampoo and telling the boss she'd just damped the hair, which, of course, you have to do before you can set it. Why, with my own eyes I've seen her put on a special application, which is three-and-six extra, but there was never any mention of it on the bill."

"That's not the kind of thing the sergeant wants to know," insisted Margaret Reith. "He wants to know if we can help with any suggestion of someone who might have killed her, and of course we don't know. To die in such a dreadful way . . ."

"How she'd enjoy all the fuss if she knew about it," commented Miss Buxton, viciously.

"You didn't like her, did you, miss?" suggested the sergeant.

"I don't like cheats, and she was one. And all that showing off! I remember saying to her once, When you have your own salon, and I suppose that's what you're looking forward to, and she laughed and said, 'Come the day, I'll be giving the orders. It 'ud be nice to have all that power. Don't you ever wish it could be you telling the others?' . . . I said, of course, I was perfectly satisfied with my job, and so I am, Inspector. Mr. Polly's a most considerate employer, and of course Linda took advantage of it. I'm sure Mr. Polly knew she wouldn't stop long anyway, which is why he didn't really bother. She'd never stop long anywhere, that girl. She was with Robinson's at one time, but it didn't last."

"We should all enjoy power if we had the chance," said Margaret Reith simply. "And she was very young."

"She knew how to get round you all right." Audrey nodded. "And she wasn't so irresistible that she didn't get herself murdered in the end."

"You have to have something to get yourself murdered," Miss Reith said.

They both agreed that the girl had left early on Thursday evening, though neither had actually seen her go. Miss Buxton said someone came in without an appointment for a trim . . . "And we generally manage to fit them in if they're regular customers, because it doesn't take long and Linda was quite clever at that kind of thing, and I could see from the book she had no appointment that evening, and then I realised she'd disappeared. Mr. Polly said she had asked if she could go a little early and as we weren't expecting anyone else he'd agreed. Just out of hairdressing school," fumed Miss Buxton, "and she got practically the same rates as experienced assistants like Miss Reith and myself. Have you any idea who's responsible, Sergeant?"

"If we knew that, miss, we shouldn't be asking questions, should we?"

"There was this one called Chris." Miss Buxton meditated, and the sergeant's attention sharpened at once. "No, I don't know his other name. I was admiring that ring she had, and she said, 'Yes, Chris has good taste, hasn't he? Though I earned it, and not the way you might think.'"

But when it came to giving a description of the mysterious Chris the sergeant got very little help. "I saw her around once or twice with a tall, fair man, late twenties, I'd say," Miss Buxton allowed. "She liked them tall, she was quite a little thing herself, which was an advantage in its way, because she could make even short men feel big."

"So where does that get us?" demanded the inspector sourly. "A tall fair chap called Chris. Well, that ties up with what Solly Gold told us, but it doesn't give us much of a lead. Of course, if Myers is right and this chap is coming to see him to-morrow . . ." But neither he nor the sergeant believed that one.

"Girl may simply have said it to keep her father calm," the sergeant said.

"Oh, and the autopsy has just come in," the inspector said. "Girl was pregnant—no suggestion from the step-mother?"

"Not a word, and if she'd known she'd have told. She couldn't hope to keep a thing like that hidden."

"Could be a motive," Crowthorne hazarded, "though in this permissive day and age it's not a very good reason for committing murder."

"Unless it's a married man," countered the sergeant shrewdly. "One who didn't want to lose his status and didn't fancy paying out blackmail."

"It doesn't have to be a premeditated crime, of course.
Well, I think we might call it a day."

The telephone rang and it was Solly Gold, ringing to
say he'd just remembered something. Several weeks earlier
he had seen some rather pleasing blue cups and saucers in
Mrs. Politi's self-styled antique store, and had gone in to
enquire how many were available. He had wanted three
but she only had two, though she had a number of addi-
tional saucers. She said she always bought in the odd
saucers because it was surprising how easy it was to sell
them. People bought them to stand under flower-pots or
for make-shift soap dishes or ashtrays. He had been reminded of the occasion this evening when his wife served
tea in the cups. He was certain that the cracked blue
saucer his son had noticed near the impromptu grave was
one of those from Mrs. Politi's store. He had heard that
there was a little elderly lady who often went out during
the week feeding the wild cats on the Common, so it seemed
possible that she was responsible for the saucer being where
it was.

"If it had been there for long it would be encrusted,"
said Mr. Gold earnestly. "So much rain, so much mud. But
the saucer was clean, licked clean my Reuben say. So perhaps the little lady heard something—no, I have no information, it is just an idea. Her name is Miss Forbes, and
she works at Robinson's."

He couldn't supply her address. "She is no client of mine,
you understand, but respectable—and kind. You would
need to be kind to go all that distance for some cats that
do not even belong to you."

By now it was 10.30 p.m., and the rain was coming
down in sheets. It was agreed that Miss Forbes should be
contacted first thing next morning. Though if she had seen
anything she would surely have reported it to the police
before now. Even the most optimistic constable would
never connect her with the violent death of a girl.

"She may not even have heard the news," one of the

force offered, but the inspector said she'd need to be as deaf as an adder not to. "By the way, didn't one of those women at the Polly shop say Linda had worked at Miss Robinson's for a time?"

It showed how desperate they were that they should snatch so easily at so frail a straw. If one of May's derelict cats had strolled in with even a whisker of evidence at that stage it would probably have been provided with enough salmon to last it for the rest of its life.

On Sunday mornings Mrs. Politi rose a little later than usual, though she didn't go to Mass till 12 o'clock. But she liked to take her coffee and rolls and sit in the window and watch the world go by. Her bedroom looked as though it had been lifted clean out of a museum, good solid Victorian furniture that was rapidly coming into its own, and large china ornaments and vases. Not very much normally went on at this hour, but if there should be anything exceptional you couldn't hope to see it by lying in bed. The usual faithful few, little black net squares in hand, went down the hill to St. Aloysius. Others, primmer, wearing what Lilli called derisively a holy look, and carrying small prayer-books as opposed to the enormous missals of the Catholics, plodded in the opposite direction. The nonconformists didn't surface until later, and last of all came the Christian Scientists, in Mrs. Politi's opinion, the best turned-out of the lot. She had no sooner settled herself than she realised that something unusual was afoot in the flat opposite. Usually May had a nice lie-in on Sundays, a breakfast tray in bed, and then off to the chapel where she helped to lay out the music. Mrs. Politi had hardly got over the surprise of seeing the light burning so early, when it was extinguished, and a minute later May emerged, not carrying a service book, but equipped with macintosh and umbrella, and she turned, not in the direction of the chapel, but up a side-street, walking purposefully and wearing the hat that she considered rather showy for chapel.

Where she go? wondered Mrs. Politi. There was only

one place where she could be going and that was the station. The few food shops that braved the nonconformist conscience and opened their doors on the Sabbath wouldn't be stirring yet—but why a train on Sunday morning? It wasn't even as though she was carrying luggage—not that you could imagine May doing a flit, and what reason had she? But Mrs. Politi's feelings were outraged. Surely if you are going to do anything so out of character as catch a train at an hour when most of your neighbours are still asleep, you would confide in your best friend, the one who lives just over the way?

"That May, she getting sly," announced an indignant Mrs. Politi to an immense china horse that served as a door-stop. Considering, she decided that the metamorphosis had started on the night that May came back from feeding her beloved cats in the company of a strange man in an unforgettable yellow car. Perhaps she go to meet him now, Lilli confided to the horse, a noble inscrutable creature, and would probably have dropped dead from shock if she had known she'd hit the bullseye.

After that everything started to go haywire. Mrs. Politi had just dressed, not because there was any reason to dress so early but because she felt restless, when a police car drew up at the house opposite and an officer got out. He rang May's bell, but of course there was no reply, and in the meantime the man who owned the lower flat had disappeared with his wife or the woman who passed as his wife, so there was nobody to answer the bell. Lilli pushed up the window-sash.

"You want Mr. Eccles?" she shouted, cunningly. "He gone out. With the car. And that woman go with him."

The officer came across the road and Lilli hurtled down the stairs to open the door.

"We're trying to contact Miss Forbes," he explained.

Lilli smirked. "She go too, but not with Mr. Eccles. I think she go to the station."

"Did you happen to notice if she took any luggage?"

Mrs. Politi looked surprised. "Why she take luggage? She have a conscience, she don't shirk her duty. Miss

Robinson expect her to-morrow, so to-morrow she go to the shop."

"You don't know where she might have gone?"

"She not tell me," acknowledged Lilli, "but I think she go to meet the man, the one who bring her home the night Linda Myers is murdered."

The police officer was about to put another question, but she grabbed him by the arm and pulled him into the passage.

"Walls have ears," she reminded him, "and sometimes they don't hear right. I think she in plenty trouble. Never before she miss the choir, a nice voice she has, sometimes she sing the anthem, and I tell you this, never before does she miss chapel. Oh, she in trouble all right."

"Who is this man who brought her home, Mrs. Politi?"

Lilli spread her hands. "Do I know all her friends? She miss the bus, he give her a lift, put her down at the corner. That I see. Maybe she tell you to-night when she come back."

"Of course," suggested the officer rather nervously, "you didn't notice the number of the car?"

To his surprise Mrs. Politi's face suddenly split into an enormous grin. "You know Elijah?"

"Elijah who?" He wondered if Elijah was the name of the mysterious driver.

"Elijah-taken-up-into-Heaven-in-a-chariot-of-fire," gabbled Lilli. "This car like that, big and yellow. And very fast."

"And she didn't mention his name? Or where he came from? Or even where she met him?"

"She wait at the bus stop, the bus has gone, he come, he give her a lift." She chuckled again. "The Gingerbread Man, that who he look like." Then her manner sobered. "I tell you, mister, someone frighten May. Friday she don't go to the Common. A man speak to her, she say, she afraid, see? Well, I tell you she damn' afraid not to go for her precious cats."

"I understand she leaves food for them in saucers."

"Saucers I give her." It wasn't quite the truth but at a

penny a time you could really call it giving them away. "Monday, Tuesday, Thursday, Friday, she go to the Common, Wednesday we go to the pictures, Saturday she go to choir practice."

"But this Friday she stayed at home. You would recognise your own saucers, Mrs. Politi?"

"Plenty saucers I don't sell," said Mrs. Politi blandly.

But she finally agreed that *the* saucer was the facsimile of those she had sold to Solly, so that was one point out of the way. The police, who felt they were competing in a snail race, sighed with relief.

"You think May Forbes bury the girl?" Mrs. Politi asked.

"Of course not. But if she was down there that night she could have heard something. This man who spoke to her . . ."

"You think he the murderer? That May! So quiet and so sly."

"I don't know that it's such an advantage to have met a man who may have killed a girl," said one of the police officers severely.

"And then she meet Mr. Elijah and he bring her back." Lilli shook her head. "No need to marry to have excitement."

"Is she on the telephone, Mrs. Politi?"

"She say she summoned by bells—a funny thing that?—all day in the shop, at home—peace."

"If she comes back before night . . ."

"She come back," prophesied Lilli serenely. "She not stay away with Miss Alice having her strokes and Miss Phyllis coping and that nephew watching like a swordfish who he pierce. Oh yes, May back in time for work tomorrow."

She half-rose to indicate that the interview was at an end. One of the officers remembered a film he'd once seen about Queen Victoria, just the same cocksure old aristocrat, though everyone knew Mrs. Politi didn't come of aristocratic stock. "She say it was her duty to come back," Lilli wound up. "I tell her her duty to herself, but no, that

May, she die for her duty and no one the better off, but—"
she shook her huge head of brilliantly black hair—"no
sense. I have a phone," she added, delicately. "Maybe I
give her a message. Maybe when you ask she tell you why
she go off so early, desert her chapel—maybe."

"We must hope so," authority agreed, thinking it would
be nice to be told something for a change. So far they were
still blundering around in the dark.

CHAPTER V

THAT SAME MORNING while Mrs. Politi was bedevilling the
police, Mr. Crook sat in his office tearing his way through
the Sunday press and looking hopefully at the telephone.
The notion that man should rest on the Sabbath had never
found a sympathiser in him. One-seventh of life idled away,
he'd have said. And "The better the day the better the
deed," and it seemed that quite a number of his clients
agreed with him. He had finished reading about an invisible wolf, a sort of Loch Ness monster of the woods, that
was ravaging a village in one of the northern counties,
when his front-door bell buzzed, and he was on his feet
with an alacrity that would have done credit to a prize
army cadet. He pressed the release mechanism that would
open the front door and came on to the upper staircase.
His flat was at the top of the building, and leaning over
the well he saw a small figure trudging purposefully up-
wards.

"Will you walk into my parlour?" enquired Mr. Crook
joyfully.

The small figure turned up a face as round as a plate.
"It's May Forbes," called a voice no louder than a ghost.

"If you're afraid of waking the other tenants, don't give
it a thought," bellowed Mr. Crook. "Judgment Day'll
hardly wake some of them."

"Perhaps I shouldn't have come on a Sunday," protested
May, "but I couldn't very well leave Miss Phyllis all by her-

self to-morrow, and though Jack Hardy means well he's something of a bull in a china-shop."

Panting slightly, she reached the top floor. "Come in, Sugar," Mr. Crook invited her heartily, "don't know when I've been more pleased to see anyone."

She blinked at what seemed to her the confusion of the room into which she was ushered, but Mr. Crook, with a wave at the uncurtained window, said, "Best view in London. All those houses, all the houses full of rooms, all the rooms full of people and any one of them might need my help any minute. Keeps you on the buzz, you know."

He looked as new-minted as if he'd been turned out from some Machiavellian machine only that morning.

"It's about Linda Myers," said May, coming to the point with a directness that delighted him. "You've seen the news, I'm sure."

"I've read the pieces in the paper," Mr. Crook agreed, "but when you're as old as me you'll know the important bits are the ones they don't print."

May nodded. She felt suddenly dizzy. "Have any breakfast?" asked the astute Mr. Crook. "Nice cup of tea, I suppose? That's what I thought. I'll give you something better than tea. Just for medicinal purposes, if that's the way you like it," he added.

He poured some brandy into a glass. "They won't give you better than that on the Health Service." He produced a box of biscuits. "My First-Aid pack," he told her, beaming. "Now, Sugar, put yourself outside that, and then come clean. You were holding out on me last time, and don't think I didn't know it."

This direct attack made May blink. "I couldn't know it was a girl he had in the boot," she protested. "I mean, you don't expect—and it isn't as if I could recognise him again, because of the mask."

"So just what did you think he was doing?" enquired Mr. Crook, taking this remarkable confidence in his stride. "Chap in a mask at dead of night with something mysterious in the boot of his car. Didn't happen to see a spade, I suppose?"

"Actually, I did," confessed May. "That's really what alarmed me."

"Must be the understatement of the year. Just tell me, Sugar, and remember you'll have to tell the police, too, so it better be good, just what did you think the chap was doing?"

"I thought it might be a dog," babbled May. "A big dog."

"You don't generally put on a mask to bury a dog," suggested Mr. Crook reasonably.

"It would depend on the dog. I mean, if it was one you'd run down and you thought it might be valuable. You're supposed to report it to the police, but it might be someone who didn't want to—I mean, he mightn't find it convenient—and you can't exactly leave a dog lying in the road, though that does happen sometimes to cats . . ."

"So the fellow put on a mask and retreated to the woods, goin' to a place where no one was supposed to hang around, and there you are—why?"

"I told you, I feed the cats."

"So you did, Sugar. You must have given him a shock."

"He gave me a shock. I explained about the kitten—well, I told you that—and I couldn't get away fast enough. I suppose if I'd heard next day that someone was missing I might have linked it up, but no one was, not till the police went digging by the canal last night, and found that poor girl. I knew then, of course, I'd have to tell them what I'd seen and heard, but I thought I should get some advice, and you had said—I mean, you gave me your card, and of course as a rule I don't need a lawyer."

"What do you expect me to tell you?" asked Crook.

"On the films," explained May shyly, "they always say, I wish to speak to my lawyer . . ."

"That's when they're bein' accused of some crime. You don't think the police are goin' to suspect you . . ."

"Well, of course not. But it's nice to feel you have someone *behind* you. Not that I don't trust the police, of course I do."

"Mentioned this to anyone else?" asked Crook.

"Only Mrs. Politi. I told her I'd seen a man by the canal and he spoke to me. I had to tell her something because she saw me getting out of your car. She's my neighbour, a very kind woman, she sometimes gives me pieces for the cats, but she does talk."

"It's when they make you talk you have to start watching your p's and q's," Mr. Crook commented.

"She's very curious . . ."

"No harm in that. Curiosity may have killed the cat but it's saved a lot of lives, whatever the moralists may tell you. Tell her much?"

"Just that I'd seen a man who made me nervous and then you saw me waiting at the bus stop and gave me a lift home. She wanted me to go to the police, but I said no one had done me any harm, the man didn't threaten me in any way, and they'd simply say I was asking for trouble, going down there by myself at night. And I suppose in a way they're right," added May honestly, "only nothing's ever gone wrong before, I mean, I've never met anyone. And it's not as though I can really help much. I wouldn't know the car again and I wouldn't know the driver. I don't know that I'd even recognise the voice. He spoke as though he had a sore throat or something, kind of muffled."

"If I was found burying a girl at dead of night I'd have a muffled voice, too," said Mr. Crook generously. "You still don't think there was something rummy about the mask? Or do they all wear masks for night driving in your part of the world?"

"I did think that a bit strange," May confessed, "but, of course, if it was a valuable dog he wouldn't want to be recognised, and that and the balaclava—did I say?—and the darkness, well, it would be difficult to know him again."

"You didn't answer my question," Mr. Crook pointed out. "Do your drivers mostly wear masks?"

"Well, of course, in the ordinary way—but this wasn't ordinary. You see, the Saturday before, I don't mean yesterday, of course, the Saturday before that, there was this Students' Rag at Ainstown, that's the next town on the map to Churchford, about eight miles away, and there was quite a pageant, or would have been if the weather hadn't turned so bad. The students were going round in all sorts of disguises to get money for the Cottage Hospital. One of them was dressed like an ape (she disregarded Crook's hearty suggestion that most likely he didn't find the change very different) and frightened an old lady out of her wits. And there was someone on one of the floats dressed as Death —the Arch-Enemy, you see—and he wore a mask. And Linda was taking part, I remember, because she came to see Miss Alice, she came in occasionally to wash her hair after Miss Alice found it difficult to get about—of course, she made it worth her while, Miss Alice, I mean, she really did love seeing Linda, and you couldn't be surprised, she was so pretty and bright, and Linda must have had a good heart, because sometimes she'd stay on and read some of Miss Alice's letters to her, she kept all her old letters, she said her life, her real life, was all in the past . . ."

"So'll mine be, at this rate," commented Mr. Crook heartily. "Are you saying that the chap representing Death thought he might as well go a step further and put the theory into action?"

"Well, of course not." May looked shocked. "I don't even know which one he was and I daresay there was more than one. I only saw the floats as they went past the window, we don't close on Saturdays. Mr. Polly does and Agnew's stay open. Of course, they get the week-end trade, but Mr. Polly gets a lot from assistants and manageresses who don't work that day."

"Once when I was a kid I went into a maze," said Mr. Crook frankly. "Believe me, I thought I was going to die there before I found the way out. I'm beginning to feel the same way now. Let's recap. You stood in the doorway and watched the floats go by and there was this chap wearing a mask, and there could have been another . . ."

"I only saw a part of the procession, because a customer came in, and I never saw the return because of the rain, it really pelted down, and broke everything up. And, of course, I'm not naming any special person, I don't even know who was wearing the mask, I'm just pointing out that it wouldn't be so difficult for someone to have one. I mean, if he'd tried to buy it, or you can make them yourself with a square of felt and a bit of ribbon, we sell squares of felt at Robinson's, people buy them to make egg-cosies or children's toys, particularly at Christmas . . ."

"And you don't remember anyone buying one?"

"Well, no, but someone else might. Or I expect you can hire them at these theatrical costumiers, people going to fancy dress parties or doing charades, I used to do quite a lot of amateur theatricals myself when I was younger, I loved dressing-up, and you don't have to believe the psychologists who say it's because you're dissatisfied with your own life and are looking for compensation, I went to a lecture at Ainstown Town Hall once, and that's what the professor said . . ."

"It's all very interesting," said Mr. Crook solemnly, "and I could listen to you all day, but it's going to be different when you're talking to a chap in uniform. Uniform does something to people—you remember the tribe in the Good Book whose yea was yea and nay nay? Well, that's what the police 'ull expect, so before we go down to set a light in their darkness, it might be as well to separate what you think it could have been from what you really did see."

"You mean——" May's eyes were brilliant, she must have been a fetching little thing as a girl, Crook thought—"you're *coming with me?*"

"I thought that was the proposition. I mean, you didn't make this journey on a cold Sunday morning just for me to warm your hands. And one more thing, Sugar. Just remember, the uniform ain't the man. There's something about a uniform that works havoc even with the innocent. But underneath it is someone who has to blow his nose and cut his toe-nails, same like you and me. The other thing to remember is that X may not have set out to murder the girl, a lot of murders I know have been no more than unfortunate accidents, but once you're loaded with the corpse, what are you to do? I don't say it's ideal to dig a pit in a dark wood, but it's generally more convenient than keepin' the body on the premises."

"I suppose she could be tiresome," May allowed, and he marvelled at her discretion. "I know she used to annoy Miss Phyllis by serving her own friends first, she said old people had plenty of time on their hands, and she did quote special prices to them. I think she really didn't understand that it wasn't honest, and Miss Phyllis couldn't make her."

"Wonder they kept her as long as they did."

"That was Miss Alice. I think she saw her as the daughter she'd like to have had. If she'd been married, I mean."

"No secret romance?" asked Mr. Crook.

"I did hear a reference once to someone she'd lost and never really got over . . ."

She looked so woebegone that Crook clapped her on the shoulder. "Window-dressing, Sugar!" he declared. "Of course, the world's changed a lot since I was a boy, but human nature don't change much, and when I was a lad every maiden lady had a gentleman friend who died on his way out to India. Funny how lethal journeys to India were in those days. Of course, we don't go there any more. And I bet there's greater mortality on the Kingston Bypass in the 'sixties, but of course the Kingston Bypass wasn't conceived or thought of then."

He wondered what the police were going to make of his client. They might start by seeing her as a woolly-minded old dear, who'd probably dreamed up half her story at least, but it wouldn't be long before they changed their minds. Even without his support he could see she wouldn't let herself be brow-beaten, and she'd hold her own, all with an air so gentle and placatory that even a bluebottle would start feeling a brute if he pushed her too hard.

The police were still at sixes and sevens when Mr. Crook arrived with his client. As soon as the plain-clothes branch heard that May had arrived they even showed enthusiasm. When they heard about her escort, enthusiasm paled a bit.

"Trust Crook to winkle his way in, even outside his own

manor," grumbled Crowthorne. "Still, she's got something to tell us to make it worth his while coming down to Churchford. We'd better have 'em both in."

When he saw May he said they'd been hoping for this meeting.

"Hope don't always pay such rapid dividends," agreed Mr. Crook.

"I suppose you'll think I should have come to you right away," May acknowledged, forgetting everything Crook had told her. "But I didn't really know anything. I just saw a man in a car down by the canal, and he had a spade, but, as I said to Mr. Crook, he might have been burying a dog."

"The police are like me," said Crook. "Imagination ain't their strong suit. I mean, they do like their facts in order. Start at the beginning, and if there's anything they don't understand they can stop you and ask."

So May told her story steadily, aware that to them it must sound absurdly melodramatic. "Mr. Crook says I might have known it wasn't a dog, I mean, he wouldn't have to display so much secrecy, but some dogs are very valuable, I met a woman once who told me she'd given £175 for a poodle, it wasn't even very pretty, one of those very sharp noses, and I don't know if insurance would cover running down a dog. And then, of course, there's the breathalyser. If it was someone whose living depended on his car, he wouldn't dare take risks."

"Did he sound intoxicated to you?"

"I told Mr. Crook, his voice sounded odd, but that might be because he was afraid I might recognise it."

"Somebody you knew, you mean?"

May looked horrified. "I didn't say that. But—well, it was an English voice, I mean, you can always tell, however they try to disguise it, foreigners still retain a trace of accent. It might have been clever if he'd pretended to speak broken English, but I think I took him by surprise as much as he took me. I told him about my kitten in case he thought I was spying on him or something. Actually, I felt rather nervous."

"But you still thought he was burying a dog?"

"I thought it could be a dog. Well, you don't go for a walk and expect to meet somebody burying a girl you know. And it's no use asking me what he looked like, because what with the mask—what they call a domino, I think—and the balaclava which hid his hair and the general darkness, well, it could have been practically anyone."

"You didn't mention this, not even to Mrs. Politi?"

"Well, especially not to Mrs. Politi, because—I daresay it's her foreign blood—she's like the poet who saw Heaven in a wild flower, if you get my meaning, only in her case it wouldn't be Heaven or a flower. And if I had told anyone else, before Linda's disappearance became public property, I mean, they'd just have thought I was crazy. You might even have thought so yourself."

"She's got you there," said Crook, grinning.

"But you didn't mind telling Mr. Crook?"

"He'd said—he drove me back that night and of course I didn't tell him then, because in a way you could say it was no affair of mine—but he said if I ever should need any help here was his card. So when I heard about Linda I remembered that—he had been so kind," she wound up.

"Oh, Mr. Crook's a very kind man," Inspector Crowthorne agreed. "But you didn't really need him to tell you where your duty lay."

"No. No, of course I didn't," May acknowledged. "But when you're on your own and you're a woman and not young any more, and you've never had much to do with the police, well, nothing really, except once when I slipped on a banana skin and an officer came up after a minute to ask if I was all right, and of course I was, and anyway someone else had helped me to my feet by then—it's rather nice to have someone *behind* you. I've always thought that was the great advantage of being married. Someone else buys the tickets and asks the policeman the way. And naturally, Mr. Crook said I should come to you at once, even if I couldn't help you much, because you might be able to read something into the situation that hadn't occurred to me."

77

"Or to Mr. Crook? That's difficult to believe."

"He said I should just tell you what I'd seen and heard and you'd understand."

"Mr. Crook's got a very high opinion of the police all of a sudden."

"You should try living a blameless life yourself," suggested Mr. Crook heartily. "Virtue may get you extra points in the hereafter, but in this sinful world it has a very constraining effect."

"Has it helped at all?" pleaded May. "What I've told you, I mean."

"It narrows the field considerably," the inspector said. "We know that Miss Myers left her employment just after five p.m. on Thursday, and you saw this stranger digging a grave—what precise time would you say?"

"I couldn't be precise," said May, knitting her brows. "I left home about seven-thirty and I walked to the Common and I didn't go very fast, because of frightening the cats . . ."

"Lady came into the Rampant Horse just after nine," said Crook.

"Mr. Crook means the Mettlesome Horse," May explained.

"Do I?" said Crook. "He'd been out to grass so long . . . how long would it have taken you to walk, Sugar?"

"About twenty minutes, I think."

"So Miss Myers was probably killed between 5.30 and 8 —those are the outside figures." 6 to 7 or 7.30 was his own idea.

"I'm sorry I can't help you more. Of course, the person you want is the person she was going to meet on Thursday when she left Mr. Polly. It doesn't prove he's the one responsible . . ."

"He?"

May looked honestly astonished. "I can't imagine Linda getting off early to meet a girl-friend," she said. "But perhaps someone will remember seeing her with an escort that night and come in and tell you."

"I can see you believe in miracles, Miss Forbes," the inspector said.

"Oh, I do," agreed May. "The difficulty is one doesn't recognise them at the time. It's like angels, who come in the strangest guises."

"If you're looking at me," said Mr. Crook, "thank you for the kind thought. Now, you're going to be asked to sign a statement, and read it through carefully . . ."

"I'm sure it'll be all right if it's only what I've said," urged May.

"That's why you have to read it."

At last he did take her away. "How does Crook do it?" the inspector murmured. "Has 'em all eating out of his hand, young and old. I could do with a miracle or two myself."

And at that moment, though he wasn't aware of it, his miracle was drawing nearer and nearer to Churchford.

CHAPTER VI

Chris Wayland, tall, fair, twenty-seven years old, a bit of a rolling stone, explaining himself to himself as a seeker for the right niche in life, came out of his lodging at Hornby that Sunday morning at about eleven o'clock and walked down the main street looking for a newsagent. He was in a strange town, shaping out one more of a series of articles—Primitive Life in the Twentieth Century, they were called—and his thoughts were running on his work. He bypassed the queue of the devout outside the Roman Catholic Church and another queue waiting for the Sunday morning bus, and found a stationer and tobacconist that was open. And went in. And, in a sense, you could say he sealed his fate.

The girl behind the counter was small and dark, some might have called her dumpy, but Chris remembered a song about a nut-brown maiden which seemed much more appropriate. When she looked up to take his order he saw that she seemed to twinkle—no, he amended, to sparkle—not just her eyes that were a kind of golden-brown—but her whole personality. He looked at her small capable hands slipping out a paper from a pile, reaching to a shelf for the cigarettes he preferred, and he asked, surprising himself as much as her, "What's your name?"

"Well, you didn't leave your tongue with the cat to-day," said the girl coolly. But the sparkle was like diamond-dew. He thought for an instant she wasn't going to tell him, then she relented and said, "It's Jennifer, since you're interested."

"And I suppose everyone calls you Jenny. Jenny Wren."

"How did you guess?"

He didn't smile, as she'd anticipated. "The inference of the obvious," he said. "How long does this shop stay open on Sundays?"

"As long as there's any call for goods. Say five o'clock."

His thick fair brows lifted. "No trade union?"

"My mum says I don't need any union so long as I've got her."

He nodded. He took the change she offered him and folded the paper under his arm, slipped the cigarettes into his pocket.

"Are you promised?" he asked her, and she stared.

"Well, there's a way to talk!"

"I can see you're not wearing an engagement ring," he elaborated, "but—are you compromised by an understanding with anyone?"

"It means something to you if I say yes?" She was still laughing, but there was curiosity in her voice.

He said, "I don't like poachers, I'd always sooner persuade a man to go peaceably."

She leaned her elbows on the counter and met his gaze clearly. "Do you talk to all the girls this way?"

"I'd be wearing manacles long before now if I did," he pointed out. "I'm twenty-seven. How old are you?"

"Nineteen." She spoke before she could stop herself. "Though what affair it is of yours . . ."

"Half a man's age plus seven, that's what the philosophers used to say."

"I suppose you realise I don't know what you're on about."

A couple of other men came in for papers, and then a girl for cigarettes, and Jennifer served them, and out they walked, showing about as much feeling as if they'd got their purchases from a machine.

"It used to be the old recommendation—well, one of them, anyhow—for a successful marriage. Half a man's age plus seven. You see how well it fits."

"If you don't talk like this to every girl, why me, why to-day?"

"It's like Sir Isaac Newton and the apple." He paused, and she said, quite without sarcasm, "I went to school, too, you know."

"The point being he must have seen bushels of apples, growing on trees, too, before the day that was the turning-point of his existence. Probably he'd watched them fall, but one had to crash right on his head to give him the notion of the law of gravity. Maybe it jolted something in his brain that was—well, a bit sluggish—before then. In the same way," he continued composedly, and how should she guess that his heart was leaping like a hooked fish under his conservative jacket, "I've been seeing girls all my life. Nice girls. In the same way as Sir Isaac had probably eaten a lot of apples."

"We're open on a Sunday to sell papers and smokes," Jennifer pointed out.

"I'm not stopping you, am I? And you didn't answer my question."

"You ask so many."

"The first one of all. Are you promised?"

Her brows, very delicate and dark, drew together. "Promises are things to be careful about."

"I couldn't agree with you more. But you still haven't answered."

"Let's say I'm choosy."

"Then—will you have dinner with me to-night?"

"I don't know what my mother would say if she could hear you."

"Let's ask her, then."

He had no sooner spoken than the door at the back of the shop swung back and a big commanding woman came in.

"Haven't we got what the gentleman wants, Jenny?" she said.

It was Chris who answered. "I want your daughter to come out to dinner with me to-night."

Mrs. Hart stood quite still. He thought Boadicea might have looked like that, watching the slaves binding scythes to the wheels of her chariot.

"What we sell here are papers and cigarettes," she observed.

"That's why I came in. Now I'm wondering if your daughter would come out to dinner with me to-night."

"I don't know what you think my daughter is . . ."

"The girl I want to take out to dinner. I've told her, and she thought I should tell you."

Mrs. Hart turned to the girl. "Do you know him, Jenny?"

"Not till a few minutes ago."

"Well, young man, you've got your answer."

"I'd like to hear what Jennifer has to say."

"My girl's a good girl and does what I tell her. I've no mind for any daughter of mine to make a fool of herself, and maybe end up like that poor girl in the papers to-day."

He moved instinctively, as if already he felt the scythes grazing the calves of his legs.

"Which girl's that?" He unfolded the paper he had tucked under his arm. A pretty face looked out of the front page. Chris could actually feel himself turning pale. "Oh no," he ejaculated. "Oh no."

"What's the matter?" Mrs. Hart demanded keenly. "Is it someone you know?"

His face seemed to have stiffened and aged by ten years in as many seconds. His eye was running rapidly down the column of print, he might never have heard the question. He didn't even move out of the way of other customers, wasn't aware he was blocking the counter. At last he looked up, he refolded the paper and pushed it back under his arm.

"I'm sorry, Jennifer, it can't be to-night, after all. I have to go to Churchford."

"You mean, you did know her?" Mrs. Hart's voice rang with indignation.

"It was my ring she was wearing." It might have been a machine rather than a man speaking the words. No feeling there at all. And then Chris turned and walked out of the shop, practically walking through a stout lady who had just entered with a yapping peke on a lead. Perhaps the young man trod on its foot, because suddenly the yapping rose to a wild crescendo.

The owner's voice was almost as piercing. "Well, really, did you see that? No manners some people, and a poor dumb beast. If that's all education does for you—the *Sunday Record* and the *Gossip*, please, dear."

"Couldn't you see," demanded Jennifer, and her voice was almost as devoid of feeling as his had been, "he's taken the knock? He didn't even see you. He's taken the knock."

"What made you say that?" her mother demanded, when the vociferous pair had left the shop.

"If he'd known—about her, I mean—he wouldn't have said. He'd have been like those soldiers in the hymn who had their armour girded on. He wasn't wearing any armour at all. I wonder why he gave her the ring."

"The sooner you forget about him the better, my girl," scolded Mrs. Hart. "Walking into the shop like Lord Himuckamuck, asking you out to dinner, and you letting him . . ."

"How do you stop people asking you out to dinner?"

"A smart girl like you knows how to put a man in his place. I've told you before, my girl, I don't want to see you make the mistake I did. Anyone would have thought butter wouldn't melt in your father's mouth. He's not the man for you, my mother said, but I didn't listen. I knew it all."

"I don't know anything much," the girl agreed, "but someone has to teach you."

"The only good thing I got out of the marriage was you," Mrs. Hart continued, "and I don't mean to see that ruined, too. Now, stop day-dreaming. We're here to sell papers, and goodness knows there's competition enough."

The girl moved a few steps down the counter to serve some newcomers. "He called me Jennifer," she said, dreamily, as they went out. "No one's ever called me that before."

Inspector Crowthorne had only just got over the shock of his interview with Crook and his intrepid companion when someone knocked on the door of his office and a constable came in to say, "It never rains but it pours, sir. There's a chap outside who says his name's Christopher Wayland and he's the one who gave the Myers girl the ring."

"What's he like?" Crowthorne asked.

"Tall, fair, late twenties, I'd say . . ."

"In short, Chris, the man of mystery."

"He says he only saw the news about two hours ago, he was staying in Hornby and he went out to get a paper . . ."

"And came right down to see us?"

"He said he wanted to hear at first-hand what we'd found out. Came in a car, sir," he added, "dark blue Martineau."

"Very considerate of him. We'd better have him in, and then send someone along to collect Miss Forbes. It's not much of a chance and I don't suppose any jury would wear it, but she just might recognise the voice or something— women are good at details—and, what's more to the point, he might recognise her."

"Shock tactics? Yes, sir. He looks a pretty cool customer."

"Oh, they're all that," the inspector agreed. "And that wretched girl's the coolest of the lot."

"I'd have come before if I'd known," began Chris bluntly within a minute of taking a chair, "but I didn't see the news till about eleven o'clock."

"And you recognised the girl from her photograph?"

Chris looked surprised. "Well, yes. But I didn't actually

need the photograph, it was all in the letter-press. And then there was the description of the ring. I haven't seen it yet, but that was described, too, and it sounds like one I bought from Mr. Gold to give to her."

Shown the ring, he identified it immediately. "We had heard from Mr. Gold about the man who purchased it," Crowthorne said. "Did it have any special significance? I mean, a ring's a rather personal thing to give a girl."

"It wasn't an engagement ring, if that's what you're driving at. There was never anything but a ships-that-pass-in-the-night relationship between us. I hadn't set eyes on her till I came to Churchford . . ."

"How did you meet her, sir?"

"As a matter of fact, she thumbed a lift. It was a wet night and there was no bus . . ."

"And after that you saw more of her?"

"Well, obviously. I don't make presents to every girl who asks for a lift. And even present is hardly the right word, it was more like payment for value received."

"What exactly does that mean, Mr. Wayland?"

"I've been commissioned to do a series of articles on ancient customs still obtaining in English village life, a sort of link-up with the past, and Miss Myers was remarkably knowledgeable. The difficulty isn't usually to find someone who'll talk about the past, but someone who can give you authentic information. The girl told me the legend of Hunter Scanes, for instance, that I was subsequently able to verify, and she knew about a number of other local superstitions. She said her mother used to tell her stories when she was a child. It was a snip for me, really, it saved me any amount of research, that is, I wasn't lunging about in the dark, I knew what I was looking for. Then a TV company bought the rights in one of the articles, and I told Linda—Miss Myers—and she laughed and said didn't she rate something or words to that effect."

"And you gave her the ring?"

"Yes."

"Did she ask for it?"

"I think she might have preferred the money, but I didn't want that. She hinted that a ring would be acceptable—I could be wrong about this, but I wasn't certain the idea wasn't to gear up some other fellow . . ."

"Make him jealous, you mean?"

"It was just an idea. If you're going to ask me for chapter and verse, then I can't supply it. I know she went around with quite a lot of men, I never thought it went very deep with any of them, she was just a girl wanting a bit of fun. I was always expecting to hear she was going to be married, she was very attractive."

"You didn't think of marrying her yourself?"

"I couldn't possibly support a wife on the standards she'd expect."

"And you don't think she could have misunderstood your attitude?"

"She wouldn't have thought of me twice in that connection, and only once if I'd put the idea into her mind. You're tied down like a donkey pegged out in a field once you're married, she said to me once. All kids and supermarkets. I don't mean to settle for that."

"And when did you last see her?"

Chris considered. "It must have been Thursday. It was the day I left Churchford. It wasn't by appointment. I'd just come from Mr. Warren, the man who has the garage at Churchford Point—but you know that, of course."

"We know Mr. Warren."

"I'd taken my car in to have a general overhaul as I was moving on and I've got the M.O.T. test at the end of this week. When I went back to Mr. Warren he said I'd never get through with the tyres she was wearing, two of them anyway must be replaced, and he wasn't very sanguine about the other two. He said he could get me two good second-hand ones and two others by next day. I couldn't wait because I had this article to do on Hornby, so I said I'd bring her in on Friday morning . . ."

"And you did?"

"That's right."

"So you've had four new tyres put on since Thursday night?"

"I'd have expected the police to commend that. You're always on about dangerous driving and careless drivers . . ."

"And you saw Miss Myers?"

"Only for a minute. I said 'I'm moving on' and she said 'Good hunting,' or words to that effect."

"And the rest of the day?"

"I was going on to Hornby. There's a place called Thurleigh Castle close by and there's a very interesting legend there, a haunted lake, where some unfortunate lady is supposed to have thrown an illegitimate child. Now she's said to walk round and round the lake after dusk, carrying the child in her arms and wailing."

Crowthorne looked openly sceptical. "You really believe that?"

"The chap who only believes the evidence of his own eyes isn't going to get far, though pretty often that's all you have to go on. I went fairly early because I wanted to see the old church there, there are some fine brasses, but my luck was out, because the church was locked and I couldn't find anyone who had the key. I didn't see the ghost either, but I've since found one or two old folk who swear they have and that enabled me to produce my article. I hung about a long time hoping the ghost would manifest herself, and also waiting to hear the nightingales, which are pretty famous there. Then I stopped at a drive-in type of café, had something to eat and got back, I suppose, about eleven p.m. I'm staying—was staying, that is—at the Bald-Faced Stag. And that," he concluded, "is the only statement I can positively prove."

"You didn't see anyone you knew in the café?"

Chris looked sceptical. "Well, hardly. I'd never been in Hornby before."

"Would anyone recall seeing you there?"

"I should hardly think so. It was one of these places where you queue for your food and wait on yourself. We might have been an army of faceless men. I doubt whether I'd recognise anyone I saw there, either."

"You didn't chance to see anyone in the wood—while you were waiting for the nightingales?"

"You're joking, of course." But Chris wasn't sure he was.

The inspector said as much. "I never felt less like humour in my life. This is a murder case we've got on our hands, a young girl."

"I had realised that. Why else do you think I came pelting back to Churchford, though it doesn't seem as though I've been able to give you much assistance. Except, of course, that I could identify the ring, but since you knew who she was . . ." he let the sentence fade out.

The detective-inspector was doodling with a rather thick black pencil. "One more thing," he said. "Mr. Wayland, were you aware that Linda Myers was pregnant?"

"What!" Chris stiffened as though he'd swallowed a poker. "The paper didn't say anything about that."

"The news will be released in the morning. There's no doubt about her condition. She was about two months gone."

"I had no idea," murmured Chris.

"You're quite certain of that?"

"Well, of course I'm certain. Anyway, why should you suppose she'd tell me?" .

"Let me put it another way. Mr. Wayland, is there any possibility that the child could have been yours?"

"Absolutely none," said Chris, as though surprised the question should have been put. "I told you, ours wasn't that type of relationship."

The inspector switched briskly to another point. "Did you ever meet any of her family?"

"No. I knew she had a father and a stepmother."

"You hadn't any intention of meeting them?"

"There didn't seem much point. I was only here for a short time."

"So if the girl told her father you were coming down from London to meet him and his wife to-day, you wouldn't agree?"

"Well, of course I shouldn't agree. There was never any such suggestion. Is that what Mr. Myers says?"

"He says it's what his daughter told him."

"He must have misunderstood her. There wasn't any sense Linda saying a thing like that. She knew I was moving on."

"Perhaps she was thinking of the child. Incidentally, she hadn't mentioned it at home."

"I've explained already, the child was no concern of mine. Look, Inspector, are you sure Mr. Myers didn't get it wrong? Linda could have told him someone was coming to-day, only it wasn't me."

"Both Mr. Myers and his wife say you were the man she named. He saw the ring and asked about the man who'd given it to her."

Chris looked relieved. "I gather he was—is—a bit of a stiffneck. It would be quite like Linda to say I'd be coming, and then when Sunday dawned she'd tell him there'd been a misunderstanding or something, or she'd had a message. Didn't anyone know about the child?"

"No one has admitted to knowing. It's pretty conclusive that her stepmother didn't know. She may have hoped to persuade the father to marry her."

"And he didn't see it like that, and they had an argument and it got a bit more violent than he intended? That's pretty Grand Guignol, isn't it? I mean, this isn't the Victorian era. Girls do actually have children without a wedding-ring, and it doesn't wreck their lives."

"So far we haven't been able to put a name to any-one . . ."

"And that surprises you? It shouldn't. Not if, as I see it, you're tying up her condition with the murder." He rubbed his hand down his face, as though he could change its expression by so doing. "It's still difficult to accept. She seemed to have the gift of eternal youth." He paused; the inspector might have been carved out of wood. "If there's nothing more," Chris insinuated, "I'll be getting back. I'm staying at the Feathers at Hornby . . ."

"You came by car, Mr. Wayland?"

Chris looked surprised. "Yes, she's outside. A blue Martineau." He gave the number, but the inspector didn't seem particularly interested. Instead he asked another question.

"You said you'd had fresh tyres fitted?"

"That's right. On Friday morning. You can check that with Mr. Warren," he added drily.

"We have to do things by the book," the inspector assured him. "Did you have the car washed at the same time?"

"I generally polish her up myself but as he was putting on the tyres . . ." He stopped. "You are trying to tie me up with this, aren't you? Well, ask him. He'll tell you he didn't find any bloodstains . . ."

"I wouldn't expect it, not when the victim's been strangled." He doodled some more. "Do you carry a rug in your car, Mr. Wayland?"

"Well, I call it that. It's more of a blanket, really. Just in case I have to spend the night in her. It has happened."

"Yes. All right, Mr. Wayland. That's all."

"You mean, I'm free to go? After this build-up?"

"Leave your address and telephone number with the sergeant as you go out," said Crowthorne. "I may take it, I suppose, you won't be leaving Hornby for a few days?"

"Not of my own free will," agreed Chris, elaborately polite.

He thought that Crowthorne might be a quite formidable enemy, though his appearance was ordinary enough. You could see him half-a-dozen times and not remember him on the seventh occasion. Coming into the general office or whatever they called it, he noticed a little woman sitting on a chair against the wall, like a rather dejected Patience on a monument. She peered at him from under the brim of a brown felt hat that half-obscured her face. He wondered what sort of trouble she was in. But as he approached the desk she suddenly came to life, jumping up and hurrying across the floor.

"Sergeant," she said, pushing back her hat with a fluttery hand, "I'm sure this gentleman's business is very important, but I have been here some time, and naturally I'm anxious. Are you sure there isn't any news about Tom Jones?"

Chris turned to her, she looked as though she might have walked out of a nursery rhyme, swaddled in a rather too heavy coat for the time of year, with a collar that came up round her ears.

He felt an urge to say something shocking, like "Another poor soul gone missing?" and was appalled at himself.

"Go ahead," he advised her. And then to the sergeant, "Have you heard anything of Tom Jones?"

"He's my kitten, you see," said the urgent voice, and he thought he might have guessed, she was the motherly sort, presumably unmarried, and so turning to an animal for company. "A Burmese. I lost him last Thursday night on Broomstick Common, I don't know if you know this part of the world, but it's a great place for wild cats and, well, he's so young and I don't know that he can look after himself—they say cats always know their way home, but it's quite a distance. I keep feeling he may have fallen into the canal."

"Oh, I shouldn't think so," said Chris. "Cats hate water as a rule."

"He could have slipped. And I'm sure he can't swim. If cats were licensed like dogs," she added uncontrollably, "there'd be a lot more notice taken if they vanished."

"If you'd sit down again for a minute, Miss . . ."

"Jones," she supplied hurriedly. "I told you."

"Is that why the kitten's called Tom Jones?" asked Chris.

"Of course. I suppose you think I'm making a lot of fuss about a cat with all the trouble there is about poor Linda Myers—you did hear about her?"

"Yes," he agreed. "I've heard about her. Well, it's in all the papers."

"Yes. Of course. Such a pretty girl."

The sergeant intervened. Women never knew where to stop. She was quite the actress, all that yap about a kitten.

"If you'd wait a little longer . . ."

91

"I don't want to take up too much of your time. But family men and women don't always understand. The difference between a house and a home, I mean."

"I know just what you mean," said Chris. "The inspector asked me to leave my address and phone number in case he thinks of anything else," he added to the man at the desk. Having concluded his business he went out. At the door he turned. "I hope you find your cat," he said to May.

His footsteps hadn't died away before she was back at the counter. "That's not the one," she said. "I couldn't be certain about the car when your officer pointed it out to me because I don't know anything more about cars than I know about horses. One has four legs and a tail and the other has four wheels and a bonnet. But that's not the man I saw in the wood on Thursday night."

"How can you be so certain, Miss Forbes? It was dark, beginning to rain, he was wearing a mask, obviously he'd do his best to stay out of sight . . ."

"He didn't know who I was or why I was here," May insisted. "Why, it stuck out a mile. I was just some poor old body who'd lost her cat, like—like La Mère Michel," she added. "That was a French book we did at school. After all, even if I didn't see HIM very well that night, he got a clear look at me, and suddenly jumping up like a djinn out of a bottle, I mean, of course, a spirit, not spirits, he must have given himself away, especially when I talked about Tom Jones, but he was absolutely *fogged*. He never turned a hair when I mentioned Broomstick Common, and do you know why?"

"You tell me, Miss Forbes."

"Because none of it meant a thing to him. He wasn't on Broomstick Common that night."

"I expect you're going to tell me just where he was," the policeman suggested.

"Oh, I daresay he hasn't got an alibi. My father used to say always mistrust a man with an alibi. Honest people don't carry them around like carnations in their buttonholes."

"Heredity," thought the sergeant, gloomily. Whole family seemed to have been round the twist.

"Thank you for your co-operation," he said, formally. "One of our cars will take you back."

"That's absurd!" cried May. "It's only ten minutes. And I shall enjoy the air. It's rather stuffy in here. I suppose you get used to it. It's like that in the shop sometimes," she added, more kindly. "I'm really quite grateful to the thoughtless customer who leaves the door open, though Miss Alice used to feel the draughts so. Anyway, people will talk enough without me being driven back in a car. Mrs. Politi started plenty of gossip when she noticed Mr. Crook drive me home that evening."

"Oh, there's always plenty of gossip where Mr. Crook is," said the sergeant.

"To tell you the truth," May confided, "I've been shaking in my shoes ever since I got here, in case anyone I knew came in. I know I'm only here to assist the police, but it's like justice, isn't it? It must not only be done it must be seen to be done." As though she had made her position crystal clear she gave him an understanding sort of nod and walked out.

"She seemed pretty sure," the sergeant told Inspector Crowthorne, "and she could be right. If she isn't, he's wasted on his present job, he should be on the stage."

"He played it cool enough," Crowthorne agreed. "Talk about the three fates. That woman and Crook and Wayland all in the same day. I want someone to go out and bring Warren in, he might remember something about the car—no hope of tracing anything from the tyres, Wayland got them changed first thing next morning, but according to him that had all been fixed up beforehand. And get someone to keep an eye on Wayland. I don't want him leaving Hornby till we say so."

Lloyd, the officer sent to collect Warren, came back to report that the man was out, the garage wasn't open on a Sunday, and Warren, a widower, had taken his eight-year-old son for a drive.

"Sister keeps house for him, she said she'd give him the message as soon as he came in. She said right off she knew nothing about his business affairs, so it was no use asking her questions."

"Wonder why she said that," the inspector brooded.

"She's the kind that thinks the police bring bad luck just by crossing the threshold. Not that I got that far. And it's probably true that he doesn't confide in her, but I'll tell you this, sir, she wouldn't tell us if he did. Quite steamed up about Albert being disturbed on his day of rest. Different for you, she said. That's what you think, I told her."

Warren, a short square man, with an open fresh-coloured face, came in shortly after six o'clock.

"You've put my sister in a rare old tizzy," he told the inspector. "Next time you want me and I'm not there, send one of your nice lady-policewomen. Martha thinks every man is an ape in human guise. I left her planning to get the priest in to exorcise the house."

"Let's skip the humour," said Crowthorne. "We all have our crosses to bear. Do you remember a young chap called Wayland coming in for a new set of tyres on Friday morning?"

"That's right," Warren agreed. "And none too soon at that, only I hadn't got the complete set. You're never going to tell me he's crashed or something?"

"Not in the sense you mean. Know him well?"

"He's been coming to me for his petrol for about three months, I suppose. A newspaper chap, goes around writing pieces for his paper." By his voice it wasn't likely to be the sort of paper he, the speaker, would subscribe to. "And there was the time some Mick ran into his car on the M.1 and he wanted a dent banging out. Not worth claiming the insurance, he said, it would cost more than the bill, and anyway, he hadn't got the other chap's number. Didn't stop, see?"

"You'd recognise his car again?"

"Why, what's up?" demanded Warren. "It's not been stolen?"

"When did you last see him?"

"Must have been when I fitted the tyres. That 'ud have been Friday."

"Just fitted the tyres—that's all?"

"I gave her a bit of spit and polish."

"Needed it, eh?"

"Nothing special. Here, what's up, Inspector? You're asking a funny lot of questions."

"You didn't notice anything unusual? She could have been involved in an incident."

"Here, wait a minute," said Warren, and he began to laugh. "I don't suppose this is what you want to hear, but when he fished out his cheque-book to settle for the tyres, he yanked out a sort of highwayman's mask, you know the kind of thing, two eye-pieces and a band to go round the head. Hullo, I said, what are you planning? Don't waste your time on my garage, I bank every night."

"Not trying to be funny, I hope," Crowthorne barked.

Warren looked startled. "Well, but it was funny."

"Didn't strike you as a bit ominous that he should be carrying a mask around with him?"

"Well, but there was this hospital rag they had the other week, he was in that. He said, Good Lord, I'd forgotten I still had it, and when he went out he stuffed it into the litter-bin I keep on the premises, don't want the station mucked up with cigarette cartons and ice-cream papers. My kid found it a minute or two later and brought it in. Martha, that's my sister, was all for chucking it away, not hygienic, she said, but the bin was practically empty and quite clean, and it's the sort of thing that amuses kids. Get more education from the telly these days they do than from their schooling, anyway they pay it more attention."

"Wasn't it a bit outsize for a boy of—how old?"

"Eight. Well, but it was rigged up on a piece of elastic, adjustable, see, all very professional. Yes, I thought he must have had it for the Student Rag."

"But he's not a student."

"They're not that fussy. I suppose someone pulled him

in. Not that it came to much, thanks to the rain, came down in sheets, sent everything flying."

Asked about the discarded tyres, he said he sold them with a lot of other similar stuff to a rag-and-bone man who came round regularly. "It's that or taking them along to the dump," he pointed out. "What does he do with them? How should I know? Sells the stuff by weight, I should think."

"Anything to distinguish them from any other tyres?" Crowthorne asked. "Well, no need to keep you any longer, Mr. Warren. We know where you are if we should need you again, and I expect your family's getting anxious."

"Not Brian," said Mr. Warren, confidently. "That kid's a regular tearaway. Will you be in handcuffs, Dad? he said. And if I was to go back in a police car . . ."

But the inspector didn't take the hint.

Chris Wayland had got nicely settled at the bar of the Feathers Inn at Hornby and was talking casually to the barman—no mention of Linda Myers on either side—when he was called to the telephone and told that Inspector Crowthorne would be glad if he could come in and clear up one or two points that had arisen. The inspector offered to send a car, but Chris said he thought the landlord probably wouldn't care for that.

But he suspected that the Hornby police had been alerted and if he tried to oil out he'd be stopped before he'd gone a couple of miles. It was a quiet night, not much traffic on the roads, a moon tilting on her back, lights in windows showing like golden squares on a dark chess-board. A night for witches, he thought, and wondered what else the inspector had conjured up.

At the station he was confronted with the domino. "Where did that erupt from?" he asked, and the inspector said, "Mr. Warren brought it in. Found it in his litter-bin. Could it be the one you wore to the pageant?"

"You don't miss a trick, do you?" murmured Chris. "I'd go a step further and say you can bet your hopes of a pension it's the identical one. I stuffed it into the bin on my way out. Funny, I hadn't thought . . ." He stopped. "Are you tying this up with Linda Myers's death?"

"We know that the man seen on Broomstick Common that night was wearing a black mask."

"Funny there's been no mention of it till now."

"We have a most reliable witness. Could you explain how it came to be in your possession?"

"I had it for the Hospital Rag," said Chris. "I was Death, the faceless enemy, confronted with Life, battling for an anonymous patient."

"I didn't know you were a medical student, Mr. Wayland."

"No more did I, but they're not that fussy. Actually, it was Linda Myers who suggested I should lend a hand. It was a tableau on a float, and if I may say it myself, it was pretty effective, or would have been if the rain had held off. As it was it came down cats and dogs, and we had to belt for shelter. I stuffed the mask into my pocket . . ."

"Didn't it belong to the organisers of the show?"

"If they had to supply all the props they wouldn't have made much for the hospital. I bought it at a theatrical costumier's near Great Newport Street in London. As a matter of fact, I'd forgotten all about it. Quite a surprise when I found it in my pocket when I was at Warren's."

"His boy found it where you'd put it and took it for a lark, and when we were questioning him—Mr. Warren I mean—he remembered and told us."

Chris grinned faintly. "Yes, I suppose he would. I don't suppose he sees one of these every day of the week."

"Highly unlikely," the inspector agreed.

"Who said your suspect was wearing it that night?"

"An unimpeachable witness. She happened to be on the Common . . ."

"Of course," exclaimed Chris. "That woman who stormed the desk when I came out to leave my name and address. Well, I can promise you one thing, whoever was wearing a mask that night, it wasn't me. Good thing for her it is a woman, isn't it?"

"What does that mean, Mr. Wayland?"

"If it had been a man I might have suggested it was a switcheroo. You know—criminal makes the discovery and informs the police. There was a case when I was a kid, a doctor had a woman die in his surgery from an illegal operation, somewhere in the East End of London so far as I recall, he dumped the body under a bridge on a black wet night and 'found' it in the small hours on his way back from visiting an emergency case. Reported it to the police, imagining they'd never suspect the chap who gave the information, I suppose."

"But they got him?"

"Oh yes, they got him. Still, you can't win them all."

"You can't supply the name of any other participant in the pageant who wore a mask?"

"How policemen love long words! No, actually I can't. But the organisers might remember. Or of course it doesn't have to be anyone connected with the pageant."

"Sheer coincidence?"

"Where would we be without it? Oh, come now, if what I think you think were true wouldn't I have got rid of the thing the same night?"

He still wasn't taking the situation too seriously. Playing it cool, the inspector decided.

"You admitted you'd forgotten you had it."

"I wouldn't have forgotten it if I'd used it to conceal a body. Besides . . ."

"Yes, Mr. Wayland?"

"That was your witness, wasn't it, that woman who yapped about a lost kitten on the Common and being afraid it might have fallen into the canal?"

"We're asking the questions, Mr. Wayland."

"And I've answered them. Now it's my turn. You ask your sergeant, he'll tell you she didn't know me from Adam. I suppose you'd briefed her? No, don't answer that. I remember, you're asking the questions. But I'll tell you this for free. She didn't recognise me because she'd never set eyes on me before, nor, so far as I know, I on her."

"It's not so easy to recognise a man wearing a mask, particularly in the dark."

"You want to get on to the organiser of the rag and ask him who else was wearing a mask."

"We've done that, Mr. Wayland. He doesn't remember anyone else."

"Then the odds are it wasn't anyone connected with the pageant. Good heavens," exploded Chris, "you can get these things anywhere. They sell them at kids' joke shops. Anything else I can do for you, Inspector?"

"I'm wondering if you'd care to make a statement. I'm sure you know your rights, but all the same I'll remind you of them. You don't have to say anything, nothing you've said to date can be used against you, because you haven't been cautioned, but I'm cautioning you now. Did you see Linda Myers on Thursday night?"

"I've already told you I didn't. I saw her earlier in the day and told her I was moving on and she said good hunting or words to that effect. I went to hunt for this ghost— well, to try to track down the legend—I went alone, I didn't see anyone I knew, I got back about eleven p.m. The mask is mine, and I can tell you where I bought it. I don't know why Linda Myers was murdered, I had no motive at all to wish her any harm. I didn't expect to see her again, and I was absolutely staggered to find her picture in the paper this morning. That's the only statement I can give you, and I'm afraid it's not going to get you very far in finding the chap who's responsible. And if there's nothing more to ask me I'll be glad to be on my way."

But he didn't get back to Hornby that night.

CHAPTER VII

THE NEWS that a man had been at the Churchford Police Station for a good part of the day, assisting the police in their enquiries, was part of the late news. (The further information that a man was being held for the murder of Linda Myers appeared in the first editions on Monday.)

"So they've got the chap who did it!" That was the general reaction, and a few people, notably those in the Churchford area who had young daughters with romantic ideas, sighed with relief. But in one household the police had never heard of officially and which, therefore, they did not connect in any way with the crime, the relief was unmistakable.

Willy Stephenson was the only son of his mother and she was a widow. He had been to some extent a thorn in her flesh but recently had atoned for all the anxiety he'd caused her by announcing his engagement to Victoria Ebury, only child of that alarming tycoon, Sir Alfred Ebury. Willy was good-looking, red-headed and enthusiastic where his pleasure were concerned. He was also the son of a man who had gambled away an inheritance and then moved out with a fascinating actress and had subsequently died abroad.

"Thank goodness you've shown a little sense at last," Blanche congratulated her son. "Now be sure you don't spoil everything by falling at the last fence."

On the Sunday after Linda's murder Blanche Stephenson rose at 11.30 and dressed with as much care as if she had been going to meet a lover, though her appointment was her usual Sunday one of having lunch with her sister, Louie. Louie was sixty-one, unmarried and blunt as a paper-cutter.

"I don't know why you always wear your finest clothes to come here," Louie said candidly. "You're not going to find your millionaire under my roof." She looked at her sister's elegant figure. "And you can't believe that you'll impress me at this time of day."

"I don't know why I bother to come," murmured Blanche restfully, accepting a thimbleful of sherry in a cut-glass goblet. Louie would not have a bottle of Scotch in the house, but there were delicious smells coming from the kitchen. "If you were a cannibal and were going to feast me on a missionary you couldn't take more trouble with your pot-roasts," Blanche went on. Her voice made the words sound like the compliment they were intended to be. "As for why I come, you know perfectly well that at our age there's nothing better than conversation with someone who remembers the world you knew when you were a child —and the people in it. It's as good as taking your hair down." She didn't mention the Hon. Theo but he was in the minds of both.

"How's the great romance?" Louie demanded.

Blanche looked grave. "To tell you the truth, Louie, I shall be glad when they've both said I will. They tell you it's difficult getting a daughter married. Believe me, it's nothing to getting your son settled."

"Particularly if his father was the Hon. Theo," Louie agreed robustly. "I hope this Ebury filly realises what she's taking on. He's the dead spit of his father—as if you didn't know."

"Oh, I know all right," Blanche agreed with a sigh, "but if he wasn't he wouldn't have girls falling in love with him all over the place."

"Falling in love with the Hon. Theo didn't do you much good."

"You only say that because you haven't been married. If I could have foreseen the future, I'd still have married Theo. Oh, I know he was reckless . . ."

"To the point of criminality," Louie reminded her sternly, and really Theo had only just escaped prosecution by the skin of his teeth. "And then going off with this bitch . . ."

"She wasn't a bitch, she was the most beautiful thing I

ever saw. And it didn't do her all that amount of good. She didn't last more than about four years, four years that wrecked her as an actress. It's no use, Louie. You can't try and judge people like Theo and Willy by ordinary standards. You remember that song Mother used to sing: 'I lift up my finger and I cry Tweet! Tweet!'? Theo and Willy hardly need to lift their fingers, the girls come running. And if I ask Willy what he wants with so many of them all he says is that you can't have too much of a good thing."

"Well, it's to be hoped Victoria will be able to keep him on the straight and narrow—for Willy's sake."

"The depressing thing is, Louie, that if she does convert him, though I admit it's unlikely, she probably will find he's no longer the man she married. I was like that with Theo. I knew he was no good before any of you told me, but I loved him the way he was. It doesn't make sense, does it?"

"You never did make sense," Louie assured her, heartily, taking up the glasses and going into the kitchen to fetch in the first course of what was to prove a delicious meal. "Still, I suppose the girl knows her own mind. If her feeling for Willy can survive two months' absence—I suppose Sir Alfred only took her on that cruise in the hope she'd come to her senses . . ."

"And marry some tycoon of his choosing?" suggested Blanche dryly. "You have such a charming way of putting things, Louie."

And the conversation passed to other subjects.

Sometime during the afternoon Louie made casual reference to the finding by the police of the body of a girl in a piece of waste land not more than fifteen miles away.

Blanche hadn't heard. "You'd better take my *Sunday Record* and read the whole story," offered her sister. "Strangled, she was."

"The usual reason?" wondered Blanche.

"The paper didn't say. She was only found last night with the aid of a dog."

Blanche shivered.

"Mind you," Louie conceded, getting up to put on the kettle for tea, "she may have asked for it. Nine times out of

ten these girls do. But that doesn't detract from the fact
that she was somebody's daughter."

Nothing was said about the killer being somebody's son.

Blanche stayed till nearly six. When she got home Willy
was out. He hadn't left a note, but she hadn't expected it.
Men of twenty-eight don't have to account to their mothers
for every hour of the day, and until he was safely married
Blanche rode him on the lightest of reins. Like his father, he
was capable of getting into trouble anywhere, but less likely
under her roof than anyone else's. That's what she thought.
Presently she put on the news. This was very much the
mixture as before, one long record of violence. And the
last item in a sense was the most violent of all, concerning
as it did the girl whose body had been unearthed by the
dog. The police, it said, were anxious to contact anyone
who could give any assistance in the search for the killer
of Linda Myers, and a picture of the girl was flashed on
the screen. Blanche Stephenson, who had risen to switch off
the set, remained standing as still as Lot's wife turned into
her pillar of salt. She had never heard the girl's name
before, but she had seen the face, and with her heart giving
sickening jolts, she remembered where.

Willy Stephenson came in shortly before eight. He said
he'd been to the cinema at Axton.

"With Victoria?" Blanche asked, like an automaton,
knowing the answer in advance.

"You're joking, of course," said Willy. "Sir Alf (his
irreverent way of referring to his prospective father-in-law)
wouldn't enter a place of entertainment on the Sabbath—
you can hardly call Chapel a place of entertainment—and
he's brought Vicky up the same way. That's one of the
things I shall have to cure her of," he added.

"Are you asking me to believe you went to a cinema
alone?"

"Well, of course not. What's up, Mater? Was Aunt
Louie more scathing than usual? I know what she thinks
of me."

"I know what I think," retorted his mother fiercely. "I

think you're a fool. Oh Willy, couldn't you even take your engagement seriously? Did you have to go running around with a girl who's got herself murdered?"

Willy stared. "I suppose you know I haven't an idea what you're talking about?"

"This is what I'm talking about." She opened her stout black leather bag, and took a bit of paper out of the zip pocket. "Now tell me you've never set eyes on this girl and I shan't believe you."

Like a man in a daze, Willy took the photograph. It showed a girl, laughing and gay, her hair blown by the wind, her eyes full of mischief, but shrewd for all that.

"Tell me that isn't Linda Myers."

"Well, of course it's Linda. Where did you get it?"

Blanche, feeling sickness beginning to overpower her, gripped the table-edge with one strong hand.

"You must have been a jackdaw in a previous existence. I found it with a lot of rubbish in the pocket of your sports coat that you asked me to send to the cleaners."

"I'd forgotten about it," Willy muttered. "Still, because I'd met the girl months ago . . ."

"You've only had that sports coat two months, so you must have been seeing the girl while Victoria was on her cruise with her father."

"Well, what did you expect?" Willy demanded. "Because I'm engaged to Vicky it doesn't mean I have to break with every other girl I know."

"A tactful fiancé would see to it that he doesn't know a girl who gets herself strangled."

"What's that you said?" Willy's voice was as sharp as the ping of a rifle.

"I told you—she's been murdered."

"So you did. I didn't take it in. Well, Ma, you must admit you are inclined to lay on your colours with a heavy hand. But murdered? Linda? Not that she didn't ask for it. Look, you're not playing some macabre joke?"

"Read it for yourself," cried Blanche, half hysterical by now and quite unable to read her son's mind. Theo had been the same, the world's most convincing liar, though even he had had too much sense to get involved in murder. She picked up the *Record* that Louie had told her she could bring home and threw it in her son's direction. Willy took the paper and opened it so that his face was concealed while he read the hideous story. "And if you'd been back a bit earlier," Blanche continued, "you could have seen her on the television. That's how I knew . . ."

"Knew?"

"That she was the same girl, of course. I suppose she's the one who has been ringing you up this last two or three weeks."

"Girls are always ringing me up. You know that." Willy sounded sulky.

"Not like this one. Willy, did she expect you to marry her?"

"Linda?" It was impossible to mistake the genuine amazement in his voice. "She wouldn't have put me at the foot of her list. She was just waiting for her millionaire to come along, and meanwhile anyone would do to go around with."

"How long had you known her?"

"I don't remember exactly. Oh, before there was any question of my marrying Vicky."

"But you went on seeing her?"

"What was I supposed to do while my betrothed was sunning herself in the Caribbean or wherever it was Sir Alf took her in the hopes of curing her of her infatuation? That's what he called it, an infatuation. Now, if he'd got himself murdered . . ."

"Willy, can't you be serious about anything? Here's a girl you've known pretty well—anyway you were carrying her picture around with you . . ."

"I'd forgotten I had it. She showed it me one day and said—and she was laughing—Take it as a souvenir. I tell you, she was no more serious than I was."

"I suppose that's why she rang you—three times."

"You didn't tell me."

"She didn't give a name. She just said, Say it's Lynn, I must try again, mustn't I? As you say, girls are always ringing you up."

And she remembered those months before Theo eloped with his Fay, who also had been ringing him up at brief intervals.

Willy was recovering his aplomb. "I warned her that one of these days she'd overplay her hand," he observed. "She seemed to think her luck could never turn. Oh Mater, that girl had as many boy-friends as she's had hot dinners. And she liked to be the one that did the ditching."

"So she didn't much care for it when you ditched her?"

"I didn't ditch her. But she must have realised that when I was married things would change."

"She did know about Victoria?"

"Of course she knew."

"Did she mind?"

"I told you, she wouldn't even have thought of me as a husband. Any more than I ever thought of her as a wife."

"It says in the paper that she was a hairdresser's assistant."

"Not quite the way she put it. According to her, she was a partner."

"At eighteen? Not even you, Willy, foolish though you are, can have believed that."

"Well, perhaps not." Willy shrugged. "But it was no skin off my nose. She was just a pretty girl I played around with. Just one of a number."

"Only none of the others got themselves murdered."

"I can't help that. It's an odd thing, seeing how unlike they are, but she and Vicky had quite a bit in common. They both expected to be able to play things their way. If I'd known at the start she was going to make such a nuisance of herself . . ."

"Willy, you're talking about a girl who's been murdered. I should have thought even you would have had the sense to leave her alone once you got engaged."

"I hadn't seen her for some time. The last time I told her my fancy-free days were over. I'm putting my head in the noose, I said. It happens to the best of us. Now, Mater, I can see this has been a shock to you, but even you can't have expected me never to see a girl for two months. It's Sir Alfred's fault, if anyone's, trying to break things up between me and Vicky. And though I mean to make her a damn' good husband—well, that's part of the contract, isn't it?—even you can't pretend she's a sex kitten."

"And Linda Myers was?"

"And how. You know, I can't quite take this in yet. When did it happen or doesn't the paper say?"

"They found the body on Saturday following up information given by some schoolboys who found a ring that had belonged to her. She'd hardly have been buried in daylight, so they think she was strangled on the Thursday. Where were you on Thursday night, Willy?"

"What on earth are you driving at, Mother?" It was only in moments of the gravest import that he ever used that word.

"It's what the police will ask."

"The police? What on earth are you talking about? They haven't been *here*?"

"Not yet. But when they know you knew her . . ."

"If they're going to follow up every chap she ever went out with they've got their work cut out till Christmas. You haven't said anything about the photograph to anyone, have you?"

"No."

"Not to Aunt Louie?"

"Least of all to her. And if you're shocked, give me a thought, too. I didn't know that the girl in the picture and the girl who'd been murdered were one and the same, not till I put on the TV."

"So," said Willy, "where do the police come in? If they'd been going to connect me with Linda they'd have been round before this."

"Perhaps they did, and no one was here."

"Why on earth should they?"

"They want to contact anyone who knew her."

"That's routine stuff. My dear Mother, I couldn't help

the police even if I wanted to. It was as big a shock to me to hear she was dead as it can possibly have been to you. After all, you'd never met the girl. She didn't seem to be made for death."

"Oh, we're all made for death," said his mother in a curiously calm voice, "only not all in such a violent shape. You didn't answer my question, Willy. Where were you on Thursday night?"

"How on earth am I supposed to remember? Hold everything. Yes, that was the night I was at home. Remember?"

"Thursday's my bridge night and has been for the past six years. I go over to Marianne's about six, and we have a snack and go on to the club. You weren't here when I left."

"That's right. I wasn't."

"You didn't mention you were going to be at home."

"I didn't mean to be, I meant to go round the pubs, you can always meet someone there—well, it's hardly likely I'd be taking a girl out with Vicky just back from her cruise. But I had this blinding headache . . ."

"At the prospect of marrying Victoria? Headaches aren't up your street, Willy."

"I'd been lunching with my prospective father-in-law, remember. That would give anyone a headache."

"I don't think the police are going to be very satisfied with that as an explanation. Unless, of course, you rang someone up to postpone an engagement."

"I told you, I didn't have an engagement. So naturally I didn't ring anyone up."

"And no one rang you? Not Linda Myers?"

"How could Linda Myers ring me if she was being murdered? Anyway she knew we were through. And she had plenty of other fish on her line."

"So you just stayed quietly at home?"

"That's right. Well, till about nine-thirty. Then I thought a spot of fresh air might clear my head, and I went for a little spin."

"That's something else the police aren't going to like."

"I've told you before, the police don't come into this, so far as I'm concerned."

"How about the people who knew you were friendly with the girl?"

"No one knew. Well, obviously I wouldn't take her around and introduce her to my friends. She was a pretty girl and good fun, but, hang it all, she was a hairdresser's assistant—O.K., O.K., I never really believed she was a partner—her father was a commercial traveller, and for some reason that's always good for a laugh and I was engaged to Vicky Ebury. She was just a fill-gap and we both knew it."

"And I suppose whoever killed her was also a fill-gap, only perhaps he didn't know it?"

"I don't know. She never talked about her other boy-friends, except to let you know she had plenty of them on a string. The fact is, that girl was obsessed by the idea of power. She liked to think she could make chaps jump to her bidding, and I daresay it was a bit of a shock to her when she found I wasn't one of them."

"I hope when you're talking to the police you'll show a little more sense," his mother said.

"I've told you, the police don't come into this. Not that I've anything to fear from them, of course, so far as Linda is concerned, but there's bound to be publicity. and though Sir Alf's nuts on it as a rule, this is the sort he wouldn't appreciate. And I don't propose to let a little gold-digger like Linda muck up my whole future." He made a swift gesture and before his mother could realise what he had in mind, he had snatched up the photograph and was applying the flame of his cigarette lighter to one corner. Like a rabbit hypnotised by a snake she watched the paper blacken and curl; the ashes fell into a small china dish on the table. When the picture was utterly destroyed he took the dish to the window and blew the blackened ash out into the darkening air.

"Goodbye, Linda Myers," he said.

Blanche was appalled. "Your father did a lot of things to shock me," she said, slowly, "some of them I couldn't find excuses for. But he'd never have done that. I daresay you were only having a bit of fun with the girl, but she was eighteen and she was living and now she's dead and in this hideous way. Can't you even show a little rational pity?"

"Well, of course I'm sorry," said Willy. "I'd be sorry if I'd never known her, just as sorry as if she'd been run down by a bus, but there's nothing I can do about it. If you brought the head of Scotland Yard in here I couldn't tell him any more than I've told you."

"He might think it odd you were so anxious to destroy her picture," said Blanche slowly.

"Not he. No one wants to carry the picture of a murdered girl around with him, particularly if he's engaged to someone else. I bet you there are quite a lot of chaps tearing up photographs of Linda Myers this week-end, and it's possible that one of them might be able to give the police some pointers. Only that chap isn't me. Now, Mother, do stop working yourself into a fever. By the time we get the late news they may have identified the chap she was with on Thursday night. Until then I propose we shelve the subject. We can go on arguing all round the clock and still meet ourselves going to bed."

The late night news carried the information that a man had spent a considerable part of the day at Churchford Police Station assisting the police with their enquiries . . . (The news that Chris Wayland had been detained for the murder of Linda Myers didn't make the Press till the next morning.) Willy was full of triumph.

"There you are, Mater. You know what that means. The police always play it cagey, but it means they've got the chap they think's responsible, so you can stop worrying yourself about an alibi for me for Thursday night."

It occurred to Blanche that he hadn't uttered one cry of pity or horror at Linda's fate, only displayed an immense relief at the thought that enquiries were virtually at an end, or, if not, wouldn't turn in his direction. And she remembered Louie saying, "She may have asked for it, but you can't overlook the fact that she was somebody's daughter."

Now, to her amazement, she found herself thinking of the unknown man who had been assisting the police with their enquiries, and remembering that he was somebody's son. And this one, this Anon, might really have cared for the girl, while she could have been running the two of them, Anon and Willy, on a string.

"God help him!" she thought.

There didn't seem to be any one else likely to do so.

CHAPTER VIII

ON MONDAY MORNING Miss Alice didn't appear in the shop. Miss Phyllis, her eyes sunk in her head, and looking like someone who hasn't slept for two nights, told May frankly, "I don't know what I should have done without Jack these last weeks. He's been a tower of strength, but I begin to think he was right, after all."

"Is Miss Alice worse then?"

May was scurrying round tidying and dusting, and rearranging stocks on hangers and stands.

"She's had another little stroke. And, of course, the news —about Linda—has upset her terribly. Is it true, my dear, that she was expecting a baby—Linda, I mean?"

"That's what the doctor says. Poor Mr. Myers! He must feel so responsible."

"I don't see that he can be blamed," Miss Phyllis objected. "He was in Wolverhampton at the time. That's two counties away."

"He'll probably feel he should have prevented it somehow. That's human nature. I wasn't with my father the day he tripped on the kerb and broke his ankle—and he was such an energetic invalid and he wouldn't hear of going into hospital—but I felt responsible just the same. If I hadn't had such a headache that morning I'd have run out myself and bought his tobacco, but he said he couldn't wait, and then—I've always felt guilty."

111

"My poor sister!" said Miss Phyllis, with great feeling, not even pretending to be interested in a crochety old man who'd been dead and gone for years, and no loss to anyone, least of all May. "She feels it quite dreadfully. Not responsibility, of course. I wished I didn't have to tell her, but if I hadn't someone else would and they might just have broken it quite baldly, but of course nothing really softens the blow."

"What did you tell her, Miss Phyllis?"

"I said a terrible thing had happened to Linda, she broke her neck in the dark on Broomstick Common, which is more or less the truth, but of course my sister has too much sense to believe you can break your neck on a piece of comparatively flat ground. A leg or an arm—yes. But a neck's different. And then we've had the police here, asking questions. We can't tell you anything fresh, I assured them, and no, you cannot see my sister, she's in a state of shock. I got Dr. Mellish to say she wasn't fit to be questioned. It's not as though she could tell them anything. I'm afraid he told them no evidence of hers would be of value, because she's so confused. Which is true. I mean, she seems to have lost her sense of time. It's what's called living in the past. She actually addressed me as Amy the other day, though Amy's been dead for years, and we were never in the least alike. I suppose it was because of Jack, it sent her thoughts backwards. I suppose I have a very selfish nature, because I know it's terrible what happened to the poor girl, but what chiefly concerns me is the effect it may have on Alice. It's not as though being distressed could help Linda now."

"I think it's perfectly natural for you to put your sister first," said May firmly.

"I wish everyone had your sense. It's odd how sympathetic people are for widows—and widowers too, of course—when they suffer a bereavement, but seem to think it's quite different if it's a sister. But if it's your sister who has made your house a home for more than thirty years, the sense of loss, of—of having your second self chopped off, as it were, is just as acute."

"Poor Miss Alice!" said May respectfully, but she really thought, Poor Miss Phyllis. Alice was protecting herself, even if unconsciously, by retreating into a past where Linda couldn't penetrate, but Miss Phyllis could seek no such consolation. Hers were the present and the future and she could expect nothing but anxiety.

"In a way it eases things for her," she murmured, but Miss Phyllis said, "Oh, no. If it had been anyone but Linda. Poor Alice, she did so long to have children, and Linda—I sometimes think she saw her as the daughter she didn't have. That's why she took to her so, because there's no use pretending she was much good in the shop. I've wondered so often what might have happened if our father hadn't put his foot down about young Percy Trivett."

"Is he the one whose letters she keeps and won't let anyone read?" asked May, frankly enthralled.

"She never minded Linda reading them, and I must say the girl was very patient, because young people don't want to hang about a sick person's room. And I think she used to confide in her. Percy was an assistant here in the 'twenties. Of course we were a much livelier concern during our father's lifetime. We had a Mrs. Gordon, who was our buyer and manageress—for years neither Alice nor I ever served in the shop, our father wouldn't permit it, though we were allowed to assist in the clerical work behind the scenes. Percy came to us after the war. He'd gone to fight very young, and when he came back there was nothing waiting for him in the way of a position, no one seemed to care after that war. It was different, of course, the next time; I suppose you might say we'd developed a national conscience. He was quite glad to take a subordinate situation here, I think he really did hope to work up, not that he was brilliant in any way, but he was very honest and hardworking and customers liked him, but even if he'd been a second Gordon Selfridge I don't think Father would ever have considered him as a husband for his daughter—well, not for Alice, anyway. He was quite devoted to her; you can't think, my dear, how lovely she was as a girl. Amy and I both disappointed him; he set all his hopes on her."

"Did she want to marry him?"

"She never wanted to marry anyone else. Father said he must have behaved in a very dishonourable fashion to have got acquainted with Alice at all, but I don't think that's true. And since, I've sometimes wondered if Father didn't regret his decision, because there might have been children, and a man to step into Father's shoes in due course. But then—" Phyllis drew a long, sighing breath— "he didn't expect to die at sixty. After that, Alice and I took things into our own hands. It was a bad time industrially, and no one was particularly interested in the shop. After 1918 Churchford developed so much, a whole new miniature town sprang up with bigger and flashier shops and restaurants, and then cars became so common, and people dashed up to town or went over to Axton and Maresford for goods. Mrs. Gordon had gone before then, and afterwards we found any amount of goods she'd bought as bargains, she said, but they weren't bargains really, because nobody wanted long-sleeved combinations and wool vests and camisoles any longer. There are boxes of them down in the cellar, together with a lot of Father's effects, as I think they're called. We really never knew what to do with them. It seemed irreverent to give them to charities—there were six pairs of trousers, think of it, my dear, six pairs, and two never even put on. We packed them all in moth-balls and they're there to this day."

"So that's what's in the boxes down there," May said. "I always wondered, when I take the wrappings and the waste-paper-baskets down for the dustman. You have to go through the storeroom to get to the back door."

"We used to carry a lot of stock, millinery, too. And at one time we had a delivery service (Miss Phyllis seemed happily, dreamily immersed in the past, and May hadn't the heart to remind her that this was 1969 and custom might be tapping on the doorstep), a boy on a bicycle with a little van in front. We used to feel so proud to see our name on the side of the van as he pedalled through the streets. But then people started having motor deliveries and our boy learned to drive and left us and we couldn't get another, so people started taking their own goods home. We got a different class of customer, too. The big houses got shut up or turned into flats, I often think it's a good thing Father can't see it now. The bicycle lived in a little shed affair, opening off the stockroom. I believe it's still there, though it must be thick with rust now."

"What happened to Percy Trivett?" asked May, who didn't care a button about the late Mr. Robinson's fads and foibles.

"We never heard. Father dismissed him at once. He did write a few times and the letters got smuggled in, then Father found out and there was a terrible scene. Poor Alice cried for days, but she wouldn't give the letters up, and, as you know, she's got them still. Father said he looked higher for his favourite daughter than an assistant in a provincial drapery, but, my dear, between ourselves, I've always thought his attitude would have been different if Percy had been after me. He thought the world of Alice. Nothing was too good for her."

"They could have eloped to Gretna Green," suggested practical May.

But Miss Phyllis shook her head. "You didn't know our father. When they arrived they'd have found him waiting for them. That was the sort of man he was."

May thought he sounded odious, never realising he was cut from the same cloth as the late Mr. Forbes, only *he'd* seen to it that his daughter never had a chance of cutting loose. Miss Phyllis was meandering on.

"It's an odd thing, nothing was ever quite the same after Percy went. Father might have kept Alice in the flesh, so to speak, but she changed, and she's never changed back. There were other men who wanted to marry her, but she wouldn't look at any of them."

"He didn't mind your other sister getting married," May pointed out.

"He didn't really have any choice there," said Miss Phyllis, simply. "Amy was some years younger than we were. And Father thought his family was complete. Alice used to say he would have liked a son, but I've never been

115

sure. Men, even when they're only boys, have a way of making themselves felt, and there's no doubt about it, Papa did like to rule the roost. And then suddenly this new baby. And, of course, her disability . . ." She paused.

"Disability?" May scarcely dared breathe the word. Next to cats, people were her passion, and she'd often wondered about the mysterious sister who was practically never mentioned.

"It wasn't anything dreadful," Miss Phyllis assured her. "And Amy never let it make any difference, I mean she never felt different from other people. It wasn't like being a mongol or anything, it was just this foot, what they call a club-foot, I believe, it made her walk—well, not quite straight like other people. But I don't believe Papa ever forgave our mother . . ."

"You mean, he thought she was responsible?" May sounded as shocked as she felt.

"Dear Father was such a perfectionist, everything had to be just so. And his family was like the rest. He never let me or Alice serve in the shop—I told you that—and really we didn't mind, but Amy wanted to stand behind the counter. I'm afraid she was rather sly, though neither of us could find it in our hearts to blame her, you see she never met anyone, and even when people did come to the house Father always tried to—to . . ."

"Exclude her," suggested May, and even Mrs. Politi would have been startled at the stony quality of her voice.

"I suppose you could say that," acknowledged Miss Phyllis reluctantly. "But—have you ever noticed that someone with a slight—a slight deformity quite often attracts a husband where the normal ones don't? Perhaps it's the law of compensation, I don't know. Or perhaps nature makes up for the deficiency in other ways. Amy was a very lively girl. And one day Tim Hardy came into the shop, he was a buyer and Papa happened to be out, but she contrived to be there. 'I am Miss Robinson,' she told him. 'I'm afraid my father's been called away. Perhaps I can be of assistance? At all events I could give him a message.'"

"But how romantic!" breathed sentimental May. "So your father . . ."

"Oh, he didn't give his consent. But Amy told me once that dear Alice was a dreadful example to her sex." Miss Phyllis blushed. "Of course, she thought Papa kept Alice at home because she took our mother's place, she really ran the household quite beautifully. So Amy did what Alice would never have done. She waited till our father was out of the way and told Tim to bring his car round to the side door and she packed a little bag and off she went. 'I'm just going for a drive with Mr. Hardy,' she told Alice. And she never came back. By the time Father had traced them they were married. But he never forgave her and he sent back her letters unopened. But it was difficult to get the better of Amy. She wrote to Alice and me and she sent the letters by registered post, and even Father didn't like to destroy them. I think she was very happy, though the marriage lasted barely ten years. Jack was only nine when she died of some local infection. Father said it was a judgment on her, but I never could understand that, because when our mother died he said it was the Will of God. He wouldn't let her come to the house or let us go up to stay with them—it sounds quite absurd now, but neither Alice nor I would have dreamed of disobeying him. Amy sent a few photographs of Jack when he was a little boy, but they were mostly snapshots, and one little boy does look very much like another."

"I'm glad she got away," May exclaimed. "If it was only ten years she had, it was more than either of you——" She stopped, colouring in her turn, but Miss Phyllis didn't take offence.

"I've no regrets," she said. "I've really enjoyed having the shop and living with Alice, and being independent. I hadn't realised what a great blow Mrs. Pankhurst struck for women when she insisted they should have the vote and be treated as individuals. Of course," she resumed, "Tim married again, you couldn't expect him to look after a boy of nine and his business, but I think the second wife must have been a very nice woman, because she saw to it that Jack didn't forget us altogether. He even went on writing from time to time after he was grown up, keeping in touch, he called it."

"But he never came to visit?" hesitated May.

"Between ourselves, my dear, I think Papa was right about Tim not being a good man of business. Of course, he never returned to us as a buyer and Amy wrote that he was opening his own business in the same line up in the North, but it can't have been very successful because after Tim died Jack sold out and wrote to say he was going to try his luck in Canada."

"The same sort of business?" wondered May. "I mean, he never talks much about it."

"Oh, I'm afraid he's rather a rolling stone. He met some man on his way out, George Something, and I always feel that this man talked Jack into putting his capital into some concern that didn't do very well. But he liked the life, though he said at first they were jeered at for what he called their limey accents, almost as though they were foreigners. Anyway, he kept in touch and when I wrote and told him about Alice he said at once he'd come back and see if he could be of any use. Well, you must agree it's not every young man would throw up everything and come home because an old aunt he'd never set eyes on wanted to see him while she still had the chance. And it's made all the difference to my sister. He's so patient, sits with her, lets her talk, even reads back some of the old letters. And even staying in quite a small inn costs money. Dear Alice—she really does love youth, and to have Jack *and* Linda dropping in . . ." She drew a deep breath. "We're going to miss her, you know, she may not have been very reliable in the shop, but it was like having a sunbeam round the house."

But practical May reflected that sunbeams are very unreliable. They vanish as unexpectedly as they come and never seem to stay five minutes in the same place. Poor Miss Alice! She hadn't had much success with her sums, never able to count on anything remaining stable for any length of time.

Miss Phyllis seemed suddenly to realise the time. "Oh dear, what can I be thinking of gossiping away like this, but you can't imagine what a relief it is to be able to recall the past—and really there was a lot of happiness, though it's difficult to put one's finger on the precise occasions— enough to make dear Father turn in his grave. You know, I think I'll run up and sit with Alice for a little, if you can hold the fort. We're never busy on a Monday, but if you need any help just press that button and I'll come straight down. Don't call out, we don't want to give the impression that everything isn't all right. I don't know where Jack is, I did so hope he'd remember it's Alice's birthday, he's always been so good, and though she hasn't said a word I know she's waiting."

"Perhaps he's gone out to buy something," suggested resourceful May.

After that brief quiet half-hour at the start of the day there was quite a bustle of customers, though May shrewdly suspected they could thank poor dead Linda for a lot of the trade. Customers came in to make inessential purchases and stopped to comment on the tragedy. What a shock for Mr. Myers! One can't help wondering . . . and they looked slyly at May under thin or artificially thickened brows, but they got no change there.

"We don't know any more than anyone else," May told them firmly. "That'll be one-and-eightpence, please, Miss Shrubb. Yes, of course Linda worked here once, but it's quite a long time ago." And she added with a rare touch of malice, "I wonder how many people are trying to get snap appointments at Polly's this morning."

"Yes," she said to another nosey old biddy, "we did hear something about Linda expecting a baby, but you can't expect us to be able to shed any light on that."

But during the afternoon the blow fell. Old Miss Marsh, who had a nose like that of the fabled princess, that ran down a long road and round a corner, came bustling in to look at dressing-jackets, and said fruitily that she understood the police had nailed the man responsible for Linda's murder. He was at the police station at this minute. "Helping the police with their enquiries—" she nodded— "and we all know what that means. I expect he'll appear before the magistrate to-morrow. It's Mr. Pantin, he's very severe on sex cases."

"I didn't know it was a sex case," said May repressively. "This is a Shetland wool, lined with nylon, four-and-a-half guineas . . ."

"You're forgetting I'm a pensioner," riposted Miss Marsh roguishly. "I must say it's a consolation to think they've got this man under lock and key. I've hardly dared put my nose out of doors since I heard about that girl. You know what they say, *l'appetit vient en mangeant*, and the first murder's always the hardest. After that . . ."

"Do we know this is a first murder?" asked May, neatly refolding the Shetland bedjacket, and feeling her heart thudding like a piston or a bird in a cage behind her plain Viyella blouse. And if he was after more blood, she thought nastily, you wouldn't be in any danger. You wouldn't yield more than about half a pint in your whole stringy carcase. She was horrified at the violence of her own thoughts. But I'm right to be violent, she reassured herself, she's just a ghoul.

Miss Phyllis had been flitting in and out of the shop all day. Jack hadn't put in an appearance. At five-thirty May locked the door and started to neaten the place against the morning, collected the empty boxes and wrappings and slipped down the stairs through the cellar to put them out for the dust collector, and it was just after six when she got back to find Mrs. Politi waiting in her own doorway. She hailed May in a voice like a fog-horn.

"I hear the news—at six o'clock," she declared.

"What news?" murmured May, who suddenly felt as though someone had removed her spine, so that she simply couldn't remain upright any longer. All she wanted was to kick off her shoes and make a cuppa.

"About this man they take for Linda Myers's murder. I light a candle for you," she added magnanimously.

"Very kind," murmured May. "I don't know why, but all the same . . ."

"You see the murderer face to face—yes?"

"If I'd done that I could give the police an accurate description of him, I might even know his name," May pointed out.

"You fortunate you not see his face or you be in another grave with that Linda. But——" she leaned her enormous bulk towards her friend, who automatically stepped backward anticipating annihilation—"maybe he see you, too."

"Since I don't know who he was . . ." May began.

"But I tell you. Why you not listen? The police have him . . ."

"Oh, that one!" said May. "He's not the one who killed her. I'm sure of that, even if he was wearing a mask. And what's more, Mr. Crook won't believe it either."

"You think this MISTER CROOK . . ." Her voice put his name in capital letters.

"He's like the man in the Bible—or Mr. Churchill," amended May, who wasn't sure that Mrs. Politi's authorities allowed her a free run of the Good Book. "The one who having put his hand to the plough, never looked back."

"Better he look back to see who follow him," returned Mrs. Politi severely. May thought she wouldn't like to be the Archangel on the Gate when Lilli's turn came up for the particular judgment. But, dropping with fatigue, she let her friend have the last word.

The next morning Miss Alice was worse and her sister said she meant to ring Dr. Mellish.

"I begin to think dear Jack is right, we shan't be able to carry on much longer, it's too much of a strain. And I could never agree to Alice going into any sort of institution. She hasn't worked all her life to be driven out of her own home at the end." The buyer from Bayman was due to-day or to-morrow and Miss Phyllis couldn't be sure how much to order or if, indeed, there was any sense ordering anything. She was more downcast than May had ever seen her. May had decided to nip out at midday and have a word with Mr. Crook. He would know, of course, about Chris Wayland and wouldn't need any advice from her, but she felt she must talk to someone, and she was certain he would understand. He might have a face like a professional pugilist, but that only went to show that you couldn't judge by appearances. At about 10.30 the shop door jangled open and Jack marched in, carrying some flowers.

"I hear they've got the fellow for that girl's murder," he said. "If you ask me, he's lucky to be inside, getting police protection at public expense."

"We don't know yet that he's guilty," said May calmly. "What beautiful flowers!"

He bowed and extended them towards her. "I had an idea you'd like this kind."

"You're getting confused," May told him. "It's not my birthday. At least, yesterday wasn't. Miss Phyllis was rather upset, because you never do forget, but Miss Alice was so poorly . . ."

He looked at the flowers in his arm. May was right, they really were beautiful. "*Amende honorable!*" he murmured. "I better go up and make my peace."

"You might offer to sit with Miss Alice for a little, if you have the time," May suggested, quite without sarcasm. It didn't seem to her natural that a young man should spend all his time with an ailing old lady he'd never seen until a short time ago, even if she was his aunt. "Miss Phyllis probably didn't get more than catnaps all night."

She'd have liked to ask him to hold the fort for ten minutes while she ran across the Green and telephoned, but she decided against it. Jack Hardy might be very good at his own job in Canada, but he was like a bull in a china-shop when it came to haberdashery. Not that she blamed him, it wasn't a young man's job. Of course there'd been Percy Trivett—but things had been different then. Life had been much drabber for the young and much more stereotyped.

"It doesn't seem very appropriate to say Happy Birthday, does it?" Jack murmured, diving for the stairs that led to the upper floor from the back of the shop. It was a dark morning with fog outside that threatened to thicken, and May put on the light, no one was going to come into a shop that looked like a cave. Jack vanished, the shop bell rang sharply. May turned, she'd always secretly resented that bell, people should be summoned by people, not a machine. An old termagant called Parrott came in to ask for handkerchiefs—the initialled kind, she explained, for my niece, her name's Queenie.

It would be, May reflected grimly, explaining there really was no demand for personal lingerie with the letter Q embroidered on it.

"Well, really," bridled old Miss Parrott, "there's Queenie and Quentin and Quarles, and my best friend had a daughter christened Quebec."

It was obvious to May that she'd come in for a gossip rather than a purchase, but "You shall buy some handkerchiefs if I have to stuff them down your throat," May adjured her silently. She ransacked a drawer and came up with a box of handkerchiefs with a coloured design of ducks in the corner.

"Quack-quack!" she explained.

Miss Parrott laughed gaily. "What an amusing idea! Still, I don't know that my niece—everyone's sense of humour is different, isn't it?"

"If your niece has the right kind," asserted May, "she'll be tickled pink."

"You really think so! I must admit they're rather ducky . . ." She suddenly realised she'd made a joke, and began to giggle. While May packed them up she wandered to the opposite counter where she began to finger gloves, disarranging the neat stand May had set up that morning. Suddenly she began to neigh like a horse.

"Think of that," she said. "We were so busy talking we never even heard the postman come."

123

"The postman doesn't call at this hour," explained May.

"He's come this morning." The old horror contrived to look positively arch. "Or perhaps it's a *billet-doux.*"

She stooped down, a great overgrown croquet-hoop of an old woman, and tugged the envelope out of the low letter-box that the postmen disliked, but where else can you put a letter-box if you have a glass shop-door?

"Why, it's for you," she discovered, more arch than ever. "And dear me—I was right—it's not stamped, so it must have come by hand."

May took the letter without even looking at it and put it in the pocket of her cardigan. She took a pound note from the clearly-disappointed Miss Parrott and returned her change.

"I mustn't keep you," Miss Parrott simpered. "I'm sure you're dying to open your letter."

"And that," reflected May, putting away the box of handkerchiefs, "is probably the first true thing you've said since you came in."

She stood well back in the shadow where she was virtually invisible from the door, but could herself keep a watchful eye on her domain. Miss Parrott was right about something else, that the letter hadn't come through the post. On such a foggy morning and with so much on her mind it wouldn't be difficult for anyone under the guise of window-shopping to stoop and slip the envelope into the slot marked LETTERS. Either it wasn't there when Jack came or else he didn't notice it, she decided. But it would be so easy to overlook. It wasn't even a white envelope, one of those cheap yellowish ones that in this light could easily go unnoticed. The address was printed in a backward sloping slapdash hand, and even May didn't suppose it was the author's normal writing. Anyway it was kind of printed, had an uneducated appearance, but that could be cunning, too. She tore the envelope open, willing everyone to stay away until she'd digested the contents. When she had read the message she stared and stared. It was composed of letters and words cut from a newspaper and stuck unevenly on to a plain white sheet. The message read:

Ask Mr. Polly where he was at 6 p.m. last Thursday.

The sender had had some difficulty in finding a capital P and Mr. Polly was fashionably named with a small letter.

May's first thought, as she pushed it deep into her cardigan pocket again, was "Now I've got to get in touch with Mr. Crook." It never once occurred to her it could be someone playing a practical joke, it was someone who had evidence and couldn't or wouldn't come forward, someone who was afraid of the police pinning the crime on an innocent man, but fearing to put a name to his or her own suspicions.

"There's no time to be lost," decided May, and as though fate grudgingly admitted that she deserved a small respite for her patience, Miss Phyllis could be heard to open a door upstairs and then down she came into the shop.

"Was that Miss Parrott?" she asked. "I thought I recognised the voice. I suppose she didn't buy anything."

"She bought six handkerchiefs with ducks on them," said May. "People talk about putting a purchase tax on goods, I think there should be a service tax, Miss Parrott would pay at about fifty per cent."

"Poor May!" But Miss Phyllis's thoughts were clearly elsewhere. "It's about a quarter to one, I think we might close the shop now."

Since Alice had been unable to serve in the shop they had closed for the midday break between one and two o'clock. "I doubt if anyone would be coming in," Miss Phyllis added, as though it didn't really matter much either way. "It's not so important. I could do with a cup of tea. I'll put on the kettle."

This was so unlike her normal courageousness, which could be brazen at times, that May found the words sticking in her throat.

"I must just run across to the chemist. My head . . ." It wasn't really a lie, it had begun to ache abominably, the world seemed to be spinning round her, and her mind must be spinning too, because she thought that if Crook stuck out his big hand and steadied it everything would be calm again.

"I have some aspirin upstairs," said Miss Phyllis. "There's no need to go out."

But May said desperately she was allergic to aspirin, Allen's kept a tablet that was just the job, she'd only be five minutes anyway.

She didn't suppose Miss Phyllis would try and check up on her, but conscience made her dive into Allen's and buy twenty-five tablets she didn't need, before slipping across the green into the Ancient Mariner by the restaurant entrance. They had a telephone half-way up the stairs which ensured privacy, not like those you saw in French films where the instrument was in the bar and you had to shout to make yourself heard. If she should be seen and recognised it would only be supposed that she was nipping up for a bit of lunch. The bar was filling rapidly and there was plenty of noise, which gave her an odd feeling of concealment. She had her money in her hand and now it only remained for Mr. Crook to be in. And this time luck was with her and he answered the phone himself.

"I've only got a minute," she whispered. "I'm in a call-box . . ."

"I could have told you that, Sugar," said Crook, who had heard the coins fall.

"There's something I've got to tell you, it's urgent."

"If it's about Young Lochinvar being taken for the girl's murder I've heard that," said Crook, and she didn't stop to wonder how it was he could be so sure of her identity.

"Well, yes, I suppose so, but this is different, I've got something to show you, only I can't get away, not this afternoon, with Miss Alice so ill, and no one but me in the shop, so . . ." She paused, because her breath had suddenly run out.

"I get the message," said Crook soothingly. "Mahomet can't come to the mountain. Well, Sugar, you're speaking to the most travelled mountain in the business. What time's your tea-break?"

"We don't actually have a break then . . ."

"You should have a word with your union," Crook advised. "Then say I come along for a pair of gloves, or . . ."

"We don't sell men's gloves."

"I didn't say I was buying them for myself. I daresay my auntie wouldn't mind a nice surprise. And if you don't serve in the glove shop she'll have to put up with a nice silk scarf or a pair of bedsocks."

She thought he was considering a comparatively long journey in bad weather with less ado than most people make about having to go down the road in the rain for a pint of milk.

"I wouldn't ask you if it wasn't urgent," she began, and he said well, it hadn't occurred to him she was ringing just because she had cold hands and wanted someone to warm them for her. Then he added, "Be seeing you," and he set down his receiver with a resolution that would have aroused the envy of King Canute who couldn't even stop an advancing wave, let alone a distracted female in full spate.

When May got back to the shop she found Miss Phyllis sitting with her hands folded in her lap and the electric kettle puffing away fit to burst. She switched it off, drew herself a glass of water and ostentatiously swallowed two tablets, then fetched some teacups from the cupboard.

Miss Phyllis opened her eyes. "I believe I was dropping off," she confessed. "But it's all right. Jack's upstairs with Alice. Did you remind him about it being her birthday yesterday? I mean, he came in with an armful of flowers."

"They were entirely his own idea," May reassured her. "I saw them. They were lovely."

"I must have given him a fright because he tried to give them to me, and they were lovely, but oh dear, they made me think of funerals, all so white, you know. Somehow it seems wrong for a young man to bring white flowers to an old woman. Youth should go in for the strong colours. And then Alice saw him and she must have been half-asleep, because she started to call him Percy, though they aren't in the least alike, and she said she'd kept all his letters, and if he didn't believe her, they were all in a box under the bed. And then she saw me and said hadn't I better make sure

Father didn't want anything. Poor Jack! I'm afraid he's not going to have very happy memories of his aunts, when he's back in Canada."

"Did Dr. Mellish come?" asked May, because the doctor naturally would go to the side door which was the private one. The shop stood on a corner, with a long narrow lane running down to some recently built maisonettes grouped round a little square.

"I talked to his partner, Dr. Mellish was out, and he said —Dr. Durant, I mean—that I should try and keep her quiet —not that she's in the least violent, you understand—he did ask if she had a temperature, but I said no, I didn't think so, she didn't seem feverish, so he said if there was an emergency to ring again and he'd tell Dr. Mellish as soon as he came in. Not that I think there's much he can do if she's suffering from loss of memory, and if she's happy believing that Jack is Percy Trivett why should any of us try to prevent her having a little pleasure? She hasn't had much in her life, poor Alice."

"She's had you," said May simply, unwrapping a packet of sandwiches, and she spoke with so much sincerity that her companion was startled.

"It's not a great deal to show for a life," she said humbly. It didn't seem to occur to her to wonder how much she herself had had.

Mr. Crook turned up about three o'clock. Miss Phyllis was at the glove counter, so he diplomatically asked for a silk scarf instead.

"Pick the sort of thing you'd like yourself," he suggested.

May produced her favourite, pale pink with a design of small groups of kittens in shadowy grey at the corners and an erect mother cat in the centre. She spread it on the counter, and Mr. Crook lifted it, bunching it in his hand in a professional manner. On the counter, underneath the scarf, lay the letter.

"Got the envelope?" murmured Mr. Crook, dropping the scarf and sleeving the scrap of paper apparently all in one movement. "I'm not so sure about the kittens, how about a nice poodle? Or a picture of Buckingham Palace? She's very patriotic, is Auntie. So maybe not a poodle, after all. French dogs, ain't they?"

"I believe they were originally seen in Russia," said May, playing up like mad, and hunting through the folder of scarves.

"When did it come?" murmured Mr. Crook, demanding of fate a fresh customer who would distract Miss Phyllis's attention. She was looking at him rather oddly, as if she thought at any minute he was going to produce a gun and yell, Put 'em up, though May could have told her that men of his calibre, even if they have criminal intent, don't waste their energy on tatty little haberdashers run by old maids. And an instant later the door-bell tinkled and someone came in to buy some Fair Isle mittens for a grand-daughter.

"This really is something," Mr. Crook acknowledged. "Make with the scarves, Sugar. Something with flowers, maybe. My auntie loves a nice bunch of flowers. Too bad all the words have been cut out of a popular morning daily. There can't be more than a thousand locals or so who take that one. Or it could even have been bought for the occasion."

"You think whoever left it knows something?" whispered May, shaking out scarves like someone plucking a fowl, they seemed to be flapping in all directions.

"Well, I don't think it's a practical joke," Mr. Crook retorted. "My guess would be that whoever sent that knows you've pulled me into the case, and you ain't done that in your own interests because you don't even know the young chap. So, if Wayland's out, someone else has to be in, and X wants to be tooting sure it ain't him."

"But why Mr. Polly? I mean, he's a married man . . ."

"That could be why. Who was it said a man with a wife and children had given hostages to fortune? He can't afford to laugh it off like some young chap might be able to. What's she like?"

"Mrs. Polly? Well, she comes to the chapel. Very— forceful—I think is the best word for her. And decorative in a sort of Roman matron way. About twice his size and very competent. I mean, if a fuse blows in the house she's the one who knows how to put it right, and if the car breaks down she could probably mend it much more quickly than he could. She was a school-mistress before she married."

"Wonder she stooped to trade," murmured Mr. Crook, snatching up a scarf with a Beefeater design, and bunching it under his chin as if he were trying to learn if he liked Beefeaters the way children hold buttercups to decide whether they like butter. "Or maybe she didn't like the notion of having Miss writ on her tombstone."

"It can't have been that," objected May. "She was a widow—she's some years older than he is—with one daughter. She's married, the daughter, I mean, and the Pollys never had any children. Did you say your aunt likes flowers? How about this one with lilies-of-the-valley on a pale green ground?"

Miss Phyllis's customer had chosen her gloves, but curiosity being strong in her too, she was making conversation in the hope of catching the sense of what the brigandish creature was saying to Miss Forbes. Mr. Crook blessed her. He said he thought not the lilies-of-the-valley, his auntie was superstitious, and May went on to explain about a customer finding the envelope, etc., etc.

"Likely to open her trap?" enquired Mr. Crook sympathetically, meaning the customer, of course.

"Well," said May innocently, "she is a Parrott." And Mr. Crook put back his head and roared like any bull of Bashan.

"Lucky she was here, though, and was the one to take it out of the box," he suggested.

"I don't understand."

"Then no one can say it didn't come straight dinkum through the slit, not a home-grown article," he elucidated kindly.

"But why on earth should I want to implicate Mr. Polly?"

"Maybe you put half a dozen names in a hat and that was the one you drew. Well, use your marbles, Sugar.

You're backing Young Lochinvar, wearing his colours, so to speak."

"Only because I know he's innocent," urged May. "You see, the police set a trap and he didn't spring it."

"You have to hand it to the police, they wouldn't let a little thing like that stop them," acknowledged Mr. Crook generously.

"Even though I didn't really see HIM that night, who-ever it was must have seen me, and if I'd sprung up at his elbow like—like a ghost, he'd need to be Sir Laurence Olivier not to show even the smallest sign of surprise."

"I'd like to see you standing up to the Attorney-General," offered Mr. Crook, meaning just that. "You know, I think I'll have the kitties, after all."

"I thought you said your aunt didn't care about cats."

"Wherever Auntie is now, God rest her soul—" Mr. Crook made a reverent gesture towards his abominable brown bowler hat—"it won't matter to her what sort of scarf I buy, so maybe I'll take this one, and if I find I need a bit more info. I can bring it back and you can find me a nice view of Lake Windermere or something. Is it a fact you ain't got a buzzer?" He sounded quite incredulous, he'd as soon have been without his clothes as without his tele-phone. "Well, then, how about your lady-friend over the way? The one like the Eye of God that never sleeps?"

"She would always take a message," May agreed, reflect-ing as she folded and packed the scarf that this was the first time in years she'd sold anything without the thrifty cus-tomer enquiring the price. "Are you going to see him now, Mr. Wayland, I mean?"

"Have to find out first if he wants to see me. May have a legal beagle of his own."

"He hasn't had much time, and he doesn't sound the sort of young man who would have a lawyer." Her voice made them sound as rare and valuable as diamonds.

"Might have a word with Mr. Polly," conceded Crook, offering a five-pound note. "Where does he hang out?"

May told him, while she made change. "But he's not a gentleman's hairdresser," she pointed out. "Mr. White, at the corner of Mill Street, is said to be very good."

"I need a barber like I need a hole in the head," said Crook graphically. He pocketed his change and picked up the little parcel. "If Auntie don't like the kitties I'll bring it back," he promised. "By the way, got a chain on your door at home?"

"No," said May. "I've never needed one."

"Maybe not, but now times have changed. You're obstructin' someone's plans by being so tooting sure the police have got the wrong man, which makes you a person of importance, whether you know it or not—important to young Wayland and important to me, to say nothing of being important to yourself. And one more thing, don't let anyone in, not even if he says he's a rozzer, not without he shows you his warrant through the crack. Faith is one of the great trilogy, as we know, but blind faith is just blankity stupidity. I sometimes think," he added more calmly, "that's one of the things that's got faith such a bad name, the faithful do have a tendency to shunt responsibility on to the Lord God, and though I ain't a theologian, I don't recall any place in Holy Writ that tells you to do that."

"Casting all your care upon Him," murmured May.

"Sounds like heaving bricks to me," said outspoken Mr. Crook. "And me, I'd have a better use for bricks. Still, you bear that in mind and drop into Woollies or whatever on your way back and don't forget to buy a chisel while you're about it. When you've finished putting in the screws just remember there are a lot of worse weapons than a chisel, if some nasty chap does manage to insinuate himself over your threshold."

CHAPTER IX

LEAVING MAY to ponder on the wisdom of that suggestion, Mr. Crook got back into the Superb and breezed along to Polly's Parlour, where he found himself confronted by a female with a face like a human lemon, who had just fitted a setting helmet over a mop of pinned-up hair. When she saw the newcomer she quickly pulled the cubicle curtain, as though it would be sacrilege for him to see a client in what might be called a state of undress, and an instant later came into the shop with a nice trimming of frost around the lemon-face.

"I'm afraid you've made a mistake," she told him, icily. "This is a ladies' salon."

"And you don't think I look like a lady? And you'd be dead right." He gave her his friendliest smile. "Boss around?"

Miss Buxton stiffened.

"If you mean Mr. Polly, he is not available."

"How do you know he doesn't want to see me?"

Her expression said that this was something beyond the bounds of likelihood.

"I mean," pursued Mr. Crook, "I might have come from Ernie, to tell him he's won £25,000 in the draw."

Miss Buxton didn't unbend. "Draws are made on Saturdays and on the first of the month," she pointed out. "In either case your timing is wrong."

"I bet the boss sets his watch by you," observed Mr. Crook respectfully. "All the same, I'd like a word."

"He is giving a blue rinse to one of our most important clients."

"Blue hair to match her blue blood?" suggested Mr. Crook. "Well, but I can wait." He dropped down on a hard chair and picked up a woman's magazine.

Miss Buxton looked dismayed. "I'm afraid it won't be any use," she said.

Crook pulled one of his fantastic professional cards out of his pocket. "Maybe if you were to get him to cast his eye over this . . ."

Unashamedly Miss Buxton read it. "Is it supposed to be a joke?" she enquired.

"Chaps who get one don't normally think so."

Miss Buxton's client who, after the way of women, realised there was something funny going on, began to fidget under her drier and call out something about it being too hot.

"Turn it down, dear," said Miss Buxton crisply. "But it'll mean staying there all the longer . . ."

"I can't find the switch," whined the client.

Mr. Polly, attracted by the unusual clamour, darted out of the cubicle where he was performing the miracle of turning drab grey into a sparkling lilac-blue. Crook was on his feet like a bouncing ball. "Mr. Polly? My card." He removed it from Miss Buxton's nerveless hand. "Representing young Wayland, if you know who I mean, thought you might be able to assist enquiries . . ."

"Are you from the police?" demanded Mr. Polly, looking baffled and outraged at the same time. "May I remind you this is my place of business . . ." Then he noticed the card in his hand and paused to read it. The bafflement disappeared, the outrage swelled.

"Really, Mr. Crook, I consider this an unwarrantable intrusion. Miss Buxton, I think your client is endeavouring to attract your attention." Miss Buxton departed. "If you have come for information, I can only assure you that I have told the police all I know about Miss Myers."

"Ah, but maybe the police and me wouldn't ask the same questions. They were thinkin' of a guilty man, I'm out for an innocent one. So, how about you and me havin' a little get-together, at your convenience, of course?"

"I repeat, this is my place of business . . ."

"Wouldn't want to do a fellow-toiler a bad turn," agreed Mr. Crook, handsomely. "How about after you shut up shop?"

"I go home—naturally."

"Maybe I could call around there." He waited for that to sink in, then continued affably, "Or if Mrs. P. wouldn't be agreeable, how about you meeting me for a nice glass of something at some convenient rendezvous? I daresay you'd know the local ports of call better than me."

"I can assure you, Mr. Crook, I have already told the police everything they wanted to know, in so far as lay in my power."

"Such as—where you were Thursday night?"

"Thursday is the night I stop late at the shop to do the week's accounts."

"Every Thursday?"

"Every Thursday."

"So if my informant says he saw you at six p.m., outside the shop, he's a liar?"

"A case of mistaken identity perhaps." Mr. Polly's hands stole out and caught at the back of the chair.

"He don't seem to think so."

"May I ask the name of your informant?"

"That I can't tell you at the moment," returned Mr. Crook, truthfully. "But he seems dead sure. And the only way of proving him wrong is to prove he ain't right."

Mr. Polly hesitated. His worst enemy couldn't accuse Crook of a threatening attitude, but the hairdresser recognised the look in that wide-open bright brown eye. He'd seen it too often (though hers were a refined shade of blue) in Mrs. Polly's. To cap everything, the titled client began to make chattering noises.

"I cannot wait," Mr. Polly said hurriedly. "A tint—a case of the little more and how much it is. Very well, Mr. Crook, if you insist—yes, Lady Pitt-Marten, I am coming immediately—the Flying Fox at the top of Aldershot Hill, it's a short distance, but my wife doesn't care for me to be seen in the local public houses, she's the Chairman of our Temperance Association—no doubt you have your car— shall we say six o'clock?"

He barely waited for the reply, but hurried back to his client, who was behaving as royalty would scorn to do.

135

Miss Buxton came popping out of her client's cubicle as the boss dived back into his.

"Not to worry," said Mr. Crook soothingly. "I'm the other side of the coin, checking up on behalf of the accused." He thought he'd better take her to this extent into his confidence, Mr. Polly had a reputation to maintain. " 'Him being the poor girl's employer, I can't afford to overlook even a trifle. It's O.K.," he added, soothingly, "I'm sure Mrs. Polly is a lady of integrity, she'll understand."

He found himself wondering whether the aforesaid lady had ever been jealous of the dead girl. A bit older than him, Miss Forbes had said. And according to the evidence the girl had been quite a beauty. All the same, there was something odd about the situation, an ancient and fishlike smell. Not for the first time Mr. Crook thanked the powers that be for his own single status. Everyone concerned seemed to him eager to cover up something, but when all the flat stones were lifted and the flat creatures they concealed revealed, it wouldn't surprise him if quite a lot of people had quite a lot of shocks. Come to that, he was prepared for a shock or two himself. He drove direct to the prison where Chris Wayland was kicking his heels, quite unresigned to his situation.

"Is Wayland expecting you?" an officer enquired when Crook had made his errand known.

"Mr. Wayland," amended Crook. "He ain't convicted yet, you know. And lots of chaps have been taken unaware, some of 'em by angels. Lawyer," he added patiently. "Even an accused man has his rights."

The officer stiffened. "We've no instructions about legal aid."

"You're getting 'em now. Want I should call the boss?"

He produced his official card, and the man gave it and him a quick, suspicious glance. It was clear he'd heard of Crook and didn't much like what he'd heard. But Crook continued to look about him with a guileless air until, after some apparent consultation, he was told he could see the prisoner. The gaoler wasn't the only person to be surprised by Crook's appearance. Chris Wayland stared at him as though he were a denizen from the deep.

Once more Crook produced his card. "My friend, client really, Miss May Forbes, asked me to come and see were you fixed up. She's the one who knows you didn't do it," he added persuasively.

"I'm glad there's someone besides me," Chris agreed.

"That makes three of us, because, naturally, my clients are never guilty. Four, if we count the chap who really is guilty, I mean. Now, Sugar—Miss Forbes to you—she's as good as gold, and you can't have better than that."

"Why should she concern herself?" Crook saw the young fellow really wanted to know.

"I'll tell you why—and hold on to your hat—because she believes in justice, and she knows the rozzers have pulled a boner. No hope of showing you couldn't have been there that night, I take it? No, I thought not. Mind you, there are probably a few chaps who did see you go by that evening, without actually *seein'* you, if you get me. Well, then, let's try another tack. Stop off at a bar or anything? Petrol station? Ask anyone the way?"

"No to all those," said Chris. "I went into a help-yourself hot-dog café—I don't even remember the name of that, though I suppose I could track it down again—but no one 'ud remember seeing me there, and then on to meet my ghost, who failed to keep her appointment. I tried to knock up the church caretaker, but she was having a day off, and no one answered the Rectory phone. I'm afraid I'm a dead loss to you, sir."

"Oh, I don't know," murmured Crook. "If you don't give the police any facts at least they can't twist 'em into the wrong pattern."

"So how do you start convincing them I'm not the chap they're after?"

"Only one way I know and that's to find a substitute. You don't want to be known as another of the chaps that got away with murder. Doesn't seem to have occurred to anyone that if you'd laid the girl in her pebbly bed the odds are you'd have removed the ring first."

"I suppose they'd argue I was panic-stricken and didn't think till it was too late, or was taken unawares by the prowler and dropped the ring and couldn't find it in the dark. You know, if Miss Forbes hadn't been out feeding her cats that night, the odds are the police wouldn't have found Linda Myers yet."

"It wasn't the police found her, it was Solly Gold's dog, but no one's going to give him a medal. I take it, by the way, you're not legally represented?"

"Well, not till you drifted in." The young man actually grinned. "It's hard to make these old chaps understand that while you're still working on your first million, the odds are you don't have any need of a lawyer—even if you could afford one."

"If you're thinking about the legal aid cert. you can forget it," said Crook instantly. "Payment by results, that's my motto, and Robin Hood was one of my ancestors."

Then he took his new client through his story in detail. "It figures," he said at last. "I mean, that's virtually what the police got, too. Now, about the young lady. I've had her stepmother's opinion, second-hand of course, and Sugar's. (Linda worked at Miss Robinson's for a while, I understand). Old lady took the news very hard. And Mr. Polly's going to open up to-night, whether he believes it or not."

"Polly? That's the chap she worked for?"

"It ain't likely there'd be two. Ever mention him?"

"She said once it was nice to be the one that called the tune. I suppose she'd got him tied to her shoestring, too."

"Ever wonder why?"

Chris looked surprised. "You never met her, of course, but she is—was—the kind that takes it for granted that whatever she wants there'll be someone to give it to her."

"If he didn't, would she try and get it by force?"

"Not force, but—I'd say she didn't give up easily."

"According to one of his assistants, she wound Polly round her little finger."

"I wouldn't be surprised."

"Never tried anything of the sort with you?"

"You're joking, of course. I mean—perhaps this isn't a thing one should say of the dead, but you're asking the questions—she wouldn't have thought I was worth it, and she'd have been right. I hadn't much to lose, living more or less from hand to mouth—the TV payment was a bonanza and it wasn't all that generous—not even much of a reputation. No, she'd reserve her energies for bigger game."

"No touch of Little Dan Cupid, I take it?" murmured Crook.

"Not on my side, and certainly not on hers."

"Knowing how many beans make five?"

"Knowing that, and knowing, too, where to pick the beans. No, I don't know in whose yard, if I did I'd tell you, I can't do her any harm now. But I gather she could pick and choose her escorts, though I couldn't put a name to any of them for you."

"Know the most difficult job the police ever find themselves up against?" Crook asked. "The murder of prostitutes. Because there's never a clue pointing in any definite direction. Same with maniacs. What the police need is motive. And if the chap stops at just one—if Neil Cream had had that sense they'd never have named him but he went on and on. It's a hard saying, but missing women are still two a penny. And that's when chaps begin to think they're safe. Smith (George Joseph) might have lived to get the Queen's telegram if he'd stopped at one bride in the bath, because one bride's a misfortune, but three is plain ridiculous. By the way—you're bound to be asked this one day or another—got any other girl in your eye?"

The question was so direct, so unexpected, that the young man looked as though he'd been kicked by a mule, and kicked practically insensible at that. After a moment during which Crook made no attempt to hurry him, he said, "You don't have to drag her in, I hadn't even met her at the time of Linda's death. And that's one thing I can prove, if I have to."

"I like a quick worker," Crook approved. "All the same, the rozzers 'ull be grasping at straws, seein' that's all they've got to grasp at. Well, that's all for the time being. I've got a date to see a man who might be able to throw a bit of light on the situation, only my guess is he's going to claim he's lost his matches."

Chris grinned appreciatively. "And you're going to do a conjuring act and produce them from behind his ear or something?"

"You catch on quick," Mr. Crook congratulated him.

"Take care of my client," he adjured the outraged officer who saw him off the premises. "And be sure you vet his visitors. Anything happens to him and British justice could go right down the drain." Leaving the man speechless, he hopped into the Superb and drove gaily off to keep his appointment at the Flying Fox.

There was no sign of Mr. Polly when he reached his rendezvous, so he perched himself up by the bar and asked for a pint.

"Not had a message from a chap called Polly, I suppose?" he offered with that first pint safely under his belt.

The barman, who had been watching him, fascinated, said, "You mean the hairdresser? No, we don't see him here. You should ask at the Black Sheep, or so they tell me."

"Mrs. P. runs the Temperance League, I hear," remarked Crook, ordering a second pint and adding, "Have one yourself."

"Strong drink is raging, wine is a mocker," intoned the barman who clearly saw himself as a bit of a wit. "Still, here he comes."

Out of his business premises, Mr. Polly looked taller and better turned-out than Crook recalled him. But then shackles of servitude hardly ever do a fellow justice, he reminded himself. Crook picked up his tankard and hopped down from the bar.

"Give it a name," he encouraged.

Mr. Polly said a glass of dry sherry, adding that he couldn't stay long, his wife was expecting him. And he repeated that he'd told the police everything he knew. He'd said it so often by this time he sounded like a gramophone record, and he wondered if that was the way he sounded to Crook, too.

"You may find it hard to believe this," Crook assured him, "but the police don't always confide in me."

The barman brought the drinks and Crook came straight to the point. "It's about Thursday."

"Last Thursday?"

"So far as I'm concerned, that's the only Thursday there is. So tell me."

"Tell you what?" Mr. Polly swallowed almost all his sherry in a gulp.

"Anything that occurs to you that could help us to track down Linda's killer. We both know the police have got their finger on this chap Wayland, but for the sake of argument, let's assume he's innocent. So—who would you suggest we might put in his place?"

"Why ask me, Mr. Crook? Linda was nothing but a temporary employee. I never expected her to stay very long, she was the restless kind, always wanting change."

"What kind of change?"

"How do I know? She never discussed her future with me. I know at one time she was anxious to go to London, only Mr. Myers prevented it."

"I didn't know they could do it, these days. Fathers, I mean."

"Well!" Mr. Polly looked down at his folded hands. "I suppose there were some advantages in her present situation. She was living rent-free, so anything she earned was hers to spend."

"Not the saving type?"

"I don't think she'd have known what the word meant."

"She was a good employee, good at her job, I mean?"

Mr. Polly considered. "I wouldn't describe her as a devoted hairdresser, in the way Miss Reith is, for instance, or, if I may say so, as I am myself. But when she gave her mind to it she could turn out a very pretty job. I sometimes wondered if there wasn't some feeling among the other members of my staff when some client of quite long standing would ask for Linda, explaining that she knew the trendy ways of doing hair, and really she produced some remarkable results. Some of those middle-aged women can't have recognised themselves when they looked in the glass."

"Didn't they like themselves the way they were before?"

"You know how women are, Mr. Crook, always something for a change. And no one likes to be thought to be stuck in a rut. Miss Buxton and Miss Reith both turned out neat, accomplished jobs, but even elderly women get tired of the tidy parting and the careful wave. I've had clients say to me, 'I almost feel as if I was wearing a wig.' Delighted they were! And they'd give Linda a bigger tip than usual. Of course, that's partly the age. The older ones are afraid to give the youngsters what they'd think sufficient for their own contemporaries."

"You seem to have made quite a study of it," said Crook. "Still—I know Jealousy's a green-eyed monster, but you need rather more motive than that . . ."

Mr. Polly looked horrified, as well he might. "You're not suggesting that I should attempt to involve Miss Reith or Miss Buxton in this tragic affair? They're—I could call them dedicated women."

Dedicated to a hair-drier, reflected Crook ribaldly. "Well, let's come on to Thursday," he suggested. "She left at her usual time?"

"Actually, she asked if she might leave a little early. She had no further appointments and she had what she'd call a date."

"And you agreed?"

"I've said she had no other appointments—and it was only a matter of, say, twenty minutes—well, perhaps half-an-hour."

"And that's the last time you saw her?"

"I've told the police that."

"And now you're telling me?"

"That's right."

"You mean, that's right, that's what you told the police, or that's right, it's the last time you saw her?"

"Well, both. Naturally."

"You couldn't have made a mistake?"

"What's all this in aid of, Mr. Crook?"

"So if my informant says he saw you together at six o'clock that night he's a liar? But I asked you that before, didn't I?"

"It must be a case of mistaken identity," insisted Mr. Polly. "She went around with a good many men."

"So I've heard. Do you know a pub called the Black Sheep?"

"The—I've told you, I'm not a drinking man. I owe it to my wife . . ."

"That wasn't what I asked."

"I've heard of it, of course."

"But the barman there wouldn't recognise you? Oh, come on, it's simple enough. He does or he don't."

Mr. Polly hesitated. Then he said desperately, "I have been there occasionally. But I've never gone there to meet Linda Myers."

"And you didn't see her there last Thursday?"

"If you're trying to link me up with what happened to her . . ."

"I'm trying to find out who killed her, if Chris Wayland didn't."

"That's a big IF, Mr. Crook."

"The Black Sheep's quite a way out from Churchford," murmured Mr. Crook.

"It doesn't do for me to be seen drinking at the locals," blustered Mr. Polly.

"So when you tell your wife you're stopping late to do the books, what you really mean is you're on a bit of a pub-crawl. Ain't you afraid she might ring you at the shop?"

"Thursday night is the night of the Temperance Meeting. That's why we decided it was a good time for me to work late. Otherwise I should have to clear the books on Saturday afternoon, and naturally she expects my company then."

"You know all the answers, don't you?" said Crook in an admiring tone. "Now let's stop going round in circles, and you tell me what she had on you?"

"Are you talking about Linda Myers?"

"She didn't make any secret of it, you know. She knew she could get off early or have an elastic lunch-hour. She told one of her boy-friends it was nice to be the one with a bit of power. Well, I suppose her stepmother ruled the roost at home."

"I've told you already, Mr. Crook, I wouldn't dream of taking that girl anywhere. She's nearly young enough to be my daughter and I'm a married man."

"I don't say you set out to meet her on the Thursday. Maybe she just turned up uninvited, knowing you often went to the Black Sheep that evening."

"I'm sure she knew nothing of the kind, it was purely fortuitous . . ." Mr. Polly, gasping and floundering like an inadequate swimmer suddenly finding himself out of his depth, stopped and picked up his empty glass to cover his discomposure.

Crook looked across to the bar. "Same again," he called. "Yes, of course you will. You're going to need a bit of Dutch courage. Not that I blame you for wanting a pull now and again. Man wasn't made to live on water. And don't tell me that all she had on you was knowing that you sometimes dropped in for a glass or two. It's who you dropped in to meet. Now just consider. It wouldn't be too difficult to get you identified, a chap as well known as you, and maybe they could identify your companion as well."

"I won't have her dragged into it," cried Mr. Polly, sharply. "The girl meant nothing to me, and Monica—my friend—knew it. Nor do I know what happened after I left the bar. I can only assure you that Linda Myers was in excellent health and about to join whoever she had come there to meet."

"What makes you so tooting sure about that? Now, let's not waste any more time. That's a nice suit you're wearing, it fits you a treat, but the coat wasn't cut for you to sleeve aces. So let's have a few cards on the table. You went to the Black Sheep, as per usual . . ."

"I was a little early, also as usual. To my surprise Linda Myers suddenly appeared at my table and sat down uninvited. She said something like, 'Someone standing you up too?' She's not the sort of girl who likes being kept waiting."

"Didn't drop a hint who she was there for?"

"I daresay I shouldn't have been enlightened if she had. But she was put out and—it was more than that. I knew that girl well enough to realise that if someone really kept her waiting she'd march off with her nose in the air."

"But instead she decided to fill in time talking to you? And you couldn't shake her off because, like I said, she had something on you. Could be she knew your friend's name?"

"No. No, I'm sure it wasn't that. But—she did see me out one Thursday evening with someone who wasn't Mrs. Polly. As a matter of fact, she tried to thumb a lift."

"Seems quite a habit of hers. That's the way she got acquainted with Wayland. If her stepmother knew so much, shouldn't she have warned her that's the way to make trouble for yourself?"

"It was unfortunate that the lights were against us, so I couldn't drive on, and of course . . ."

"She got a good dekko. And she didn't see why she shouldn't turn her knowledge to good account. She sounds a real charmer. What did she take you for?"

"You make it sound so melodramatic," stammered Mr. Polly. "Blackmail and all that. But there was never anything of that sort, she just liked to be able to pull a string, like asking to get off early, and, well, subbing on her salary."

"And forgettin' to pay when Friday came round?"

"Quite small sums," Mr. Polly insisted. "A pound or two here and another pound or two there. I think in a way she thought it was all rather a joke, the sort of thing she'd seen on T.V."

"From what I hear of her she was never home often enough to watch T.V. And it ain't my idea of a joke. Anyway, it must have been pretty important to you." He had a sudden vision of Mr. Polly's existence—the salon where he worked and bowed and booked appointments, and the home where he wasn't even allowed to take a bottle over the threshold. No kids, May had said, no stake in the

145

future, and for entertainment endless chitchat with elderly dames all fancying themselves the Jersey Lily or Miss Floradora. It shouldn't happen to a dog, he thought.

"Not just to me. There was Monica to consider."

"Never thought of asking Mrs. P. for a divorce?"

"It wouldn't have been any good. Monica's husband wouldn't have let her go, and there's the boy, Teddy. He's fourteen, you can't drag a fourteen-year-old through the Divorce Court. I'd always been sorry that Mrs. Polly and I never had any family—her daughter by her first marriage is married and in the States—but I wouldn't do that to a child, even if Monica had been prepared to take the chance, which she wasn't."

The aces were falling out of his sleeve all over the table now.

"Know anything about Linda's baby?" Crook asked. It was brutal, but you can't afford kid gloves in his line. Knuckledusters are more like it.

"I don't think anyone knew. It's a funny thing, even the police haven't been able to turn up a doctor who told her what her trouble was."

"Could be because she didn't see a doctor. Could be she came to the Black Sheep to meet the father and hear what he had to say. Sure you didn't see him come in?"

"The place got pretty full, it's a popular bar, which is one reason we used it. There are so many people coming in and out—it's near a station and quite a lot of customers drop in and have a quick one while waiting for a train—I wouldn't notice any particular person. But I'm sure he had arrived, because suddenly Linda became much more animated, she threw her voice out and waved her hands, and laughed in a confiding sort of way, wanting to let him know he wasn't the only pebble on the beach."

"She sounds just a kid," Mr. Crook exclaimed, surprising himself as much as his companion. "Showing off. How about your friend?"

"I saw her come in. Of course. She went to sit at a table by the wall, as she always did. Then I'd go to the bar and get the drinks. By that time the barman would have served an orang-utan without noticing. Of course she saw Linda with me, so she couldn't come up. She must have recognised her from that meeting in the car. I don't think Linda saw her, she was too much engaged in her act. Are you sure your friend hasn't come? I asked her, and she said, without moving her head, I don't see him. And even if he is here it doesn't matter. Do him good to see he isn't the only daisy on the patch."

"Didn't occur to her you might be keeping your friend waiting?"

"That sort of consideration wouldn't weigh much with her. I said I couldn't stop long, and she laughed. Let her wait for once, she said. It's what we all come to. Really, I could have—well, you know what I mean."

"If you have to give this evidence in court," suggested Crook, "leave that last bit out. It's the sort of thing juries are so inclined to misconstrue."

Mr. Polly, who had been plugging along like a man trying to climb a steep hill without sufficient breath for the ascent, came to a dead stop.

"What do you mean—juries? I can't afford to appear in this case. And I won't have Monica's name mentioned."

"Tell me something," said Crook so earnestly that the question was robbed of offensiveness, "how did you expect it all to end? Not allowing for Linda, I mean, but you and the two ladies?"

"One doesn't look ahead in a situation like that. One doesn't dare. But it means a great deal—everything, in short—to me. Well, I couldn't actually get up and leave Linda—I wasn't absolutely certain that she would recognise Monica, and I certainly didn't want the two to meet, we were always so careful, two short drinks, and then we'd leave—not even together—she always had to be home before 10.30—that's when her husband's train came in, he had these Rotary meetings . . ."

"Everything happens on Thursday. Well?"

"After a while I saw Monica get up and go towards the door. I suppose she thought she looked too conspicuous, sitting there alone. I couldn't let her go without a word. I said to Linda, 'In that case, how about the other half?' and I snatched up our glasses and marched up to the bar. I just dumped them and slipped out, and there was Monica waiting beside my car. She doesn't have a car of her own, comes in by bus and I drive her back to the nearest bus stop and let her out at the corner, so if she does meet anyone they'll think she's just alighted."

"Do you mean to say her husband never tumbled?" asked Crook.

"She tells him she goes to an upholstery class, and now and again when I couldn't make it, things crop up in spite of yourself, she really went. And when the classes were over she'd say she was meeting her sister . . . Oh, it was balancing on a knife-edge but what choice had we? If he had an inkling of the truth he wouldn't hesitate, he'd take the boy from her—I don't know who spread the story about the delights of illicit love, but it was someone who'd never been through that particular mill. Sometimes she'd even wonder if the game was worth the candle—what with her husband and my wife, and never being sure if we'd be recognised . . ."

"And you have been," capped Mr. Crook neatly. "And it can't have been Linda this time, because she's past all mischief-making, and it wasn't my client because he was in durance vile . . ."

"You mean, you don't actually know—you've been leading me up the path all this time?" Mr. Polly was as white as the proverbial sheet.

"This arrived at Robinson's, by hand, this afternoon," Crook said, producing the anonymous letter.

Mr. Polly stared. The white gave place to red. "You mean, that's all you had to go on?"

"You're a glutton for punishment. How much more did you want?"

"You tricked me," Mr. Polly accused him wildly. "You let me think . . ."

"Calm down," Mr. Crook advised him. "Suppose I hadn't called you up, just consider the alternative. The finder of the letter would have taken it to the police, they might have thought it was somebody's idea of a bad joke, but they'd have had to make enquiries, and it's my belief you'd do better to talk to me than to them."

"They wouldn't have taken any notice of it," Mr. Polly declared thickly.

"You don't do them justice, honest you don't. I don't say me and them always see eye to eye, but they're no slouches."

"Who do you suppose wrote it? The murderer?"

"I think it was someone who knows I'm on the trail and thinks it would be a good idea—realising that my clients are always innocent—to point the police to a different direction."

"Why not go to the police station, instead of all this mayhem?"

Crook stroked his big pugnacious chin. "It's a funny thing—how shy even the most boastful chap can be when it comes to taking the limelight, particularly where the law's concerned. You note there's no signature. You or me could have sent that if we'd been daft enough."

"Mr. Crook, promise me one thing, you will keep Monica's name out of this? That girl was alive and well when I walked out of the pub. Sam, the barman, may have seen me. He must have known me by sight at least, we'd been going there quite a long while."

"Point is, would he know Linda by sight? Well, Mr. Polly, thanks for your help. And try and have a bit of common. I mean, an accident with your razor wouldn't be any use to anyone. If we can get an alibi for Linda, you're home and dry. Only—you might remember she's your alibi if awkward questions are asked."

"I've told you already . . ." He glanced at his watch. "I must get back. Mrs. Polly will wonder what's happened."

"Simple enough. Defence counsel—not that it quite amounts to that, but it sounds well—wanted to ask you a few questions. Come now, you've been juggling quite a long time, a little thing like that shouldn't unseat you. I won't be getting along myself right away," he added, cheerfully. "I'll stay and have another pint. You never know, the stuff at the Other Place may be what they keep to drown the mice in." He smiled, a big, affable, alligator smile, and called for another pint.

The door had hardly swung to behind Mr. Polly when a young man who had been standing at the far end of the bar moved as it were casually in Crook's direction.

"Come right up and take a pew," invited Mr. Crook. "Feel like declaring an interest or is it just that I've got a smut on my nose?"

"You don't miss much, do you?" said the young man. "Is your name really Crook?"

"So my mother always told me, and I've never had any reason to doubt it," returned Mr. Crook, heartily.

"I'm Hardy, Jack Hardy."

"The nevvy from overseas. Yes, I've heard of you from Sugar. Fill the gentleman's glass, Sam. Do things always happen when you're around or is it just chance?"

"Just chance. I say, though, you're not trying to pull Pretty Polly into this, are you?"

"Pretty . . ."

"That's what Linda used to call him."

"So you knew the young lady."

"Seeing Aunt Alice looked on her as a sort of dream-daughter—grand-daughter really, I suppose—oh yes, I heard a lot about her. Mind you, I don't think the old lady really knew Linda at all, but there's no doubt about it she got a lot of pleasure out of the acquaintance. Poor Aunt A., she's gone downhill definitely since she heard what happened to her. They talk about cushioning the shock, but there's a limit to the amount of cushioning you can do."

"Any chance of me seeing her?" Crook enquired.

Young Mr. Hardy frowned. "The police 'ull have your guts for garters if you do. They weren't accorded the privilege." He thought. "I don't believe she'd seen Linda just recently, but Aunt Phyl might know more about that than I do. She could fill in a few gaps, unless, as I say, you've got your eye on Polly."

"It occurred to me that, as the girl's employer and the last person who admits to seeing her, he might be able to give me a pointer or two."

"I thought he'd confided everything to the police."

"Everything he was willing to tell," Crook conceded, "but the police and me could have the same facts, and the results 'ud be quite different."

"Must be a fascinating job, yours."

"So long as you're well insured. But he couldn't help me much."

"I don't suppose he could. Mrs. P.'s a terror by all accounts. Any husband of hers would have about as much freedom as a cat with a tin can tied to its tail."

"If I was a cat and anyone tied a tin can to my tail I'd go around with my claws unsheathed day and night. Young lady didn't confide in you, I take it."

Hardy grinned. "She made it clear from the start I was no more than a fill-gap while she waited for Lord Himucka-muck to come riding along and carry her off to his castle. For a hard-boiled girl she was really very romantic. Funny thing is she believed what she told you. I'll surprise you all yet, she'd say. A Mini's all right for them that like small cars . . ."

"But her taste was more for a Rolls?"

"Got it in one. And, talking of Rolls, there's a remark-able specimen outside, a big yellow job . . ."

"Don't say it," begged Crook. "If I had a sovereign for every time I've been asked which museum I've been rob-bing, I could retire to-morrow."

"Not you," scoffed Jack Hardy. "All the same, I wouldn't mind getting my hands on her wheel."

"I'll put you on the waiting list," promised Crook, generously.

"And I suppose I could hope for a Council house before you reached my name."

"Don't look round," said Crook with no change of tone, "but you're a native, temporarily anyway, so—what's Coppernob's name when he's at home?"

"Coppernob?"

Crook indicated the broad sheet of glass behind the bar. He'd heard that publicans put it there so that even when the barman had to turn his back on his customers he still had 'em in view, and a very wise precaution too, in his opinion.

Jack's glance followed his. "Oh, you mean the Dishonourable Willy. It's only a joke," he added quickly, "I don't suppose he does any more fiddling than the next man, but his mother's the Honourable Mrs. Stephenson, so you see?"

"I'm not so sure I would in his shoes," murmured Crook. "Come here often?"

"I couldn't say," Jack acknowledged. "I'm not often here myself. Hullo, you seem to have flushed him."

For the red-headed man had pushed back his chair and was moving towards the door.

"He's got better hearing than a bat if he could hear what I was saying," Crook protested. "Unless, of course, he lip-reads. Anyway, why should he care?"

"Don't overdo it," begged Jack. "The modesty, I mean. Everyone knows you aren't even temporarily a native, and I reckon most of them know why you're here."

"Don't see why that should bother him, unless he was a friend of the dear departed."

"That's another thing I wouldn't know," Jack conceded, "but it 'ud surprise me if there was a chap under forty Linda didn't know. Not that he'd be much good to her. For one thing, he's engaged, and for another—if you were going to suggest that engagements have been broken off, he'd be even lower on the list than yours faithfully. Any worldly goods he has will come to him through marriage."

"Like that?" murmured Crook. "I didn't know."

"I suppose if the Archbishop of Canterbury were to walk in and take any notice of you you'd put him on your list of suspects, too," hazarded Jack. "Hullo, look who's here!"

As he thrust powerfully against the swing-door Willy found himself practically barging into another chap who was coming in.

"What's up, Mr. Polly?" enquired Crook, cheerfully. "Thought of something you forgot to mention just now?"

"I—I seem to have mislaid a glove," muttered Mr. Polly. "Just wondered . . ." He dropped down and made a feint of looking for it under the bar.

Crook obligingly dropped down beside him. "I should take another look in the car," he murmured. "What's the real reason?"

"It's just—if you should meet Mrs. Polly—I'd be obliged if you wouldn't mention where we met, I mean. I'm not suggesting she's an unreasonable woman, but . . ."

"Mum as an oyster," promised Crook, generously. "Well, wherever you dropped it, Mr. Polly, it wasn't here."

"I must take another look outside, only it's part of a pair Mrs. Polly gave me and . . ."

"If you had to lose it she'd prefer it to be Ann's Parlour or Prue's Pantry. Well, good hunting."

He went out. Willy was staring at the big yellow Rolls. "That's Mr. Crook's car," said Polly, going past.

"I knew it wasn't local," Willy agreed. "That was Crook inside?"

"That's right. A Londoner, I understand."

"They say in London you could go about naked and no one would notice you," Willy agreed.

He watched Mr. Polly get into his neat blue Rover and drive off. When Jack Hardy came out a minute or two later Willy had disappeared, too.

Mr. Crook was still sitting up at the bar. "Give you a toast, Sam," he offered. "You choose your own vintage."

When both glasses were charged he lifted his a little and, looking Sam in the eye, announced, "We'll drink a toast to X, the mystery man in the Linda Myers case. Because it's my firm belief you've had him drinking in your bar this very night."

CHAPTER X

BY THE TIME Mr. Crook had finished drinking his toast Mr. Polly's smart dark blue Rover, Willy Stephenson's racing model and Jack Hardy's jalopy, as he liked to call it, had all disappeared from the car park. It was an inhospitable sort of night, a damp mist turning to fog, and Mr. Crook found himself hoping that at the Black Sheep, where he proposed to follow up Sam's tip, they'd have a nifty steak-and kidney pie with all the trimmings. Or, failing that, a nice steak would do. And, seeing he was going to grill Joe or whatever the barman's name might be, it could be appropriate if they were to grill something for him in turn. (This was the crude sort of pun he enjoyed.)

Of course, he told himself, turning the Superb out of the yard and facing her down the hill, there's steak *and* steak. The name was like charity, it covered a multitude of sins. There was goat steak, whale steak, and he remembered a place where he was convinced they kept a stableful of mules for the dubious benefit of clients.

"And there was that chap who always swore he had a kangaroo steak at a lush-up in Brighton," he reminded himself, looking down to the distant lights in the valley, which seemed to be approaching him rather more rapidly than he expected. "Whoa, Emma," he adjured the Superb, but for once she seemed as deaf as the famous adder that laid one ear to the sand and put the tip of its tail into the other. "This ain't the Monte Carlo rally," he protested. But if it wasn't that it seemed to him uncommonly likely it might turn out to be the Churchyard Stakes.

Mr. Crook wrestled with brakes that mysteriously failed to respond. "I'm not fussy," he protested to no one in particular, "but I do aim to reach the bottom in one piece."

Only by this time he was pretty sure someone else didn't intend that he should. His original plan had been to pay a call at the Black Sheep, get some sort of a meal, and maybe leave a note in May's letter-box to report progress. It might be a bit late to go paying calls, with that Komodo dragon over the way. Now it seemed more than probable he'd be paying a call himself in a quarter he'd never contemplated for this evening at least.

The Superb was winging her way downhill, like a drunken bird. The hill was long and pretty steep—Crook found time, still trying to keep the car under control, to wonder if that was why Polly had chosen the Flying Fox. The Superb herself had been made in a day when everybody expected value for money, good solid metal and insides made to last, not like the tin and wire contraptions you saw all round you nowadays. Two-Ton Tessie ain't in it with her, reflected Mr. Crook, grimly. Mind you, he hadn't the smallest doubt what had happened. Cars like the Superb don't put themselves out of action for a pettish whim, they don't go on strike or work to rule, in short, they're a lot more dependable than many of the human agencies responsible for their make-up. One of these days, he supposed, some genius would invent a car that went bleep-bleep if she'd been interfered with, but long before then he (Crook) would be bones and dust in some anonymous churchyard. With so many chaps coming and going no one, particularly on such a night, was going to notice just one chap standing beside a car in the car park, with the bonnet raised, doing a bit of repair work. That's how it would look to the man in the street. And he himself, like the braying ass of the Scriptures, had sung out to all and sundry that he'd be staying on and having another pint or two, which would give an enemy all the time he needed. And when the crash came it wouldn't be easy to say just when the damage to the brakes occurred, and there'd be the fellow at the Flying Fox to remember how many pints he'd had, and another victory would be chalked up for Demon Drink, which he wouldn't deserve.

Biter bit, thought Mr. Crook, his mind working almost as fast as the car. Going to see a man, I said. Person I'm most likely to see to-night is the Recording Angel.

He remembered there was a sharp bend at the foot of the hill, and at the rate she was going even the Superb wouldn't be able to negotiate that.

"Eternity, here I come," announced Mr. Crook, remembering with the clarity of desperation one of his late Mum's favourite aphorisms about dealing with a fool according to his folly. Even in this extremity he couldn't really blame anyone but himself. A chap with the most rudimentary notions of preservation doesn't drive with his eyes shut, which was precisely what he had been doing.

He heard a furious yell behind him, and in the driving

mirror he saw a lorry thundering down the hill. The driver's lips were moving, though Crook couldn't distinguish what he said. Still, you could forgive him anything in the circumstances. The Superb was bouncing all over the road. Then the door of the cab opened and a few words became audible.

"You blurry fool!" said a voice. "Pull in, can't you?"

It was too much to suppose there were two of them out of control at the same time and in the same place, but no sense both of them getting clobbered, so he pulled in recklessly towards the wide ditch to his left. The Superb would crash into that and then through the narrow hedge, and it would be curtains for Arthur Crook and quite likely a lifer for young Wayland. He was aware of a great dark bulk on his right-hand side, for an instant he thought the lorry was going to crush him, just to make sure of the job, only it wasn't reasonable to suppose everyone was in league to put out his light, then he tipped sideways into the ditch. But the Superb didn't make the break-through he'd anticipated, because the great bulk of the lorry was there to slow him down. It was a chance in a thousand, and like many reckless chances it brought home the bacon. And he needed bacon now as he'd seldom needed it before. Automatically he'd shielded his head—hands were given men for more than lifting tankards—he'd shut off the engine without realising what he'd done, he felt like a porpoise in a gulf stream, any moment he'd go over and over, always assuming porpoises haunted gulf streams. He heard glass shatter, and the world darkened, someone screamed, he couldn't think who. The lorry-driver hadn't seemed the hysterical type, and anyway hysterical night drivers don't last long on the roads of Britain. He wasn't, he assured himself, a murderous type, just a cosy hard-working chap who liked his job, but at this instant if he'd had a carving-knife in his hand, it would have been bad luck for the chap who'd put this insult on the Superb.

A voice broke through the mist that had assumed a reddish tinge. "He's coming round," it said.

"About time, too. Wake up, mate."

Crook opened a cautious eye. He wondered if these were the holy angels he'd heard about in his childhood; they sounded uncommonly like members of the base-born human race. He opened a second eye, now he could see a girl with a long shining tail of fair hair bending over him.

"Crummy!" he ejaculated, reverently. "They do exist, then?"

"And you can thank your perishing stars they do," said a voice that clearly never emanated from a celestial being. "Lucky for you there isn't a copper waiting around with his breathalyser apparatus. Who did you think you were? Waltzing Matilda?"

To his surprise Mr. Crook found he could function comparatively normally. He looked at his hands, they were both there, like outsize chestnut-coloured starfish. He moved one foot, then the other. They were cramped, but at least they hadn't fallen off. True, one of his arms felt as though a giant had twisted it, and at the same time had mistaken his conk for a tenpenny nail and tackled it with a hammer with angelic zeal. He shook it experimentally.

"Take care it don't come off," said the same grim voice.

Mr. Crook swerved slightly. The angel was still in evidence wearing a sort of abbreviated skirt that came nowhere near her knees and what his mum used to call a smicket. Behind her the lorry bulked very solid and dark in the half-light.

"It wasn't you driving that?" he suggested vaguely.

"For Pete's sake!" It was the avenging angel again this time. "Women have enough daft ideas in their heads without you giving 'em any more, free, gratis and for nothing. Here, Beryl, you nip back into the lorry before some Nosey Parker comes along and starts calling the police."

Mr. Crook drew a deep breath. "Praise the pigs!" he said. "At least you're no angel, even if you are wearing your invisible cloak."

A tall cool young man came into his line of vision. "What's she made of?" he asked, touching the Superb with a reverent hand. "Cast-iron? I wouldn't have backed my lorry to come through that, and she's brand-new."

"I've got a refrigerator at home," Mr. Crook confided. "Comes with the flat. I had it—let's see—1935—still works a treat, and strong enough to stand on if you feel like painting the ceiling. 'Lectricity chap tried to sell me a new model last time he was around. I swear, you only had to lean on it, and there was a dent where your elbow had been, and if even the young lady had put a toe on it, it'ud have gone through the roof."

"Well, that's progress for you," said the lorry-driver. "If every chap got a fridge that 'ud last thirty years how about redundancy? Anyway, no sense being greedy and expecting strength *and* grace. These modern fridges, they make 'em so you can keep 'em in the lounge."

"What's the sense of a fridge in the lounge?" asked Mr. Crook. "Here, give me a hand out of this thing and we might try and assess the damage. Maybe, if you could give her a tow she might run down the hill on her own."

The lorry-driver looked at him in admiration. "You don't half expect miracles, do you, mate? Anyway, she's about as safe on the road as a charging rhino."

"If you found yourself deprived of the law of gravity you might be hanging upside down in a tree," pointed out Mr. Crook, defending his darling with spirit. "And that's what's happened to her. No use blaming a fellow whose foot's been chopped off for not coming in first at the relay."

With some difficulty and with assistance from Rod, whose second name he never learned, he got himself into a perpendicular position, and they examined the extent of the damage. This was less than might have been anticipated. She'd lost a good deal of paint and her bonnet and front mudguard were a bit cockled and she wouldn't have passed an M.O.T. test, but given a bit of expert doctoring she'd soon be on the road again.

"'Tain't so easy to put the Superb out of action," exulted Crook.

"What's that you called her?" said Rod.

"The Superb. Comes out of a poem, so they tell me."

"I did you a right bad turn when I stopped you diving into space," said the young man frankly. "Do you know

158

who that car belongs to? I'd sooner have the D.P.P. on my
trail than that chap. You take my tip and have yourself
tucked up nice and comfy in hospital before he learns
what's happened to her. He's a real tearaway by all accounts."

Crook was patting himself all over to find out if there was
an odd bone sticking up somewhere that he hadn't noticed.
Now he said, "How about a few introductions?" and produced one of his fantastic cards.

It was a pity really that visibility was so poor, he couldn't
see Rod's face properly in the light of the pocket torch the
fellow produced, but his voice filled in all the gaps.

"This straight up?" he asked. "Here, Beryl, come out a
jiff and meet someone who might be useful to you one of
these days."

"Not in with the police, are you?" asked Beryl. Crook
didn't think it worth answering that one.

"What happened?" Rod enquired.

"Some chap's been reading the statistics about over-
population and thought he'd rid the world of one specimen.
Lucky for me you were taking the same road. I don't know
what your work of mercy has done to her innards, but
there's something screwy about the brakes that was done
beforehand."

He looked thoughtfully at the Superb who, even in her
hour of defeat, maintained her air of dignity.

"Any hope of pulling her out?" he enquired.

"No harm trying. There's a tow-rope in the van. Here,
Beryl, be a doll and fetch it out. Don't mind travelling
heavy, do you?" he added to Crook.

"Hark who's talking!" murmured the lawyer.

"What's it feel like, driving a Rolls?" Rod continued.

"If she wasn't in the towing-class this 'ud be your chance
to find out," said Crook generously.

Beryl reappeared with the rope and between the three
of them—and never tell him no more that ladies don't know
how to pull their weight, reflected Crook—they got the
Superb back on the road and hitched up to the lorry.

"Here, doll, you keep a weather eye open," Rod told his

companion. "I reckon I know something about the inside of a car. Fact is," he confided to Crook, "we're not supposed to take passengers, even the non-paying kind. The bosses think we talk to ourselves to keep us awake. I suppose. There's the radio, of course, but they don't even like that much. Bad for the concentration. And if they knew I had a girl up with me . . ."

"Would they know the difference?" asked Mr. Crook. "Honest, I saw a chap down Fulham way last Sunday, ever such pretty brown hair, parted and plaited over the shoulders, two-thirds to his middle, and tied with a blue bow. And he *was* a chap, what's more."

"There's nothing of that sort of chap about my girl, only I don't want to marry her on the social security, and if you're outs with one lorry boss, you're outs with the lot. The word goes round. Mind you, it's not your morals they're troubled about, or the doll's for that matter! No, they're afraid something may happen to their precious van. Well now, let's take a dekko."

He had the bonnet up and was peering inside with all the ardour of a Jacques Cousteau investigating some newly-found denizen of the deep. "You're right, Mr. Crook," he acknowledged. "She never did this to herself. Someone don't love you, Mr. Crook."

"Point is—which one?" But he had a pretty fair idea. With all the coming and going at the Flying Fox—and him calling out about stopping on—why, if everything had gone according to plan the Recording Angel would have had a job to say when the real damage was done, before she started belting down the hill at breakneck speed or after she crashed.

" 'Christian, seek not yet repose,' " he recited solemnly, and the girl's voice took him up, shaking with laughter. It 'ud take a dame to laugh in circumstances like these, he reflected.

" 'Thou art in the midst of foes . . .' "

"Too right," he admitted. Though watching and praying weren't exactly his strong suit, so he didn't complete the verse.

"Going to report this to the police, Mr. Crook?" Rod enquired.

"And see 'em split their sides laughing, those who ain't weeping into their mooshwars—handkerchiefs to you—because the plot didn't come off? Not something likely. Besides, me and the police so often don't see eye to eye they might take steps I wouldn't approve. No. Heaven helps them that helps themselves, and Heaven's on my side, wouldn't you say?"

"Don't mix me up," pleaded Rod. " 'Rithmetic was never my strong suit."

"If you hadn't been coming down the hill some undertaker might be having himself a ball," Crook pointed out. "Had you thought of that?"

"Tell me something," asked Rod, in the voice of the man who really wants to know, "do you have much difficulty getting life assurance?"

"What for? When I hand in my dinner-pail there'll be no one to benefit but the State, and why should I pay premiums to cosset them? And over and above that, it's tempting Providence."

"What are you going to tell the garage that puts that right for you, then?"

"I had a breakdown—brakes wouldn't work—or will they now?"

Rod lifted his head from under the car's bonnet. "If all the rest of her was as good as her brakes you could drive her off yourself," he promised. "Funny how simple it is to put a car out of action if you've got the know-how."

"Lucky for me you carry the spare parts," said Crook.

"My old man runs a garage, wanted me to come in with him. I've got better things to do with my time than fetch and carry for all the barmies who drive a car these days, I told him. Anyway, it 'ud be a case of always the bridesmaid, never the bride, if you read me."

"Loud and clear," agreed Mr. Crook. "All these nits driving cars on the petrol you supply 'em with . . ."

"And me with no more than a motor-bike. You tell a girl you work for your dad and you've only got a motor-bike and she doesn't want to know. Now we'll tow you down to the bridge, there's an A.A. phone there, you tell anyone who you are and they won't be able to come fast enough." He would hardly have been surprised at this juncture if the Superb had unfolded invisible wings and taken off on her own account.

"You from the Smoke?" asked Mr. Crook, getting behind the wheel, an operation that gave him a bit more difficulty than usual.

"However did you guess?"

"They know me and the Superb in my own local, and maybe in a few farther out, but this is beyond my normal perimeter, and you recognised her right away. Sure you ain't making trouble for yourself, bringing her along?"

"Well, she can't stay there, brother, not without you want to be run in for obstruction," Rod explained. "And then there's the Highway Code. Remember the chap next door, He's got as much right (or more) To stay alive, So when you drive, . . . two gallons of free petrol and green stamps for the best last line. Out of sight, doll, we're on our way. There's a caff on the corner beyond the bridge," he added to Crook. "Mostly only serves drivers, but they'll let you in, I'll pass them the word."

"Well, you've been in the wars," commented the A.A. man candidly. "What did you do? Try to jump a wall?"

"Don't confuse me," begged Mr. Crook. "I was tooling down the hill as nice as you please when suddenly she went out of control, never ask me why. Next thing there was this chap stopping and giving me a hand, no, I don't know who he was, he didn't say, but we got her out of the ditch and he helped me roll her down, risked his own future, I wouldn't wonder. Something wrong with the brakes, he thought," he amplified vaguely.

"And you didn't get his name?"

"There's no record that the Good Samaritan left his name, either. Now, if I can get her back to Churchford Mr. Warren 'ull doctor her for me, if he has to stop up all night."

"Don't mind expecting miracles, do you?" suggested the A.A. man. And that made two of them in one night.

"You want to look out for yourself, Mr. Crook," offered Warren. "That's a nasty bang you've got on the head. You should see a doctor."

"Join the Army and see the world. Visit the doctor and see the next," improvised Mr. Crook. He dropped into a late-night chemist and got a bit of plaster and some more advice (which he left behind on the counter), tracked back to the Bald-Faced Stag and decided to call it a day. May Forbes and the chap at the Black Sheep could both wait till the morning.

"Someone's precious anxious young Wayland shan't get off the hook," he reflected. "Still, we're coming along nicely. Funny how often chaps think they're blocking your road, when all the time they're giving you a hefty shove in the backside that gets you over some of your worst bumps."

Having been assured the next morning that he couldn't expect the Superb, even at double time, before midday, Crook mounted the bus for Axton and paid his promised visit to the Black Sheep. The fellow behind the bar was loath to help him till Crook suggested that his boss would probably prefer to answer his (Crook's) questions to those of the rozzers. Then he acknowledged, a bit churlishly, that he knew Polly by sight and that he came in from time to time.

"Always the same time the same day of the week," Crook suggested. "Think, man, this is a murder case, some chap's going to get life and I'm out to see it ain't my client. Try and put yourself in his shoes . . ."

"I get bunions enough with the ones I am wearing," said Joe, still only half-mollified. "We don't like answering questions about clients, Mr. Crook, not if they're well-behaved and don't cause any trouble."

"Someone caused me a hell of a lot of trouble last night," Crook observed, more grimly than usual. "And I don't want to make trouble for innocent chaps any more than you do,

163

but you know what they say, we're all one big family,
members one of another . . ."

Joe gave up. "You'd talk the hind leg off a goat, Mr.
Crook. All right then, he used to come in Thursday nights,
not every Thursday but if he did come it would be a Thursday. When chaps are that regular you get to notice, and of
course he's lived in Churchford a long time."

"And the lady? O.K., he's admitted she exists."

"I can't tell you anything about her. They just used to
have a couple of drinks and off they'd go. I didn't think
much about it, you get all sorts in a bar, and, like I said,
they never made trouble."

"This girl who got herself murdered . . ."

Joe looked horrified. "You're not on about her?"

"Ever see her here?"

"Not that I recall, which isn't to say she never came. But
she's not the one *he* used to meet."

"No, I didn't think she was. Well, it's a wicked world,
you have to check up, don't you? You a believin' man?"

"Come again," said Joe.

"Our Father which art in Heaven," amplified Mr. Crook.

"With the world in its present state? You're joking."

From which Crook deduced it mightn't lie too heavily
on the fellow's conscience to bend the facts a bit, if it suited
the management. But the way things were going at the
moment there didn't seem much sense trying to involve
him.

He had reached the Black Sheep soon after opening time
and hadn't stayed long, so he reckoned he could squeeze in
his red-headed neighbour of the previous night before
returning to Churchford and giving May Forbes the wigwag. Since the mysterious "accident" to the Superb it
occurred to him that May herself might do with a bit of
protection. If both of them were out of the way X could
count on going as free as air, and Chris Wayland would
likely languish in gaol, having no one to speak for him.

She, he reminded himself, referring to May, is as trusting

as a puppy. Look at the way she came with me that first night. All this mock-up about seeing, hearing and believing no evil might have been all right in the days of Victorian innocence, but it was out of date in the twentieth century, when the fellow to survive is the one who never lets his ears or eyes off duty.

He didn't phone to announce his coming. It's not only trick-cyclists who believe in the value of shock treatment.

The Hon. Blanche Stephenson might have what Crook in his plebeian way called a handle to her name, but her house looked like anybody else's, and when he rang the bell she herself came to the door. She had two "obliging" women four mornings a week, but this didn't happen to be one of them.

When she saw Crook she started to close the door at once, but something seemed to have got in the way—in fact, the toe of Crook's glossy chestnut Oxford shoe.

"We don't buy on the doorstep," she said crisply.

"Suits me," Mr. Crook agreed, "seeing I've come to get rather than give. You'd be Mrs. Stephenson?"

"That is so, but I don't think . . ."

"It was really your son I came to see," Crook explained.

"My son is out."

"Expecting him back soon? I could wait."

"I really couldn't tell you. I don't keep tabs on the comings and goings of a grown man."

"Saw him in the Flying Fox last night," offered Mr. Crook.

Blanche's face froze, though the fascinated Mr. Crook hadn't thought it possible it could assume a wintrier aspect.

"If you have come to collect a debt or anything of that kind . . ."

"No money involved," Crook promised. "Well, I'm not mug enough to play cards with a chap I don't know."

"I don't understand what you intend to insinuate, Mr. . . .?"

"Crook—Arthur Crook." He didn't offer her one of his cards. He knew she'd simply drop it in the nearest trash-bucket. "Had an idea he might be able to give me a bit of info."

"Really, Mr. Crook, I cannot imagine . . ."

"What me and your son could have in common? Well, for one thing, we're both human, and for another I fancy he might be able to help me about some enquiries I'm makin' on behalf of a chap called Wayland."

Blanche Stephenson looked at him as though she couldn't believe the evidence of her own eyes. "It's not possible—I mean, you are not here in connection with the man who murdered that girl, Linda Myers?"

"Got it in one," beamed Crook.

"It is quite impossible for my son to be able to help you."

"Go on," invited Crook. "Tell me he never knew the young lady and I shan't believe you. Why, he had his ears on sticks last night when two or three of us went into a huddle. Anyway, it ain't likely an enterprising girl like Linda Myers would overlook a distinguished-looking man like Mr. Willy Stephenson."

"Have you any proof that this—this Wayland is innocent?"

"If I had proof I wouldn't be bothering to ask questions, would I? But the Courts won't take my word, they want facts, and facts is something your son might be able to give me."

"In what connection?"

"Well, for instance, he might have seen the chap who tried to disable my car last night. You don't do a thing like that for fun, and whoever was responsible was pretty keen I shouldn't continue to cumber the earth and wreck his future."

"If, as I suppose is the case, you are a lawyer, you must be aware of something called slander."

"I should, seeing how much I've experienced it. But you tell me how I slandered your son. I just said he might be able to give me some gen—might have seen someone showing a bit more than normal interest in the Superb. If he gave me a few particulars I daresay I'd be able to fit a name to them."

Somewhere in the house a telephone rang. Blanche hesitated. It rang again. She looked pointedly at her visitor.

"You go right ahead and answer it," Crook assured her blandly. "I'll wait here. Even if you don't like my mug or my moniker, you must admit I couldn't uproot one of the pillars." He looked about him with a glance that said there was nothing else worth pinching.

Blanche Stephenson acknowledged her first defeat. "You had better come in, though I warn you, you may have to wait a long time."

But if he was going to wait it would be better to do it inside where he was invisible to passers-by. A man like Crook can't hope to escape comment, and she didn't fancy the kind of comment she would get if he were seen lurking about on her doorstep.

Crook looked interestedly about him. Gracious living, he supposed, observing the copper bowl of spring flowers, the scarred rug-chest and the rug itself, so shabby it had to be valuable or a rag-and-bone-man wouldn't give you the time of day for it. He was examining a Victorian lithograph entitled *Twixt Love and Duty* when Blanche came back, closing a sitting-room door behind her. It was clear he wasn't going to graduate farther than the hall.

"You spoke of a second attempted crime," she began.

"Well, not successful, or I wouldn't be here now, would I?" beamed Crook. "But that's not to say the chap won't try again."

He could read her thoughts like goldfish swimming in a bowl. She was inwardly cursing the bungler who'd messed up his first attempt.

"You make it sound very melodramatic, Mr. Crook."

"Well, but murder is melodramatic. Maybe it ain't come your way much to date."

There was the rattle of a key behind him, and Willy came in. When he saw Crook he blinked as though he were seeing visions and not the kind you'd hanker after. When he'd recovered he said, "Didn't know you knew Mr. Crook, Mater. If I'm interrupting anything I can push off."

"Mr. Crook came to see you, Willy. He appears to think you met at some bar last night."

"Flying Fox," explained Crook. "Chap I was with told me your name. You shouldn't have sat there drinking on your owney-oh, you should have joined us at the bar."

"My son is not in the habit of joining people he doesn't know." Blanche again, with the temperature below zero.

"How does he come to enlarge his acquaintance?" Crook wondered aloud. "Happen to notice anyone in particular in the bar last night?" he added to Willy.

"The Flying Fox isn't actually one of my pubs."

"So it was just chance you were there last night?"

"It's a free country, isn't it?"

"So they say, but you don't have to believe all you're told. Couldn't have anything to do with the fact that I was goin' to be there last night?"

"How on earth should my son know where you, a perfect stranger, would be drinking last night?"

Willy wished the old girl knew when to keep her mouth shut.

Crook was cheerfully answering her question. "Well, not because I told him," he agreed, "but you know the one about the chap who was following a tiger and all the time another tiger was following him?"

"My son being the second tiger?"

"I see you catch on," said Crook. "Most people around here know why I left the Smoke—London town to you," he added, seeing her perplexed expression. "On Linda Myers's account. So it's easy to guess I'd be of interest to anyone who knew the young lady, if only to keep tabs on my movements."

"That's the second time you have suggested that my son knew the girl. Are you not aware such a statement might be actionable?"

"You take the action, go right ahead," Crook advised her. "What interests me—I can find out about the girl for myself—is who went mucking about with my car last night. Your son was there—came by car, I suppose?" he added to Willy.

"I didn't walk," Willy agreed.

"And you could hardly have flown. Funny—even a sparrow can do that, and yet we go around thinking our-selves superior to the bird world. And you left the Flying Fox before I did. Happen to notice a yellow Rolls standing in the forecourt?"

"You could hardly miss it," said Willy.

"Anyone else taking any interest in it?"

"Some chap told me it was yours. Not many fellows about."

"It's like the Ancient Mariner," explained Crook, who could sport a culture-vulture hood himself on occasion. "He stoppeth one of three. Point is, which one should I be stopping?"

"If your car was really damaged, wilfully damaged, which I take it is what you mean to imply . . ."

"I said you caught on quick," interpolated Crook admir-ingly.

"How is it you were not injured?"

"The Lord looks after His Own," said Crook, piously. "Likewise, angels come in strange disguises. Mine wore denims and talked a language that might fox even the Heavenly Host. Well, so you don't think you can help? But you don't blame me for trying, do you? I mean, she was O.K. when we got there, and a car like the Superb don't put herself out of action. So I'll have to enquire in another quarter, won't I?"

Willy, who was expecting questions about the dead girl, was looking a bit dazed. "Oh!" said Crook, turning back from the door, "don't happen to have a bus time-table handy, I suppose?"

"I'll run you back," offered Willy suddenly.

Crook looked more like an alligator than usual. "I may not look it," he said, "but I'm about the downiest bird in the business and I wouldn't dream of troubling you. There's bound to be a pub near a bus stop where I can hang around, and having come so far on the road it 'ud be a pity to fall at the last fence. Oh, and two gems I leave with you. If you're thinking it's a thousand pities I didn't get fatally tangled up with the Superb last night, let me tell you, that wouldn't have been the end of it. There'd still be Sugar, Miss Forbes to you, and out and beyond her there's Bill Parsons, my partner. Remember the king in the Old Testament who said his father had chastised the mob with whips but he'd chastise them with scorpions? Well, Bill's the original King Scorpion, and it don't pay for anyone to forget it. No," he mused happily, opening the door, "I wouldn't say there was anything civilised about Bill."

He went out, leaving mother and son speechless. When they were past that phase Blanche enquired, "What do you make of that?"

"Man's as mad as a hatter," said Willy.

"It's the mad ones who do the most mischief. Was he really in the bar of the Flying Fox last night?"

Willy nodded. "Carrying on like nobody's business about Linda Myers. That chap was born to put his feet into things; lucky for some people, I suppose, he only has two."

"Willy, you didn't say anything that he could get hold of?"

"I didn't speak to him, and I wouldn't have spoken to him to-day if I hadn't found him over your threshold. What d'you mean, Mater, by letting a chap like that in?"

"It's what he means that matters," retorted Blanche, "and a blind man could see that what he means is trouble."

It was ten minutes' walk to the pub and twenty-five minutes to wait when he got there, but he thought he'd just make Robinson's before it closed for the half-day. He remembered that May usually spent Wednesday afternoon with the redoubtable Mrs. Politi, and he'd prefer not to muscle in on any private arrangement of hers. But when he reached the shop he found it closed already, and a handwritten notice on the door to the effect that the business would be closed temporarily for family reasons. He rattled the handle but nobody came, he rang the door-bell, which seemed to be out of order; and then he went round to the side, where the private or family door was, but the blinds were still open, which seemed to him to prove that though the Angel of Death might be flapping his wings on the threshold he hadn't yet gained entry. May, presumably, had gone back to her own place, so he beetled round to Main Street, but when he pressed the bell nothing happened. No one looked out of a window or opened it and shouted, there was no sign of life there at all. Still, the woman had to be somewhere. Probably gone direct to Mrs. Politi. He recalled May telling him that she and the junk-shop proprietress often went to the cinema together on a Wednesday afternoon, so possibly May was over there, knocking up something for their lunch. The junk-store bore an imposing scroll over the door—"Antiques, China and Glass." Mrs. Politi was clearly getting ready to close down; she regarded one or two stragglers who had just stepped up from the pavement, where the cheapest goods were laid out along the floor, with some asperity. She had a desk at the back of the shop where she could see everyone, without actually thrusting her presence upon them. People who were going to buy cheap damaged goods didn't like to feel they were under too close an inspection. Crook picked up a plate decorated with an improbable tiger-lily, with a bit of the rim missing, and marched up to the desk.

"Seen anything of Sugar?" he asked casually, handing the dish across. It was marked two-and-sixpence.

"Why you want this?" demanded Mrs. Politi, wearing her Rock-of-Gibraltar air. In a rainstorm at that.

"Wanted a word with you," explained Crook carefully. "Cheap at the price." He put his hand in his pocket and produced a half-crown.

"And you're not going to see a lot more of those," he went on cheerfully. "All, all are going, the old familiar faces."

"What word?"

"What I came for was Sugar, or news of her. She ain't at the shop, they've shut down temporarily owing to illness of proprietor, I rang the side-door bell but no soap."

"They put a piece of paper between the clapper and the wall," explained Mrs. Politi. "Then the bell not ring."

Crook nodded. "That figures," he said. "Still, don't tell

me no one would be watching the street—well, they'd send for the doctor, wouldn't they? Anyhow, occurred to me you might know where she was."

Mrs. Politi didn't touch the half-crown. She laid the dish on the table.

"You make a joke?"

"Never felt less like joking in my life."

"So—you ring me up, you say Miss Forbes not able to meet me this afternoon, she is lending you a hand, and then —but perhaps you forget," she added, elaborately sarcastic.

"Who's the philosopher who says you can't forget what you never knew? Look, is this straight up? I mean, you got a message said to come from me to the effect that Sugar and me—it's all baloney, you know."

Mrs. Politi looked over Crook's shoulder and bellowed, "You take that wolf off my premises. You think they a zoo?"

The startled customer, who was leading a Labrador not much larger than a Shetland pony, said stiffly, "Bruce wouldn't hurt any of the junk you've got here. Difficult to see how he could. A rag-and-bone-man wouldn't make you an offer for this stuff."

"You go before someone make an offer for you," threatened Mrs. Politi. To Crook she said, still speaking in a loud voice, "I show you a better dish, perfect condition, those I keep here." She backed him into a room behind the desk where there were some quite good pieces of china and glass. But she remained with her gaze on the street.

"I take off my eye," she explained. "What happens? Someone help himself to a glass, a jug, a little dish, maybe. They talk of the magpie being a thief, like the one at Rheims . . ."

Crook opened his mouth to point out it had been a jackdaw, then prudently shut it again.

"I tell you," Mrs. Politi continued, "I not insult the magpie likening him to some I see go up and down this street. One of these days, believe me, some magpie write his story and let us know what he think of the human race. That will be worth reading." She nodded and her four chins quivered.

Regretfully Crook abandoned a desire to take her up on the subject of literary magpies, and got back to his first question.

"What's this about me and Sugar?"

"You don' remember? Perhaps you take a little drink."

"I could drink the sea dry before I forgot a date with her," replied Crook, simply. "When was this?"

Lilli considered. "I hear the church bell ring for Mass of the Dedication—that will be twelve o'clock. I have a customer about ten minutes later, the telephone ring, 'Excuse me,' I say, 'please to wait.'" She indicated the telephone that was strategically placed so that she could get a reasonable amount of privacy and still be able to keep the shop under her eye. "Then the voice said, 'Mr. Crook? You remember? May's friend. She ask me to tell you she cannot come this afternoon, she will be helping me.'"

"You're sure that's what he said? May's friend."

"That is right."

"No, it ain't," contradicted Crook. "If it had been me I'd have said Miss Forbes or Sugar. I don't call a lady by her first name, not without I'm invited. What did he sound like?"

Mrs. Politi flung out her big arms. "He sound like a man." She said it in the same way as she might have said, "He roar, like a tiger."

"Where did you suppose I was ringing from? Or didn't I say?"

"You ring from a call-box. I hear the pips."

"Any reason why Miss Forbes shouldn't ring you herself? I mean, she didn't say she was bein' pressed into service with the invalid, only that I wanted her. Why bother to ring at all?"

"Because if May not come I ring the shop."

"And X don't want you to do that. How about doing that very thing now. They may not answer the front-door

bell, but . . ." He looked at the huge watch he wore on his
wrist, gift of a grateful client—and about as reliable, he
sometimes reflected. "It's time you shut up shop," he added
encouragingly.

Lilli looked at her watch, and surged forward, turbulent
as a wave of the sea. She swept away the last of the lingerers
and started to pull out huge faded green shutters. You
wouldn't have believed a woman of her size could have
handled them so deftly. Mr. Crook, on a point of honour,
went to help her and was immediately made to feel like
some beetle that's got in the way of an Amazon forebear.
Lucky if he only got his wings bruised, he reflected ruefully,
wasn't completely trampled underfoot. Mrs. Politi locked
the shutters, pulled another key from a chain she wore
round her neck, and opened her side door.

"A private phone for my room," she assured him, as the
stairs creaked under her monumental tread. It was a good
thing it was an old house, a new one, run up as so many
of them were, would have crackled like a twig in the
smoke, and precipitated them both into the cellar.

Either both Miss Robinsons were incapacitated or there'd
been a wholesale holocaust at the house, for even Crook
could hear the bell shrilling away while no one answered.
Lilli hung up, waited a couple of minutes and dialled
again.

"Bet you an even pint you get the engaged signal," prophesied Crook, and that's just what they did get.

"I'll do the next call," Crook offered.

"You not put the police on to May," threatened Mrs.
Politi.

"Who said anything about the police? I'm going to ring
the doctor. If the Angel of Death has run amok in that
household it's time someone found out. If not, I want to
know why no one's answering the phone."

Mellish was in, but in no very good mood. "Don't you
know I don't take calls between one and two?" he demanded. "If it's an emergency, there's the hospital, if not,
this happens to be Wednesday when there's no surgery."

"So far as I'm concerned there don't have to be any surgery Monday to Saturday either," Crook assured him briskly. "The police have got their knife into me and I don't need any medicos doing likewise. Just want an answer to a question."

"Who's calling?" demanded the belligerent voice. "If it's you, Petersen . . ."

"If that's who I am my mother never told me," Crook assured him. "Who's Petersen, anyway?"

"Miserable little pipsqueak acting as garbage-collector for the local *Argus*," shouted the doctor. Give himself blood pressure if he carries on all his conversations at this pitch, Crook reflected. Nice, though, to find a chap out in the wilds who spoke your own language.

"Name of Crook, representing Miss Forbes," he introduced himself. "Been round to the shop—Miss Robinson's, that is—no answer. Tried to phone—there's someone there because the receiver was taken off, but no dice conversation-wise, been to Miss Forbes's place in Mill Street, no dice there either, and a neighbour says she had a message can-celling a regular date."

"So?" suggested the doctor, but with rather more inter-est, and rather less ferocity. "What are we supposed to make of that?"

"I don't know about you," returned Crook at his blunt-est, "but my guess would be murder."

"You do like your dishes with parsley round them, don't you?" the doctor approved. "Or do you really have any-thing to go on?"

"Don't they say three's a magic number? Listen, then. We've had one murder, even the rozzers agree to that. Last night someone took a swipe at me, well, the Superb, if you like, but it comes to the same thing, and it ain't his fault it's no case of 'The angels in Heaven are singing to-day, Here's Johnny, here's Johnny, here's Johnny.' And now Miss Forbes goes into a vanishing act."

"She could be doing some shopping or something," mur-mured the doctor vaguely.

"Or saying her prayers in the parish church, I suppose," amplified Crook tartly. "You tell me how she could be going round the markets on a Wednesday with the boards up everywhere? And why ain't she with Mrs. Politi, because they have a standing date every Wednesday afternoon? And, no, I ain't finished yet—here comes the crunch. Who rang Mrs. P. and said, in my name, *my name, mark you*, that her and me 'ud be walking out together to-day?"

Crook's breath ran out, to the doctor's relief, as he'd been trying to get a word in edgewise for the past thirty seconds.

"Are you suggesting she's joined Linda Myers?" he demanded brutally.

"Not X's fault if she ain't."

"And this plot against you—sure you don't write whodunnits in your spare time?"

"You give me some," challenged Crook, "and maybe I will. And, for your information, cars like the Superb don't put themselves out of action. What's the situation at Robinson's, anyway? There's a notice on the door—Closed till further notice—old lady taken another step downhill?"

"Whizzing down on a toboggan," agreed the doctor grimly. If chaps talked Choctaw to you you had to talk Choctaw back to them. "Miss Robinson had another and to my mind a final stroke this morning, no sense trying to keep the shop open. I told the sister I'd try and get her a nurse, but with all this 'flu about I'd need to make one myself with cardboard and a gold-paper halo. And by the time the glue was dry you'd find it was too late, her services wouldn't be wanted."

He stopped abruptly, startled to realise he'd been so confiding to a perfect stranger. Still, he reflected, the news 'ud be public property by to-night, unless he was much mistaken. So no harm done, and anyway his correspondent didn't seem the sort of chap to take No for an answer.

CHAPTER XI

AT THIS JUNCTURE they were interrupted by the operator saying, "There is an urgent call for Dr. Mellish. Will you hang up your receiver, caller, please."

"Ringing from Mrs. Politi," added Crook rapidly.

"What he tell you?" Lilli demanded as Crook put the receiver down.

"He don't know much, just that this Miss Alice had another stroke, and he reckons it'll be her last. Shop closed by his advice. Next visitor likely to be the undertaker; and I only hope," he added savagely, "it'll be for Miss Alice and no one else."

"He tell you about May?" Mrs. Politi insisted.

"He don't know anything. Still, he'll come through again, seeing I told him where I was ringing from. Yes, of course he will. He's human, ain't he, and that bein' the case, he's bound to be curious."

Sure enough, within five minutes the doctor was on the line. "On my way to Miss Robinson," he said. "I'll ask her about Miss Forbes. Not that she'll probably know much—gone shopping, perhaps, Miss Forbes, I mean. Anyway Miss Phyllis is on her own. You didn't happen to mention who you were," he added.

Crook told him. "And at the moment I'm standing in for Sugar's guardian angel."

To Mrs. Politi he said, "We know Sugar didn't come home right away from the shop because you'd have seen her. And she didn't stay behind to hold Miss Phyllis's hand. I'm away to the House of Usher," he added, coming briskly to his feet. "I don't say that doctor ain't twenty-two carat, but I do like to come in on the ground floor. I don't suppose Miss Phyllis will be able to tell me much, but if young Clyde should surface . . ."

"No one called Clyde living there," insisted Mrs. Politi, stubbornly.

"Bonnie and Clyde—Yankee gangsters," supplied Mr. Crook. "Well, if he should put in an appearance he might be able to fill me in a bit. Y'see, it ain't no joke. After last night's little adventure I rather fancy Sugar 'ull be the next on the list. Come to that, X may not know I'm still breathin'. Be a bit of a shock, I wouldn't wonder."

"You not breathing?" commented Lilli scornfully. "You breathe so hard you blow open the lid of your coffin."

"I don't know when I've had a compliment that's pleased me more," said Crook. "Well, I'll keep in touch."

"You keep in touch," repeated Lilli scornfully. She seized a sort of black mantle from a hook and swung it round her huge shoulders, she jammed a black woollen scarf on her head, and, her fingers digging into Crook's arm like an outsize crab, she demanded, "Why do we wait?"

Crook recalled that somewhere in the dear, dead past there was a chap who had his liver chewed up by a vulture; he felt a strong affinity with him. Vultures wouldn't be in it with Lilli Politi.

Feeling as conspicuous as if he were walking with his own guardian angel, Crook processed up the street and round to the side-door of Robinson's Drapery.

"Why the private door?" demanded Lilli, trenchantly.

Crook explained, "Miss Phyllis might know where Sugar's gone. Hullo!" For the private door had opened suddenly and Jack Hardy appeared.

"How you do get about!" he said. And then had the grace to look ashamed. "It's not exactly the best day for visiting, you know."

Mrs. Politi fixed him with an avenging eye. "What you done with May?"

"I was just going to try and fetch her back," the young man told them. "Aunt Phyl said to shut the shop at midday, she was expecting the doctor, well, it was obvious it was just a matter of hours, and she felt it wouldn't be respectful to carry on business in the circumstances, so she asked me to put up a notice on the door."

"We saw that," Crook agreed.

"I'll tell you something," Jack added with a sudden sparkle, "your friend Coppernob is on the warpath."

Crook for once was taken off balance. "You mean, he's been here?"

"Well, not here, but in Churchford. Miss Forbes was just putting up the notice when his car went by—well, either of them is noticeable, but the two together—and Miss Forbes said a rum thing. 'I've wondered sometimes if he knows more about Linda than he'll say'—meaning about the baby, I suppose. There isn't much she misses, for all she looks so innocent."

Hearing voices from below Miss Phyllis came down the stairs. She seemed surprised but not outraged to find she had visitors.

"Do you know where Miss Forbes is?" she asked her nephew. "Not that I think Alice will recognise her again, she seems to have gone past a sort of curtain without looking back, but I think Miss Forbes would like to be here."

"As a matter of fact, I thought the same thing," Jack agreed. "I was going down to collect her."

"You know where May is?" Mrs. Politi spoke like a great brooding bird of prey.

"She said, as she had a bit of unexpected spare time, she thought she'd nip down to Mr. Polly and see if he could fit her in. She's quite an old client of his and says he's very obliging."

Miss Phyllis looked distressed. "When I said I didn't want the telephone used I didn't mean May to carry it to that extreme. She could have rung up Mr. Polly, and perhaps saved herself a fruitless journey."

"Well, I did suggest it," said Jack, "but she thought she might only get one of the juniors who'd say right off it was no good coming without an appointment, whereas if she came down in person she might see Mr. Polly and he might squeeze her in. They don't shut Wednesdays," he added for Crook's benefit. "Saturday's their half-day."

"And perhaps Mr. Polly phone me that May not come this afternoon because she out with Mr. Crook."

Jack shook his head. "Why on earth should he?"

"I ask you."

Jack looked hopefully at Crook. "I don't quite get the drift."

"Someone rang Mrs. Politi, a voice she didn't recognise . . ."

"Some man," bayed Mrs. Politi disdainfully.

"And said the afternoon's entertainment was off—on my account."

"But—was that meant to be a joke?"

Mrs. Politi gave an impression of the Three Weird Sisters rolled into one, rising to her feet. "So you think it a joke! Miss Alice all but gone, Miss Phyllis left with no protector, May vanished, and you think it a joke."

"Let's you and me go along to Polly's and fetch Sugar," suggested Crook diplomatically. "We might look in at Warren's on the way and see how the Superb's coming along."

"I was in there this morning getting juice," reported Jack, "and she was being given V.I.P. treatment. You must have had a nasty smash—on the hill, was it?"

"Not as nasty as X intended." He clapped on his horrid brown bowler hat. "You keep your auntie company until we get back," he suggested.

"I don't know what we should have done without Jack," said Miss Phyllis simply. "Sitting with my sister this morning . . ."

"She thought I was Percy Trivett," confessed Jack, looking a bit sheepish. "I hope it was all right, Aunt Phyl, she made me tear up all those old letters, his, mine, the whole caboodle. 'Now I have you I don't need them any more,' " she said.

"May say Miss Alice say she have them buried with her," intoned Mrs. Politi.

"I'm sure there's a precedent for it," agreed Miss Phyllis hurriedly. "There was a poet or someone . . ."

"That's right," agreed Mr. Crook, "I read about him in the papers. Only it wasn't letters, it was his original unpublished manuscript, and later, a lot later, when the wolf came baying at the door, he wanted to dig up the coffin and get the poems back. For the lolly," he explained. "I don't think they let him, though, and serve him right. All this shilly-shallying."

"I do hope I haven't pulled a boner, Aunt Phyl," said the young man anxiously. "Miss Forbes was here when I brought the waste-paper-basket down and she looked a bit blue. Was I sure I'd torn them up very small, it wouldn't be nice to think of strangers reading them."

"Well," observed Mr. Crook heartily, "I've never been a dust-collector, but it's news to me they'd have either the time or the inclination to piece together a lot of old letters . . ."

"You did quite right, my dear," said Miss Phyllis to her nephew. To tell you the truth, for many years now Percy has been more of an—an amorous ghost to her than a real person. I don't think she ever accepted the fact that if he were alive now he would be a man of about seventy. She remembers—remembered—him as he was when they were both young. And one of the tragic things about bereavement is the clearing up of the lost one's possessions. Alice and I never had the heart to destroy our dear father's lares and penates, as he liked to call them."

"Is that all his stuff down in the basement, Aunt Phyl? I took the rubbish, the torn papers, I mean, down there, Miss Forbes told me that's where they should go . . ."

"A lot of it is old stock, quite worthless now, I suppose, but there are his personal clothes there, too. We knew we should give them to a charity, he always had the best of everything, but somehow we couldn't feel he would agree—it's strange how some people don't seem to disappear just because you see them no more . . ." She conjured up a vision of the horrid old man lurching over a cloud, prepared to transfix his daughters with thunderbolts if they dared give away so much as a shirt he couldn't use any longer. "And by now, of course, they'll all be so outdated even the Salvation Army wouldn't take them."

"It was while I was down there I heard the shop door close," Jack continued. "Miss Forbes had told me about trying to muscle in on Polly, and seeing she wasn't around when I came back I assumed she'd gone off. You did say," he added to his remaining aunt, "there was nothing more that she could do."

"Our exit line, I think," murmured Crook, getting to his feet. "You're sure she didn't phone or anything before she left?"

"Not that I heard, and I don't think she had the time. I just heard the door clang . . ."

"No voices?"

Jack looked surprised. "Unless she was talking to herself . . ."

"O.K.," said Crook. "How long does it take a dame to get her hair fiddle-faddled?" he added to Mrs. Politi when they were on the pavement.

"You ask me?" demanded Lilli scathingly. "I don't have to pay no man to do my hair. I brush, I pin—not more than ten minutes, say, maybe less. But that Polly . . ."

"Say an hour," suggested Mr. Crook peaceably. "And she'd get down 12.30 at latest. Should be pollydoodled all right by now."

When Mr. Polly saw his visitors he looked like a man perceiving the opposite of the Heavenly Vision.

"Mr. Crook?" he whispered, as though he feared all the élite of Churchford would pop their semi-dressed heads out of their cubicles and see the type of person now invading their privacy. "This—this is a surprise. I mean—I had heard you were involved in an accident last night, no details, mind you, but I did see your car, a striking machine, if I may say so, being—er—doctored at Warren's this morning. I left mine there for a small adjustment—not much of a mechanic myself," he added in the voice of one who puts art at the head of his list and manual dexterity nowhere.

"She's been havin' a face-lift, too," Crook agreed cheerfully. "Sorry if we gave you a shock. Did you think I was a ghost?"

Mr. Polly offered him a sickly smile. "I think you do know we don't have a gentleman's salon," he whispered.

182

"Wouldn't find me in it if you did," Crook assured him ungallantly. "No, we've come to see if Miss Forbes is through."

"Miss Forbes?" Either the man was genuine or he'd have put Henry Irving in the shade. "But why should you suppose you would find her here?"

"Mainly because she left a message that she was on her way. Mean to say she never surfaced?"

"But she had no appointment, Mr. Crook, and Wednesday is a particularly heavy day, because of all the other establishments that close at one o'clock. We get positively swamped."

"She thought you might manage to fit her in."

"Dear me, that sounds remarkably unlike Miss Forbes. In any case, I can assure you . . ."

"Couldn't be that one of your staff . . .?" hinted Mr. Crook, leaving the sentence unfinished.

Mr. Polly looked outraged, but he crept from one cubicle to another putting the question.

"No one has seen her and there is no message," he announced on his return. "In any case, in the circumstances, poor Miss Robinson, a final stroke, I understand. She would not be thinking of personal beauty treatment at such a time, I do assure you."

"My, my, you're on the grapevine all right," commented Mr. Crook. "Nothing escapes you, does it? Me last night, Miss Alice to-day."

"Perhaps that young man get it wrong," interposed Mrs. Politi, speaking in the sort of voice that once summoned Moses to the mount of Sinai.

"Somebody got something wrong, that's for sure." Of course, May might have told the young chap a tarradiddle to account for wherever she did propose to go, and wherever that was he was willing to bet it wasn't doing Sugar any good. Obviously she knew something or thought she knew something or X believed she knew something, you could play the cards half a dozen ways. Crook was well aware that a number of people die every year, by violence or by stealth, because they possess information they don't know they've got or whose value they don't appreciate, and murderers, by and large, are a cowardly lot, sneaking up behind the unsuspecting and doing a bit of garrotting (only nowadays it was more likely to be karate) or pulling a gun on an unarmed man, if they could find him or coax him in a sufficiently remote place, or even asking a neighbour to wet his whistle and lacing the drink with something that never came out of any honest bottle.

"Maybe the young man not listen," suggested Mrs. Politi.

"And maybe the moon's made of green cheese, though the lunarnauts seemed determined to prove otherwise. And how about the message you got? Come on, sugar, we'll collect the Superb and go back to Square One."

CHAPTER XII

"YOU BACK AGAIN?" exclaimed Jack. When they returned they found the house-blinds drawn. "Aunt Phyl thought you might be Mr. Erskine."

"He bury you," explained Lilli, "like a beetle or a king, according to what you pay. Poor Miss Alice!" She sketched a cross.

"You must have misunderstood Sugar," Crook told the young man. "She never went near Mr. Polly. And don't tell me he had her bundled away under a washbasin, because that's plain daft."

"I only told you what she told me," expostulated Jack. "Anyway, why should anyone want to do her harm? She's the most inoffensive creature living."

"She's the one who saw X in the Wild Wood," Crook reminded him.

"I thought the trouble was she didn't really see him?"

"Could be X is afraid that when the police have given her another going-over she may remember something that 'ud point in his direction. And if you've already killed a lamb you may as well get picked up for killin' the sheep, too."

"So we are talking about sheep now, is it?" said Mrs. Politi.

"Skip it," Crook begged. He had the feeling of a man in a darkened room with the shutters fastened and bolted from the outside. Down in the street below vigorous life goes on, and the very chap you want may be standing on the step, but it don't matter a row of buttons to you if you can't see him.

Mrs. Politi intervened in a fine deep mannish voice that could have been heard a couple of streets away.

"You talk and you talk like the Houses of Parliament and all this while no one looking for May."

"Where do you suggest we shall look?" Jack enquired. "We know she left the shop . . ."

"Well, not exactly," murmured Crook. "You heard the door clang. That's all you heard? No voice, no nuffin'?"

Jack thought. "That's all," he agreed.

"She might have been shutting the door after putting up the notice."

"But in that case . . ." Jack sounded as puzzled as he looked.

"She'd still be on the premises," concluded Crook.

"The toilet!" exclaimed Mrs. Politi, suddenly. "Maybe she go to the toilet and the door stick."

"She's got a voice," objected Crook.

"Then maybe she faint." She darted away to investigate.

Hearing voices, Miss Phyllis reappeared. If anyone was going to faint she looked the chief candidate. Her one-time rosy face had a crumpled look, as though someone had taken a piece of pale brown paper and scrumpled it up and half-heartedly smoothed it out again. Jack hastily pushed a chair in her direction.

"You look absolutely tuckered up, Aunt Phyl. How about me putting the kettle on?"

Mrs. Politi came back, her big hands spread.

"No soap?" murmured Crook.

"Where is she, if she didn't go?" Jack demanded. "When I came back from putting out the debris the shop was empty, and she wasn't up with Aunt Phyl because I went straight up to see if there was anything I could do."

"You don't really think anything—terrible—can have happened to her?" whispered Miss Phyllis. "Losing dear Alice is bad enough, though not unexpected, but May is a tower of strength."

Mrs. Politi had her second brainwave. "Maybe she go down to the cellar, she slip on a stair . . ." But Jack demurred.

"She can't have done that, I'd have seen her. Besides, why should she want to go down to the cellar? It's like going into a world of ghosts," he added candidly. "All those overcoats hanging on hooks—were they my grandfather's? The sort they called redingotes?"

"It was fashionable at one time for gentlemen to wear their coats very long," Miss Phyllis explained.

"So perhaps you think May play a trick, she hide in an overcoat."

Mr. Crook didn't seem to have heard. "Whatever it was she knew it made her suddenly dangerous," he said. And he had a vision of himself saying to the Stephensons, mother and son, "Blotting me out wouldn't do the trick (or words to that effect), because there'd still be Miss Forbes." He wandered over to the door where the notice was still displayed. "She put this up when she'd written it . . ."

"I wrote it," murmured Jack.

"And gave it to her. And you think you saw Willy Stephenson's car go by. Then you went down the stairs and while you were there you heard the door close, but not anyone come in or any voices. It don't make sense."

"Unless, when she saw Willy, it went through her mind that he could have been the one in the wood that night."

"So she went out, complete with bag and brolly, to accuse him?"

'She might have gone to the police," Miss Phyllis said. "Jack, dear, we shall have to put up another notice to say that my dear sister has passed away. And add something about no enquiries either at the door or by telephone."

"Well, so she might," agreed Crook, answering Miss Phyllis's unexpected supposition. "We shall look the greatest if that's where she is all this time and we've got our thoughts on Murder Mile."

"Here, hold on," exclaimed Jack. "You're alarming Aunt Phyl."

"No harm giving them a word," Crook went on, taking no notice of the interruption. "They might have caught a glimpse of Coppernob, too. Anyone know if he has any sort of record?"

But, like Pilate, he didn't wait for an answer.

"I wonder what he is saying to the coppers," speculated Jack, who was carefully printing out the fresh notice. The original one had been in ordinary longhand, but it had been written in a hurry; or perhaps he thought death commanded the utmost respect. He looked hopefully at the door through which Crook had passed, leaving it slightly ajar. The telephone was in a narrow passage behind the shop, an old-fashioned instrument set on a table with a plain wooden chair for the benefit of users.

To his surprise, Miss Phyllis rose and closed the door. "If Mr. Crook has something private to say to the police he would prefer us not to listen," she said. "In any case, eavesdropping . . ." She left the sentence unfinished.

Jack was unabashed. "I'd say that one was born with his ear to a keyhole."

"That man think he God," asserted Mrs. Politi. "Perhaps he tell the police to pick up Mr. Polly."

"But we know Miss Forbes didn't see Polly. She never turned up at the shop," protested Jack.

"That what Mr. Polly say."

"I thought all the assistants agreed."

Mrs. Politi merely shrugged.

There was an uneasy silence until Crook came stamping back. "No, she didn't turn up at the station, and if she had I doubt they'd have rung Mrs. Politi to say she was spending the afternoon with me. So we're left with one solution." He looked at them expectantly.

"She take wings and fly into a tree?" offered Mrs. Politi scornfully.

"You don't think she legged it to the railway station and just ran off?" suggested Jack.

"Why should she?" enquired Miss Phyllis simply.

"A very good question," corroborated Crook.

"If she was being threatened," suggested Jack uncertainly.

Mrs. Politi intervened. "You think May run out on her friend in time of trouble?" she demanded.

"I know she never carried much money with her," Miss Phyllis added.

"Well, of course she ain't run out," said Crook. "Leopards don't change their spots this late in the day. Well, there seems only one answer and that is that Sugar never left the premises."

"Well, but I heard the door," protested Jack.

"But you didn't see her go out. Which way did you leave the house yourself?"

"Well, through the private door, the side door."

"So if she'd still been in the shop . . ."

"If she was in the shop why isn't she there still?"

"I was wondering," confessed Crook. "These letters you destroyed. She knew Miss Phyllis set a mort of value on them?"

"I only destroyed them at Aunt Alice's request."

"But maybe she thought the old lady might have second thoughts. Which day does your dust-collector call?"

"To-morrow," Miss Phyllis told him.

"So if she got the notion she might rescue a few of the letters and piece them together . . ."

"Isn't that a bit improbable?" murmured Jack.

"I think she may have done just that thing."

"Why didn't she stop me chucking them out, then?"

"She may not have thought of it right away. When did you say you gave her the notice to put on the door?"

"I brought down the basket of torn-up letters from Aunt Alice's room, and I wrote out the notice, and gave it to her, and while she stuck it up I went downstairs."

"And meantime you'd seen Coppernob?"

"He flashed past. I recognised his sporting model, well, it would be hard to miss."

"So . . ." Crook took the newly-printed notice and moved towards the door. "Sugar goes this way, you didn't actually see her put it up?"

"Well, no. I'd gone down to the basement. She told me where to dump the stuff, and while I was down there I heard the door shut."

Crook tore down the original notice and affixed the later one. He walked slowly back with the first slip in his hand.

"She wouldn't be carrying the brolly and bag while she put up the notice, so she'd come back here, collect her things—you're dead sure you only heard a door close, no other sound at all."

"No," said Jack consideringly. "That was all."

"And you didn't look in the shop on the way back?"

"I went straight up to Aunt Phyl. Well, I thought Miss Forbes had gone."

Mrs. Politi took a hand. "If May go down to the cellar, why she not leave by the back door?"

"The only reason I can think of is that she couldn't," Crook told her.

Miss Phyllis stood up rather shakily. "You mean, you think she may have gone down to the cellar, and had an accident, and—but this is terrible, Mr. Crook. She may be lying there now, unconscious."

"Those steps are like precipices," Jack agreed, looking anxious.

Mrs. Politi had already waddled over to the door that cut off the cellar stairs from the ground floor of the shop. "This way?"

"But surely, wouldn't she have called out?" suggested Jack.

"Again, maybe she couldn't. I don't say she is there, but she ain't home, she ain't at Mr. Polly's and nobody's seen her. When you've tried all the likely places you have to start looking in the unlikely ones. Now," to Jack. "Lead on, Macduff. Ladies stay upstairs," he added. "Yes," this to the protesting Lilli, "Miss Phyllis is waiting for a caller, and she don't want to wait alone. In times like these one member of your own sex for company is worth a dozen bumbling males."

CHAPTER XIII

THE CELLAR STAIRS stretched dark and forbidding and, as Jack had observed, almost as steep as the side of a cliff.

"Youth before beauty," said Crook, pushing the young man in front of him. "This way, if I fall, I'll have something soft to fall on."

The two women remained doubtfully at the stairhead. Mrs. Politi started to call like some giant bird trying to attract her mate.

"May! May! Why you play hide and seek?"

"If Sugar had the use of her voice we should have heard it before now," was Crook's rather grim comment.

The cellar seemed an eerie place. Boxes of goods, years and years old, yellowing and probably all mouldering within, Crook thought, were piled on shelves. There was a stone floor, but, at this moment, at all events, no signs of even inferior life—rats, mice, beetles. From some nails in the wall hung the late Mr. Robinson's coats, three of them, a long dark speckled frieze with a velvet collar that suggested the era of Edward the Peacemaker, a green tweedy affair, though no one had ever suggested that its once-owner had been a sporting type, and a plain faced black cloth—"Moth and rust do corrupt," said Crook oracularly. "What's wanted down here is a nice fire, with all the goods insured first." The floor was cold to the touch, yet the cellar seemed less icy than he'd have anticipated. Patches of damp showed on the walls. "Talk about a charnel atmosphere!" Crook ejaculated. The cellar seemed singularly devoid of hiding-places, unless, of course, some of the paving-stones were loose.

"There was a story I read once," Crook told Jack, "about someone else missing, a little chap this was, practically had the Town Crier out for him. Know where they found him eventually?"

"I'm sure you're going to tell me," said Jack.

"Hangin' on the hatstand under an outsize ulster, like it might be here." He twitched one from its hook. "Not that one." He made the same experiment with the green tweed.

"Third time lucky," gibed Jack Hardy. "Honestly, Aunt Phyl, the chap's daft."

From her place at the head of the stairs Miss Phyllis came down a couple of steps. "Are you saying—are you telling us—that May is *there*?"

"Well, no," acknowledged Crook, "she ain't. But she's been down here, that I do know, at least . . . Mrs. P., come down a minute, can you?" He was standing with his back to the area door. "Catch," said Crook, and he tossed something in her direction.

Lilli caught it neatly. "That May's handbag."

"That's what I thought. And I daresay this is May's umbrella. And where did I find them? Hanging under a gent's overcoat. And who put them there? Well, not Miss May Forbes. That's for sure." He turned to Jack.

"It all sounds very elaborate," murmured Jack. "How do you work it out? Or do you think Miss Forbes, putting up the notice, saw someone—or someone saw her—and came in—only why didn't I see them when I looked into the shop? You don't suggest they were both hiding under the counter or something? I go on up to speak to Aunt Phyl—and—what does he do to persuade her to come down here?"

"Well, he don't take her out for a nice spot of lunch, we know that, and maybe she came down here of her own free will and he followed. Where does that door lead to?" He pointed to the door in the whitewashed wall.

Miss Phyllis, who had come down two or three steps after the finding of the bag, answered quickly, "That's where we kept the delivery cart in the old days, and later on our bicycles. It hasn't been opened, oh, for years."

"I wouldn't be too sure," said Crook. "Ain't there a key?"

"There's a nail beside it," offered Jack. "Shouldn't it be there?"

"Oh no!" said Miss Phyllis, quickly. "I mean, it did at one time. Then some tramp came in by the back—we never quite knew how—and he—well, he camped down there— dossed, I think, is the right word. It was extraordinary that no one knew he was there, but it wasn't as though we came down to the cellar often. Then one day we heard the police were looking for an escaped convict, it was thought he'd been seen in the neighbourhood, and Father said, 'If that man's in my cellar . . .' but of course it was meant to be a rather dreadful sort of joke. But the police came round and when we went down—it was clear that someone had been there, though we never knew if it was that man. It must have been very uncomfortable, there was no light once the door was shut. But we found a little old rusty brazier and a tin kettle and one ragged sock. I've always believed it was a tramp myself, it was terribly cold weather, and as soon as it warmed up—or perhaps it came to his ears some- how that the police were making a search, anyway he'd disappeared. Or—we had a woman to scrub and so forth in those days, and one of her sons got into trouble, it could even have been him, and she could have smuggled food in. But you were asking about the key. After that, Father locked the shed, that's what we called it, and kept the key in a drawer upstairs, and so far as I know it's there to this day. It's so rusty it probably wouldn't turn in the lock now."

"Let's try it, shall we?" said Crook, and Bill Parsons would have realised how strung up he was by the very quietness of his voice.

Miss Phyllis pushed past Lilli and hurried up the stairs. Crook stayed where he was, Lilli did likewise.

"It's a bit far-fetched, isn't it?' murmured Jack.

"He must have forgotten about the umbrella and bag or found them afterwards and thought it would be pretty safe to leave them there. Any luck?" he called up the stairs to Miss Phyllis.

"It isn't here, and I've no recollection of moving it. But, of course, Alice—but we can't ask her. Or I may even have thrown it away, it was a big key, and I suppose I decided we'd never need it again . . ."

Something like the hissing of a mighty serpent filled the cellar. "You think May in there?" hissed Lilli Politi. "You get a locksmith—pronto."

"Oh, I don't think that'll be necessary," demurred Crook. "I think a certain chap may have got it in his pocket."

He stuck out an immense hand right under Jack's nose. "Give," he said. "Unless you want to go to quod in sections."

Jack stared. "Have you gone stark raving bonkers?"

"Maybe up till now, but not any more. Give me that key."

"I didn't even know there was a key," Jack protested.

"So you won't mind turning out your pockets. Come on, man, we haven't got all day."

"Aunt Phyl," exclaimed Jack, "this man's a raving maniac."

"You know what they say about madmen," said Miss Phyllis, and even Crook was shocked by the change in her voice. "They should be humoured. Besides, it will save a lot of time . . ."

But she got no further. Mrs. Politi, moving with a speed of which even Crook wouldn't have believed her capable, hurtled from her position near the foot of the stairs and fell on the young man like a tidal wave. One hand caught him by the necktie, half-choking him.

"You tell where May is," she hissed.

"He can hardly do that while you're throttling him," Mr. Crook pointed out. He put two fingers in his mouth and emitted a whistle that might have been heard on the other side of the town. Heavy footsteps sounded outside, and someone pounded on the door. Jack made a gurgling noise.

"Hold him, Ma, but don't quite kill him, we're going to

need his evidence," implored Crook, tearing open the back door. A uniformed bobby stood outside.

"What's going on?" he demanded, just like any stage policeman.

"Don't they brief you before they push you out?" Crook demanded. "We've some reason to believe a missing lady —Miss Forbes to you—is incarcerated in the Black Hole of Churchford—" he indicated the locked door in the wall— "and equally we've reason to believe the key may be in this gentleman's pocket. All we're asking him to do is prove we're wrong by turning out said pockets."

"Do you know anything about the key, sir?" said the constable to the red-faced and dishevelled Jack Hardy.

"Of course I don't," gasped Jack. "If only they'd listen— I told them I didn't even know the door had a key."

"Then, just to save time, you won't mind obliging this gentleman by showing us the contents of your pockets."

"Mind you," put in Crook, "it don't have to be in his pocket. He could have slid it down the back of his neck. A good-sized key, would you say?" he added, turning to Miss Phyllis.

But before she could answer the volatile Mrs. Politi had taken matters into her own hands. She had little respect for men at any time, and even less when they wore a uniform, and now she created a diversion by banging the wretched young man's head against the wall.

"Here, you can't do that," cried the constable, jumping forward. Quick as lightning Lilli thrust her hand first into one pocket, then into the other.

"By the living God," said Crook in a soft, reverent tone, "she's got it." He held up the key. "This right?" he asked Miss Phyllis.

But Miss Phyllis seemed to be beyond speech.

Silence gives consent, they say, so Crook shoved the key into the lock of the shed door.

"It'll be rusty after all these years," whispered Miss Phyllis, finding her voice, or at least some semblance of it. It sounded as rusty as she claimed the key would be.

"And keep your hands off that chap, Ma," Crook added over his shoulder. "If he's going to be knocked about, let the Law do it. It's what we pay 'em for."

"Will it open?" whispered Miss Phyllis again, in that thread of a voice.

"You'd be surprised," said Crook. He had fists like legs of mutton, but he could manipulate even a key that looked as if it might have come out of one of the Grimm Brothers' grimmer tales, with a surprising delicacy. After a moment's struggle the key turned, the door swung back, releasing a great wave of warm air. It was too warm, though. It had a suffocating effect.

"My God!" ejaculated Crook. "You don't believe in doing things by halves, do you?"

He dashed into the sealed-off apartment and came out, coughing a bit, and carrying a lighted brazier in his hand.

"Years since I've known anyone use this method," he gasped. "Must be—oh, better part of thirty years ago—in Norfolk. Here—" he extended the brazier to the startled constable—"take care of this, and for the Lord's sake don't let Lady Macbeth get at it. She's quite capable of dowsing the young man with the contents, and he don't give me the impression of being the martyr type."

The constable gingerly accepted the burning brazier, and Jack, seeing his opportunity, wrenched himself free and went flying up the back steps.

"You let him go," screamed Mrs. Politi.

"He won't get far," promised the constable. "We've got one of our men leaning on his car, and if he goes the other way there's another officer at the Main Street junction."

He thought if Jack had any sense he'd be grateful for police protection. This harpy would like to see him torn limb from limb, and wouldn't object to initiating the exercise.

Lilli said something about bulls trying to catch eels, but no one was listening. Against the wall of the shed-room leaned an ancient bone-shaker, stiff with rust, and behind the bone-shaker, flung down on the floor, partially concealed, and looking like a bundle that should have been deposited outside for the garbage-collector, was the missing woman. There was a strip of material over her mouth, her wrists were bound behind her back, her ankles were fettered.

"We want an ambulance," said Crook, not taking his eyes off the figure. "Not you, Miss Phyllis, they'll come quicker for the police. But first of all give me a hand with this. Where's that blasted brazier?"

The constable indicated he'd put it outside the area door, where it could do no harm.

"Except collect a pack of ghouls all hoping for a drop of blood," grumbled Crook. "Well, if any blood's being shed, let's hope it's theirs."

Together they bore the unconscious form into the cellar, where the door was left wide open. Crook had his arm under her shoulders.

"Feel in my pocket," he invited Lilli. "Maybe a snifter would help her to come through."

"You want to make her drunk?" But Lilli was deft enough in withdrawing the flask and unscrewing the top.

"Are they building that ambulance?" Crook demanded of the policeman who had reappeared. "Don't hover, man. Get some coffee."

"I think the lady . . ." the constable began, and when Crook looked up he was surprised to see Miss Phyllis coming rather shakily down the stairs, carrying a tray with a coffee-pot and some cups on it. The constable moved forward to take it from her.

"I'm sure I've always heard that black coffee with plenty of sugar is what the doctor ordered," she said.

"Well, but Sugar ain't suffering from a hangover. Ambulance coming?" he repeated belligerently. The constable thanked his stars that men like Crook didn't come in pairs. He tried to sound reassuring.

"On its way. How is she?"

"She the cat's grandmother," interpolated the fierce Mrs. Politi. "Miss Forbes have a name."

"She's breathing," said Crook, "and lucky at that. A

lighted charcoal brazier in a cupboard, which is more or less what that place is, asphyxiates in a matter of hours. Don't ladies carry smelling-salts or anything these days?"

To everyone's surprise, Miss Phyllis dashed at one of the yellowing packages and tore open the end. An instant later she had yanked out a pillow, its cover rotten with age, and with a minute pair of scissors that she apparently carried round her neck, she started to make a jagged hole in the ticking. Feathers began to float. Mrs. Politi, who seemed to read Miss Phyllis's mind, started to gather them up.

"Burnt feathers," said Miss Phyllis, piling them on to the enamelled tray containing the coffee pot. "I know it's an old-fashioned remedy . . . Has anyone got a match? If not, I can get a spill from the brazier."

Crook thought they must look good enough for Grand Guignol. While Miss Phyllis started to wave the scorching feathers under May's nose—and if ever he'd come across a kill-or-cure remedy, decided Crook, this was it—someone pushed a cup of coffee into his hand.

"If that's for Sugar it's a waste of good coffee," said Crook sensibly. "If she can't take the real article—" he indicated the flask whose contents she had rejected—"she won't be likely to take a substitute." He took a mouthful or two of the coffee himself. It was hot, strong and sweet. "Very acceptable," he pronounced. Now came sounds from without as an ambulance drew up, stared at in owlish or ghoulish fashion, take your choice, by the few passers-by who always seem to spring up from the paving-stones or drop out of a tree whenever anything melodramatic's in the offing. Two young men in blue uniform ran down the steps carrying a folding chair. Getting a stretcher up even half-a-dozen steep stairs would probably result in the unfortunate patient standing on her head.

They stopped for an instant, though they'd have told you they were immune from the quality of surprise. Mrs. Politi had dropped on her knees beside her friend, and was breathing at her.

"May, you not die, you not *dare*," she proclaimed fiercely.

"Lady isn't conscious," said one of the ambulance men, but "By Golly, you've done the trick," ejaculated Mr. Crook. For May had sleepily opened her eyes. She looked about as sane as a March hare. Her gaze moved from Lilli to Mr. Crook. It was obvious she was trying to focus. She opened her mouth, Crook made a sign to the ambulance attendants and they waited meekly.

"He told me," she said in a voice like a wandering wind. "Only I didn't get the message."

Her lids drooped again over her eyes. "She's all yours," said Crook. Lilli followed the men up the steps, puffing like a great black porpoise. She made it clear that she intended to accompany her friend to the hospital.

"When May wake up," she insisted, "she want to see some woman's face that she knows, not some man in a UNIFORM." Her voice put the last word into capital letters.

"You a relative?" one of the men asked.

"That's right," interposed Crook. "The kind that sticks closer than a brother. And it 'ud be a waste of breath tryin' to prove otherwise."

Lilli climbed ponderously into the ambulance and seated herself upright on the second bed, as though awaiting the Day of Judgment.

"You be careful," she adjured the driver. "You not jolt or run like a Derby horse."

"Don't dilly-dally on the way, either," chimed in Mr. Crook. "O.K., Ma, unto each man his destiny, and theirs is to rescue the wounded so to speak, and they'll do it a lot better without any advice from outsiders."

"Fancy you thinking of that, Mr. Crook," said one of the ambulance men, but he was drowned by Lilli declaring, for the benefit of Heaven to judge from the size of her voice, "Who you calling an OUTSIDER?"

CHAPTER XIV

WHEN CROOK went back to the store-room in the cellar he found Miss Phyllis seated on the bottom step, looking as though at any minute she might be the next candidate for a stretcher. It occurred to him they'd completely forgotten Miss Alice, who was missing all the bun-fight, as Crook would have put it, much as she'd missed it during her life-time. But that was the way the system worked—nothing happens for weeks and weeks and then everything comes down like bombs from a raiding plane, so that you hardly know if you're standing on your head or your heels. He put his hand tentatively against the side of the aluminium coffee-pot. It was still warm, so he poured out a cup and fitted it into the stricken woman's hand.

Obediently Miss Phyllis lifted it to her lips. "I can't believe it, Mr. Crook," she said at last. "It would be dreadful whoever it was, but my own nephew!"

"I wouldn't be too sure of that," murmured Crook. And he added gently, "The object of the exercise is to get the coffee down your larynx, not dye your smicket."

Like an automaton Miss Phyllis straightened the cup. "But he did it, Mr. Crook. The key was in his pocket, we all saw you take it out."

"Sure you did. Question is—whose pocket? Now, your nephew. Never set eyes on him till he turned up a few weeks back and announced he'd come to look after his dear aunties' affairs, and call on him, and no trouble too great, and he'd reap his reward? Right?"

"Yes. Yes, I think so," agreed Miss Phyllis, looking rather dazed as well she might.

"Ever had any photos of him?"

"Not since he was a small boy. And one little boy looks very much like another. Mr. Crook, what are you trying to tell me? That Jack Hardy wasn't my nephew?"

"Well, of course Jack Hardy's your nephew," responded Crook. "Point is, was this chap Jack Hardy?"

"But—where would be the sense of him pretending, I mean it's not as though we were rich people, and Jack, the real Jack, only gets on in quite a modest way, so we've always been given to understand."

"You can inherit other things besides money," Crook pointed out. "Like a name f'rinstance, that ain't on the police record. I begin to wonder if the Canadian police would recognise a picture of our Jack Hardy, only in that case they wouldn't know him under that name."

"But—he knew about us, things he couldn't have known if he hadn't been one of the family."

"Oh come to that, you served him butter in a lordly dish, so to speak. Didn't you say your sister got him to read all the old family letters, and I daresay she added a comment or two. It wouldn't be difficult for him to play ball, and if he said he was your nephew and had all the right papers, why wouldn't you believe him?"

"But Jack—our real nephew—that is, if you are right, Mr. Crook . . ."

"Well, I don't think he'd have taken the chance of the genuine article turning up or even starting enquiries, knowing, you see, just where to look. No, I think he saw his chance . . ."

"You can't mean that he—killed—Jack?"

"I mean, I think your Jack's joined the great majority and the phony one knows it. And he saw his chance and jumped for it and to hell with the consequences. That's the way most chaps become millionaires and look how we're always bein' told to make the most of our opportunities."

"But—Mr. Crook—this is just guesswork. I mean, no one has suggested . . ."

"I'd say two people had," Crook amended in his grimmest voice. "One of them died—on Broomstick Common—and we don't know yet about the other. Though if Sugar don't pull through after this I'll lose my faith in human nature."

"I still don't see how May knew . . ."

"I'll tell you," said Mr. Crook, kindly. "It seems pretty clear she'd only just found out, or she'd have said something—not to you, maybe, but to me, because I'm her legal adviser. And she knew she could get me on the blower any time, so—why didn't she? There's only one answer I can see, that she never got the chance. Because X saw to it that she didn't."

"But what did she know?" insisted poor, bewildered Miss Phyllis.

"Let's take it step by step," suggested Crook. "Sugar's in the shop, when down comes Jack—we'd better go on calling him that—with his basket of scraps. He tells Sugar that you want a notice put on the door and he sits down and writes it out and gives it to her to stick up. Then down to the cellar. O.K. so far?"

Miss Phyllis nodded.

"She goes over to the door." Crook suited the action to the words. "And something happens. Either she sees someone . . ."

"And thinks it might have been the one who was on the Common that night?" hazarded Miss Phyllis.

"Well, but in that case why didn't she call Jack? Or go out and try to trail him? But we know she did neither of these things."

"Perhaps he saw her," suggested Miss Phyllis, "and came into the shop."

"But no one came in," Crook insisted. "Because—listen." He put out his hand and opened the door, and the bell that May had secretly resented rang out full and clear. "Remember I asked Jack not once but twice if he heard anything beside a door close, and he said No. But if that door had opened or closed he must have heard the bell. So, if he heard a door at all, it was the cellar-door and Sugar 'ud only shut that if she was going down below. No, here's the answer." He put out a big hand and tore down the notice Miss Forbes had affixed not long before. "Recognise the hand? I mean, ever seen that writing before?"

Miss Phyllis looked at it with perplexity. Before she could reply Crook shoved his great hand into his pocket and brought forth a few scraps of torn paper, two of which were clearly the tailpieces of correspondence, and both were signed Jack Hardy.

"But it's not the same writing, it's not a bit the same," Miss Phyllis demurred. "This is a good firm hand, Jack's was—well, my sister and I used to say it was the hand of a dreamer, rather vague. There's nothing vague about this. You mean, they were written by two different people." The penny had dropped with a crash like a time bomb.

"That 'ud be my guess," agreed Crook, modestly. "And I'll tell you something else. I don't think Sugar was the first to rumble our villain. You remember tellin' me how much pleasure young Linda gave your sister reading through all the letters. Now, she seems to have known how many beans make five, and where to look for said beans."

"And she realised that Jack was an *impostor*?"

"I said I wouldn't be surprised."

"And—and blackmailed him?" Miss Phyllis's voice had dropped to a whisper.

"I wouldn't put it as strong as that," said Mr. Crook. "I don't suppose there was much cash in it for her, but what she liked was the sense of power, making the other fellow jump to it. Same like with Mr. Polly."

Miss Phyllis staggered him by saying, "You mean, you think she knew about this woman he used to meet."

"Well, blow me down," exclaimed Crook, "you consume your own smoke, don't you?"

"Thursday is the night my sister and I used to go to our Women's Meeting," Miss Phyllis explained, "and even after Alice couldn't get about she liked me to go. 'Let me have a little life at second-hand,' she said. And my way ran past Mr. Polly's boutique, as he calls it. And there was never any light burning in the shop. And then one evening I saw them together. I don't mean I should have known her again, but I knew perfectly well she wasn't Mrs. Polly. How did Linda find out?"

"Same way you did. Just chance. Only she got a better look at the lady, and not being one herself—a lady, that is, and you know what I mean—she thought it was fun to jerk the wires a bit—oh, nothing very violent—a little time off here and there, subbing and maybe forgetting to pay back, just reminding Polly who held the whip-hand. She didn't want to beat him black and blue—but Jack was a different thing altogether. She was swimmin' out of her depth there, though I daresay she didn't know it. And that," he added, "is why I think she was found on Broomstick Common, not because she was going to put up the birthrate."

"Was Jack the father of her child?"

"Well, if she wouldn't throw herself away on Polly I doubt if she'd risk her all for a man she knew was a fake. I'd be inclined to hold Coppernob responsible, but that's something we'll never be able to prove. Anyway, Coppernob couldn't have been responsible for trying to put out Sugar's light, and me, I doubt if Master Jack ever saw him driving by. I was up at the house this morning, saw him and his lady-mother, and I don't think he'd be anxious to show his face hereabouts right away."

"Poor silly child!" whispered Miss Phyllis. "Talk about playing with gunpowder! Why didn't she go to the police? Or tell her father?"

"Why should she?" asked Mr. Crook, genuinely puzzled. "Defeated her own ends, that would. She didn't see it as vicious and I doubt she ever worried about you bein' deceived. To her—believe it or not—it was just plain fun. Watch me crack the whip and jump for it, me lad, that sort of thing. She wouldn't give a thought to the real Jack Hardy. And when X comes to tell his story—because he'll sing like a canary, that sort can never keep their mouths shut to the end—you'll find he never really meant to put out her light, she just got under his skin—anyway that's how he'll tell it, and it could be true."

His quick ear caught a sound. "What's that? Someone calling?"

"That'll be Mr.—oh dear, I don't seem able to remember names nowadays—the man from the undertaker's. I did tell you my dear sister passed away—yes, just before I came down, and then Miss Forbes was missing—I'm so glad Alice can't know, about Jack, I mean the one she thought was Jack. He can't be wholly bad or he wouldn't have spent so much time with her, reading those letters . . ."

"Well, he had to do his homework, hadn't he?" suggested Crook, bluntly.

The front-door bell rang again, but it wasn't the man from the morticians, but Detective-Sergeant Bailey, who asked Miss Phyllis very respectfully if she felt up to answering a few questions.

"Got the bad boy under lock and key?" enquired Crook, and Bailey gave him a baleful stare and seemed to suggest that he'd prefer to do business with Miss Phyllis solo, but Crook cut in that he was representing the lady, and anyway he might be able to help.

"If you have any information, Mr. Crook," began Bailey in formidable tones, but Crook said that he and Miss Phyllis had only just worked it out.

"Tell me," he went on, "when your lot collected Sugar— Miss Forbes to you—did she have anything clutched in her hand?"

"What sort of thing had you in mind?" asked Bailey cautiously. He knew something of Crook's way of persuading the other chap to give him information that he then proceeded to turn to his own use.

"I thought maybe some scraps of paper, bits of torn-up letter. You see." He turned to Miss Phyllis without waiting for a reply. "She did suspect this chap. That's why she was down in the cellar. Well, can you think of any other reason? Like I've said all along, she's got all her marbles, and she couldn't understand why Master Jack should want to destroy the real nephew's letters. It's funny," he continued thoughtfully, ignoring the police officer who looked as if he'd cut his head off with a bread-knife if he had one handy, "no one's asked yet *why* Miss Forbes was in the cellar."

"I'm sure you're going to tell us, Mr. Crook."

"My guess is that when Jack came up the stairs he

didn't look in the shop at all, and he didn't hear any door shut while he was down there. And when he did hear a door he knew tooting well it couldn't be the door of the shop, because of the bell, see, so it had to be the cellar door. And —guilt makes chaps very sensitive for their own security, so down he came and, so to speak, caught Sugar red-handed. She'll be able to fill in the details later. He'd know where the key was kept, I daresay?" He looked enquiringly at Miss Phyllis.

"It was always in the drawer and he used to use the telephone. I may even have told him—my poor wits—I don't seem to remember as I used."

"You're doing fine," Crook assured her.

"That brazier," whispered Miss Phyllis. "I do blame myself for leaving it there. I should have thrown it out long ago."

"Maybe it's lucky for Sugar you didn't," Crook consoled her. "If he hadn't thought of that way of putting paid to her affairs he might have been a bit rougher. Must have been a shock to him when he noticed the brolly and bag, but then he was counting on no one going down there, coats probably hadn't been moved for a decade. Later on —you made a will in his favour?"

"Now that Alice has gone I certainly intended to make a will, and of course I should have left the bulk of anything I had to Amy's son—I still find it hard not to think of him as that. A little something to May Forbes, of course, she's been a tower of strength to me all through these difficult times, but the rest to Jack."

"Mind you," said Crook, "I don't say that's why he came over in the first place. Wouldn't surprise me to know it was mighty convenient for him to get a new moniker and a new life story—chancy, of course, but then it's chancy getting born in the first place."

"The letter," discovered Miss Phyllis. "He said something about a letter involving Mr. Polly. The first I'd heard . . ."

"Now I wonder who could have told him that," marvelled Crook. "But, of course, them as hides knows where to find. He shoved that letter through the flap while Sugar was engaged with her Parrott, and in he breezes carrying a book-ay . . ."

"That explains something else. When he brought the flowers upstairs he tried to give them to me as if he thought it was *my* birthday . . ."

"Maybe he did."

"Why did he try to turn the limelight on Mr. Polly? I mean, he can't really have believed he was the father of Linda's child."

"Well, he had to substitute someone for Young Lochinvar, and there wasn't anyone else handy at the start. I daresay the young lady had dropped a hint or two—she seems to have been like that hymn, The sower went forth sowing—and that 'ud provide a possible motive. And though Mr. P. did have an alibi for that Thursday night, as he's admitted, it wasn't one he wanted to bring up in open court. I mean, there wasn't anyone else could have left the letter, except old Poll Parrott, and it wasn't likely to be her. And once Sugar had uncovered his mystery, as they say, he really didn't have any choice. Five thousand pounds, if he'd had it, which he didn't, wouldn't have buttoned her lip."

"I see you've got it all worked out, Mr. Crook," said the police officer.

"Just an idea," offered Crook. "Up to you to get the proof, of course."

"And if the proof doesn't tally?"

"Then I'm wrong, ain't I, and we're back to square one."

But you could tell from his bearing he didn't believe it. "Feeling better?" he asked Miss Phyllis kindly.

"I shall be perfectly all right now, Mr. Crook, and Mr. Erskine will be here at any minute, so I know you won't misunderstand me if I say I would prefer to see him alone. I don't want my sister to—to play second fiddle, as it were, to a man like that." Crook realised she no longer gave him a name.

He couldn't think of any adequate reply and felt it might be a bit insulting to look for one. Miss Phyllis might appear a bit frail, and she could never have been a contestant for a Beauty Queen competition even as a girl, but she was, in the old-fashioned parlance of his youth, captain of her soul, and mentally he saluted her.

The front-door bell sounded, a discreet note, as if it, too, wore mourning. "That will be Mr. Erskine," Miss Phyllis said.

"O.K.," Crook agreed. "You let him in and I'll melt away like the famous Arabs once you've got him upstairs."

The way women could effect quick changes was always something that flummoxed him. It wasn't a quarter of an hour since Miss Phyllis had sat on the bottom step looking more like a ghost than a woman, watching her friend being rescued from the death-pit. Since when she'd had one shock after another. But as she moved towards the door she said quite firmly, "I will not have 'Now the labourer's task is o'er' at the funeral. Even if it were true, and we have no reason to suppose it is, it has such a—such a supine sound."

"How about 'Fight the good fight'?" suggested Crook. "A nice rousing tune. I never had the honour to meet Miss Alice, but if she's anything like her sister, she'd appreciate it."

"Dear Father!" said Miss Forbes, regretfully.

She was sitting up in bed with Crook on one side and a police officer on the other. Of course, the authorities would much rather Crook hadn't been there, but apart from the difficulty of dislodging him, he'd laid so much of the foundation of their case they felt they owed him something, and in any case Miss Forbes had said clearly, "I should prefer my lawyer to be present."

"You're lucky Mrs. Politi hasn't taken it into her head to come too," Crook assured the officer. "She'd gobble up even that Dracula of a Ward Sister in her stride."

"Dear Father!" repeated May. "He always said women had no logical intelligence. They had knowledge of a sort, details, he meant, but they didn't know how to put them together into a logical pattern. Lacking in a capacity for mental arithmetic," she elaborated.

"I was never much of a hand at foreign lingos," acknowledged Crook frankly. "Can't you get your tongue round a few words of plain English that Robert here and me can understand?"

"I mean, that young man gave me the clue, and I was so stupid I didn't notice. It was one day when we were talking about nothing in particular, and he said I reminded him of his mother, always on the go. You should have been born a Greek, he said, or something like that. Then you'd have been a marathon runner. But, Mr. Crook, she had a club foot. However insensitive you were, you'd never say a thing like that to a woman who was even a little crippled. And then, she died before he was ten, and his father married again, but he never mentioned a stepmother."

"Because he didn't know the real Jack Hardy had one," said Crook.

"And the day he brought the flowers, I said thank goodness he'd remembered her birthday, but I'm sure he thought I meant Miss Phyllis not Miss Alice. Only—I never put the pieces together. I daresay there were a lot of other small things that I don't recall, but until I saw the handwriting, that notice to go on the door—well, it was like a flash of light, because I actually saw him writing it, and I'd seen the real Jack Hardy's handwriting quite often, and this wasn't even a bad copy. Of course I told myself I must be crazy, so when I thought he'd gone I slipped down to the cellar and opened the back door and pulled in the rubbish bin. Miss Phyllis has the plastic kind that anyone can lift, she says it's not fair to expect men who're as human as we are to carry those big dirty metal bins up the steps. But he must have seen me go down or heard me, because suddenly there he was and I had the papers in my hand.

" 'Looking for something?' he said, and I told him I wanted to find Percy's letters. I was sure Miss Alice never meant him to throw them away.

"But of course he could see the scraps I was holding hadn't been written by Percy, and—oh, I can scarcely think of him as a human being—he smiled and he said,

'Don't you remember what happened to Bluebeard's wife? The story has a moral, you know.' And suddenly I was sure he was the one I'd seen on the Common that night, the night I lost the little cat. And it was as if he read my mind. I mean, he knew what I was thinking."

"Did he say anything, miss?" asked the policeman who, after a reasonably good start, now felt himself an Also Ran in the Execution Stakes.

"I don't think so, that is, I don't absolutely remember, only when you're quite sure of a thing yourself it's very difficult to realise other people don't know, which is why, I suppose, it needs so much practice to become a good liar. I was never any good, I couldn't even deceive Father, not in quite small ways, which seemed a good idea at the time. I started to say something—to Jack Hardy, I mean, but his hand came over my mouth. 'We don't want to disturb Aunt Phyl, do we?" he said. 'She's got trouble enough.' And I remembered that was probably how Linda died. It was surprising what a big hand he seemed to have. I think he must have knocked me out or something, I don't remember too clearly, I think his arm came round my neck . . ."

"The old neck-lock," murmured Crook, "best and quietest way to stop anyone talking."

"I don't remember his gagging me," added May in a wondering tone, "but presently I found myself all tied up, most uncomfortable, like—like a tortoise or something—and everything was very hot. Stiflingly hot. Then I saw the brazier and I wondered why he should particularly want to keep me warm. I thought of the most absurd things, like those stories one used to read where you light a fuse or something and it's attached to a home-made bomb—I wasn't really myself."

"He counted on no one looking for you there," Crook commented grimly. "He had his story all pat. Must have had a bit of a shock when he found your bag and brolly in the shop—he had to put 'em somewhere and even he seems to have been a bit delicate about opening that door again, or maybe he was afraid a draught would put the fire out. Anyway, he hid them very nice and thoughtful, and seeing no one goes to the cellar except to put the rubbish through the back door, no reason why they should be found, either. A case of 'The little toy dog is covered with dust'— my mum used to recite that at chapel reunions, not a dry eye in the place, and she wasn't what you might call a sentimental dame."

"I suppose he was the one who telephoned Mrs. Politi pretending to be you. What luck you should have come looking for me."

"All things work together for them as follow the right," intoned Crook rapidly. "You look as if you could do with a good meal, Sugar, and as soon as you're out on your owney-oh again that's what you're going to have."

"But," persisted May, "if he wasn't—isn't—Jack Hardy, who is he?"

But Crook said, Let patience have her perfect work and they were waiting for information from overseas.

CHAPTER XV

THE CANADIAN POLICE proved extremely helpful. Furnished with the finger-prints of the pseudo-Jack Hardy, they were able to identify these with a similar print found in the house of an old lady who'd been banged up to such an extent that she'd died in hospital forty-eight hours later without recovering consciousness. The print in their possession had been traced to an Englishman called George Jardine who had passed through their hands on a minor charge about a year previously. This man had emigrated to Canada from his native country about three years before.

"About the same time as your nevvy left to better himself and for where?" Crook asked, feeling the familiar thrill of satisfaction warm the cockles of his heart. "Why Canada? Mind you, I don't say he was your nephew's partner, but it would explain him knowing so much about your affairs, wouldn't it?"

"There was an occasional reference to someone called George, in his earlier letters," Miss Phyllis recalled.

This Jardine's line was to visit elderly women, preferably living alone, posing as a buyer of modern and antique jewellery. His victims were solitary and for the most part gullible and he had a well-oiled tongue, with the result that he seldom came away empty-handed. But the last of his victims had proved more spirited than the rest, had rounded on him and assured him with injudicious candour that she'd set the police on his trail.

Jardine, who, as Crook had prophesied, eventually broke down, swore he'd never meant to do her permanent harm. It was her own fault he said. "She asked me in, didn't she? I never break into premises, but once I was inside it was up to her to take the consequences."

("You can't argue with chaps like that, Sugar," Crook was to observe to May later. "They've got a sense lacking, like the ones that are born deaf or blind. Only we haven't developed any apparatus yet to cure them even in part.")

"Silly old fool," Jardine insisted. "What were a few brooches and a necklace to her at her age?"

The manager of a motel near the coast had seen the picture of George Jardine in the paper and had informed the police that it resembled that of a man calling himself Smith and speaking with a British accent, who had spent a night in one of the chalets. At a place on the beach some miles farther on police found an abandoned car and some clothes and documents in the name of George Jardine. Of the man himself there was no sign. It was assumed that the chap had stopped to have a bathe and been carried away by the currents which ran very strong along that part of the coast. The body had not been recovered, and Jardine's death from drowning was assumed, and the hunt for him called off. Fresh enquiries uncovered the fact that another man of British descent and speaking with an English accent had spent the night at a second motel farther along the coast. He had signed the book in the name of Jack Hardy, and had told the motel-keeper that he was on his way to England to look up his remaining English relatives. The airline had a flight booked in this name and the reservation had been taken up in due course. Nobody remembered the passenger particularly, but there was nothing outstanding about him, the flights were pretty fully booked, he didn't create any sort of disturbance, he was everybody's John Doe or Richard Roe.

"This is where you can make your own pattern," Crook told May Forbes. "I guess that Jardine, who'd kept in touch with his old pal, wired him when he was in trouble, probably needed some dough. The real Jack Hardy don't seem to have been much more successful in Canada than he was over here. A nice likeable chap—like a long drink of water, I'd say. Water's O.K. for keeping clean, but it don't have much fortifying power, wouldn't you agree? Anyhow, we suppose that he got the S.O.S. from his old chum and along he came, full of his story about going home. Well, it was a gift from on high—or the depths whichever way you like to put it—to our pal, George Jardine. According to the evidence, though you'd distinguish the chaps easily enough if you saw 'em together, they were much of a height, similar colouring—ah, and the real Hardy wore thick-rimmed glasses."

"But the one we knew as Jack didn't," May protested.

"Because he chucked 'em away as soon as he was through the Customs. It's wonderful what glasses 'ull do for a chap, and it's noteworthy there was no mention of any glasses being found on the beach."

"You mean," said May who, woman-like, had little sense of logic or mathematical accuracy, "they met and Jack Hardy, Miss Phyllis's nephew, talked about coming home, and somehow he got drowned and the substitute took his place. As you say, it was a risk, but I suppose he thought it was worth taking. Is there any evidence that anyone ever saw the two together?"

"If there is it ain't been uncovered," said Crook. "And we won't ever know for sure if Jardine had the wigwag all fixed when he called on his old chum. I doubt he could have hoped to keep up the pretence in Canada, where someone was bound to recognise him somewhere. He was a bit of a drifter, you know, was Jack, I daresay the invitation to come home was a pot of honey for him. He just had to raise the fare—it was a night flight, remember—he comes innocent as Johnny in the orchard to meet his old friend, probably spills all the beans, and Jardine would know a bit already. Just how the real Hardy died ain't susceptible of proof. I hear Jardine's saying it was his, Hardy's, notion they should go for a swim, having time on their hands, and according to him Hardy swam like a seal and went out quite far, so that our Mr. X shouted was he planning to swim the Atlantic. He says the chap suddenly disappeared."

"And he did nothing about it? His own friend?" May sounded shocked.

"He did a hell of a lot about it, Sugar. There he was, police on his tail, no future he'd care to contemplate, and here was a lost man's passport, air ticket, papers, the bundle. He says he couldn't call the police—well, you do see his point there—if he phoned them odds were they'd trace him —the old ladies had never set eyes on their nevvy—oh, it was served him on a plate. Chaps don't normally go swimming in specs, so Hardy had left his on the beach. Put those on, wear Hardy's gear, drive his car, produce his documents—I don't know if you've noticed, Sugar, but these Customs wallahs mostly look for similarities, not differences, and then the passport authorities help them all they know. Why, they could even make me look like someone's just escaped from a concentration camp, and if they see a tallish chap, right colouring, right accent, wearing glasses, having all the appropriate papers—no reason really why they should think he was anything but what he pretended to be. Then Miss Alice played right into his hands, letting him pry among her papers, and I daresay she talked more than a bit about the dear old days. My guess 'ud be the passport went down a drain once the situation was established, well, he wouldn't be planning the return journey, would he? All his hopes 'ud be settled on what Auntie might leave him when she handed in her dinner-pail."

And, of course, leading gullible old women up the garden path was his forte.

"If he'd been satisfied with his original plan," Crook speculated, "they might never have uncovered him. Everyone in Churchford accepted him, his aunties treated him like the prophet of old taking his meat from the Biblical raven, and best of all, nobody in England was interested in a chap called Jardine who'd socked an old lady overseas so enthusiastically that she passed out.

"Nobody appeared to be around who could or would identify the real Jack Hardy, and of course if the elder sister died the second might be persuaded to sell the business, which would help to line the pockets of the self-styled nephew.

"You were the nigger in the wood-pile," Crook assured May. "He hadn't allowed for you, and that's one thing he can't be blamed for."

"But Miss Phyllis is in very good health, all things considered," protested May. "He might have had to wait years and in the meantime the law could have caught up with him."

"The trouble with second-rate sharpies, which is the way I'd describe him, is they don't know the meaning of patience. I don't want to chill your blood, Sugar, but if it had gone the way that chap planned, I fancy Miss Alice would have had a companion in her solitary grave a lot sooner than she anticipated. Now you can get all these pills and whathaveyou on the National Health it shouldn't be difficult for a chap who's got his heart, to say nothing of his financial interest, in the job, to do a bit of switching. You know the sort of thing—I've got a chronic head, give me my aspirin, there's a dear boy—and Heaven knows, half these tablets are as alike to the layman as a pair of Siamese twins. Still," he added quickly, "that's just my surmise. Not bein' a criminal myself, and even the police have never tried to pin that label on me, I couldn't be expected to know precisely how they tick. Well, there it is, Sugar. Anything I've left out?"

May considered. "I don't think . . . I suppose he bought the mask at a toy-shop or somewhere. That and the bala-clava—did you know, Mr. Crook, those helmets are called after the battle of Balaclava? I should think they needed them there—those Russian trenches must have been icy."

"We didn't say No to them in the trenches in Flanders," Crook assured her. "One thing, we ain't ever likely to set eyes on *that* helmet or *that* mask again. Maybe he made that himself, the mask, I mean. He seems to have been quite useful with his hands—and I don't mean just Linda Myers," he elaborated quickly. "There was my car."

"You think Jack Hardy disabled her that night?"

"It had to be one of those three, and I was pretty sure that whichever one was responsible was the one who left Linda on Broomstick Common. Y'see, he'd be the only one who had any real reason for wanting me out of the picture. I never really thought it was Polly, I don't fancy that chap could mend a fuse, let alone fiddle with a car like the Superb, which left me with the two others."

"What made you choose Jack?"

"I didn't, not right off. My trouble was motive. Mind you, I didn't think in what's called our permissive age, any chap in his senses would have to strangle a girl because he'd got her in the family way. All these societies and a waiting list for adoption—no, it had to be something more than that, and that's what I didn't know. Only Mr. Polly gave me a lead. If she was putting pressure on him she might be putting it on one or both of the others."

"If it was Willy Stephenson's baby," offered May rather diffidently, "that could be a motive. I'm sure I've heard he's engaged to a very rich woman and he hasn't anything of his own. I don't think Linda could have thought he would marry her or that it would do her much good if he did . . ."

"And if she could prove the kid was his," added Mr. Crook. "She seems to have racketed around more than some-what—of course, in nine months' time it could be a different story, kids do have a way of taking after their dads—no, all I could do was wait for X to show his hand. Trouble in cases like these is you can't guarantee control of the situation. I mean, he'd had a shot at Linda and that came off, he had a shot at me and that didn't, and the next in line of fire . . ."

"Was me," discovered May.

"I never thought of him trying anything on the premises," confessed Crook, in a voice she'd never heard before.

"It wasn't your fault," May assured him, earnestly. "Even you can't expect to be in three places at the same time. And though, of course, it's awful, that poor girl, and poor Miss Phyllis, it's been a great shock to her coming at the same time as Miss Alice's death, I can't help feeling that when the dust's settled—I mean, Mr. Crook, it will be something to remember, won't it? Nothing so dramatic has ever happened to me before."

"That's the spirit," said Mr. Crook, heartily. "Take it by and large, Sugar, you come out of this the best of the lot. I hope young Lochinvar's grateful."

"You mean, Mr. Wayland? How dreadful of me, I'd quite forgotten about him. And I'm the one to be grateful. If it hadn't been for you . . ."

"And Mrs. Politi. By the way, any notion what Miss Phyllis is planning for the future?"

May looked surprised. "She'll carry on with the shop, of course. And I shall help her, that'll suit us both. You see, Mr. Crook, when you're getting on, and if you don't keep house for anyone, and don't work for your living, you must feel you're a charge on the community."

Crook looked at her with respectful admiration. "That's something you'll never have to worry about, Sugar," he said. "Now, don't let's have any more of who owes what to who. All this talk of debts would get an astronaut down. Open the newspaper and it's stocks down, exports down, credit down, value of the pound—let's not you and me add to the general gloom. You remember I said we'd have a nice cut off the joint together when you felt like it, well, no time like the present, so . . ."

"Oh, Mr. Crook," cried May, "you wouldn't mind if we made it a threesome, would you?"

"If you mean Miss Phyllis, she's got a date."

"Oh, I didn't mean her, I meant Lilli Politi."

Mr. Crook actually paled. "That woman! Honest, Sugar, she makes me shake in me Number Nines."

"Of course she doesn't," said May comfortably. "She may look a little fierce, but underneath she's the kindest creature."

"Too bad I wasn't born with a spade in my hand," mourned Crook, but he knew when he was defeated. May Forbes, he reflected, was just the reverse. Soft as butter on the surface and pure cement below. No wonder even a villain like George Jardine hadn't been able to dispose of her.

"I hope I'm always ready to learn," said Mr. Crook resignedly.

"You see," explained May, eagerly, "it would be such *fun* for her, and she doesn't have a lot of fun these days. Hearing you tell it, I mean."

"You could tell it as good as me," pleaded Mr. Crook, aware that he was on a losing wicket.

"Oh, I expect I could," agreed May, modestly, "only it would be more exciting for her coming from you. I mean, she can talk to me any time."

So they took Lilli with them.

As soon as he was released from durance vile Chris Wayland recovered his car and drove to Hornby. It was another Sunday morning and enough had happened in the interim to fill a book. He stopped outside the newsagent's and went in. Jennifer was behind the counter as before. He looked round him in some surprise that everything should seem so unchanged.

"What can I get you?" Jennifer said, and he came back to earth.

"I called in to know if you were free to have dinner with me to-night," he told her. "I said I'd be back."

"You've got a long memory," said Jennifer.

"What else have I had to think about? I mean, Mr. Crook had matters in hand . . ."

The door behind the counter flashed open and Mrs. Hart appeared.

"You?" she exclaimed unbelievingly.

"I said I'd be back. I've come to invite your daughter out to dinner."

"And I don't care for her to go," retorted Mrs. Hart bluntly. "Girls who get mixed up with you find themselves murdered."

"Only one," demurred Chris.

"Isn't one enough?"

"Others get offers of marriage," pleaded Chris.

"Only one?" asked Jennifer demurely.

"Jenny," said her mother, sharply, "we've got customers." Two men had come in and were waiting expectantly farther down the counter.

"It's astonishing," Chris marvelled. "You haven't changed a bit." Mrs. Hart might have been not only invisible but inaudible.

"In a week?"

"It seemed like a lifetime."

"You, too?"

"No sense waiting here, mate," said one of the men. "Lummy, some chaps seem to enjoy hard labour seven days a week."

"Should get on to the Union about it," the other agreed.

"He's the one," exclaimed the first. "Just like his pictures."

Chris turned his head slightly. "If I'd had time I might have grown a beard."

"Could be the young lady doesn't fancy beards."

"What did you want?" snapped Mrs. Hart.

She came back from serving them in time to hear Chris say, "And I thought we might ask Mr. Crook to be our best man."

"Mother was saying only the other day she'd like to meet that man—weren't you, Mother?"

"It's quite an experience," Chris agreed. "Lucky, really, he's not the marrying kind. I wouldn't like to be cut out on

218

my own wedding day. We ought to ask Miss Forbes, though."

"Don't mind me," said Mrs. Hart icily.

So they didn't.

>>> If you've enjoyed this book and would like to discover more great vintage crime and thriller titles, as well as the most exciting crime and thriller authors writing today, visit: >>>

The Murder Room
Where Criminal Minds Meet

themurderroom.com

Alicia Pope

Alicia Pope is a teacher and writer. She studied English and Drama at the University of Glamorgan, and trained to be a teacher in Bristol in 1999. She has taught GCSE and A-level English, Drama and Theatre Studies, and currently teaches Drama in Bath. Alicia is a Bristolian from a mixed Caribbean background with a dad who was a long-standing Bristol bus driver, which made writing about *Princess & The Hustler* a very personal look into issues relevant to us all.

Sharon Wells (*Consultant*)

Sharon Wells has been an English teacher for over twenty years in Bristol, teaching both English Language and Literature at GCSE and A-level. She gained her BA in English Literature from the University of Bath, and her MA in Victorian Literature from the University of Liverpool.

**Study Guides
from Nick Hern Books**

GCSE Study Guides

Winsome Pinnock's *Leave Taking*

Chinonyerem Odimba's *Princess & The Hustler*

Page to Stage Study Guides

Jessica Swale's *Blue Stockings*

Henrik Ibsen's *A Doll's House*

Diane Samuels' *Kindertransport*

Timberlake Wertenbaker's *Our Country's Good*

Anton Chekhov's *Three Sisters*

GCSE STUDY GUIDE
FOR ENGLISH LITERATURE

Chinonyerem Odimba's
PRINCESS & THE HUSTLER

Alicia Pope
Consultant: Sharon Wells

NICK HERN BOOKS
London
www.nickhernbooks.co.uk

A Nick Hern Book

Princess & The Hustler: The GCSE Study Guide
first published in Great Britain in 2024 by Nick Hern Books Ltd,
The Glasshouse, 49a Goldhawk Road, London W12 8QP

Cover image: Kudzai Sitima as Princess in the 2019 original production of
Princess & The Hustler at Bristol Old Vic. Photo by The Other
Richard/ArenaPAL (www.arenapal.com)

Designed and typeset by Nick Hern Books, London

Printed and bound in Great Britain by
Mimeo Ltd, Huntingdon, Cambs PE29 6XX

A CIP catalogue record for this book is available from the British Library

ISBN 978 1 83904 137 2

Contents

Themes

Structure, Form and Language

Essay Questions and How to Answer Them

Glossary

Further Reading and Research

For R, J and K

Foreword
Chinonyerem Odimba

Writing this play, it felt like an important and personal mission to tell this story – but really it was a story that belonged to a whole city, and in fact the whole country.

I had lived in and around Bristol for over twenty years before writing the play, and as someone who worked with and volunteered for lots of community and grassroots organisations, such as St Paul's Carnival, I knew how important the story of the Bristol Bus Boycott was for historically excluded communities in Bristol.

It was a nerve-wracking play to start, as I had already met and was in awe of many of the campaigners involved in the boycott – who had been instrumental to its momentum and success.

To ease my nerves, I started by visiting Paul Stephenson and his wife Joyce in their home. They were very welcoming and excited that I was writing the play, and shared some of their archive with me that afternoon. That was the day that I knew that writing *Princess & The Hustler* was important, but also that it was about writing Black British history into the theatrical canon. The play almost wrote itself from that point.

Princess and her family were a joy to write, and the heart of the play – which is about how racism robs us all of our love and our dreams – seemed to beat even louder for me as a writer.

Since writing the play, rarely a day goes by that I don't feel a great sense of pride that I brought those characters and that history to audiences, and now to students across the country.

This play is not unique in telling the hidden histories of Black lives and experiences in the UK, but its magic is that somehow it now sits beyond what it was intended for. Telling stories is about us using our greatest human attribute – the imagination

– but reading and seeing ourselves in those stories is a greater magic and force for change. I believe for *every* student that studies *Princess & The Hustler*, there is something to see in yourselves in Princess's story. Something to discover about ourselves and our collective histories.

I hope more than anything else that the names and the courage of those that led and supported the Bristol Bus Boycott are never forgotten.

And I hope that we learn.
Learn from history.
Learn from stories.
Learn from the power of justice and dreams.

Princess lives 'ere!

Introduction

Welcome to your study guide for Chinonyerem Odimba's *Princess & The Hustler*. This book is designed to guide you through the text, looking in detail at context, plot, structure, characters, language and themes. This book will offer you guidance on the key areas of the play and show you samples of writing to help you prepare for your own exam.

How to use this study guide

This book is designed to help you in a few different ways.

You can use it to guide you through the play when you are reading and after you have read it. There is plot summary and scene-by-scene analysis of the whole play.

When you have read the play you can use the sections on character, themes, context, language, form and structure to focus your understanding of the play.

You can use the exam questions when you are ready to start practising how to answer questions in the exam.

At the back of the book is a glossary of keywords for you to refer to as you are learning, or to use for revision, and there is also a list of suggested further reading if you'd like to do more research around topics in the play.

What happens in the exam?

Your work on *Princess & The Hustler* will be assessed in Paper 2 of the AQA English Literature exam: Modern Texts and Poetry.

It's a written exam lasting 2 hours and 15 minutes, and worth 96 marks or 60% of your GCSE.

Only Section A of the exam is about *Princess & The Hustler*. You should spend 45 minutes on this section, and your essay will be worth 34 marks. You will answer one essay question from a choice of two.

You will be marked on four assessment objectives (AOs):

Assessment Objective	What do I need to do?	Things to consider	This Assessment Objective is worth:
AO1	Read, understand and respond to texts. You should be able to: • maintain a critical style and develop an informed personal response. • use textual references, including quotations, to support and illustrate interpretations.	How well do you know the play? What is the play about? What happens in the play? What journey do the characters go on? What do you think about the main ideas in the play? How can you support your views? What quotations will you use? When? Why?	12 marks
AO2	Analyse the language, form and structure used by the writer to create meanings and effects, using relevant subject terminology where appropriate.	What choices has the writer made in this play and why? How does she use language for impact? Why do certain things happen when they do? What is the effect of these things happening when they do? Tension? Humour? Excitement?	12 marks

AO3	Show understanding of the relationships between texts and the contexts in which they were written.	What can you say about society from reading this play, e.g. What does it tell you about what it was like to be an immigrant in 1960s Britain?	6 marks
AO4	Use a range of vocabulary and sentence structures for clarity, purpose and effect, with accurate spelling and punctuation.	Are you writing clearly and accurately using a range of vocabulary and sentence structures? Are you using spelling, punctuation and grammar accurately?	4 marks

Top-level responses

AO1: You will give a critical conceptualised response to the task and the text. You will use thoughtful references and quotations to support your answers.

AO2: You can analyse the writer's methods and use careful subject terminology. You can explore how the writer uses their methods to create meaning.

AO3: You can explore different ideas, perspectives and contextual elements.

AO4: Your spelling and punctuation is very accurate. Your writing shows strong control of meaning.

Mid-level responses

AO1: You will give a clearly explained response to the task and the text. You use reference effectively to support your answers.

AO2: You can clearly explain the writer's methods and use appropriate and relevant subject terminology. You understand the effects of the writer's methods to create meaning.

AO3: You show a clear understanding of some ideas, perspectives and contextual elements.

AO4: Your spelling and punctuation is mostly accurate. Your writing uses a good range of vocabulary and sentences.

Low-level responses

AO1: You will give a clearly explained response to the task and the text. You use references effectively to support your answers.

AO2: You can clearly explain the writer's methods and use appropriate and relevant subject terminology. You understand the effects of the writer's methods to create meaning.

AO3: You show a clear understanding of some ideas, perspectives and contextual elements.

AO4: Your spelling and punctuation is reasonably accurate. You are beginning to use a range of vocabulary and sentence structures.

Context

The UK in the 1960s

The 1960s are often called the 'Swinging Sixties'. Life had been hard for people in the 1930s, and this was followed by the Second World War. By the 1960s, Britain was starting to recover from these events. The teenagers of the 1960s were the first group that were not affected by conscription.

What is conscription?

In the spring of 1939 the British government needed to start preparing for war with Germany. Single men aged twenty to twenty-two were approved to have six months' military training, and 240,000 men registered for service.

When Britain declared war on Germany in September 1939, the National Service (Armed Forces) Act meant all men between eighteen and forty-one had to register for service. Those who were medically unfit were exempted, as were men who worked in key industries, such as engineering, farming and medicine.

In December 1941 a second National Service Act was passed which led to all unmarried women and childless widows between twenty and thirty being eligible to be called up. Men now had to do National Service up to the age of sixty, which included military service for those under fifty-one.

National Service ended in 1960, with the last national servicemen discharged in 1963.

Many parents had spent their youth fighting and were pleased that their children were free from the shadow of war. Young people were starting to want more freedom and there were lots of cultural changes in the 1960s.

The economy was also starting to recover from the war years, and with this recovery came items that changed people's lives. The more widespread introduction in the 1950s of household washing machines, fridges and telephones had a big effect on people's lives. People had more money to spend, which meant they could spend some of it on entertainment and holidays.

> 🔗 **Link to the play:** Weston-Super-Mare is a seaside town in the south-west of England. It was a very popular holiday destination in this period. Although it is only twenty miles from Bristol, Princess and her family have never been there and it has exotic and exciting associations for Princess.

There were also big changes for women. In 1961 the contraceptive pill was made available on the NHS, and the Abortion Act of 1967 legalised termination of pregnancies under twenty-eight weeks.

There was also the Sexual Offences Act 1967, which decriminalised homosexual activity between two men over twenty-one. The Sexual Offences (Amendment) Act 2000 made the ages of legal consent for gay and straight people equal at sixteen. (This change came into effect in Northern Ireland when the Sexual Offences Order was passed in 2008.)

Capital punishment was abolished and there was also a relaxing of laws regarding prostitution and divorce.

> **Capital punishment** is the death penalty. The last executions in the UK were in 1964 and capital punishment for murder was suspended (paused) in 1965, and abolished in 1969. Although it wasn't used, the death penalty was still legally a punishment for offences such as treason until it was totally abolished in 1998.

> 🔗 **Link to the play:** When Wendell and Mavis arrive in the UK, capital punishment is still legal: can this be linked to Wendell's fear of being lynched? Despite Wendell knowing that murder is against the law, would the way he is made to feel isolated and outside of society make him feel vulnerable?

TV became much more popular in the 1960s, with around 75% of homes owning a television by 1961. Nearly everyone owned a radio, and there were also changes there, with more options for news and music. British music changed a lot: rock and roll and pop were both introduced in the 1950s. One of the most popular bands at the time were The Beatles. 'Beatlemania' swept across both Britain and the United States.

In 1964, Labour leader Harold Wilson became the youngest prime minister in 150 years. His government brought in many changes that helped working-class people, such as more university places and help to buy houses.

The 1960s also saw big changes in fashion. Most notably, designer Mary Quant introduced the miniskirt and brought affordable fashion to people. Although women had worn trousers before, it was during the 1960s that women began to wear trousers more frequently and in larger numbers.

> **Research task:** Research fashion designer Mary Quant and the influence she had on British fashion. Who were the Teddy boys, mods and rockers?

The Windrush generation

The 'Windrush generation' refers to people who arrived in the UK between 1948 and 1971 from the Caribbean. The name comes from the ship the *Empire Windrush*, which arrived at Tilbury Docks in Essex on 22nd June 1948, bringing workers from Jamaica, Trinidad and Tobago and other islands. Thousands of buildings and homes had been destroyed by bombs in WWII and it all needed to be rebuilt. Many countries in the Caribbean were still under British rule and many Caribbeans had served in the British army, so a lot of people answered an advert inviting them to come to Britain to help with the labour shortages.

> 🔗 **Link to the play:** In Act One, Scene Seven, Wendell refers to when he first came to Britain: 'When mi come to dis country I was ar good man. Ar soldier. Fight far King an' country.' (page 53)

Treatment of Black people in Britain in the 1960s

The 1948 British Nationality Act gave full right of entry and settlement to people born or naturalised in the UK or one of its colonies. However, despite being invited to Britain, many immigrants faced racial discrimination.

> 🔗 **Link to the play:** Although it could be argued that Wendell doesn't make as much effort as he could to find work, it was still hard for Black people, especially men, to get jobs. As he says in Act One, Scene Seven, Wendell was 'ar good man' as a soldier, 'But it never make far respec'. Fram dis Englishman' and he struggles with how he is treated when he is looking for work: 'Even now everywhere mi go looking far work, dem look at mi so so... An' grown men wit ar family scratching around far even ar paper round.'
>
> People who were well-qualified professionals in the Caribbean were refused work or offered low-paid jobs in the UK, and Mavis is frustrated with Margot not understanding the difficulties she and Wendell face: 'It's not Wendell's fault that the world look at us [...] somehow as second-class citizens. This country call upon us to work. Call us! And now we're here they're telling us only certain work suit us. Who do you think runs the hospitals and schools in the Caribbean?' (Act Two, Scene Four, page 82)

Quite often the only housing available was overcrowded, shared accommodation that no one else wanted to rent. Black people were often turned away from accommodation because of their race, and the colour bar was in full force. The colour bar was a policy that meant that Black and Asian people were stopped from entering pubs and bars and from working in certain jobs even if they were qualified for them. This led to many people having to take any work they could get.

> 🔗 **Link to the play:** Wendell says to Junior 'Wha' kinda world put men in de same sentence as dogs?' (Act One, Scene Seven, page 54). This refers to signs frequently seen in windows turning Black people away from jobs and

accommodation. The phrase 'No Blacks, No Dogs, No Irish' represents the idea that racism was widespread.

'With respect to...'

At the start of the printed playtext, Odimba offers respect to a variety of prominent people. The first person listed was a member of the Windrush generation who overcame great obstacles to succeed in her career in Bristol:

Princess Campbell was born in Jamaica. When she arrived in Bristol in 1962 she applied for a job at the Wills Tobacco Factory and became their first Black employee. Princess trained as a nurse, and fought to become Bristol's first Black ward sister.

Immigrant children in education

Lots of the children who arrived from the Caribbean were bullied at school because they were not white.

🔗 **Link to the play:** In Act Two, Scene Two we are given a hint as to how Princess is treated by children at school: 'My name is Phyllis Princess James. I want to wear this crown... I want to be the prettiest girl in the whole of Weston-Super-Mare and Bristol... But everyone in school says I can't be...' (Act Two, Scene Two, page 66)

In the 1960s, hundreds of immigrant children were labelled as 'educationally subnormal', often simply due to their differing use of language or dialect, and were wrongly sent to schools for pupils with special needs. In addition, many children were part of the controversial 'bussing out' policy, where non-white schoolchildren were taken by bus to schools outside their local area to try to limit the number of ethnic minority children in schools.

🔗 **Link to the play:** When Princess comes home from school crying in Act Two, Scene One, Mavis assumes that her teacher has been acting on a racist bias: 'That teacher saying meanness to you again? Those teachers need to realise they can't keep putting my children on some dunce table.' (page 59)

Windrush scandal

In 2017 it was discovered that many people from the Windrush generation had been wrongly sent back to the Caribbean. Lots of the people involved had arrived in the UK with their parents when they were children and did not have their own passports. In 2010, the landing cards that they arrived with proving that they were allowed to be here were destroyed by the Home Office (the government department for security including immigration and passports), and many people were wrongly deported even though they had been told that they could stay for good. In 2018, the UK government apologised and said they would give compensation to people who were affected, but many people did not receive payment.

Geographical context: Bristol

Bristol, situated on the River Avon, is a large port city in the south-west of England.

Historically, Bristol was a well-defended port and by the Middle Ages it was well known for cloth and leather. By the fourteenth century, Bristol was England's second largest port; the harbour was bustling and busy, but the streets were dirty and most people lived in cramped, unsanitary conditions. In 1348, Bristol was one of the first places to be hit by the Black Death. It spread rapidly and wiped out vast numbers of the city's population.

Italian explorer Giovanni Caboto (John Cabot) sailed west from Bristol on his wooden ship the *Matthew* in 1497 searching for a new route to Asia. Cabot eventually landed in Newfoundland, North America.

Bristol's trade with Europe and America made the city's merchants wealthy but the trade also attracted pirates, the most famous of whom is Edward Teach, known as Blackbeard.

By the seventeenth and eighteenth centuries, the port was incredibly busy, and ships set off with cloth and other goods for Africa where they traded for spices, gold, ivory and slaves.

The enslaved people were then taken to British-owned lands in the Caribbean and sold to work on plantations. The ships then returned to Bristol with tobacco, coffee, rum and sugar. Tonnes of sugar was transported from the West Indies and by 1760 Bristol had more than twenty sugar houses. By the mid-eighteenth century, people were starting to realise how wrong slavery was and after much protest and many years of appalling suffering, slavery was abolished in 1807.

In the 1600s, Edward Colston was a prominent figure in Bristol who made his money from the slave trade. He worked for the Royal African Company, which it is estimated sold around 100,000 West African people in the Americas and Caribbean. To reinforce their 'ownership', the company branded the enslaved people, including women and children, on their chests. Colston made most of his money this way, and used his wealth to fund schools, churches and hospitals in the UK, giving him a reputation as a **philanthropist**. A bronze statue was erected in 1895 as a memorial to Colston's good works, however in recent years many people in Bristol campaigned about the statue, suggesting that because of Colston's link to the slave trade he should not be memorialised. On 7th June 2020, during a Black Lives Matter protest in Bristol, the statue of Edward Colston was pulled down and thrown into the docks.

> *Keyword:*
> **Philanthropist** – a person who wants to encourage the wellbeing of others, especially by the generous donation of money to good causes.

St Paul's

St Paul's is an inner suburb of Bristol, just north-east of the city centre. The striking Georgian architecture in parts of St Paul's clearly shows that in the 1800s the area was favoured by wealthy people. In the 1870s, the Brooks Dye Works opened, becoming a large employer and attracting people to the area, making it quite a fashionable place to live.

During the Second World War (1939–1945), Bristol was very heavily bombed and this had a big impact, with people who could afford to move leaving the area. Things didn't get repaired, and the area became neglected. During the 1950s, when Black migrants started to arrive, they often ended up in run-down areas because they could not afford to rent houses elsewhere or were refused accommodation by white landlords.

St Paul's is a diverse community, well known for its carnival which has been running since 1968. The carnival was created to challenge negative stereotypes of the St Paul's area. It started as a community event called the St Paul's Festival, with residents selling home-cooked food from their front gardens. The organisers wanted to bring communities together. It became very popular and in 1991 was renamed St Paul's Afrikan Caribbean Carnival. Thousands of people attend the event to enjoy its spectacular parade, sound systems and food.

St Paul's also made national news in April 1980 because of a riot which took place there.

> **💡 Research task:** What can people expect from St Paul's Carnival today? What sparked the riot in 1980? What happened?

Mavis lives with her children in a flat in St Agnes, which is the area directly next to St Paul's. Many of the grand houses in these areas were turned into flats and several families might have occupied one house.

'With respect to...'

Many of those listed by Odimba in the front of the playtext lived in or were connected to St Paul's. Seven of them (labelled here *'Saint' mural) are depicted in large murals which were painted on buildings in the suburb or in nearby St Agnes, and Montpellier, by artist Michelle Curtis. The murals are referred to as the 'Seven Saints of St Paul's':

Alfred Fagon was born in Jamaica. He came to England in 1955 and worked for British Rail before joining the army. He began working as an actor in Bristol, where he lived in St Paul's, and he went on to write and produce his own work, becoming one of the most notable Black British playwrights of the 1970s and 1980s.

Clifford Drummond (*'Saint' mural) was born in Jamaica and moved to the UK with his wife Mavis in 1954. Drummond was involved with many community organisations and helped immigrants from the Caribbean and Asia with legal and bureaucratic difficulties they faced. Alongside Owen Henry, also listed by Odimba, he founded Homelands Travel Service in 1962, chartering cheaper flights to the Caribbean.

Delores Campbell (*'Saint' mural) was born in Jamaica. She thought equality, integration and community were really important, and she co-founded the St. Pauls' Festival and the United Housing Association. Delores really cared about children and she became a foster parent; over eighteen years she fostered approximately thirty children.

Tony Bullimore was a white British man from Southend-on-Sea who moved to Bristol in the early 1960s and married Lalel, a West Indian immigrant. The mixed race of the couple caused a lot of controversy and they were very badly treated. In 1966, they opened The Bamboo Club. The club was open to everyone regardless of their race, which was very unusual at the time. The club became very popular; people could meet and enjoy themselves regardless of their race, and the club allowed mixed friendships to flourish.

> *𝒫* **Link to the play:** In Act Two, Scene Two, when Mavis, Margot and Wendell return from their night out, Wendell says: 'De club welcome everybody for sure. Only inna Bristol yuh see so many different different people in same place.' (page 68) Could this club be The Bamboo Club?

The docks

Today, Bristol's harbourside is a vibrant, bustling hub with bars, restaurants, museums and many places to explore, including Brunel's SS *Great Britain* and a replica of John Cabot's *Matthew*. Historically, the docks were busy and dangerous. The water was busy with vessels and the area was full of large warehouses that stored goods for manufacturing and trade. In the 1960s, shipping goods in containers became much more economical, and Bristol Docks were too small for the large container ships. This led to the docks beginning to decline. It would not have been a nice or safe place to be.

> *𝒫* **Link to the play:** In Act One, Scene Six, Junior is angry that Wendell has left the girls alone at the docks. 'He brought you here? Where is he now? Why are you waiting for him all alone like this?' (page 43). Leon also thinks it's no place for the girls to be by themselves: 'This is no place for young girls. There is grown men and dirt and machinery.' (page 44).

Bristol accent and dialect

Bristol has a distinctive **accent**, and many people use features of its **dialect**. We see evidence of this in the play, with Margot's use of words such as 'lush' (lush is a positive word that can mean many different things in different contexts. If a person is lush they might be attractive or a nice person or both. Lush food is delicious, a lush day might refer to a great day out, or nice weather. The word 'lovely' is a good substitute) and 'babber' (baby/my love), and phrases such as 'Ark at ee!' (Listen to that/you).

> *Keywords:* **Accent** – the way you pronounce words; **dialect** – the words that you use.

Bristol bus boycott

In the 1960s, the Bristol Omnibus Company refused to employ any Black or Asian workers as conductors or drivers. The West Indian Development Council (or WIDC), which included Owen Henry, Roy Hackett, Audley Evans and Prince Brown, joined forces with Paul Stephenson to fight the decision. Stephenson arranged for Guy Bailey to have an interview; he was well-qualified and should have got the job, but when the bus company found out he was Black they refused to interview him. In April 1963, Stephenson got the WIDC to call for a boycott of Bristol's buses. The boycott began on 30th April and asked for people to stop travelling on the buses and to walk instead. Sometimes people blocked the roads to stop the buses too. Some white people were angry, thinking that if the bus company employed Black workers there wouldn't be jobs for white people, even though they were short-staffed. The protestors did, however, have people on their side and the newspapers were full of letters in favour of the boycott as well as against it. There were also some high-profile supporters, including Sir Learie Constantine, and Labour MP Tony Benn who involved the prime minister at the time, Harold Wilson. Students and tutors from Bristol University also held a demonstration.

> **Sir Learie Constantine** was a professional West Indian cricketer, and was the High Commissioner of Trinidad and Tobago. In 1943 he won a case against the Imperial Hotel in London because they refused to honour the reservation he had made for himself and his family.

On 28th August, the bus company was forced to end the colour bar. On the 17th September 1963, Raghbir Singh became the first non-white bus conductor. He was soon joined by Norman Samuels and Norris Edwards from Jamaica and Mohammed Raschid and Abbas Ali from Pakistan.

The success of the Bristol bus boycott led to the passing of the 1965 Race Relations Act which made racial discrimination illegal in public spaces. This was followed by the 1968 Race Relations Act which extended the ruling to housing and employment.

> ✏ **Playwright insight:** Odimba was initially hesitant to write a play about the Bristol bus boycott as she felt that the story had been told many times. However, she wanted to highlight how important Black British Bristol was to the whole country, because the boycott led to the Race Relations Act.

'With respect to...'

All of the key figures in the Bristol bus boycott are named by Odimba in her list at the beginning of the printed playtext:

Paul Stephenson was born in Essex to a British mother and a West African father. He arrived in Bristol in 1962. In 1964, Stephenson was asked to leave the Bay Horse pub in Bristol because he was Black. Stephenson refused and the police were called. He was arrested and taken to the police cells. Stephenson was a prominent civil rights activist and was a social worker at the start of the bus boycott. In 2007 Stephenson was the first Black person to be given the honour of the Freedom of the City of Bristol. He is mentioned by name on pages 71 and 75 of the play.

What is a social activist?

A social activist is a person who works to achieve political or social change, especially as a member of an organisation with particular aims.

Roy Hackett (*'Saint' mural) was born in Jamaica and moved to the UK in 1952. After living in Liverpool and London, Hackett moved to Bristol. Roy Hackett, Owen Henry and Clifford Drummond established the Commonwealth Coordinated Committee to challenge the racist policies of the Bristol City Council and other institutions in the city. Roy Hackett is mentioned by name on page 75 of the play.

Owen Henry (*'Saint' mural) was born in Jamaica. He was committed to helping his community and fighting for equal rights. To fight housing discrimination, he co-founded the United Housing Association and, together with Clifford Drummond, he started the first Black-owned travel agency in Bristol.

Audley Evans (*'Saint' mural) was born in Jamaica. He settled in Bristol with his wife Delores, and became active in civil rights. In 1967, he helped establish the St Paul's Festival.

Guy Bailey was a central figure in the struggle to end the unofficial segregation – the colour bar – prevalent in the UK in the 1960s, Bailey took part in the Bristol bus boycott and went on to found the first Black housing association in Bristol.

Prince Brown was the fourth prominent member of the bus boycotters.

Raghbir Singh was born in India and had been in Bristol since 1959. He became Bristol's first non-white bus conductor.

Hackett, Henry, Evans and Brown formed the West Indian Development Council, determined to tackle the hostile working environment faced by Black and Asian workers. Paul Stephenson became their spokesperson. The men set out to overturn the bus company's colour bar. They wanted proof that the colour bar existed, so they helped eighteen-year-old Guy Bailey secure an interview for a job as a bus conductor. The hiring manager was surprised when Bailey arrived; he had assumed that Guy would be white, and he refused to interview him. This moment sparked the bus boycott.

Joyce Stephenson was Paul Stephenson's wife. The couple met when Stephenson knocked on Joyce's door to ask her to sign a petition he was taking to the House of Commons on the Bristol housing situation. They met in May and were married in October.

Carmen Beckford was born in Jamaica and was only seventeen when she arrived in the UK and trained to become a nurse. Her job as a midwife kept her busy but she was also a social activist. Beckford was Bristol's first Race Relations Officer and in 1982 the first Black woman in the south-west to be awarded an MBE. Beckford began the West Indian Dance Team and held events that encouraged groups from different cultural backgrounds. Beckford was also known as the 'Carnival Queen' as in 1968 she was one of the people involved in setting up the famous St Paul's Festival.

What is an MBE?

MBE means Member of the Most Excellent Order of the British Empire. It is an honour given to people to recognise and reward their contributions to arts, sciences, charity and welfare work, and public service.

Barbara Dettering (*'Saint' mural) was born in British Guyana. She worked as a social worker and dedicated much of her personal life to helping her community. She is one of the longest-serving members of the Bristol West Indian Parents and Friends Association.

In December 2022, Roy Hackett, Guy Reid-Bailey, Barbara Dettering, Owen Henry, Audley Evans and Prince Brown were also granted Freedom of the City for their role in the Bristol bus boycott.

Tony Benn was a Labour MP during the bus boycott. Benn lobbied Prime Minister Harold Wilson to help race relations.

Weston-Super-Mare and beauty pageants

Weston-Super-Mare is a seaside town twenty miles from Bristol. Weston (as it's known for short) was a popular Victorian holiday destination, and many Bristolians have spent happy summer days playing on the beach and the Grand Pier.

Weston's lido, the Tropicana, dates from the 1930s when it first opened with the largest open-air pool in Europe. The Modern Venus beauty contest was hosted at the Tropicana from the 1930s until the 1960s, with the accolade of having Hollywood stars Laurel and Hardy as judges in 1947.

In 2015, artists including Banksy and Damien Hirst created a temporary art project called Dismaland, a 'Bemusement Park' on the disused site of the Tropicana, which attracted over 150,000 visitors.

The idea of a beauty pageant might seem outdated, but pageants were extremely popular in the 1960s, with millions of people watching Miss World on television. Many UK holiday resorts held their own competitions and by the 1980s the prize money for Miss Great Britain was £10,000. Contestants tried to mirror what was considered to be the ideal picture of female beauty and, as fashions changed, so did that ideal. In the fifties, Marilyn Monroe was who women were meant to aspire to look like, with a fuller figure and hourglass shape, but in the 1960s super-slender fashion models, such as Twiggy with her iconic blonde pixie cut, were seen as more desirable. Princess is enchanted by the idea of pageants, despite the fact that the ideals of beauty in her time do not reflect her own appearance.

𝒫 **Link to the play:** Princess's 'Beauties of the West' fantasy pageant is a reference to the Modern Venus beauty contest.

Research task: Beauty contests and pageants were very common in the past. For Princess, the idea of taking part in the beauty contest in Weston would be like a dream come true. How did people react to the idea of this sort of competition in the 1960s? How do we feel about the idea now? How do contests like this represent women?

Geographical context: Jamaica

The island of Jamaica is the third largest island in the Caribbean Sea. Jamaica is 160km west of Haiti, 150km south of Cuba, 1,214km from the central American country of Belize and 1,142km from Florida.

Capital city: Kingston

Population: 1.6 million in 1960, 2.8 million in 2023

People: The majority of Jamaicans have African ancestry, descended from enslaved people brought to the island by European colonists. Jamaica became independent from the UK in 1962 but is still part of the Commonwealth.

The first settlers in Jamaica came across the sea from South Amercia. These settlers were part of the Arawak tribes known as Tainos. The Tainos were well established by the time Christopher Columbus arrived in 1494. The Europeans enslaved the Tainos and they became infected with diseases carried from Europe, such as smallpox. Descendants of the Tainos have disappeared.

Religion: Religious freedom is written into the Jamaican constitution. Most Jamaicans are Protestant, wth Pentecostal and Seventh Day Adventist churches being the most popular. Rastafarianism has been an important religious movment since the 1930s.

The **Seventh Day Adventist Church** is a Protestant Christian denomination. Seventh Day Adventists believe that Jesus Christ will return to the earth. Adventists live modest lives, they observe the biblical Sabbath on Saturday and feel that it is important to share their beliefs with others.

The **Pentecostal Church** is a branch of Christianity that focuses on the Holy Spirit. Pentecostalism is often energetic, and people believe that they have the power of God within them. This power can be shown through speaking in tongues, prophecy and healing.

Rastafari is an African-centred religion that began in Jamaica in the 1930s. Rastafarians believe that Haile Selassie I, the King of Ethiopia in 1930, is God and that he will return exiled members of the Black community to Africa. Rastafarians don't cut their hair, and wear it in distinctive dreadlocks.

Language: The official language of Jamaica is English, but Jamaican patois is most widely spoken. Jamaican patois is a **creole** language which developed when enslaved people learned forms of English spoken by slaveholders and combined it with aspects of their own language. There is lots of Jamaican patois (pronounced 'patwah') in *Princess & The Hustler*. Patois is mainly spoken by Wendell, but we do see examples of it in Mavis's speech too.

> *Keyword:*
> **Creolisation** – when two or more languages and cultures blend together to create a new one.

Jamaican Culture

Food

Some of the most popular Jamaican dishes include:

- Jerk chicken – jerk seasoning can be used on a range of foods. It often consists of allspice, habanero or cayenne pepper, garlic powder, salt, black pepper and thyme.
- Goat curry.
- Rice and peas – the peas are actually beans. Usually gungo beans but often substituted with kidney beans.
- Ackee and saltfish – ackee is a fruit, saltfish is usually dried and preserved cod.
- Patty – similar to a pasty with a spicy meat filling.
- Fried plantain – plantains are similar to bananas but have a more savoury flavour.

Music

Traditionally, Jamaican music had two styles: mento and Jamaican blues. Mento is a Jamaican folk music that is similar to the calypso music of Trinidad and Tobago. After the Second World War, blue beat developed, which led to ska music. Ska led to a slower style called rocksteady, which then developed into reggae, which is the Jamaican music that most of us are familiar with. Britain's biggest ska artist during the 1960s was Prince Buster, who arrived in the UK in 1963. Reggae music was a way for people to deal with their feelings about being isolated and not accepted in British society. The music often had political themes that young people especially could identify with. In the 1970s the rise of punk led to an unexpected alliance between punk and reggae, and Britain saw music breaking the barriers between Black and white youths.

Dance

Jamaica has a strong heritage of traditional dances, including burru, dinki-minni, ettu, gumbay, jonkunnu, kumina, maypole, quadrille and tambu. These traditional dances have very specific movements and meanings and are influenced by Jamaica's African ancestry and history, as well as traditional dance from migrants from other places. Some dances are for couples, some for an ensemble, and others are considered children's dances.

Burru: This fertility masquerade includes rotating the hips and bending the knees, and small jumps.

Dinki-minni: This dance is usually performed as part of the nine night ritual after someone has died, to cheer up the grieving family.

Jonkunnu: This group dance is performed with a band playing traditional songs. Characters include King and Queen, Horse Head, Devil and Belly Woman.

Quadrille: A dance for couples. The Ballroom Quadrille is similar to the eighteenth-century European ballroom dance, while mento music accompanies the Contra Quadrille.

As music has changed, so has dance. With ska music came fast hips and flailing arms between the legs, followed by rocksteady with the arms held closer to the body and slow hips. The next stage was dancehall which includes the bogle, world dance and wine (or whine). Dancehall has continued to evolve and is still hugely popular.

> $\mathscr{O}$ **Link to the play:** Mavis whines her hips to imaginary music in Act Two, Scene Two (page 68).

Sport

Cricket is very popular in Jamaica and many players have represented the West Indies internationally. Jamaica has also produced many successful athletes, including Olympic champion Usain Bolt.

> **'With respect to...'**
>
> Three names remain on the list of people to whom Odimba offers respect in the opening of the printed playtext:

Mary Seacole was born Jamaica in 1805. Her mother was Jamaican and her father was a Scottish soldier. Mary learned nursing skills from her mother, who kept a boarding house for invalid soldiers. Seacole travelled to the Crimea and set up the 'British Hotel', a hospital on the front line to treat soldiers who were fighting there. She also visited the battlefield to nurse the wounded, and became known as 'Mother Seacole'. Mary Seacole experienced racial prejudice: despite her experience, her offers to serve as an army nurse were refused. Her reputation rivalled that of Florence Nightingale.

George Odlum was born in Saint Lucia. He studied economics at Bristol University and became the first Black head of the University of Bristol Union before moving to Magdalene College, Oxford. He then returned to Saint Lucia where he became a left-wing politician and served as Deputy Prime Minister and Foreign Minister.

The Crimean War, 1853–1856, saw the Russian Empire defeated by an alliance of Britain, France, the Ottoman Empire and Sardinia.

Mrs Mavis Bowen is the mother of a friend of Odimba. Odimba says that she wanted to honour an ordinary woman whose name was unlikely to appear anywhere else, to offer thanks for the unrecognised work that so many Black women did and still do to improve the lives of those around them.

The Playwright

Chinonyerem Odimba is a Nigerian British playwright, screenwriter and poet. Her plays include *Black Love* (2021), *Unknown Rivers* (2019), *Amongst the Reeds* (2016) and *The Birdwoman of Lewisham* (2015). Odimba preceded Roy Williams as Writer-in-Residence at Royal Welsh College of Music and Drama, and in April 2021 she became the new Artistic Director and Chief Executive of theatre company tiata fahodzi, 'theatre of the emancipated'.

Production history

Princess & The Hustler was first produced as a co-production between Eclipse Theatre Company, Bristol Old Vic and Hull Truck Theatre. It premiered at Bristol Old Vic on 9th February 2019 and was followed by a UK tour.

The cast and creative team was as follows:

PHYLLIS 'PRINCESS' JAMES	Kudzai Sitima
MAVIS JAMES	Donna Berlin
WENDELL 'JUNIOR'	Fode Simbo
WENDELL 'THE HUSTLER' JAMES	Seun Shote
LORNA JAMES	Emily Burnett
MARGOT	Jade Yourell
LEON	Romayne Andrews

Director	Dawn Walton
Designer	Simon Kenny
Lighting Designer	Aideen Malone
Composer and Sound Designer	Richard Hammarton
Movement Director	Victoria Igbokwe
Fight Director	Stephen Medlin
Voice and Dialect Coach	Joel Trill
Assistant Director	Emilie Lahouel
Dramaturg	Ola Animashawun
Casting Director	Briony Barnett
Producer	Ros Terry

Photographs of this production appear after page 82 in this book.

Plot

Act by act

Act One

It is Christmas Day 1962. Ten-year-old Princess James is wearing a swimming costume and a sash, pretending to take part in a beauty pageant. Her game is interrupted by her mother Mavis calling her to help prepare their meal. Princess's brother, Wendell Junior, arrives home from a trip to take photos with his friends. There is a knock at the door. Mavis opens it and immediately shuts it. The visitor is Mavis's estranged husband, Wendell 'The Hustler' James, who left when Princess was a baby. Mavis is shocked and horrified by Wendell's arrival. She is even more shocked when he reveals his nine-year-old daughter, Lorna. Mavis agrees to take Lorna in but refuses to allow Wendell to stay. Princess is surprised to meet her father and Junior is furious at his return.

Act Two

Lorna starts to go to school with Princess and is easily accepted by the other children, while Princess is isolated. Mavis has allowed Princess to persuade her to let Wendell move in, and Junior tells Mavis that he is going to join the students on a march in support of the bus boycott. Mavis, Wendell and Margot enjoy a night out at a club where people of all races are welcome, and Mavis begins to soften towards Wendell. In contrast, tension rises between Margot and Wendell. Margot struggles to empathise with the Black community and this leads to a breakdown in her friendship with Mavis. Junior offers Wendell money to leave. Lorna also struggles with the tension and her place in the family and wants to go home to her mother.

Act Three

Princess goes missing and Mavis and Junior set off in search. Margot discovers Princess hiding in her flat and returns her home, repairing the friendship with Mavis. Wendell also returns after two days, to a frosty reception from Mavis. The bus boycott has been successful and the colour bar has been lifted. The family feel connected and positive that the future looks brighter.

Scene by scene

Act One, Scene One

Christmas Day 1962, St Agnes, Bristol.

Mavis's home.

'The stage opens like a big box – as though opening the front of a doll's house.' The play begins with Princess in the cupboard room wearing a swimming costume and a sash. She places a crown made of tinsel and cardboard on her head as the voice-over announces her to be the winner of the Weston-Super-Mare Beauties of the West Contest. The cupboard room explodes into full pageant as Princess takes to the mic and accepts her win.

Princess's dream is interrupted by Mavis calling her to help prepare their meal. Wendell Junior arrives home and Mavis questions him about where he has been. She is annoyed at him for going out with his camera on Christmas Day. Junior talks Mavis round by telling her he wants to take her photo. Junior upsets Princess by saying he doesn't want to break his new camera taking pictures of her, and Mavis reprimands him.

Princess asks Mavis why there are no presents under the tree and Mavis explains that no one is ordering curtains at this time of year. Princess understands and they dance.

As Mavis exits, Junior and Princess argue. Mavis returns as Princess tells Junior that she hates him. Mavis berates her and Princess returns to her task as Junior slumps on the sofa. Mavis mocks him and starts a cushion fight.

There is a knock at the door. Mavis, thinking it is a neighbour, opens it. She immediately shuts the door and returns to clearing the table.

Act One, Scene Two

Ten minutes later.

The knocking at the door is persistent. Junior and Princess watch Mavis and the door. Princess says she thinks there is someone at the door and Junior offers to answer it. Mavis tells him firmly to stay where he is and suggests it must be children from upstairs. Junior suggests that maybe it's the police at the door and Princess becomes anxious. Princess vows that she won't let anyone take Mavis and opens the door wide to reveal Wendell 'The Hustler' James. As he greets the children, Mavis gathers them in her arms and then tells them to go to their room. Princess asks if Mavis knows the man, Junior asks Mavis if she wants him to stay. Surprised, Wendell comments that Junior's voice has broken. Mavis points a warning at Wendell and says she won't tell the children again. Princess complains that they haven't had lunch or done Christmas, and Mavis slaps her across the face. Princess and Junior exit, leaving Mavis staring at Wendell.

Act One, Scene Three

As Wendell enters the flat, Mavis holds up a cautionary hand. She tells Wendell to take himself away and threatens to call the police. Wendell says he knows it's a shock, and as he moves closer Mavis walks to the kitchen and pulls out a knife, causing Wendell to back off. As Wendell tries to calm Mavis, she gets angrier and angrier and starts to wave the knife. Mavis suggests that Wendell leaves before she does something he will regret. Wendell tells her that he has nowhere else to go. Wendell backs out the door and Mavis slams it and puts the knife away. Wendell knocks again and Mavis grabs the knife and marches to the door, threatening to cut Wendell's throat. As Mavis jerks the door open and raises the knife, she is met with Wendell holding the hand of a girl only just younger than Princess. Wendell introduces the girl as his daughter, Lorna.

Act One, Scene Four

In the bedroom at the same time.

Junior is listening at the door while Princess sits on the bed holding back her tears. Princess is scared that Mavis hates her and is going to send her away. She starts to cry and Junior comforts her, telling her Mavis didn't mean it and giving her a lollipop. Princess tries to understand what she did wrong and, despite Junior's explanations, Princess becomes angry and threatens to run away. Junior struggles to explain to Princess because she is only ten.

The bedroom door opens and Lorna is pushed into the room. Princess introduces herself and Junior tells her to sit down if she wants to. Princess starts chatting to Lorna and Junior gives her a lolly. Princess begins to fire questions at Lorna until Junior stops her. Princess continues to talk, telling Lorna why you shouldn't keep secrets. Princess asks again about the man Mavis is talking to and struggles to understand Junior's change in mood. Junior tickles Princess and she laughs. Princess notices Lorna's eyes and starts to show Lorna her pageant dance.

Act One, Scene Five

Half an hour later.

Mavis, Princess and Junior sit together on the small sofa while Wendell sits in the armchair with Lorna on his lap. Mavis suggests that they eat, and they all move to the table. Lorna immediately tries to start eating but Wendell stops her. Mavis rejects Wendell's offer to say grace and asks Princess to. They begin to eat and Lorna surprises Mavis again by asking what's for dessert. Lorna then makes Princess gasp by leaving the table and flopping onto the sofa. Wendell tries to engage Mavis in conversation, but she struggles to allow it. As Princess questions Wendell having the same name as Junior, Mavis reveals that Wendell is her father. Wendell then reveals that he is also Lorna's father. Junior becomes increasingly snappy at Wendell's presence. Mavis suggests to Princess that she shows Lorna her beauty queen pictures and the girls become engrossed.

Junior questions how long Wendell plans to stay and Mavis warns him against his rudeness. Mavis sends the girls to look at their pictures in her bedroom and Mavis tell Junior that she plans to give Wendell and Lorna food for the day, but that's all her Christian duty can stretch to. When Wendell says they have nowhere to go, Mavis says that she will make a bed for Lorna. Wendell assumes that Mavis is also planning to let him stay, but she tells him that he can come and get Lorna in a few days, and if he doesn't then she will hand her over to the Salvation Army. Wendell questions what has happened to make Mavis so cruel. Outraged, she slaps him and tells him that the Mavis he sees now is a product of the man who left her alone with two small children without a word. As Wendell is leaving, Margot arrives, curious about whose voice she can hear.

Margot introduces herself to Wendell and tells Mavis that she has returned early from visiting family after a fight. Mavis tries to suggest gently that she is busy, but Margot doesn't take the hint and makes herself comfortable. When Wendell leaves to buy some drinks, Mavis tells Margot who Wendell is, and Princess introduces Margot to Lorna. Margot takes Princess and Lorna to her flat to play dressing up.

Act One, Scene Six

Three days later.

At the docks.

Princess and Lorna sit waiting for Wendell, complaining that they are bored. Wendell has been playing cards with some of the dock workers, and he enters concealing a bundle of money. He leaves out a single note and tells the girls that he'll take them for a treat after he has spoken to one more man, and he leaves them alone.

The girls sit and wait, and Lorna reveals that her mum is 'having a rest'. Junior arrives with his friend Leon. Junior is annoyed that Wendell has left the girls alone at the docks and asks Leon to take them home while he waits for Wendell. Wendell is pleased to see Junior, but Junior is angry. He tells Wendell that he wants him to leave, and in his anger he grabs hold of Wendell by the neck and they struggle. Wendell pins Junior against the wall and warns him that he can't put his hands on his father. Wendell explains that he's back to be a good father and Junior can do nothing about that. Wendell leaves Junior in tears.

Act One, Scene Seven

St Agnes, Bristol, January 1963.

Mavis's home.

Margot is sitting with Princess and Lorna when a shivering Wendell enters. The girls greet him enthusiastically, but Margot is surprised to see him. Margot is unsympathetic to Wendell's cold and penniless condition and tells him that he should be getting a job to support his family. We sense the underlying tension between them.

Junior enters with Leon and is not pleased to see Wendell. Leon tries unsuccessfully to flirt with Margot. Margot asks Junior to watch the girls while she goes to a rehearsal. Wendell offers to stay so that Junior can go out with Leon, but Junior angrily refuses. This is the first mention of the colour bar. Junior tells Wendell that Leon's dad is more of a father to him than Wendell is, and that he's a good man for helping others. We learn that Leon and his father are involved in the protests, and Junior laughs at Wendell when he suggests getting involved himself. As Leon leaves, he pulls Junior aside and tells him to calm down with Wendell.

Leon leaves and the tension rises between Junior and Wendell. Wendell explains how he was invited to England but treated badly when he arrived, and that jobs are hard to find. Wendell tells Junior about Lorna's mother helping him and then getting pregnant, and how her mental health issues led to Wendell being threatened by graffiti and a rope tied to the tree outside the house. Junior is angry about Wendell leaving them, and as he is shouting Mavis returns and tells him to stop shouting or he will give them a bad reputation. Princess and Lorna come in and Princess tells Mavis how much she loves having a sister. Wendell still hasn't found a place to stay so Mavis says she is happy to look after Lorna until he does. Wendell goes to leave but he is feeble and unsteady. Princess suggests that if Wendell shared a room with Junior, Lorna wouldn't cry at night. With some rules in place, Mavis agrees.

Act Two, Scene One

St Agnes, Bristol, May 1963.

Mavis is sewing when Princess and Lorna come home from school. Princess is sobbing loudly. Lorna tells Mavis and Wendell, who has just arrived with a large box, that Barbara has invited Lorna to her birthday party but not Princess. Lorna wants to go but both Wendell and Mavis agree that if Princess is not invited then Lorna can't go. Lorna stomps off. Wendell tries to sweet-talk Mavis, reminding her of how things used to be between them. Mavis at first gets angry but then as Wendell spins her round in a dance she laughs and lets him pull her close. Junior enters and Mavis jumps away from Wendell. Wendell hands Junior the box which contains a piece of photography equipment that he has been reading about. Junior tells Mavis and Wendell that students are going to march in support of the bus boycott.

Act Two, Scene Two

St Agnes, Bristol, June 1963.

Princess is in the cupboard room wearing her swimming costume and a sash as she gives her acceptance speech as the winner of the Weston-Super-Mare Beauties of the West Contest. Princess hears a key in the front door and opens her cupboard door. Mavis arrives laughing and a bit tipsy with Margot and Wendell. They have enjoyed a night out at a club where people of all races were welcome. Wendell comments on Margot's behaviour in the club and again we see the tension between them. Mavis says that she had thought the club was a place of sin but she might go back, and how she enjoyed dancing with 'her people'. The trio begin to discuss the bus boycott. Wendell sees this as a time to stand up but Margot voices her opinion that the boycott is a bad idea. Mavis goes to bed and Margot and Wendell continue to talk. Margot expresses that she can go where she likes because people know that she is friends with Mavis. Wendell suggests that Margot is happy to be seen with a Black person when it suits her but in the end she would choose her own people. Margot leaves. Mavis comes in complaining of a headache and Wendell speaks passionately about the boycott. Mavis is proud of Wendell and they become flirtatious with each other; he slaps her backside and she giggles. Princess closes the cupboard door.

Act Two, Scene Three

St Agnes, Bristol, June 1963.

Mavis and Wendell are sitting with Princess and Lorna. The girls want to see Margot but Wendell tells them that she is no longer welcome. Junior enters bleeding and hurt after he and his friends were attacked on their way home from the protest march. Furious, Wendell leaves. Princess is worried and asks if they will need to hide so they don't get attacked. Lorna tells Princess that she won't need to hide because she is not like Princess; she is only 'half'. Lorna says she wants to go home, and exits. Mavis holds Princess tightly.

Act Two, Scene Four

St Agnes, Bristol, July 1963.

Mavis and Margot meet for the first time in a while. Mavis says she feels that people are looking at her differently and Margot suggests that it's because Wendell and others are causing trouble. Mavis defends Wendell and asks Margot who she thinks runs the schools and hospitals in the Caribbean. Margot questions why Mavis has let Wendell stay. Mavis tells Margot about her life with Wendell: how hopeful they felt when they arrived in England and how hurt they were when Wendell was treated badly. She also tells Margot how she felt when Wendell left, but how if a city can try to change then one man can too. Margot leaves and Mavis doesn't look up.

Act Two, Scene Five

St Agnes, Bristol, 24 August 1963.

Junior is cleaning his camera when Wendell returns from measuring for curtains with Mavis. Junior questions why Wendell can't commit himself to the boycott and get a job. Junior hands Wendell a bag of money and tells him there is enough for him and Lorna to find a place to live. Wendell can't believe that Junior really wants him to leave so much, and Junior recounts how he heard Mavis crying after Wendell left and how he felt when she stopped. During this exchange, Princess is lying on the sofa with her eyes closed. Wendell leaves and Princess takes a pair of tailor's scissors, goes into her cupboard and destroys her cupboard world.

Act Three, Scene One

St Agnes, Bristol, 24 August 1963. Evening.

Junior and Leon arrive at the flat to find Mavis distressed that Princess is missing. Mavis has found Princess's hair in the waste bin. Mavis asks Leon to watch Lorna while she and Junior go to look for Princess. Junior tells Mavis that he asked Wendell to leave and gave him his savings. Mavis exits to search for Princess.

Act Three, Scene Two

St Agnes, Bristol, 24 August 1963. Even later that evening.

Margot's home.

Margot undresses in her flat. She feels uneasy and picks up a shoe with which to defend herself. Princess appears from her hiding place by the side of the bed. Her hair is short and uneven. Margot questions her and Princess tells her she has run away. Margot offers Princess a ball gown to wear and tucks her into bed. Princess goes to sleep, and Margot exits saying she has an errand to run.

Act Three, Scene Three

St Agnes, Bristol, 25 August 1963.

Mavis's home.

Margot enters with Princess. Margot admires the photos that Junior has been hanging up. Mavis is still cold with Margot, who turns to leave, telling Mavis that she wants her to be happy. Mavis thanks Margot for bringing Princess back and tells her she is always welcome.

Act Three, Scene Four

St Agnes, Bristol, 28 August 1963.

Wendell staggers in, having not been home for two days. Mavis asks him to leave. Junior enters with the girls and accuses Wendell of theft, assuming he took Junior's money but then didn't leave. Wendell tells Junior that he returned the money to

Junior's room. Princess reveals that she was listening to Wendell and Junior and, upset, calls him a hustler. Margot enters with the bag of money. Wendell says he's been with some boycott people and they feel hopeful that they might win. Junior and Mavis can't believe it. Wendell says he wants to talk to Mavis, and kisses her. She sends the children to their rooms. Wendell pulls out a ring and proposes to Mavis. Mavis tells him that what he has done cannot be easily forgiven, but she doesn't say no.

Act Three, Scene Five

St Agnes, Bristol, 28 August 1963. A short while later.

Mavis is dressed to go out and is trying to hurry the children. Princess feels like she can't be pretty and Mavis gives her a pep talk, telling her that she can do and be whatever she likes. They hug, and Princess returns to herself and dances. Wendell enters, clean, smart and sober, and he and Mavis dance. Junior, also smartly dressed, takes a picture of the family. The radio announces the lifting of the colour bar.

Act Three, Scene Six

St Agnes, Bristol, September 1963.

Princess is wearing a swimsuit and waiting outside Junior's bedroom door. Wendell comes out of the bedroom wearing make-up, a skirt, a shawl and a turban. Princess is excited and Wendell warns her not to tell anyone. Wendell enters the cupboard and is speechless. Princess tells Wendell that he needs to crown her, and he does. The room explodes into a world of pageantry, with fireworks, flags, and people jumping into a swimming pool, and Princess imagines a pageant where all the beauty queens look like her. Black women of all shapes, sizes and nations parade before her and assemble around Princess. Princess stands in the middle and takes a bow.

Close Analysis

Act One, Scene One

❝ *The stage opens like a big box – as though opening the front of a doll's house.*

PRINCESS, eyes closed, stands in the cupboard room.

Princess is immediately depicted as the protagonist 'My name is Phyllis Princess James' (page 6), and we are inside her imagination. It is clear that Princess aspires to win the Beauties of the West Contest as we listen to her acceptance speech.

❝ VOICE-OVER. *Ladies and gentlemen, I present to you the winner of the year's Weston-Super-Mare Beauties of the West Contest – Princess James.*

PRINCESS. [...] I want to thank my mummy, my friends, Margot and Junior... (page 6)

> *Language:* The focus of Princess's thanks shows us the important people in her life. Her use of language also reinforces the idea that she is on a stage playing a role. She has obviously rehearsed the language used in this situation, and this highlights her familiarity with the beauty pageant, showing her undertaking the role both physically and verbally.

The play opens on Christmas Day, a significant day for many people in Britain. Christmas is considered a special time for family and we immediately relate to how the family would be feeling and their expectations for the day, so we understand why Mavis is unhappy that Princess isn't listening and that Junior has been out.

> *Form:* The stage opens like a doll's house, which suggests the idea of a child's toy. As we enter the doll's house we enter both the story and Princess's imagination in the form of the cupboard room. The cupboard room is a recurring image. What does it represent?

> *Character:* What does this tell us about Princess? Why would winning a contest like this be important to her?

> *Theme:* **Race and prejudice** – what would it say about Princess's place in her world if she won?

43

Keywords:
Exaggeration and **hyperbole** are English and Greek words meaning almost the same thing – but 'hyperbole' is particularly used when writing about literary technique: it means 'exaggeration used for effect'.

66 MAVIS. If I have to carry on with this hollering at you then the next thing you will hear will be my hand against your backside. You hear me chile? (page 7)

66 MAVIS. You turn the handle on that door and it will be the last thing you do on this God-given earth. (page 8)

Language: The language that Mavis directs towards Junior demonstrates her clear expectations of what she wants from him: 'it will be the last thing you do' – Mavis uses **exaggeration**, or **hyperbole**, to gain the desired reaction from her children.

Keywords:
Personification is a type of **metaphor**, where something which is not a person is described as if it is.

66 MAVIS. I am done waiting for an explanation as to what reason you might have for leaving this house early today of all days. You better having a conversation with the leather of the belt instead. (page 8)

Language: Mavis's use of **metaphorical language** brings the belt to life – she **personifies** it, and therefore makes it appear more threatening.

Theme: **Parenting** – Mavis is a single mother. Consider the fact that the belt is a man's belt and kept in the cupboard, rather than being Mavis's own.

66 MAVIS *moves to a cupboard. She opens it up and pulls out a man's leather belt* [...] MAVIS *flexes the belt.* (page 8)

Mavis's threats here are casual, suggesting that physical discipline is something that is commonly used in the James household.

Context: It was not uncommon for parents to physically discipline children with objects such as belts, canes, slippers or paddles, and this type of punishment was also used in schools. Corporal (physical) punishment was only made illegal in state schools in England in 1986.

Keyword: **Subtext** means information that is suggested by the words on the page, without being said directly.

Both Princess and Junior respond quickly to the threats, which tells us that such discipline is both frequent and effective. We see further evidence of Mavis's strict discipline when Junior complains about having to tidy up and stomps his foot in frustration. The **subtext** of Mavis's comment: 'You got something else to say Junior?' tells us that the belt isn't far away and that Mavis does not have any problems disciplining her children. As a single parent, this could also suggest that Mavis adopts a rigid form of discipline, as she feels it is necessary to control her children.

Junior talks Mavis around with flattery, and in her responses we see the connection between them.

> 66 WENDELL JUNIOR. [...] Going to take real pretty pictures of you.
>
>   MAVIS *puts down the belt* –
>
> You gon' shine like a queen!
>
>   MAVIS *pats her hair* – (page 9)

Physical discipline was commonplace at the time both in West Indian and British families, and so Junior and Princess move on quickly from Mavis's threats. Junior's compliments to his mother are genuine and her responses show her affection for him. We also see Mavis's affection for Princess later in the scene when she is gentle with her about her Christmas list, and when they laugh and dance together.

Junior has been out with his friends taking photos, and we see his ambition to become a photographer:

> 66 WENDELL JUNIOR. [...] you know I'm trying to learn everything I can...
>
> I'll be an apprentice one day in one of them photography studios / (page 9)

Mavis is also creative in her work as a seamstress and Margot comments that Mrs Bowen has said Mavis 'made better curtains than 'em in Marks and Sparks.' (page 37). We also see how imaginative and ambitious Princess is, in her cupboard room.

In Scene One we are made aware of the difficulties that the James family face financially. Princess asks 'Why don't we have any presents under the tree?' and in the corner of the room there is a 'sad withering Christmas tree'. The tree can be seen to **symbolise** the family's financial situation. Although the family don't go hungry, there is no extravagant Christmas feast either.

Structure: This could be linked to later in the play when Wendell also uses flattery to alter the behaviour and attitudes of Mavis.

Theme: **Ambition** – Junior is determined to become a photographer and spends much of his spare time pursuing this. It's interesting that he has chosen a creative path and that he has been taking photos at the docks: an industrial working environment.

Keyword: **Symbolism** is when symbols are used to represent ideas.

Theme: **Poverty –** the Jameses don't have much but they manage. Mavis and Junior both work hard but it is clear that there isn't anything to spare, e.g. the sad Christmas tree, the lack of presents, the modest dinner. Despite this, Mavis doesn't hesitate to take Lorna in and provide for another mouth to feed.

66 MAVIS. I did read your list baby. I did. Every single word of it...

It's just...

Nobody ordering curtains this time of year. (page 11)

> *Language:* Mavis's use of language is softer here and calling Princess 'baby' shows her affection. Her repetition of 'I did' shows that she wants to emphasise that Princess's list is important to her and her hesitation with 'It's just...' demonstrates that she is thinking carefully about what she says to explain the situation to Princess.

Princess's response to the absence of presents: 'Who needs any of it?' (page 12) shows us her maturity to accept the situation and be glad of what she does have. It also tells us that she is used to not having the same things as some of the other children she knows.

Junior and Princess's arguments are what we would expect from any sibling relationship. The fact that they go from being angry at each other to a play-fight further shows this. Junior has already made Princess cry by telling her he doesn't want to break his camera by taking her photo, and they argue again when Junior threatens Princess's dream of going to Weston-Super-Mare:

66 WENDELL JUNIOR. [...] I'm going to tell Mummy about some of the ungodly things that go on there. They say at night boys and girls go on the pier there to do sin... [...]

PRINCESS.[...] Margot says we can watch them all day. Watch all those women with perfect straight shiny hair all down to their waist / (pages 12–13)

> *Language:* Princess's use of the adjectives 'perfect' and 'straight' to describe the beauty queens' hair suggests that she holds this in high regard. The straight hair alludes to their race: the beauty queens don't have curly hair like Princess, and later in the play she cuts her hair when she is upset.

66 WENDELL JUNIOR. Well none of that is going to happen when Mummy hears that Weston is worst than the devil's playground. (page 13)

Theme: **Religion** – there are references in this scene that let us know that religion is important, especially to Mavis. What other references to the importance of religion can you find?

66 MAVIS. You wan ar lickle shut-eye is wha' ya say?

[...] Which food yuh gon' nyam?

Which table yuh gon' sit down 'pon?

[...] Yuh two children fool fool fram mawnin' till night!

Understanding patois

lickle = little

what food yuh gon' nyam = what food are you going to eat

fool fool = silly

On the last page of Scene One, Mavis's use of patois becomes heightened. Why? Is it because she is joking with the children and feels more relaxed? Or is she playing a character and changing her voice to suit this role?

The loud knock at the door interrupts a fun, family moment, and the transition from the Mavis laughing with the children to opening and then quickly closing the door is significant. Princess and Junior don't hear the knock at the door, so it's left to the audience to make conclusions about the unexpected Christmas visitor. We know it's not a neighbour with mince pies as Mavis expected, as she would not have closed the door, so we are left to conclude that the visitor is unwelcome.

Structure: The ending of the scene with Mavis shutting the door and ignoring the visitor creates suspense for the audience as we wonder who it is and why they are unwelcome.

Act One, Scene Two

66 *Ten minutes have passed.*

The knocking at the door is persistent and Junior and Princess are '*motionless, watching their mother. Watching the door.*' (page 15)

The knocking at the door continues, and Mavis firmly tells Junior not to answer the door. She tries to change the subject to the children from upstairs, their lunch, and Princess laying the table. Mavis is working hard to ignore the knocking.

Form: The family watching each other and the door feels tense. The '*beat*' before anyone speaks adds to this tension, as does the second beat when Mavis tries to deflect the children's attention.

47

❝ WENDELL JUNIOR. One time when we at Deejay's house the police came to ask him a few questions about some business he say he never heard of. They come knocking in this same way. [...]

PRINCESS. [...] They're going to take you away Mummy? (page 16)

> *Themes:* **Race** – members of Black communities have often had a tense relationship with the police, so the idea of it being the police at the door is unsettling for Junior and Princess.
>
> **Family** – as a single mother, Mavis is solely responsible for Junior and Princess, so the implications of her being taken away are quite serious. There is no mention of family members living close by, so Mavis doesn't have a support network around her and carries her responsibilities alone.

> *Context:* Members of Black communities had a fraught relationship with the police in the 1960s, turn to page 21 for the example of the St Paul's riot, and research to find more information on this topic.

When Princess opens the door, she is wary of Wendell because she doesn't know who he is. This tells us that it has been a very long time since Wendell has been a part of the James family. This is also emphasised later when Wendell says 'De bwoy gon' broke 'im voice' (The boy's voice has broken) on page 16, suggesting the passing of a lot of time.

> *Form:* The **stage direction** describing Mavis's action shows us that she feels protective of her children in Wendell's presence. Previously the closed door was the barrier; now Mavis can only use her arms as a means of protection.

❝ PRINCESS *backs away from the door slowly – never taking her eyes off* WENDELL –

WENDELL *straightens himself out –*
Looks further into the room –

MAVIS *gathers her children in her arms –*

WENDELL. Blouse an' skirt is dat Junior?

MAVIS *pushes them towards the door of the other room –*

MAVIS. You children go to your room /

PRINCESS *and* WENDELL JUNIOR *remain still – frozen by curiosity –*

You gone deaf? Your room now! (pages 16–17)

> **Understanding patois**
> Blouse an' skirt = an exclamation of surprise or frustration, like 'Oh my goodness.'

Mavis's reaction to Princess's complaints is extreme: '*Mavis turns and slaps Princess across the face*' (page 17). Although the threat of physical discipline has already been mentioned in Scene One, it feels as if this slap is out of character for Mavis. It suggests desperation and could be linked to her lack of control over the situation. The idea of motionlessness is also tackled twice in this scene. The children are '*motionless*' as they look between Mavis and the door at the beginning of the scene, and also '*frozen by curiosity*' on page 17 when Wendell has come in. This physicality in the **stage directions** reinforces Mavis and the children's lack of control at this point.

Act One, Scene Three

As Wendell enters the flat in the opening of the scene, Mavis holds up a 'cautionary hand':

66 WENDELL. Mavis /

MAVIS. No.

WENDELL. Lissen /

MAVIS. No. (page 18)

In this moment Mavis is in shock and is trying to work out how Wendell can possibly be here after all this time. As we see her belief in God in other areas, we see the other side of this here.

Theme: **Family** – the breakdown of a relationship can be extremely difficult for parents and children. Mavis's life as a single parent is hard and she hasn't heard from Wendell since he left, so his surprise arrival will have stirred up a lot of feelings.

Keyword: **Stage directions** are written into play texts to tell the director and actors what should happen physically on stage.

Language: Odimba's use of **repetition** reinforces Mavis's lack of control over the situation. Mavis's repeated 'no' shows both her disbelief that Wendell has appeared on her doorstep after so long and also that she does not want to see him.

66 MAVIS. Ha! What kind of thing Satan bring to my door today. Unless you his ghost? (page 18)

Mavis's reference to Satan sending Wendell shows the strength of her feelings towards him.

Mavis tells Wendell to take himself away and threatens to call the police. Wendell says he knows it's a shock, and as he moves closer, Mavis walks to the kitchen and pulls out a knife, causing Wendell to back off. These actions link back to the previous scene. When Mavis feels like she lacks control, her reactions are extreme; here she grabs a knife, in the previous scene she slaps Princess.

Wendell's language is gentle and persuasive in contrast to Mavis's forceful language:

66 WENDELL. Let mi juss come in an' tark...

Far a lickle while...

Mi an' you...

Dat's all mi asking. (page 18)

Mavis's feelings are clearly expressed:

66 MAVIS. Mi nuh *vex* Wendell. Mi beyon' vex.
Mi angry.
Mi angry nuff to kill yuh right 'ere an' den go tell yuhh modder why.
Mi angy nuff to go to jail far dem years, an' still be laughing. (page 19)

When Wendell says 'Tink of de children' (page 19) this is **ironic** because Mavis has done nothing but think of the children in Wendell's absence.

In this scene we see a different side to Mavis. Up to now we have seen her stern and in charge with Junior and Princess, but we have also seen a soft, fun side to her. Mavis is very protective when Wendell arrives, but his arrival also causes her to slap Princess, which

Structure: Utterances from Mavis and Wendell are often short, highlighting an intensity of emotion, for example 'Children?' (page 19), or curt/factual responses, e.g. 'Thank you for your visit.' (page 20)

Language: The repetition of 'vex' and 'angry' emphasises the strength of her feelings. Mavis's move away from standard English highlights her lack of control and anger.

Understanding patois

Vex = angry

Keyword: **Irony** expresses meaning that is deliberately the opposite of what is meant or what is true.

feels out of character. In Act One, Scene Three, Mavis is initially lost for words and in shock at Wendell's arrival, but then she is furious.

> MAVIS *laughs out loud – hysterical – dangerous –* [...]
>
> MAVIS *waves the knife wildly –* (page 19)

Mavis suggests that Wendell leaves before she does something he will regret, and Wendell backs out the door. When Wendell knocks again Mavis is pushed to her limits.

> MAVIS. Mi gon' cut 'im rass throat!'
>
> MAVIS *jerks the door open –*
> *She lifts the knife up –* (page 20)

Form: Mavis's anger is shown through her use of language and also through her actions. These actions suggest a lack of control from Mavis, and Wendell is the **catalyst** for it.

Keyword: **Catalyst –** a person or thing that causes an event.

Understanding patois

Mi gon' cut 'im rass throat! = I'm going to cut his damn/bloody throat!

'Rass' can mean different things, depending on the context. In this case it's used to intensify the way that Mavis is feeling. It can also mean buttocks/bottom; to strike viciously; a derogatory term for someone; or an exclamation of shock, surprise or anger.

When Mavis opens the door, Wendell is holding Lorna's hand and he introduces her as his daughter. Mavis was already shocked at the appearance of Wendell but this is a double shock. Firstly, her rage disperses because there is a child on the doorstep, but this is also how Wendell tells Mavis that he has had a child with someone else.

Theme: **Family/ Relationships –** things are further complicated here because not only has Wendell fathered another child, he has been raising that child while Mavis has struggled raising Wendell's first two children alone.

Act One, Scene Four

While Mavis is dealing with Wendell, Junior and Princess are in the bedroom. Princess is upset and at first Junior is too focused on listening at the door to comfort her. Junior does eventually comfort Princess and we see from his reaction: 'she didn't mean it' (page 21) that he understands why Mavis has reacted in the extreme way that she has. Junior struggles to put into words what is happening. He understands the situation but knows that Princess does not.

Language: Junior's hesitance shows that he wants to protect Princess from what she doesn't know, but it also shows Junior can see that Princess learning Wendell's identity is unavoidable.

Form: Consider the **symbolism** of doors used in this first act to create separation between characters. Doors separate them physically but also separate them from the knowledge/ understanding linked to other characters.

Structure: There is **dramatic irony** in the scene when Lorna is cautious of Junior's offer of the lollipop, because the audience know that Lorna is Junior and Princess's sister, but at this point the children do not.

Keyword: **Dramatic irony** – a literary technique where the readers or audience know something that the character(s) in a scene do not.

  WENDELL JUNIOR. She's trying to...
> She wouldn't do it if she didn't have to...
> Don't think she will again...
> She only did it because she's needing to protect us / [...]
>
> You're going to have to start understanding things different soon. (page 22)

Junior is hesitant here and keeps stopping in his explanation because he is not sure what to say. It shows that Junior understands Mavis's need to shield her children from Wendell, not because she is physically scared of him but scared of how much he has hurt the family.

Partway through this scene, the door is opened and Lorna is shoved in with Princess and Junior.

Princess is friendly and welcomes Lorna into the bedroom. Junior treats Lorna is the same way as Princess and offers her a lollipop. Although Lorna is cautious, we see that she is like any other child and the threat of losing the lollipop causes her to snatch it.

  LORNA. Daddy says I can't take anything from strangers.
> (page 23)

Lorna is shy and quiet in this moment, which is the opposite of Princess who fires questions at her. This scene gives us some insight into Princess who is friendly and chatty. Junior is exhausted by the situation and lies down. Princess, keen to know who the man is, makes to open the door, and Junior warns her that she might get slapped again.

  WENDELL JUNIOR. She wouldn't if it wasn't *him*. (page 25)

The emphasis on 'him' highlights how he feels about his father. We see the close relationship between Princess and Junior as he comforts her and tickles her when she is upset.

❝ PRINCESS (*to* LORNA). You're pretty. And your eyes are almost
blue... [...]

I wish my eyes were blue or green or... (page 25)

The description of Lorna's eyes highlights that she looks different
to Princess. Princess's wish for a different eye colour links to her
view of the classic beauty queens of the time.

> *Context:* To read more about what was considered 'beautiful' in the
> 1960s and how this is linked with racist ideas, turn to page 27.

Act One, Scene Five

The opening of this scene feels tense.

❝ MAVIS, WENDELL JUNIOR *and* PRINCESS *sit tightly
together on the small sofa.*

WENDELL *sits in the single armchair with* LORNA *perched
next to him.*

Mavis suggests that they eat, and they all move to the table. Junior
and Princess are watchful in this moment. Junior watches Wendell
and Princess watches Lorna take up places at the table that up until
now have only been occupied by them. Junior continues to make
his point when he sits at the table.

❝ WENDELL JUNIOR *moves to the table –*
*He scrapes the chair noisily away from the table and sits as
far away from* WENDELL *as possible –* (page 26)

Form: The **proxemics** of the characters highlights the separation of
the two family units. Mavis sitting 'tightly' with her children shows her
wish to keep them close and protect them as if Wendell is a threat.
Lorna being 'perched' next to Wendell suggests that she is
uncomfortable. How might Lorna feel in this situation? It's a big shock
for her too. Junior's use of proxemics at the table highlights his
disapproval of his father.

> *Keyword:*
> **Proxemics** is the
> use of space on
> stage and the
> distance between
> characters.
> Proxemics can tell
> us a lot about how
> characters feel
> about each other.

Lorna tries to start eating but Wendell puts a hand on Lorna's arm and stops her.

66 WENDELL. No Lorna! (page 27)

Wendell's exclamation shows us that Lorna is about to make a big mistake. The **subtext** here is that Lorna's way of behaving is quite different to Junior's and Princess's. From Wendell's actions we can also tell that he remembers Mavis's expectations and does not want Lorna to go against them, reinforcing the awkwardness at the table and the idea that they are not a family unit.

Theme: **Religion –** the saying of grace is important to Mavis, as a rule for her family but also as a connection to her home and community. She wants to continue to keep to traditional rituals.

66 MAVIS. We still do this the old-fashioned way.
    Our people way.

WENDELL. Yuh wan' me to /

MAVIS. Not your place / (page 27)

Mavis rejects Wendell's offer to say grace and asks Princess to. Mavis's rejection of Wendell's offer shows both the importance of prayer and its significance as the beginning of the meal. It is an honour to be asked to give the blessing and not one Mavis thinks Wendell deserves. Consider Mavis's behaviour at this point. Why might she want to control what is happening?

In this scene the difference between how Mavis is raising Junior and Princess and how Lorna has been raised by Wendell and her mother are highlighted.

Understanding patois

Juss de way har modder bring har up = Just the way her mother brought her up

66 LORNA *eats ravenously –*

The others eat in silence – […]

LORNA. What's for dessert? […]

WENDELL. Juss de way har modder bring har up.
    (pages 27–28)

> *Theme:* **Family** – Wendell feels the need to excuse Lorna's behaviour by blaming her mother, suggesting that he either wants to deny his part in Lorna's manners or that he hasn't been very involved in her upbringing. This could be seen as a typical characteristic of Wendell. He takes no responsibility for the behaviour of Lorna and showed a lack of responsibility in leaving Mavis to bring up Junior and Princess.

Wendell tries to engage Mavis in conversation, but she struggles to allow it. Their conversation is clipped, and Mavis is battling with both Wendell and Junior to express herself. Mavis is usually animated and articulate and here we see her struggle to say what she needs to say, resulting in her bluntly revealing Wendell's identity:

> MAVIS. Because he is your father! [...]
>
> PRINCESS. –
>
> WENDELL. Yes Princess.
>   Mi yuh daddy / [...]
>
> All of yuhs daddy.
>
> *All eyes on* LORNA – (pages 29–30)

> *Language:* Wendell's calm words are in contrast to Mavis's outburst. Mavis's use of standard English and Wendell's use of patois is a further way in which Odimba reinforces the separation between the two characters.

Junior questions how long Wendell plans to stay and Mavis warns him against his rudeness. Junior is on the edge of being a man. He has had to be the 'man of the house' and he is fiercely protective of Mavis. Unlike Princess, Junior can remember Wendell leaving and how hurt Mavis was, and he feels angry that Wendell has just walked back into their lives. When Wendell reveals that they have nowhere to go, Mavis says that she will make a bed for Lorna but refuses to let Wendell stay. Until now we could argue that Mavis has been quite patient. She has recovered from threatening Wendell with the knife and as soon as Lorna was involved she invited them in and shared the family's Christmas dinner. She sees it as her Christian duty to help a child.

> WENDELL. What 'appen far yuh to get so cruel Mavis? [...]
>
> MAVIS *stands up and slaps* WENDELL *across the face* –

> *Form:* Wendell's question pushes Mavis over the edge. We see that she has been trying to keep control but the implication that she is in the wrong is too much. The physical action of the slap heightens the drama and is a climax for the tension of the scene.

MAVIS. De Mavis you leff you mean? She dead!

WENDELL *jumps to his feet – backing off all the time – whilst* MAVIS *walks towards him – pushing him –*

An' today dis cold-heart woman… she born de day mi wake and find my husband gone! (page 32–33)

> *Language:* Mavis's angry use of language slips into Jamaican patois. This use of non-Standard English now has her speaking in the same way as Wendell and serves to highlight the connection between the two characters, the fact that they do have a past together, even if Mavis is reluctant to admit it.

Theme: **Family –** Margot's description of her family suggests that she is isolated from them and living a different life. Margot's small, lonely room highlights that she is not surrounded by people who love her and she craves this from Mavis and her children.

As Wendell is leaving, Margot arrives. This is our first introduction to her and she appears quite flirtatious as she '*glides over to Wendell*' (page 34). Her introduction implies that although Margot looks innocent, we should sense that she is not. This is also our first introduction to someone outside of the complex James family unit. Margot tells Mavis that she has returned early from visiting family after a fight. Mavis tries to suggest gently that she is busy, but Margot doesn't take the hint and makes herself comfortable. It is likely that Margot does realise that Mavis wants her to leave but her alternative is being alone on Christmas Day. Margot has clear affection for the James family. She loves Princess and this is reciprocated, as shown by Princess's reaction to Margot's arrival.

Princess introduces Margot to Lorna and she is surprised to learn that Lorna is Princess's sister.

Understanding Bristol dialect

Ark at ee! = Listen to that/you

66 MARGOT. Ark at ee! [...]

(*To* MAVIS.) I mean look at that!
She must be half half / (page 39)

> *Theme:* **Race and prejudice –** Margot's comments to Mavis suggest that she is surprised by Lorna's mixed race, suggesting that it was unusual at the time. At the time, the term 'half half', along with many other terms to describe mixed-race people, would not have been seen by most people as derogatory in the same way that it would be now.

Margot clearly spends a lot of time with Princess, as she doesn't hesitate to agree to Princess coming to play dressing up at her flat, even on Christmas Day and with a new sister in tow.

Act One, Scene Six

Princess and Lorna sit at the docks waiting for Wendell, complaining that they are bored.

The docks at this time would have been a place of industry and work; dirty and dangerous and not a place to leave two young girls unattended.

> PRINCESS *and* LORNA *sit on a couple of crates – looking extremely bored.* [...]
>
> LORNA. We've been waiting for ages.
>
> PRINCESS. You said we were going to the park... [...]
>
> You said we could feed the birds...
>
> LORNA. And have chocolate.
>
> PRINCESS. We haven't had chocolate...
>
> LORNA. Or been to the park. (page 40)

Language: The fact that Princess and Lorna are using similar language and completing each other's sentences highlights their closeness and also their being in a similar position in regard to Wendell. They are both his daughters, and here he is showing that neither of them can rely on him.

> WENDELL *enters full of cheer – a bundle of money in his hands. He stands with his back to* PRINCESS *and* LORNA. *He carefully folds the bundle, and puts it into his pocket – leaving a single note out.* (page 41)

Wendell hiding his winnings from the girls suggests that he wants to keep the money to himself. This small deception suggests that deceit comes quite naturally to Wendell, and may also suggest to the audience that Mavis is right not to allow Wendell back into the family home. Wendell tells the girls that he'll take them for a treat after he has spoken to one more man, and he leaves them alone again, reinforcing his unreliability.

The girls wait and chat amicably. Princess asks Lorna about Liverpool and tells Lorna about Weston-Super-Mare.

> PRINCESS. [...] You will see it really is magic. It has a beach and sand. Golden sand. And they don't have just ice cream, Margot says they have *choc ices*. And donkeys. And everyone there is beautiful that is why they have the pageant there. (page 42)

Language: When Princess describes Weston she uses heightened language. The sand is elevated by the use of the adjective 'golden' and Princess's use of the pronoun 'everyone' shows how much she associates Weston with her pageant dreams.

Princess's description of Weston is a contrast to the area where the girls are waiting for Wendell. Weston-Super-Mare was a popular leisure and holiday destination in the 1960s, a desirable location for families to spend time together, whereas Princess and Lorna have been taken to the docks by their father, which was an extremely industrialised environment.

> PRINCESS. Where is your mummy Lorna?
>
> LORNA. Having a rest Daddy said. (page 42)

Structure: When Princess questions Lorna about her mum she is told that she is 'having a rest'. Princess readily accepts this explanation but it leaves the audience wondering about Lorna's mum. The **subtext** of 'having a rest' suggests that perhaps Lorna's mum is unwell.

It is only three days since Lorna arrived, but Princess is already feeling connected to her.

When Junior arrives with Leon, the girls run to Junior and he hugs them both, showing the affection Lorna and Junior now have for each other. Junior asks Leon to take the girls home and wait for Wendell. When Wendell returns, he is pleased to see Junior, but Junior is angry. Wendell's first instinct is to check the girls are okay, but he can't see any issue with leaving them unattended. There is a sense of **irony** here: although Junior is the child, his behaviour towards Princess and Lorna is more responsible than that of Wendell, the adult.

> WENDELL *reaches out and grabs* WENDELL JUNIOR*'s arm –*
>
> WENDELL JUNIOR *jerks away from* WENDELL*'s grasp – stands up –* [...]
>
> *Quicker than imaginable,* WENDELL JUNIOR *grabs* WENDELL *by the neck, they struggle with each other until* WENDELL *has* WENDELL JUNIOR *pinned up against the wall –*
>
> WENDELL JUNIOR *doesn't resist –* (pages 45–46)

Form: There are examples in this scene of Wendell trying to make physical contact with Junior but Junior not accepting the contact. When physical contact happens, it is aggressive. The image of Junior rejecting Wendell's affection, followed by a quite physical altercation, is quite a shocking image between father and son.

Wendell recognises where Junior's anger comes from, and we sense some paternal feelings when he tells Junior that he is proud of him. The scene ends with Wendell telling Junior that he is back for good and that he wants to make Junior proud by making some money.

> WENDELL. [...] De Hustler back!
>
> WENDELL *fixes the hat on his head and moves to leave –*
>
> An' when mi start making big big money yuh soon be telling everybody in dis Bristol who yuh daddy be. Yuh be proud son. [...]
>
> WENDELL JUNIOR *slumps back down on the crate – and cries hard hot tears –* (page 47)

Form: Wendell fixing his hat seems like a casual almost cocky gesture which really contrasts with Junior's physicality. Wendell is feeling buoyant in this moment while Junior feels very deflated.

Wendell is excited and uses the noun '**Hustler**' with a sense of pride and confidence, which contrasts to the meaning of the word. Wendell here is glorifying the fact that he is able to successfully cheat at cards and gain money from other players.

Keyword: **Hustler** – a person skilled at aggressive selling or illegal dealings. Somebody who gains money from another person using deceit.

What does it suggest about Wendell that this is something that he feels his son should respect him for?

Act One, Scene Seven

Margot is looking after Princess and Lorna when a shivering Wendell enters. He is quite a different figure from the proud and cocky 'hustler' at the end of the last scene. Wendell makes a rather pathetic figure and we sense that the time that has passed has not been easy for him.

Theme: **Family –** the girls greet Wendell enthusiastically, showing that despite his absence, Princess has accepted Wendell as her father.

66 PRINCESS *and* LORNA. Daddy!

> *Both girls run to throw their arms around* WENDELL – (page 47)

We learn in this scene that Margot and Mavis look after each other, and it is implied that Mavis is held in high regard and this gives Margot certain credentials in the community. Margot raises the point here that Wendell has not and is not providing for his family.

Theme: **Race and prejudice –** Wendell's experience of not being able to get a job was not uncommon. Many Black people were overlooked for jobs that they were easily qualified for.

66 MARGOT. [...] You look after *your* family. You go out. You get a decent job /

WENDELL. Fram where? [...]

> If rumours true den dem nuh wan' us far any work! (pages 48–49)

> *Context:* To read more about how Black people were treated in the jobs market in the UK at this time, turn to page 18.

When Junior enters with Leon he stares at Wendell, and Leon feels awkward in the tense atmosphere. Margot tries to lighten the mood and Leon's attempt at flirting with her adds to this lifting of tension, but Wendell warns Margot when she is suggestive:

Theme: **Race and prejudice –** Junior's separation between being a man and being a Black man highlights the different experience that he is having as a young Black man.

66 MARGOT. [...] Even though I wouldn't mind the caretaker taking advantage once in a while /

WENDELL. Watch yuh words, dem juss boys. [...]

JUNIOR. I'm not a boy! You think I don't know about the world. About what it means to be a man... a Black man / (page 50)

Life for Junior is different to life for Wendell. Junior was born in England and wants a creative career as a photographer. This scene contains the first mention of the colour bar (on page 51), and Wendell, Leon and Junior are united in their interest in the protests.

As with all of their interactions so far, Junior is angry at Wendell. Junior feels that Wendell is treating him like a child but also highlights that he feels a strong difference between being a man and being a Black man. Junior's comment here shows that he feels his father only views him as a child and that society only views him in terms of the colour of his skin.

Junior and Leon's friendship is strong. They spend a lot of time together and there is trust between them, shown earlier when Junior asks Leon to take the girls home from the docks. Leon is also honest with Junior when he feels that he is going too far with Wendell.

66 LEON. [...] Cool it Junior.

> You dig? [...]

> He's your daddy. He deserves a little...

> Stay cool.

> Yeah? (page 53)

Language: Leon's use of language includes slang words from the 1960s, e.g. 'dig' meaning 'understand'. This use of British slang contrasts with Wendell's use of Jamaican patois.

Despite his anger, Junior does stay to listen to Wendell as he tries to explain some of the difficulties that he has faced since he came to England – especially when looking for work:

66 WENDELL. [...] Even now everywhere mi go looking far work, dem look at mi so so...
> An' grown men wit ar family scratching around far even ar paper round.
> Wha' kinda world?!
> Wha' kinda world put men in de same sentence as dogs? (page 54)

> *Context:* Turn to page 19 to learn about the signs Wendell is referring to here, reading 'No Blacks, No Dogs, No Irish'.

Wendell tells Junior about Lorna's mother and her mental health issues leading to her being hospitalised. Wendell reveals that when Lorna was born he felt that he couldn't leave another child after what he had done to Mavis, Junior and Princess, but that his relationship with Lorna's mother broke down because of her health, and her illness led her to say things that were dangerous for Wendell.

Language: Wendell uses the **metaphor** 'strange fruit' to suggest that he felt scared that he would be hanging from a rope.

Keyword: A **metaphor** is a form of imagery where a thing is described indirectly by referring to something it resembles, without using 'like'.

Keyword: **Lynching** is when a mob illegally carry out the execution of someone accused of a crime, without giving them a trial.

66 WENDELL. [...] Har heart good, but har mind trouble beyon' help.
After she done screaming de street down 'bout de black devil who come an' possess her.
Rape har. [...]

People start writing all sort of nonsense 'pon mi door.
On de house.
Windows break every day till one day mi come back to find ar rope hanging fram de tree outside de house.
An' I never plan to be nuh strange fruit. (page 55)

Context: 'Strange Fruit' was the title of a 1937 poem by Abel Meeropol under the pseudonym Lewis Allen. It was recorded as a song by Billie Holiday in 1939. It was written in protest to the **lynching** of Black Americans in the American South, and 'strange fruit' refers to the bodies hanging from the trees.

When the audience hears these comments from Wendell, does this change our attitude towards him? Does it allow us to feel sympathy towards him?

Wendell still hasn't found a place to stay, and Princess suggests that if Wendell shared a room with Junior, Lorna wouldn't cry at night. With some rules in place, Mavis agrees, giving Wendell a clear list of instructions to abide by. Mavis's giving in to Princess's request puts Wendell in a good mood, and he tries to lighten the mood with Mavis – but she is unmoving:

66 WENDELL. Mi know de temptation dat come over woman
when mi inna small vest.

MAVIS *gives him the coldest stare imaginable* – [...]

WENDELL *sits back down at the table and smiles wryly to
himself* – (page 58)

Language: During Mavis's list of rules, Wendell's only response is to
smile to himself. The **adverb** 'wryly' means in a way that expresses
dry, especially mocking humour, suggesting that Wendell has got
exactly what he wanted.

In contrast to his gaining sympathy from the audience earlier in
the scene when he describes the fear of lynching, does
Wendell's behaviour and Odimba's use of 'wryly' here once
again make us distrust him?

Form: Wendell's
position at the table
is **symbolic**, and
links to the idiom
'getting your feet
under the table' –
meaning to establish
yourself firmly in a
new situation.

Keyword: An **adverb**
is a describing word
for a verb.

Act Two, Scene One

At the start of this act, Princess and Lorna arrive home from school.
Lorna being enrolled in school with Princess gives us the
impression that life is somewhat settled.

66 PRINCESS *has her head down.*
*She runs to the sofa and throws herself across it sobbing
loudly.*

MAVIS. What happen *today*?
That teacher saying meanness to you again?
Those teachers need to realise they can't keep putting my
children on some dunce table. (page 59)

Mavis's reaction shows us that Princess is usually badly treated at
school.

Context: To read more about how immigrant children were treated
at school turn to page 19.

The **subtext** of the scene suggests that Princess is already badly treated by the teacher so it would not be surprising if she was badly treated by her classmates too.

As Lorna has only just joined the school it is unlikely that she has made strong friendships. The suggestion is that it is her being more like the other girls that has got her the invitation, and Princess being Black that has prevented her getting one. Lorna's revelation that Barbara 'can't' invite Princess implies that this is Barbara's parents' decision.

The separation between Lorna and Princess is also emphasised by Lorna revealing that: 'Barbara says that I can even wear my hair like hers if I like' (page 61) which is something that perhaps Princess can't do because of the texture of her hair.

Lorna does not understand why she can't go to the party without Princess and it seems that with his warning for Mavis not to question Lorna, Wendell is trying to shield her from the knowledge that people are racist.

Theme: **Race and prejudice** – Mavis's comment suggests that Lorna has no understanding of the underlying issues here. Wendell's response hints that Lorna's life in Liverpool is in a white area where these racial issues aren't tackled.

66 LORNA *stomps off in a huff – exits.*

Beat.

MAVIS. You don't think to educate that girl?

She is going to learn the hard way one day.

WENDELL. Where she come fram dese things nuh spoken 'bout Mavis / (page 62)

Racial passing

Historically, 'racial passing' was when a person from one racial group was perceived or accepted as part of another. Mixed-race people often chose to 'pass' because they were then treated more favourably and were able to escape many forms of racism. In the context of the play, can Lorna 'pass' for white and therefore be accepted by the children at school in a way that Princess can't?

66 WENDELL. [...] Remember how it used to be?
    Remember how wi used to laugh. Like children ourselves.
    Yuh sitting on mi knee.
    Drinking rum.
    Yuh face all bright...
    Still is...

    Yuh lips always juss de right shade of pretty.
    An' yuh legs Mavis... [...]

MAVIS. You want to talk about my legs?
    What about these hands that been doing the work of two
    people? [...]

    Wendell how you think we have food? When mi nuh here
    sewing till my fingers turn blue, mi out there asking every
    woman if she need a new dress. Then I come back and sew
    them ones too! (pages 62–63)

> *Language:* Wendell tries to sweet-talk Mavis, reminding her of how things used to be between them. We see a contrast between them. Wendell is focusing on the past ('Remember...') while Mavis is fixed on the present ('mi nuh here sewing... mi out there asking'). Wendell's references to Mavis's body use positive words about how she looks, Mavis focuses on how hard her body has to work to provide.

Mavis is surprised when Wendell grabs and spins her, but she allows it and laughs, letting him pull her close. This is the first time we have seen Mavis relaxed around Wendell and allowing physical contact. Her acceptance of his touch implies that she is warming to him. Mavis's relaxation when they spin changes abruptly when Junior enters, suggesting that the entrance of Junior has reminded her of the reality of the situation.

> Does Mavis feel guilty for allowing Wendell to break down the barriers that she has put up to protect herself and her family?

Wendell's gift of the Tully flash for Junior's camera is the first example of Wendell attempting to connect with his son. Wendell has taken a genuine interest in Junior's life and interests, and brought home something that he really wants. The feeling of connection continues when Junior tells them that the bus boycott has been announced and Wendell wants to support, united with Junior.

Act Two, Scene Two

The opening of this scene exactly mirrors the opening of the play.

> *The cupboard room explodes into a world of pageantry –*
> *seems less alive... still there... but somehow subdued.*
> (page 66)

The cupboard can be seen to symbolise escapism for Princess: in there she can imagine herself as a beauty queen. That it is now '*less alive*' reflects the reality of her life and the racism that she is experiencing, which makes her realise that she is not what a conventional and white beauty pageant at Weston-Super-Mare would see as beautiful.

> PRINCESS. [...] I want to be the prettiest girl in the whole of Weston-Super-Mare and Bristol...
>
> But everyone in school says I can't be...
>
> PRINCESS *picks up a small round mirror –*
> *She stares at her reflection in it –*
>
> Because...
>
> PRINCESS *touches her lips –*
>
> And my hair? And my skin is...
>
> *Beat.*
>
> Maybe I don't want to look like everyone else...
> (pages 66–67)

Form: The beauty contest is Princess's happy place and so the change in this part of her life suggests a change in Princess.

Theme: **Beauty standards** – the children at Princess's school would have a clear idea about what beauty queens should look like according to beauty standards of the time, and Princess would not have fitted into this idea.

Language: Princess performs an acceptance speech that mirrors Act One, except that this time it focuses on what her peers are saying at school. This change in Princess feels like a huge shift and she is hesitant and uncertain, but we also see her trying to be positive.

This idea of a definite beauty aesthetic hasn't changed very much. What comments can you make about the lack of change in beauty standards for women since the 1960s?

Mavis returns laughing and a bit tipsy with Margot and Wendell. They have enjoyed a night out at a club where people from all backgrounds were welcome. Mavis thought the club was a 'place of sin', but she has enjoyed dancing with 'her people'. Margot admires Mavis's dance moves and Mavis unsuccessfully tries to teach Margot how to whine.

Whining is a form of Caribbean dance where dancers thrust or rotate their hips and pelvis in a rhythmic pattern. It is seen as a natural way to dance to a calypso or soca rhythm.

66 WENDELL. De club welcome everybody for sure.

> Only inna Bristol yuh see so many different different people in same place. (page 68)

The tension between Wendell and Margot rises in this scene:

66 WENDELL. [...] No place safe fram de white woman *attempts*. [...]

MARGOT. I am a very friendly person if you must know.

WENDELL. Especially with de Black man it seem / [...]

MARGOT. Well you clearly not shy with the white woman... (pages 68–69)

Theme: **Race and prejudice** – a multicultural venue was very unusual at the time and Black people were often turned away and refused service. In Bristol, The Bamboo Club was a safe and welcoming place for people of any race to meet, drink and dance together without prejudice.

Keyword:
Euphemism –
an indirect word or expression that is substituted for one which is considered rude or embarrassing.

Language: Wendell objects to Margot's behaviour in the club. He uses 'attempts' as a **euphemism** for Margot's sexual advances. His reference to Margot as 'de white woman' puts a barrier between them and makes Margot seem different.

Wendell objects to Margot being 'friendly'; his double standards are interesting, even hypocritical, as Margot points out in reference to Lorna's mother.

When the trio begin to discuss the bus boycott, we see a difference of opinions arise. Margot sees the boycott as 'silly' and thinks Mavis and Wendell should 'accept how things are'. Wendell challenges these opinions and we see that he is ready to stand up and fight for equality. Margot is trying to be positive towards Wendell but her choice of language, including 'your lot' and 'foreigners', alienates Wendell and feeds into the idea of 'them and us'. Margot's suggestion that people should find other jobs 'better suited to them' (page 73) highlights the ignorance of the time that immigrants could only do menial, low-paid jobs.

66 WENDELL. Mi see it all before Margot.
  Yuh nuffin special.
  As stale as de week's bread.
  Happy to be seen wit ar nigger.
  Even do de missionary ting for ar nigger but when it come down to it Margot, yuh always stand by yuh own. (page 74)

Keyword:
Pejorative – a word expressing contempt or disapproval. This particular word should never be used today.

Language: Wendell's use of a highly offensive term suggests that he sees Margot as racist and accepting of prejudices, such as using **pejorative** language. The fact that Margot does not react to Wendell's use of language also indicates how commonly this term was used in reference to Black people at the time.

Wendell's response that Margot will be seen with Mavis and help her but in the end will not support her against discrimination shows that he does not see Margot as the ally that she claims she is.

Wendell talks to Mavis passionately about the boycott, and this passion, alongside the night out, is a turning point in their relationship. Mavis's pride in Wendell shows her change of feeling, and her use of "'usband' (page 75) is significant. This leads Mavis to accept Wendell's flirtation, and their relationship begins again here.

> " PRINCESS *closes the door to the cupboard again –*
> *She sits with her back firmly against the door –*
> *Sighs heavily –* (page 76)

Princess listening and watching through a crack in the door suggests that the two worlds are now not so separate. Princess sitting against the door and sighing perhaps suggests that Princess does not want this insight into the adult world. It also separates the audience from Wendell and Mavis and what is happening on their side of the door.

Form: Princess has listened to the whole exchange between the adults. Again, the use of a door to separate the adult and child world in this moment is relevant.

Act Two, Scene Three

By now, the bus boycott is well underway. The scene opens with Mavis, Wendell, Princess and Lorna in an image of domestic contentment, with Wendell and Mavis discussing the reactions to the boycott.

Keyword: A **simile** is a form of imagery where something is described as resembling something else. It is usually signalled with the word 'like' or 'as'.

> " LORNA. Daddy can I go and see Margot? [...]
>
>   I want to say thank you for my doll.
>   She gave it to me yesterday.
>   Because my hair is as pretty as a doll's she said / [...]
>
>   PRINCESS. Is my hair pretty too Mummy?
>
>   LORNA. She said she's going to do them into ringlets for me.
>   Nice like t' other girls at school. (page 77–78)

How has symbolism been used before to separate Princess and make her feel like an outsider?

Language: Lorna's use of the **simile** to describe her hair, and the mention of the other girls, places Princess on the outside again. Princess's question is not answered, and this adds to her feeling of isolation.

Junior enters bleeding and hurt, after he and his friends were attacked on their way home from the protest march. His comments on the march show solidarity across the community but the attack on Junior and his friends shows the opposite side of people's feelings. Wendell wants to deal with the situation with force, and his words as he exits show his desire to protect his son. His anger could also be seen as his own personal response to the racism that he has experienced, and his frustration and anger because of this. Princess is anxious about the violence and looks to Lorna for comfort.

> **Language:** Lorna pulls away from Princess physically but also metaphorically with her words. This is another example of Princess experiencing separation and can be linked to the earlier comments in the scene regarding Lorna's hair.

66

PRINCESS *attempts to take* LORNA's *hand* –

LORNA *pulls away hard* –

LORNA. I won't get beat up.

PRINCESS. But we're sisters /

LORNA. I'm not Black like you.
I'm only half.
Half of everything.
Half-sister.
Half-caste.
Everyone says so.

MAVIS *looks up* –

I don't want a sister.
I want my mum.
I want to go home!

MAVIS *runs to* PRINCESS *who is standing in the middle of the room. Holds her tighter than she's ever held her before.*
(page 80)

> **Form:** Lorna ends the scene wanting to separate herself from Princess. The combination of Lorna's comments and her anxiety over Junior makes Mavis very protective of Princess, and she holds her close in an attempt to shield her. This could also be linked to Wendell's desire to protect Junior earlier in the scene from the white boys who attacked him.

Lorna's reference to herself as 'half-caste' highlights how language was used differently in the 1960s, as the term 'half-caste' is now considered an offensive way to describe someone who is mixed race. This labelling of herself also suggests that Lorna has become much more aware of her race and how race is seen and experienced in her environment, both within her family and her community.

Act Two, Scene Four

In this scene we see the divide between Margot and Mavis widen.

> ❝❝ MARGOT. There's a lot of bad feeling at the moment. If Wendell hadn't brought all this talk /
>
> MAVIS. People looking at me a bit stranger in those houses these days. I see something different in them eyes. (page 81)

> *Theme:* **Race and prejudice** – Margot blames Wendell and 'those *others*' for what is happening, as if he and Mavis are not connected, and we see that Mavis has started to feel alienated. Mavis and Margot's friendship is based on their mutual liking and respect for each other, but Margot is unable to see Mavis and the James family's struggles as a Black family.

Mavis tells Margot about their arrival in England and how Wendell, a second lieutenant in the army in Jamaica, had to work as a junior clerk when he came to England and was made to feel invisible.

> *Context:* Turn to page 18 to read about the treatment of migrants seeking work in the UK in this period.

Mavis tells Margot about how Wendell changed after he gave up his job and describes how she tried to keep control. Mavis's lack of power over Wendell's choices perhaps explains why she is so disciplined with the children.

66 MAVIS. [...] I nagged. I controlled. I made sure he didn't make a move without me knowing. [...]

But The Hustler was back. Lying. Scheming...

And when he left. Disappeared just like that one night. I cry of course! Cry like I never cry before. (page 84)

Act Two, Scene Five

Form: Junior cleaning his camera with such care highlights its importance to him. In contrast to Junior's deep interest in his task, Princess has further retreated into herself.

66 WENDELL JUNIOR *is sitting at the kitchen table in front of a dismantled camera, meticulously cleaning it.*

PRINCESS *lies on the sofa – a blanket almost covering her entire head and face.*

Wendell views himself as the man of the house again and finds Junior's challenges about getting a job as well as joining the bus boycott frustrating. Junior points out that Mavis works every day which suggests that Wendell could also do both, but chooses not to. Junior offers Wendell money to leave; Wendell struggles with this as he feels the strength of Junior's feelings. Junior's response shows us how much he loves Mavis and Princess, and that he will do anything to protect them.

66 WENDELL JUNIOR. I remember hearing her crying [...] It was like some kind of sad song [...] I thought it was never going to stop. But it did. One day it did. That one day Princess was walking around the kitchen with a pan on her head, hitting it with a stick and dancing to her own music like she didn't know it was her making it [...] Mummy laughed [...] It was like a new song being played for the first time. (page 87)

Language: Junior uses music as a **metaphor** to describe Mavis's sadness and her recovery after Wendell left. Junior also uses music when he refers to Princess. Here his reference is literal as Princess is making music by banging a stick on a pan, but also metaphorical because 'dancing to her own music' also suggests that Princess is doing things her own way.

Junior leaves and Wendell considers the bag of money before leaving. During this scene Princess has been lying motionless on the sofa under a blanket. As soon as Wendell has gone Princess immediately sits up, objecting to Wendell referring to her and Lorna as Junior's 'baby sisters'.

> " PRINCESS *moves to a drawer – opens it and takes out a pair of tailor's scissors – too big for her small hands. She walks to her cupboard – but now her world of pageantry doesn't come alive. Instead we see it for just what it is. A dark room, strewn with mop and bucket, brooms and other rejected items from the household.* […]
>
> PRINCESS *stands for a beat, feeling more alone than ever. She picks up costumes/dresses from her box and starts to cut them up. She kicks and screams – and destroys her cupboard world.* (page 88)

Form: The image of Princess taking scissors that are too big for her hands makes her seem even more childlike. Princess's cupboard world does not come alive this time, and this signifies a huge change in her.

Language: It seems significant that as Princess feels at her lowest, the cupboard room is revealed to be the place for 'rejected items' from the household – echoing how Princess feels about herself.

Theme: **Growing up** – the cupboard world has been a safe space for Princess and a place of joy and imagination. Her destruction of it is suggestive of her being forced to grow up into a world that is cruel and does not accept her.

In this scene, are both Junior and Princess forced to grow up due to the harsh realities of life? What does Junior realise about his father? What does Princess realise about Weston-Super-Mare beauty pageants, symbolised by the cupboard?

Act Three, Scene One

Junior and Leon find Mavis frantic that Princess is missing. Mavis has found Princess's hair in the waste bin. This is significant because the 'perfect' hair of the beauty queens was important to Princess. It's also notable that Princess has used Mavis's tailor's scissors to cut her hair. Hair also plays a part in dividing Princess and Lorna; Lorna is able to have her hair like the girls at school and Princess is not.

Junior admits to Mavis that he told Wendell to leave.

> WENDELL JUNIOR. [...] I told him to go. I gave him all my savings and I told him to go.
>
> MAVIS. What you say? Why would you do such a thing? [...]
>
> WENDELL JUNIOR. But he's showed his true colours now hasn't he?
>
> LEON. Junior! Mrs James, Junior doesn't mean it. (page 90)

Language: There is a clear contrast between how Leon and Junior view Wendell. Junior assumes that Wendell has taken the money, but Leon thinks he is absent because he is collecting signatures for the petition. Here we see how the boys' experiences with their fathers have shaped their reactions, with Leon only seeing the good in Wendell and Junior assuming the worst.

Structure: As the play has continued the audience has seen more outward affection from Mavis towards Princess. At the end of Act Two, Scene Three, Mavis held Princess *'tighter than she's ever held her before'*.

> MAVIS. We have to find your sister. I can't lose my Princess. My joy. (page 90)

Is Mavis more emphatic in showing affection to her children as she realises how important they are to her?

Act Three, Scene Two

Princess has destroyed her safe place and we see here that she views Margot's flat as somewhere else she can go when she is in need. Margot's reaction to Princess when she is upset shows us that she cares deeply for her. Margot's offer for Princess to wear a ball gown to bed also highlights Margot's understanding of what is important to Princess. Margot lets Princess stay but also knows how frantic Mavis will be, and leaves to let her know that Princess is safe.

> PRINCESS. They say mean things to me. They only like Lorna now.

They tell me to go away.
Go back to where I came from.

What does that mean? (page 92)

Theme: **Race and prejudice** – Princess's experience at school was common. Many Black children were isolated by their peers, and being told to go 'back to where they came from' was frequent.

For immigrant children, being told to return to the Caribbean would have been hurtful, but it is clearly confusing for Princess as she was born in England. Princess has as much right to be in England as any of her friends but this isn't recognised because of the colour of her skin.

Both Princess and Margot have lost their hair in this scene. Princess has cut hers as she sees it as one of the reasons that she is not accepted by Lorna and the other children at school, so here the audience can see Princess as losing part of her identity. For Margot on the other hand, her wig allows her to be something that she isn't, as her real hair hangs '*limp and lacklustre*' – Margot uses the wig to create an identity for herself. Hair is thus an important **symbol** in the play.

Act Three, Scene Three

Margot brings Princess home and there is relief that she is safe. Wendell is absent from this scene and there is the suggestion that once again he has left the family, and that this time he has also left Lorna. Junior has been hanging up his photos and Margot admires them. Princess is happy to see an image of herself in her sash and crown, and Lorna smiles as Junior points out a photo called 'My Other Sister'.

Keyword: A **noun** is the type of word used for a person, place or thing.

66 MARGOT. [...] I just wants you to be happy... remember that. You know where I am if you need me. [...]

MAVIS. Thank you for bringing Princess back home safe to me. And you're always welcome here. Any time. Girls say bye to your Auntie Margot. (pages 96–97)

Language: All is forgiven between Mavis and Margot. The use of the noun 'Auntie' reinforces the chosen family connection between them. Margot's tears highlight her emotional connection to the family and her desire to be a part of it.

Form: Junior holding both girls close shows that Lorna is now part of the family unit and Junior feels as protective of her as he does of Princess.

Act Three, Scene Four

When Wendell staggers in after not being home for two days, Mavis asks him to leave. This time the children do not hide behind the bedroom door but come straight into the room.

66 WENDELL JUNIOR *holds his sisters close* – (page 98)

Junior believes that Wendell took his money, and he is angry and upset that he has returned.

66 WENDELL JUNIOR. You're the worst father any family can ask for.

WENDELL JUNIOR *bursts into full tears* –

WENDELL *grips* WENDELL JUNIOR*'s arm hard* – [...]

MAVIS. You don't touch *my* son. (pages 98–99)

Keywords: **Emphasis** is indicated using italics or bold fonts in written text. It is when the speaker or writer wants to highlight something important.
Possessive pronouns are words that refer to things that belong to people, such as 'my', 'your' and 'their'.

Language and structure: Mavis's **emphasis** of the **possessive pronoun** 'my' shows how she has distanced herself from her relationship with Wendell. She has returned to being a solo parent.

Keyword: **Contrast**, which highlights a point of difference, is often used to emphasize ideas in literature.

Things are heated in the family when Wendell reveals that it looks like the bus company might back down from the colour bar. He is emotional and energised by the news, and the excitement of the likely victory seems to calm the tension. Wendell wants to talk privately to Mavis and she sends the children to their room. Princess objects and Mavis's hard stare reminds us of Act One, Scene Two, when Mavis slapped Princess. The children are sent to the bedroom to allow the adults to talk. Wendell pulls out a ring and proposes to Mavis. Although she tells him 'what you done to us cannot be easily forgiven' (page 102), she doesn't refuse.

66 MAVIS. [...] Mi 'ave dreams too Wendell. Small quiet dreams but dem still alive in 'ere...

And every day, mawning and night mi fall on my knees and pray that dis country Hingland truly see de possibilities of our children... (page 102)

Understanding patois
Hingland = England

Language: We see how Mavis is changing her thoughts about her future with Wendell. Her use of the pronoun 'our' directly **contrasts** with her use of 'my' earlier in the scene and shows that she is willing to let Wendell in.

In Mavis's words to Wendell, she lays out what family means to her and what he must help her provide for the children. Mavis wants Wendell to know all of Princess's dreams and understand that they are important. It's also important to Mavis that Wendell can teach Junior how to be a good man.

Act Three, Scene Five

66   LORNA *enters.*

She is dressed elaborately in a dress from MARGOT's — (page 103)

Form: This mirrors Princess's style and suggests that the gap that had formed between them has closed. This is also shown with Wendell and Junior being dressed smartly.

66 PRINCESS. I don't feel it any more Mummy. I don't think I can be pretty again. Ever. Now my hair is like this and... [...]

MAVIS. [...] Us... girls and women with our skin dark as the night, every shade of brown, glowing like fresh-made caramel, or legs spindly like a spider, we are everything that is beautiful on this earth.
And *you*... you the prettiest of them all because you are *my* girl. [...]

So you take that pretty and you never let anyone tell you what or who you can be.

You free to be *anything*.
That freedom.
You never forget you have that freedom Princess.
(pages 104–5)

> *Language:* Princess is struggling with how she feels about herself, especially her short hair. Mavis's use of positive, appealing language builds her up, and her expression of love ties her and Princess together with Princess's ideals of beauty. Mavis's reference to 'freedom' refers to Princess's opportunities in life, but also the struggle that Black people have endured to be 'free' and, historically, to rise from being enslaved.

Princess dances and we feel like she has returned to herself, and the world of fantasy that previously she experienced in the cupboard is now a part of her life outside of it. This suggests that now it can be a reality for Princess.

> 66   WENDELL *enters.*
> *He is looking clean, smart and sober. He holds out his hand*
> *for* MAVIS –
> MAVIS *takes his hand –*
> *They dance – together – joyfully –* (page 106)

> *Form:* Throughout the play, dance has been used as a **symbol** to signify happy times: Princess enjoys her dances; Wendell, Mavis and Margot enjoy a night out dancing; Mavis trying to teach Margot to whine reminds her of home; and Mavis and Wendell dance when they begin to reconnect.

Junior takes a photo of the family before they leave. It is significant that Junior takes this photo as we understand that he has started to accept Wendell. The ending of the colour bar coincides with the feeling that the family has come together. We feel positive for the future of the James family as this example of discrimination has ended and they feel connected.

Act Three, Scene Six

Wendell and Princess are playing together.

> WENDELL *appears – he is wearing make-up and has a skirt over his trousers – a shawl around his shoulders, and a makeshift headdress/turban –*
>
> PRINCESS *claps excitedly.* (page 107)

Theme: **Parenting** – Wendell agreeing to dress up as woman and join Princess's game shows a huge shift in the family dynamic.

By entering her world, Wendell is showing Princess that her dreams are important, which links to Mavis's request in Act Three, Scene Four when she tells Wendell that Princess needs Wendell to know all of her dreams because they are important. By agreeing to dress up in women's clothes, Wendell overcomes both his discomfort and traditional masculine stereotypes to do something just for Princess.

Wendell feels uncomfortable initially: 'Yuh better not tell anybody 'bout dis. Yuh hear?' (page 107), but as he enters her cupboard world he sees and feels the magic that Princess has created, and he is speechless. Princess is crowned as the winner of the pageant and the '*room explodes into a world of pageantry*' again (page 109). This return to the pageant feels as if Princess has returned to where she should be. The use of the iconic Union Jack suggests that Princess's British nationality plays a part in her ultimate happiness.

> [...] *scenes of people jumping into a swimming pool, Union Jacks, music and fireworks – fill the room – and as* PRINCESS *watches her world come to life, for the first time she imagines a pageant where all the beauty queens look like her.*
>
> [...] *a line of the most beautiful Black women of all sizes and nations appear before her.* (page 109)

Form: As the beauty queens gather around Princess it feels like she really is part of her dreams, and Wendell being by her side also reinforces his commitment to her.

Structure: The cyclical nature of the play, which begins and ends in Princess's cupboard, highlights the significance of her dreams. At the end of the play, when Princess is joined by her father, this highlights that he has been allowed into the secret world of her imagination and aspirations. This could show that he has been accepted and is now trusted by Princess. Princess's willingness to share her dreams could also suggest that she has confidence in achieving them.

How to write about the play: sample paragraphs

Act One

Writing about the introduction of Wendell to the play

[*Point*] Wendell is introduced to the play at the end of the first scene via Odimba's use of the **stage direction [*Evidence*]** 'a loud knock at the door'. In reaction, Mavis 'shuts the door quickly'. **[*Analysis*]** The **adverb** 'loud' highlights the intrusive nature of Wendell's desire to come into the family's home, and Mavis's shutting the door before any conversation takes place reveals her strong desire for him not to enter.[1] This is further reinforced in Scene Two where the audience see Mavis's reaction to the entrance of Wendell to the family home.[2]

Writing about Mavis's relationship with her children

[*Point*] Mavis is presented as a mother who has strict expectations of both of her children, **[*Evidence*]** 'I am done waiting for an explanation as to what reason you might have for leaving this house', and it is clear that her threats, 'you better having a conversation with the leather of the belt' are taken seriously by her children: 'No! Mummy! Hold on a minute'.[1] **[*Analysis*]** Odimba's use of **exclamation marks** here highlight that Junior is truly concerned by his mother's threats.[2] Yet later in this scene the audience are clearly shown Mavis's love and concern for her children's wellbeing: 'I did read your list baby. I did. Every single word of it...'[3] The use of 'baby' highlights the maternal feelings of Mavis, and the **ellipsis** at the end of the sentence suggests that she feels guilt at being unable to buy Christmas presents for her children, something she finds it difficult to talk to her children about.

Sidebar notes:

1. Embed your quotations into your sentences, and then zoom in on individual words and phrases: use technical terms and explain why the playwright's choice is effective.

2. Comment on the structure of the play by making links to other moments.

---

1. Embed quotations that support your point.

2. In your analysis, zoom in on techniques such as punctuation.

3. Comment on the structure of the play by making links to other moments.

Keyword: **Ellipsis** is the literary term for the symbol '...'

Act Two

Writing about Princess and rejection

[**Point**] At the end of Act Two, Scene Three, the audience are shown Lorna's rejection of Princess, and her wish to emphasise the difference between them. [**Evidence**] Lorna's use of 'Half of everything/Half-sister/Half-caste' to describe herself is contrasted with 'Black' which she uses to define Princess.[1] [**Analysis**] The fact that she **repeats** 'half' suggests that she wishes to reinforce to Princess the difference between them.[2] Odimba further highlights this separation between the two sisters as 'Princess attempts to take Lorna's hand – / Lorna pulls away hard', the use of the **adverb** 'hard' emphasises Lorna's strong desire to separate herself from her sister[3] and the racism that Princess experiences.[4]

> 1. Make comparisons between quotations.

> 2. Zoom in on techniques such as repetition.

> 3. Use linguistic terminology to analyse the writer's choice of words.

> 4. Make links to the context you have studied for the play.

Writing about effects

[**Point**] At the end of Act Two, Scene Five, Princess destroys 'her world of pageantry' within the cupboard. [**Evidence**] This act can be seen to symbolise the fact that Princess wishes to be treated as a grown-up, which is reinforced by her comment 'I am not a baby!' just after the exit of her father. Another interpretation of Princess's destruction[1] is that the innocence of her magical world which now 'doesn't come alive'[2] mirrors the innocence that has been taken from her due to the return of Wendell and the racist attitudes that she is forced to experience.[3] [**Analysis**] Her anger and frustration is shown by Odimba: 'She picks up costumes/dresses from her box and starts to cut them up. She kicks and screams.' The **stage direction** that describes her as cutting up her 'costumes' and the manner in which she does this, 'kicks and screams', emphasises how her childish innocence is being taken from her.[4]

> 1. Offer counterpoints or alternative interpretations.

> 2. Embed quotations within your own sentences.

> 3. Make links to the context you have studied for the play.

> 4. Highlight techniques that are specific to the form of the text – drama.

Act Three

Writing about symbolism in the play

Keyword: A **verb** is a word that expresses an action.

[**Point**] Odimba uses the setting of Princess's cupboard at both the beginning and ending of the play to highlight how it is important **symbolically**. [**Evidence**] At the beginning it is described as 'explod(ing) into a world of pageantry', [**Analysis**] the use of the verb[1] 'explodes' highlights the intensity of this environment and shows how significant it is in the life and imagination of Princess.[2] This language is used again at the end of the play to reinforce that it has once again come alive for Princess.[3] At the end of the play Wendell joins Princess in the cupboard and 'gently places the crown on Princess's head', joining in with her imaginative games. Odimba's symbolic use of the cupboard shows that what was just a dream for Princess at the beginning of the play is made to seem more real by her being joined by her father. 'The crown' suggests that Wendell believes in his daughter, and her 'taking a bow', possibly to the audience, implies that she also is confident in herself as an individual.[4]

1. Use grammatical terminology to analyse the use of individual words.

2. Analyse the significance of the evidence you've presented.

3. Make links to other parts of the play to comment on structure and development.

4. Make reference to techniques that highlight the dramatic form of the text.

Comparing the characters of Princess and Margot

[**Point**] The similarities between the characters of Princess and Margot are reinforced at the beginning of Act Three, Scene Two. [**Evidence and Analysis**] Underneath her wig, Margot's hair is described as 'limp and lacklustre', she only takes this wig off when she is alone; this is the first time that the audience have seen the real Margot without her gaudy outfits, as she chooses to hide her real self in public.[1] Princess, who has been hiding in Margot's room, appears with her hair, 'cut short and uneven',[2] Princess has chosen to cut her own hair due to the racist reactions she has received to it.[3] This highlights that like Margot, Princess is also unhappy about her real self and takes action to change this.[4]

1. Demonstrate your understanding of structure (first time) and form (drama).

2. Embed quotations in your own sentences.

3. Make links to the context you have studied for the play.

4. Make links and comparisons in your analysis.

All photos are of the 2019 original production of *Princess & The Hustler* at Bristol Old Vic, directed by Dawn Walton, and show the following scenes in the play (page numbers refer to the Nick Hern Books edition of the text):

- *Photo 1*: **Act One, Scene One (*page 6*)**, Kudzai Sitima as Princess
- *Photo 2* (*right to left*): **Act One, Scene Five (*page 26*)**, Seun Shote as Wendell Senior, Emily Burnett as Lorna, Donna Berlin as Mavis, Fode Simbo as Wendell Junior and Kudzai Sitima as Princess
- *Photo 3*: **Act One, Scene Five (*page 33*)**, Jade Yourell as Margot and Seun Shote as Wendell Senior
- *Photo 4*: **Act One, Scene Seven (*page 53*)**, Romayne Andrews as Leon
- *Photo 5* (*right to left*): **Act Two, Scene Two (*page 68*)**, Seun Shote as Wendell Senior, Donna Berlin as Mavis and Jade Yourell as Margot
- *Photo 6*: **Act Two, Scene Three (page 80)**, Kudzai Sitima as Princess and Emily Burnett as Lorna

All photos by The Other Richard/ArenaPAL (www.arenapal.com)

Characters

Phyllis 'Princess' James

Princess's role in the play

Princess is the ten-year-old daughter of Mavis and Wendell James. She lives with her mother Mavis and her seventeen-year-old brother Junior. Princess likes to play make-believe in her cupboard room where she pretends that she is competing in a beauty contest. Princess is one of the two named characters in the play's title and much of what happens in the play centres on her. Princess immediately introduces herself as Phyllis Princess James but she is mainly referred to as Princess. The use of her nickname perhaps highlights her as the one of the children in the family as well as linking to her fantasy life: a princess is a young (beauty) queen.

Significant moments that involve Princess

- She opens the door to reveal Wendell 'The Hustler' James, but doesn't know who he is. *Theme:* **Family** – what does it say about the family situation that Princess does not know her father?

- She gets slapped across the face by Mavis when she complains about going to her room. *Context:* This feels extreme and Princess is shocked. What does this tell us about parenting and the use of physical force at the time?

- She is welcoming and friendly when Lorna gets pushed into the bedroom, and asks Lorna lots of questions. *Form:* In this moment the audience know who Lorna is but Princess and Junior do not. Why has Odimba done this?

- She thinks secrets are bad things that make people do bad things. (page 24)

- She wishes her eyes were green or blue. *Theme:* **Race** – what does Princess's wish tell us about how she sees herself in the world she lives in?

- She is happy to have Lorna as her sister and wants her to stay forever.

- She loves Margot and enjoys spending time with her. *Theme:* **Family** – Margot is Mavis's and the children's 'chosen' family. 'Like family I am. And they abouts the only family I've got so...' (page 73) What does this suggest about the importance of Margot as a friend to Princess?

- She suggests that Mavis should let Wendell move in and share a room with Junior. *Form:* Why might it be significant that it is Princess who makes this suggestion?

- She is upset when Lorna gets invited to Barbara's party and she does not.

- She watches Margot and Wendell argue and Mavis and Wendell flirting. Princess changes after this night. How would Princess feel about seeing the adults argue? What information does she find out from listening to their conversations?

- She is upset when Lorna rejects her and tells her that she doesn't want a sister. *Theme:* **Family** – in the light of Lorna's status at school why might Lorna's rejection be even more hurtful?

- She uses Mavis's tailor's scissors to cut her hair. *Form:* Why is it significant that Princess cuts her hair with Mavis's scissors?

- She runs away to Margot's.

- She dresses Wendell up as a beauty queen to join her game. *Context:* What does Wendell allowing this suggest about his feelings for Princess?

Why Princess is important to the play

Princess gives us a child's perspective throughout the play. The big battle of the bus boycott is happening outside the flat, while Princess is experiencing her own conflict in how she is being treated by other children at school.

> *Context:* Turn to page 19 to read about how the children of the Windrush generation were treated in the education system.

Princess is playful and optimistic, and when Lorna arrives she happily welcomes her firstly into the bedroom and then into the family. Even when Lorna says hurtful things to Princess, she does not retaliate and we get the impression that she is a kind and loving child. The essence of Princess's character and her place in the centre of the family highlight how important love and kindness is at the centre of a family unit.

How does Odimba present Princess?

Princess is a vibrant character full of energy and enthusiasm. She is happy and content in her small family unit, and we see that she is thoughtful and curious. The cupboard room, which represents Princess's internal self, '*explodes into a world of pageantry*' (page 6) which is exciting, and we see Christmas and the world through the eyes of a child. The James family don't have much, but they manage, and Princess is accepting of the lack of presents under the tree and grateful for what the family do have. When things change, Princess is adaptable and accepts Wendell and Lorna into her life. Princess has a lot to deal with at ten, and the tension that Wendell causes with Mavis, Junior and Margot, the three people that she loves the most, is unsettling for her. As the bus boycott ends and the adult relationships begin to heal, Princess is able to return to her energetic self.

Character development and symbolism

Princess's mood and the symbol of her imaginary cupboard room mirror the mood of the play in many ways.

As the play progresses and Wendell and Lorna arrive, unsettling the James family's way of life, Princess's cupboard room '*seems less alive… still there… but somehow subdued.*' (page 66)

By the end of Act Two when the tension is at its highest, especially between Wendell and Junior, '*her world of pageantry doesn't come alive.*' (page 88)

Princess destroys her costumes and we later learn that she cuts off her hair. Hair is something that Princess sees as really important in her beauty queen fantasy and her cutting hers off suggests that her fantasy is over.

Later in the play as the bus boycott comes to an end and the bus company back down, the family start to repair their relationships. Mavis helps to boost how Princess feels about herself, and there is positivity in the family dynamic.

At the end of the play, the cupboard room explodes into life again, but now it reflects Princess's fantasy – with women who look like her at the heart of it.

AO1 Writing about Princess

Point	Evidence
Princess looks up to Junior and his opinion matters to her.	'*Princess bursts into heartbreaking sobs*' (page 10) Princess's feelings are hurt by Junior's unkindness, even if it is a joke.
Princess is a sensitive child who understands that things are hard for Mavis.	'Who needs presents all wrapped up in the sparkly paper and a pink ribbon? Who needs any of it?' (page 12) Princess is trying to show Mavis that she understands their circumstances and she is okay with them.
Princess easily welcomes Lorna into her life.	'If you stay here forever I will be happier than the sky Lorna.' (page 43) Princess is a kind and loving child who adapts well to the changes in her life.
Children at school are unkind to Princess.	'They tell me to go away. Go back to where I came from. What does that mean?' (page 92) Princess is only ten, and finds it hard to deal with the unkindness of the children at school. She doesn't understand what their comments mean.
Princess becomes very low after she destroys her cupboard room and cuts her hair.	'I don't feel it any more Mummy. I don't think I can be pretty again. Ever. Now my hair is like this and / ' (page 104) Princess is the centre of her pageant fantasy, and how she looks is an important part of it. Her short hair makes her feel like she can't fulfil her role in the pageant and she finds this hard to deal with.

Example

[Point] Princess is a sensitive and thoughtful girl who wants to be like the other children at school. She has a difficult time at school because she is not accepted by pupils and teachers. **[Evidence]** When Princess comes in from school upset in Act Two, Scene One,[1] Mavis says 'What happen *today*? That teacher saying meanness to you again? Those teachers need to realise they can't keep putting my children on some dunce table.' **[Analysis]** Mavis's emphasis of the adverb 'today' suggests that the teacher's 'meanness' happens often. The reference to the 'dunce's table' highlights that at the time immigrant children and children whose parents were immigrants were often misjudged at school and considered to not be as clever as the British children.[2]

[Point] Lorna's acceptance by the children at school because she physically fits in with them isolates Princess further.[3] In Act Three, Scene Two, Princess says **[Evidence]** 'They say mean things to me. They only like Lorna now.' **[Analysis]** This shows that for Princess there is a direct link between how she is treated and her sister. This makes it even harder for Princess because she loves Lorna.

[Point] Princess also feels isolated because she doesn't fully understand what the children at school mean when **[Evidence]** 'They tell me to go away. Go back to where I came from. What does that mean?'[4] **[Analysis]** It is hard for Princess as a typical ten-year-old who just wants to makes friends and fit in, to be shunned by the other children for reasons that she doesn't understand. Princess was born in Britain so the common insult 'go back to where you came from' doesn't make sense to her. Immigrant children and the children of immigrants who were born in the UK were frequently insulted in this way.[5]

1. Put your quotations in context to show where they fit in to the play.

2. Go into detail about individual words and phrases in your quotation. Use technical terms and explain why the playwright's choice is effective.

3. The word 'further' shows how this point links to the point before as well as to the main topic of the essay.

4. Embed your quotations into your own sentences so that your writing flows.

5. Include context to demonstrate your understanding of the world of the play and its characters.

Mavis James

Mavis's role in the play

Mavis is the thirty-eight-year-old mother of Wendell Junior and Princess. She is a single parent because her husband Wendell left her when Princess was a baby. Mavis makes her living as a seamstress sewing curtains and clothes for people. Mavis is strongly protective of her children and is shocked when Wendell unexpectedly arrives on her doorstep with another child in tow. Mavis is angry at Wendell for disappearing from their lives, and she has struggled and had to work hard to provide for her children. Mavis is practical and realistic but she has been lonely and she has dreams for herself and her children.

Significant moments that involve Mavis

- The play opens with Mavis busy preparing the Christmas dinner. She threatens both Princess and Junior with the belt in this opening scene. *Theme:* **Parenting** – the use of physical threats and punishments was not unusual at the time.

- When there is a knock on the door, Mavis opens it and then shuts it quickly. *Form:* What does Mavis's reaction tell us about the visitor?

- She is shocked and unhappy to see Wendell. She tells the children to go to their room. When Princess argues Mavis slaps her across the face. *Form:* Although Mavis has threatened physical punishment she hasn't carried it out. How do we feel when Mavis takes the extreme action of slapping Princess's face?

- She is furious with Wendell and threatens him with a knife.

- She invites Wendell and Lorna in to join them for Christmas dinner. *Theme:* **Religion** – Mavis sees it as her Christian duty to help, especially when there is a child involved. What does this say about her character and the importance of her Christian values?

- She allows Princess to persuade her to let Wendell stay, but puts a list of firm rules in place. Why does she allow herself to be persuaded by Princess?

- She is protective of Princess when she comes in from school upset. *Theme:* **Race** – Mavis thinks Wendell should teach Lorna more about the issues that the family face.

- She is frustrated that Wendell wants to dwell on the past and how they first got together but he does not acknowledge how she has struggled to raise the children alone.

- She enjoys the night out dancing with Margot and Wendell. *Context:* Why is the club that they go to significant especially for Black people at the time?

- She starts to feel pride in Wendell as he starts to show interest and motivation in the bus boycott. This is a significant turning point in their relationship, emotionally and physically.

- She is very unsettled when Junior is beaten up and when Lorna rejects Princess. *Form:* Mavis 'holds Princess tighter than ever before'. How does this reaction indicate how Mavis is feeling?

- She struggles in her friendship with Margot because Margot cannot accept and understand the need for the boycott. *Theme:* **Race** – how far do Margot's opinions reflect popular opinions at the time?

- She is frantic when Princess is missing and grateful to Margot for taking care of her. This leads to their reconciliation.

- She feels hope for her children and their future and wants to give Wendell a chance to be part of that.

- When Princess is feeling uncertain about herself, Mavis builds her up with powerful imagery. *Language:* How does Mavis's use of language build Princess's confidence?

Why Mavis is important to the play

Mavis is the strength behind the James family. Princess starts the play bright, energetic and happy; a testament to the life she lives with Mavis. Junior is eager and ambitious, reflecting a life where he has been encouraged to pursue his dreams. In the background, Mavis has worked through her feelings of abandonment and works hard to provide a good life for her children.

When Wendell unexpectedly arrives it is a shock for Mavis, and her feelings of anger and resentment are immediately brought to the surface. She is fiercely protective of her children and the life that she has built for them.

Mavis is a mother, so when Lorna enters the story she can't help but want to protect her too, and despite her feelings about Wendell she welcomes Lorna and vows to take care of her.

Mavis is central to the play and the relationships revolve around her; mother to Princess and Junior and then to Lorna, wife to Wendell and friend to Margot. Although she isn't the protagonist, she is fundamental to all of the play's relationships.

How does Odimba present Mavis?

Odimba presents Mavis as a strong, independent woman who will do whatever it takes to provide for her family. She is a caring mother but also a strict disciplinarian who demands high standards from her children. Mavis is thrown off balance when Wendell arrives, and her forceful reaction shows us that she has a lot of feelings that she hasn't been able to deal with. Odimba also presents Mavis as a woman; we see her friendship with Margot and how important that is to her, and also her struggles with Wendell. She did love him and he betrayed her; she was and is attracted to him and we do see flashes of this attraction. Odimba also presents Mavis as hopeful: despite all that she's been through both in her personal life and as a Black woman in 1960s Britain, she can still be hopeful for a better future.

Character development and symbolism

At the start of the play we immediately see Mavis's expectations of her children and how their family dynamic works. We know that Christmas is a special day for the family but also that it is not lavish.

Mavis shows her sense of humour when she jokes with the children, and a softer side when she allows herself to be flattered by Junior's suggestion that he takes her photo.

Wendell's arrival shakes Mavis's confidence and her reaction with the knife highlights how she does not want him back in their lives. Mavis slapping Princess also demonstrates that his arrival has pushed her to extremes.

Mavis can't help but be motherly, and the arrival of Lorna stops her violent reaction to Wendell. Despite Lorna being a symbol of Wendell's infidelity and desertion, Mavis still doesn't hesitate to take her in.

As the play progresses and the tension rises, Mavis's physical affection for her children becomes more pronounced.

Wendell and Junior are very vocal about their support of the bus boycott, and while Mavis's support is strong, she supports quietly – in the way that mothers often look after the family and keep things running in the background.

As Wendell begins to prove himself, Mavis becomes more open to him – and as she lets her guard down we see that she has been lonely. As she begins to let him in we hear more about her hopes for the future.

AO1 Writing about Mavis

Point	Evidence
Mavis is strict with the children but also likes to joke with them.	*'Mavis swipes at Wendell Junior with the cushion again – Princess giggles...'* 'Yuh two children fool fool fram mawnin' till night!' (page 14) This silly behaviour shows that Mavis has a sense of humour, and the ease of their play tells us that it is not unusual for her to be silly with Princess and Junior.
Mavis is angry and shaken at Wendell's unexpected arrival.	'Mi gon' cut 'im rass throat! *Mavis jerks the door open – She lifts the knife up – '* (page 20) Mavis is pushed to an extreme reaction when she reaches for the knife and jerks the door open. This highlights how emotional she feels in this moment. Her use of non-standard English is a contrast to her earlier speech and this also shows us that her emotions are running high.
Mavis finds it frustrating that Wendell wants to talk about the past and her body, but doesn't acknowledge how she has struggled alone.	'You want to talk about my legs? What about these hands that been doing the work of two people?' (page 63) Wendell has commented on how Mavis's legs look but she wants to emphasise how hard her body has worked to support the family. The **subtext** of her reference to 'two people' is that Wendell should have shared the work.
Mavis is tired both physically and emotionally, but puts her children first.	'Only so many battles I can fight Margot. I want to survive long enough for my children to feel like this their home too. That's all I have the strength for these days.' (page 84) Mavis's words tell us that she has had to fight many battles before Wendell [cont.]

> returned. We see her strength because although she is drained, she will keep on fighting for her children. This line also alludes to the difficulties Mavis has had to be accepted in England, and that despite this she thinks of England as her home and wants the children to feel the same way.

Example

1. Put your quotations in context to show where they fit in to the play.

2. Go into detail about individual words and phrases in your quotation. Use technical terms and explain why the playwright's choice is effective.

3. Include references to the play's structure to demonstrate your understanding of the play and the writer's choices.

[*Point*] Mavis's main objectives are to protect her children and try to provide the best life that she can for them. As she becomes more open to Wendell being a part of this life, Mavis needs him to be focused on what the children need. [*Evidence*] In Act Three, Scene Four, when they know the colour bar has been lifted, Mavis explains her hopes to Wendell when she says 'What you done to us cannot easily be forgiven Wendell and you see these children, they the ones that need you to change.'[1] [*Analysis*] Mavis's use of the pronouns 'us' and 'you' separates Wendell from her and the children, emphasising the distance between them and that they are the victims of Wendell's behaviour. Her use of the verb 'need' highlights the importance of Wendell changing his ways.[2] Mavis continues to emphasise not what *she* wants but what her children need from their father when she says 'Princess needs you to know all her dreams because they are important' and 'Junior… you need to teach him what a good man look like.' Here we see how significant Princess's dreams are to Mavis, and the importance of Junior having a strong male role model. Before this scene Princess's cupboard-room fantasy had disappeared; afterwards, when Wendell makes a true commitment to the family, Princess's fantasy becomes more animated than ever.[3]

Wendell 'The Hustler' James

Wendell's role in the play

Wendell is the forty-year-old husband of Mavis and father of Junior, Princess and Lorna. Wendell 'The Hustler' is the second title character of the play, highlighting his significance. The fact that he is called 'The Hustler' adds mystery to his character as he is not named, but it also offers negative connotations, as 'hustler' is not a positive description, implying that Wendell is a person who cheats or deceives to get what he wants. Wendell left Mavis when Princess was a baby and arrives unexpectedly on Mavis's doorstep on Christmas Day approximately ten years later with his other daughter Lorna in tow. Wendell is almost surprised at Mavis's violent reaction to his arrival and he clearly expects that Mavis is going to take them both in. He is surprised when Mavis tells him that she will take Lorna but that he has to go. Wendell also gets a cold greeting from Junior who remembers how hurt Mavis was by his abandonment. Although it was hard for Black men to find work, Wendell does not make much effort, which adds further tension. Wendell is keen to be involved in the bus boycott, and as he begins to realise that he has a lot of bridges to build, Mavis begins to accept him back into the family.

Significant moments that involve Wendell

- Wendell arrives unexpectedly on Mavis's doorstep on Christmas Day with his nine year old daughter from another relationship. *Theme:* **Parenting** – Wendell has been absent from Junior and Princess's life. What message does his arrival with Lorna send them?

- He is surprised at the cold welcome that he is given and that Mavis slaps him and tells him to go.

- He leaves the girls alone at the docks while he socialises and plays cards. *Theme:* **Parenting** – what does Wendell's choice tell us about his priorities?

- He argues with Junior and pins him against the wall.

- He struggles to find a job because employers don't want Black workers. *Context:* Many Black workers struggled to find jobs, and many people had to work in low-paid jobs that they were overqualified for.

- He is keen to be involved with the bus boycotts.

- He left Lorna's mother because he didn't feel safe after her mental health issues caused her to make accusations that could put Wendell in danger. *Theme:*

Race – why would Lorna's mother's accusations have been especially dangerous for a Black man?

- He doesn't get on well with Margot. *Theme:* **Family** – what do think is the issue between Wendell and Margot?

- He is angry when Junior and his friends are attacked after the protest.

- He starts to realise what is at stake when Junior offers him money to leave. *Theme:* **Parenting** – how does Wendell feel when Junior offers him the money? He doesn't take it, but does he consider it?

- He feels really excited and hopeful about the momentum of the bus boycott and the likelihood that it will be successful. *Context:* The bus boycott was a community effort; people affected by the colour bar and other Bristolians joined forces to change what was happening.

- He proposes to Mavis again to show his commitment to her.

- He allows Princess to dress him up as a beauty queen to join her game. *Context:* Why is this such a big step for Wendell?

Why Wendell is important to the play

Keyword: The **rising action** in a story refers to the things that happen that build to its climax. This includes the development of the characters and things that create suspense.

Wendell is the immediate **catalyst** for the **rising action** in the play. Before his arrival, the scene is showing a glimpse of family life; when he arrives, tension immediately rises and from Mavis's reaction we know that Wendell isn't welcome.

Wendell is the reason that Mavis is the person she is in the play. She is strong and determined but she is also strict and authoritarian because she has had to play Wendell's role as well as her own. Wendell expects that Mavis will allow him to stay, and this presumption shows him to be thoughtless and self-centred.

Wendell shows the audience the struggles that immigrants were facing at the time, and his lack of work and the toll it takes on him are significant. Wendell talks about wanting to make up for his mistakes, but his actions, certainly earlier in the play, do not echo this.

Wendell and his role in the family represent society in some ways. Mavis highlights that if society can change by lifting the colour bar then Wendell can change too.

How does Odimba present Wendell?

Wendell is presented as his nickname suggests, as a hustler. He arrives and expects that Mavis will take him in; he seems taken aback by Mavis's violent reaction towards him. Wendell is pleased to see Junior and Princess but he is ill-equipped to deal with Junior's reaction. He doesn't know how to respond to this angry young man who immediately steps up to protect his mother and sister. Odimba presents Wendell as irresponsible; he leaves the girls alone at the docks while he entertains himself. Wendell is also presented as impatient. When Junior confronts him and things get physical he doesn't try to reason with Junior but rather physically puts him in his place. When Princess persuades Mavis to let Wendell move in, Odimba presents him as devious; his reaction suggests that he felt it was only a matter of time before she gave in, suggesting that he has finally got his way. He is also presented as being self-centred, as he doesn't understand how hard things have been for Mavis. Wendell is also presented as a proud man; he was well respected in the army and finds the idea of doing low-paid work hard to accept.

Character development and symbolism

At the start of the play, Wendell gives the impression that he was not expecting Mavis to be angry with him. He asks to come in and talk, and when she responds angrily, he tries to make her feel guilty.

Wendell is quite casual when he introduces Lorna, and there is no sense of remorse in him for leaving Mavis, or for bringing up another child while Princess and Junior went without a father.

Wendell struggles to communicate with Junior as a young adult with strong opinions. It is much easier for Wendell to appeal to the girls with promises of sweets and park visits. As the play progresses, Wendell is able to communicate with Junior through sincere actions. Junior starts to understand Wendell when he confides in him about Lorna's mother, and we see that Wendell made a conscious decision to stay for Lorna because he had left Princess and Junior and he didn't want to make the same mistake again.

When Wendell shows commitment to the bus boycott and gets involved to help others as well as himself, there is a change in him. He feels connected and part of a bigger cause, leading him to feel more committed to his family.

A further turning point for Wendell is when Junior offers him money to leave. It would be easy for Wendell to take the money but he chooses not to and instead to commit to his family. This decision and the success of the bus boycott push Wendell into a much more positive frame of mind.

AO1 Writing about Wendell

Point	Evidence
Wendell appears to have no understanding of how Mavis feels about seeing him again after so many years – and after he abandoned her and the children.	'What 'appen far yuh to get so cruel Mavis?' (page 32) Wendell accusing Mavis of being cruel shows his complete disregard for her feelings and for what he has done.
Wendell doesn't know how to communicate with Junior and doesn't understand how Junior feels.	'Mi here to do what mi kyann to be ar good fadder and ar 'usband. Nuthing yuh kyaan do to change dat. So yuh need to fix up yuh attitude Junior.' (page 47) Wendell is demanding that Junior change and accept Wendell's wishes, but he shows no regard for Junior's place as man of the house. Junior has protected his mother and sister and Wendell expects him to step aside.
Wendell finds it hard to accept Margot, and after their night out he has an issue with her behaviour.	'Yuh making plenty attempts yuh self. No place safe fram de white woman *attempts*.' (page 68) Wendell was pleased to find a place where people from all backgrounds could mix together, but seems to have a problem with Margot flirting with the Black men at the club. Wendell's double standards are hard to justify.
Wendell is excited and invigorated by the success of the bus boycott.	'Yuh see dem men dat make dis happen, dem heroes. If this come off, it ar victory far de Black man. De brown man. Every kinda man dem.' (page 101) Wendell's excitement and relief that the colour bar will be lifted pushes him to fully commit to his family. His reference to the men making it happen includes men of all backgrounds who were part of the protest and the fight for change.

Example

[Point] From the start of the play we see that Wendell is selfish. He arrives after ten years away and expects a place to stay and for Mavis to be happy to help. Wendell is clearly finding it hard to look after Lorna and has run out of options. **[Evidence]** In Act One, Scene Five, after the family have had Christmas dinner, he says 'Yuh know only so much a man kyaan do when it come to looking after children dem.'[1] **[Analysis]** In the first instance, Wendell is referring to him looking after Lorna since her mother went into hospital, but the wider meaning can be linked to the limited care he provided for Princess and Junior. At the time it was unusual for men to be single parents[2] and so to Wendell, returning to Mavis with Lorna seems logical as he sees Mavis as she was, a doting mother. Wendell's soft memory of Mavis means it's a shock to him when she says he can't stay. Wendell's response 'What 'appen far yuh to get so cruel Mavis? De Mavis I remember never tark like dis' shows that he's living in the past and has given no thought to his actions or their consequences but only considered his own memories and feelings.

> 1. Put your quotations in context to show where they fit in to the play.

> 2. Include historical context to demonstrate your understanding of the world of the play and its characters.

Wendell 'Junior' James

Junior's role in the play

Wendell Junior is the seventeen-year-old son of Mavis and Wendell James. He lives with his mother Mavis and his ten-year-old sister Princess. Junior is a keen photographer and spends much of his time taking photos with his friend Leon. Junior is shocked and upset at Wendell's return because his lasting memory of his father's departure is how upset Mavis was. Junior has tried to be the man of the house and is very protective of his mother and sister. Junior is very involved, along with Leon, in the bus boycott, and feels that being part of the movement is helping to change attitudes in society. Junior is a caring and sensitive boy and looks out for Lorna as readily as he looks out for Princess. We see from what Junior says about his relationship with Leon's father that he has missed having a male role model in his life.

Significant moments that involve Junior

- Junior risks Mavis's wrath when he sneaks out to take photos on Christmas Day. *Theme:* **Ambition/Hopes and dreams** – what does this risk tell us about the importance of photography to Junior?

- He immediately recognises his father and is wary of him and protective of Mavis. *Theme:* **Parenting** – why does Junior feel wary of Wendell?

- He tries to comfort Princess after Mavis has slapped her.

- He is confrontational with Wendell at the dinner table but responds to Mavis's requests for him to stop. What comparisons can you make between Junior's responses to his parents?

- He is angry when he finds Princess and Lorna alone at the docks. He challenges Wendell and things get physical, leaving Junior upset.

- He is very involved in the protests and the bus boycott. *Context:* What does Junior's involvement in the protests tells us about his character?

- He reveals to Wendell how he remembers Mavis being upset for a long time after he left them.

- He offers Wendell money to leave. How do we feel about Junior offering Wendell the money?

- He is elated when the colour bar is lifted.

- He includes Wendell in his family photo. What does Junior's inclusion of Wendell tell us about his feelings towards his father by this point in the play?

Why Junior is important to the play

Junior represents the space between the adults and the children. He is aware of how Mavis feels when Wendell returns but does not fully understand the depth and complexity of her feelings as a wife and mother. He remembers clearly how Mavis felt when Wendell left and is afraid that his father will hurt them again, so he is not willing to accept Wendell. In contrast to Junior, Princess happily accepts Wendell into her life because she has no memory of him.

Junior also represents young adults at the time of the bus boycott. Many young people of different races came together to protest about the colour bar, and Junior's enthusiasm to try to make changes in society is reflective of the way many young people felt at the time.

Junior constantly pushes against Wendell and asks for him to justify his actions, highlighting that Wendell's choices have impacted him deeply.

How does Odimba present Junior?

At the start of the play, Junior's behaviour is what you might expect from a teenage boy with a younger sister; he teases Princess and easily upsets her. We see that he has household responsibilities and his complaints about doing them show him to be a fairly typical teenager. Junior is an intelligent and sensitive young man. Although Junior shows a lot of maturity he is often emotional, especially with his reactions towards Wendell, highlighting that he is still young. The way that Junior speaks about Leon's dad suggests he has missed the support of a father in his life. Junior is ambitious and hopeful for the future, and is keen to take action to make things change in society. Junior is a protector. He does his best to take care of Mavis and Princess, and later he extends this protection to Lorna.

Character development and symbolism

Junior begins the play in some respects as the man of the house, helping Mavis to take care of things. When Wendell arrives, Junior struggles emotionally as he battles to deal with his feelings about his father.

Junior's ambition to become a photographer is symbolic of the life that is possible for him. Many immigrants had to take manual jobs and often had very little choice; Junior's wish to follow his creative passion symbolises the hope for his generation of young Black British people to follow their dreams.

Junior becomes increasingly desperate for Wendell to leave; as the tension in the play rises, Junior's efforts increase. It is significant when Junior offers Wendell money; it would have taken Junior a long time to save the money, and offering it to Wendell demonstrates the strength of his feelings and his wish to protect the family.

As the bus boycott makes progress and Wendell starts to prove his commitment to the family, Junior relaxes and eventually begins to accept Wendell.

AO1 Writing about Junior

Point	Evidence
Junior is thrown by Wendell's arrival and he finds it hard to process what is happening.	'She's trying to... She wouldn't do it if she didn't have to... Don't think she will again...' (page 22) When Junior and Princess are sent to the bedroom he struggles to explain Mavis's actions to Princess. He is trying to comfort his sister and protect her from the information that Wendell is their father, but he is also shocked and confused by his arrival.
Junior is not interested in Wendell's apologies or what he might have to offer.	'Only thing I want is for you to go! [...] You heard me. You want to be down here playing cards then go ahead but keep us out of it. We're doing fine without you.' (page 45) Junior is hurt and betrayed by Wendell and he doesn't want to have any connection to him. He does not see Wendell as part of the family at all, only someone who wants to hurt them.
Junior is caring and responsible. He quickly accepts Lorna as his sister and seeks to protect her too.	'It's just... I can't... leave my sisters / ' (page 51) Junior really wants to go to the meeting with Leon but refuses to leave the girls with Wendell. His decision to stay with them highlights the girls' importance to him. His inclusion of Lorna also shows how easily he has accepted her.
Junior is proud to be a part of the protests.	'So many people. Walking proud. Students all shouting – *"No to the colour bar. Not in our name."* It felt good.' (page 79) Junior feels good to be an active part in the protests; being part of a mixed group showing solidarity shows how he fits in with the students and feels part of a community.

Example

[*Point*] Junior is shocked by Wendell's arrival and struggles with a range of feelings. He wants to protect Mavis but also knows that he has to be respectful and to do as he is asked. Junior feels worried because all of the hurt that Wendell has caused comes flooding back to him. **[*Evidence*]** In Act One, Scene Five, when the family are at the dinner table,[1] Junior makes his feelings clear when he says 'It takes more than a word to make a father'. **[*Analysis*]** Junior shows here that he doesn't think that Wendell has been much of a father to them and he struggles to stay polite when faced with Wendell. When Junior says 'How long are you planning to stay?' he knows that he is being rude but he risks Mavis's disapproval to get an answer to his question. The **subtext**[2] of his question is that he doesn't want Wendell to stay at all and feels angry at his intrusion. Junior's feelings are also emphasised because being disrespectful your parents was frowned upon in the 1960s even more than it is now, and society was still in a stage where often children were 'seen and not heard'.[3]

> 1. Put your quotations in context to show where they fit in to the play.

> 2. Use technical terms to explain why the playwright's choice is effective.

> 3. Include historical context to demonstrate your understanding of the world of the play and its characters.

Lorna James

Lorna's role in the play

Lorna is the nine-year-old daughter of Wendell, and the half-sister of Junior and Princess. Lorna has been brought up in Liverpool with Wendell and her mother. When Lorna's mother has a mental health crisis and is taken into hospital, Wendell leaves Liverpool with Lorna and arrives in Bristol. Lorna is shy at first but soon comes out of herself when she is accepted by Mavis, Princess and Junior. Lorna fits in well at school and settles into life with the Jameses well. As time passes, Lorna starts to miss her mother and struggles as the tension in the family rises. Lorna wants to be accepted by Junior and is delighted when he places a photo of her in his display.

Significant moments that involve Lorna

- Lorna is concealed when Wendell first knocks on Mavis's door.

- She is a surprise to Mavis, Princess and Junior when she is introduced. *Theme:* **Family** – how would it feel for Lorna to be away from her mother on Christmas Day and thrust into a new and unfamiliar family?

- She fits easily into life with Princess and Junior as her brother and sister.

- She gets invited to Barbara's party when Princess is excluded. *Theme:* **Race** – why is it implied that Lorna is invited and Princess is excluded?

- She rejects Princess and says she's not like her after Junior is attacked and Princess is worried.

- She misses her mum and wants to go home.

Why Lorna is important to the play

Lorna represents Wendell's other life. She is a product of the relationship he chose after he had left Mavis and her children, and the child he has raised instead of Princess and Junior. Lorna is well cared for by Wendell because he is mindful that he hasn't cared for his other children.

Lorna represents resilience. Her mother is ill and she has been moved away from the only home that she knows, yet she adapts and finds happiness in her new circumstances despite missing her old life.

Lorna is a way into the Jameses' life for Wendell. If it weren't for Lorna, Mavis would most likely have closed the door in his face and not opened it again.

Lorna's quick acceptance at school highlights how hard school life is for Princess; she is not accepted at school but Lorna is immediately welcomed.

How does Odimba present Lorna?

Lorna seems shy at first when she is shoved into Junior and Princess's bedroom, but also fairly typical when she snatches the lollipop from Junior. At the dinner table Odimba's writing suggests that Lorna has been brought up differently to Princess and Junior, and that Wendell's expectations of her are not the same as Mavis's. Lorna quickly establishes a friendship with Princess and they bond. Odimba's portrayal of Lorna suggests that she has not had difficult experiences in her life due to her race. This is highlighted by her invitation to Barbara's party; Lorna struggles to understand Princess's feelings of rejection as she has just started at school and immediately taken up a higher position in the social hierarchy than Princess. The implication that Princess is not invited to the party because she is Black is not clear to Lorna like it is to Mavis and Wendell. Wendell's suggestion that they didn't talk about those things implies that they hadn't needed to, as Lorna's experience of race has been different.

Character development and symbolism

Lorna is very quiet in contrast to Princess's quickfire questions, but she responds to Princess's friendly chat and opens up when Princess compliments her green eyes. The mention of Lorna's eye colour establishes that although she is Wendell's daughter, she is different. This difference is further highlighted by Lorna's table manners and from Mavis's reaction we see that Lorna's upbringing has been different to that of Princess and Junior. Lorna relaxes into being a sister easily and enjoys the same interests as Princess. She settles into school and seems to makes friends, indicated by the invitation to Barbara's party. As the play progresses and the tension in the play rises, Lorna becomes unsettled and misses her mother. As the tensions begin to resolve and the bus boycott has been successful, Junior including Lorna in his photos makes her feel happy and part of the new, blended family.

AO1 Writing about Lorna

Point	Evidence
Lorna is wary of Princess and Junior when she is pushed into the room.	'Daddy says I can't take anything from strangers.' (page 23)
	In this moment, Lorna doesn't know who Junior and Princess are and is nervous of them. The audience understand the irony of the moment because they know that Lorna is actually Princess and Junior's sister.
Lorna likes being with Princess and feels connected to her.	'Princess do you want me to stay here forever?' (page 42)
	Lorna's question suggests that she wants Princess to want her to stay, demonstrating that she feels close to Princess and is accepting the changes in her life.
Lorna finds the racial tension hard to understand, especially when the family feel threatened after Junior's attack.	'I don't want a sister. I want my mum. I want to go home!' (page 80)
	Lorna feels very emotional here and reacts as we would expect a young child to when they feel overwhelmed. We see that although she has started to settle down, she does not see Bristol as her home.

Example

1. Put your quotations in context to show where they fit in to the play.

2. Include historical context to demonstrate your understanding of the world of the play and its characters.

[*Point*] Lorna represents Wendell's other life; she has been brought up differently to Junior and Princess and hasn't had the same experiences because of her race. She wants to be included by the other children at school, even if that means Princess is excluded. Lorna has not been in the family long enough to have developed loyalty to her sister. [*Evidence*] In Act Two, Scene One, when the girls return from school,[1] Princess is upset. When Mavis questions Lorna as to why Princess is crying, Lorna hesitates: 'I think it was...', showing that she is reluctant to reveal that Princess hasn't been invited. Lorna focuses on the positives of the party: 'there's going to be a big cake and a clown. A real-life clown!' [*Analysis*] Lorna's focus on the cake and repetition of 'clown' show that she is really excited to have been invited. The invitation is symbolic that Lorna has been accepted by Barbara, and Lorna's reference to Princess's real name 'She didn't invite Phyllis' also aligns Lorna with the children at school rather than the family. Lorna struggles to understand why Mavis and Wendell don't want her to go, and when she says 'But Barbara says she can't invite Phyllis' we see that she doesn't understand the problem. The subtext is that Princess has been excluded because of her race: it's not explicitly revealed but we can tell that Wendell and Mavis think that's the reason, and immigrant children were often excluded and treated differently by their white peers.[2]

Margot Barker

Margot's role in the play

Margot is the forty-two-year-old neighbour of Mavis, Junior and Princess. Margot and Mavis have been friends for some time and they are a great support to each other. Margot spends a lot of time with Princess and encourages her interest in Weston-Super-Mare and the beauty pageants. Margot finds it difficult to get on with Wendell and there is often tension between them.

Significant moments that involve Margot

- Margot is passing on Christmas Day and hears unfamiliar voices.

- She has been to visit her own family but had to leave early due to an argument. *Theme:* **Family** – Margot clearly does not get on with her own family. Why would Mavis and her children be so important to Margot?

- She goes dancing with Mavis and Wendell. *Theme:* **Race** – why is the club that welcomes everyone significant?

- She argues with Wendell and is not supportive of the bus boycott. *Theme:* **Race** – do you think Margot's opinions represent the opinions of most people at the time?

- By not supporting the boycott and condemning the treatment of Black people, Margot doesn't support Mavis, and their friendship suffers. *Theme:* **Family** – what does Margot's lack of support for the boycott say about her understanding of Mavis and her life?

- She doesn't think that Wendell can change.

- She finds Princess hiding in her flat when she has run away, she looks after her and takes her home the next day.

- She returns Junior's money that she finds in her flat.

- She becomes emotional when the girls call her 'auntie'. *Theme:* **Family** – why is Margot so emotional when the girls are permitted to call her auntie?

Why Margot is important to the play

Margot is the only white character in the play and so she represents white people in a number of ways. Firstly, her friendship with Mavis is important. Margot and Mavis have been friends for some time and are very close. They feel genuine affection for each other and this shows us how many Bristolians not only accepted immigrants but formed deep and meaningful relationships with them. This is also highlighted in Margot's close relationship with Junior and Princess. Margot is also accepted into the Black community and we learn that she is proud to be able to go to places where other white people can't, because of her friendship with Mavis. Margot's enthusiasm after her night out with Mavis and Wendell also shows how she is happy to integrate with all communities. Margot's opinion of the bus boycott is that it's silly, and people should accept the jobs they are offered rather than taking jobs from white workers. Margot's opinions represent those of many Bristolians at the time, and although there is no real malice intended, she shows a real lack of understanding of Mavis and her community.

How does Odimba present Margot?

Odimba presents Margot as confident, forthcoming and nosy; when she hears Wendell's voice she invites herself in, and then stays despite Mavis hinting that she should leave. It is soon made clear that Margot is lonely, and after arguing with her own family she does not want to spend the rest of Christmas Day alone. Margot is caring and happily takes the girls to her flat, letting Mavis know she is nearby if she needs her, as well as looking after the girls on other occasions. Odimba presents Margot as fun, she entertains the children and she shows that she knows how to enjoy herself when she goes out with Mavis and Wendell. Margot is protective of Mavis and the children; much of the tension between Margot and Wendell is because she believes that Wendell will hurt them.

Character development and symbolism

Margot is brash and opinionated but she is also energetic and caring, looking out for Mavis and the children with genuine care.

Although Margot cares for Mavis, and they rely on each other, she doesn't fully understand Mavis and this is highlighted in her lack of empathy for Wendell and the bus boycott.

Later in the play, Margot seems lonely – especially after Mavis distances herself from her. When Princess is hiding we see Margot reveal her true self under her wig and eyelashes, and she seems tired and old. We also see that she truly understands that what is important to Mavis is that her children are happy.

Mavis accepting Margot back into the family and telling the girls to call her auntie symbolises the return to normality for the women.

AO1 Writing about Margot

Point	Evidence
Margot is curious about the arrival of Wendell.	'And you know I'm not one to poke it where it's not wanted but...' (page 33)
	This line is **ironic**. As Margot has burst in, the suggestion is that this is not true: she is very likely to poke her nose into Mavis's business. Her curiosity is partly driven by her being protective of Mavis, and partly because she is prying.

Margot feels strongly that Wendell should take care of his family.	'That's what you do for family. You look after *your* family. You go out. You get a decent job' (page 48) Margot has no patience for Wendell's excuses about why he hasn't got a job, and doesn't show much understanding of his genuine struggles.
Margot doesn't believe that Wendell can change.	'And what if nothing comes of the bus boycott? What then Mavis? Think he's still going to be a changed man?' (page 84) Margot is worried for Mavis because Wendell has done nothing to show that he has changed. Margot is also worried that things will change for her and her place in Mavis and the children's lives if Wendell returns.

Example

[Point] Margot has a very close relationship with Mavis and the children. She spends a lot of time with the family and when Lorna arrives she welcomes her happily. Margot's close relationship with Mavis represents how accepting many Bristolians were of immigrant families. **[Evidence]** In Act One, Scene Five, when Margot arrives back from visiting her family[1] she says 'You know that fur I'm always promising Princess? Nearly lost that in the scrap. Where is my Princess? Missed that little chicken.' **[Analysis]** Margot's use of the adverb 'always' suggests that she sees Princess a lot and her use of the possessive determiner 'my' shows that she feels as close to Princess as she would her own child.[2] The affectionate use of 'little chicken' adds to the sense of warmth.

> 1. Put your quotations in context to show where they fit in to the play.

> 2. Go into detail about individual words and phrases in your quotation. Use technical terms and explain why the playwright's choice is effective.

Leon

Leon's role in the play

Leon is Junior's nineteen-year-old friend. Leon and Junior spend time together taking photos around Bristol. Leon is a more experienced photographer and Junior enjoys learning from him. With Leon and his dad, Junior gets involved in the protests about the colour bar and the bus boycott.

Significant moments that involve Leon

- Junior asks Leon to take Princess and Lorna home from the docks when he finds them alone.

- Leon tries to flirt with Margot.

- He tells Junior to calm down when he is angry at Wendell.

Why Leon is important to the play

Leon represents the life that Junior is leading outside the family. He is a loyal and caring friend to Junior, and their involvement with the protests and the bus boycott represents the real-life context of how involved many young people were with wanting to make changes in society. Leon is a trusted friend; when Junior needs someone to take Princess and Lorna home he doesn't hesitate to trust Leon with the task.

How does Odimba present Leon?

Odimba presents Leon as friendly and loyal. Junior trusts him and we feel that Leon has Junior's best interests at heart. Leon is also presented as a young man stepping into adulthood and we see this when he tries to flirt with Margot. Leon is respectful and courteous; he refers to Mavis as 'Mrs James' and tries to warn Junior about going too far with Wendell when they argue. Leon clearly looks up to his own father and doesn't want to disappoint him. Leon is kind to Princess and Lorna, which also shows his caring side.

Character development and symbolism

Leon symbolises young, Black men in 1960s Britain. He is ambitious and proactive, working hard towards a creative career in photography and actively involved in the protests, trying to make life better for others.

Leon tries to see the best in people. When Princess is missing, Leon is the one to suggest that Wendell is out collecting signatures rather than believing that he has left again.

AO1 Writing about Leon

Point	Evidence
Leon is a trusted friend to the James family.	'Is this a real-life Princess talking to me? [...] *Leon bows – picks Princess up and spins her around – puts her down again – '* (page 43) Leon is clearly very familiar with Princess and his physicality with her shows that they have spent a lot of time together.
Leon tries to advise Junior when he is angry with Wendell.	'He's your daddy. He deserves a little... Stay cool. Yeah?' (page 53) Leon's good experiences with his own father make Junior's reaction to Wendell seem extreme. Leon doesn't want Junior to get into trouble.
Leon is calm and reassuring when Princess is missing.	'I'm sure Princess is fine. She's probably someplace playing her Princess thing.' (page 90) When Mavis and Junior are starting to panic they turn to Leon for help. He stays to look after Lorna and tries to reassure them.

Example

1. Put your quotations in context to show where they fit in to the play.

2. Make comparisons between characters or moments within the text.

3. Go into detail about individual words and phrases in your quotation. Use technical terms and explain why the playwright's choice is effective.

[*Point*] Leon is a loyal and caring friend to Junior and his family. When Junior is angry at Wendell, Leon tries to stop him saying too much. [*Evidence*] In Act One, Scene Seven, Leon feels awkward about the atmosphere created between Junior and Wendell. When Junior ignores Wendell trying to talk to him,[1] Leon whispers 'Look I better be going.' [*Analysis*] Leon lowering his voice suggests he doesn't want to draw attention to himself in this tense moment. We see that Leon wants to help his father: 'Told my dad I'd go help him set up for this meeting thing', and he doesn't want to let him down: 'You know what his "disappointed in you" face is like.' This is a huge contrast to how Junior feels about his own father.[2] Leon is shocked by Junior's outburst and tries to advise him against being disrespectful. 'Leon grabs Wendell Junior by the shoulders and pulls him towards the front door – out of Wendell's earshot – ' The use of the verbs 'grab' and 'pull' suggests a strong physical reaction, highlighting that Leon feels serious about his warning to Junior.[3] Leon wants to protect Junior and sees his behaviour as disrespectful and likely to get Junior in trouble.

Themes

Race and prejudice

Race and prejudice underpin the whole play. Mavis and Wendell have come to England from Jamaica and, although Junior and Princess were born in England, they are seen as different because of the colour of their skin. The family all have experiences that happen because of their race.

- It is implied that Princess is poorly treated and isolated at school because of her race.

- Mavis, Wendell and Margot being able to enjoy a night out together was very unusual in the 1960s.

- When Lorna rejects Princess and says she isn't the same as her, she means because Princess is Black.

- Wendell struggles to get a job because employers don't want Black workers.

- The bus boycott is because of the colour bar banning back people from driving the buses.

- Junior points out that he not only understands what it means to be a man but also a Black man.

- Wendell left Liverpool because accusations made by Lorna's mother made him feel in danger, especially as a Black man.

- Margot doesn't support the bus boycott, and this reflects many people's attitudes at the time.

- In Princess's final pageant, beauty queens that look like her appear.

Writing about race

1. Showing Margot's opinion.

In Act Two, Scene Two, tension rises between Margot and Wendell when she learns that he intends to get involved with the bus boycott. Margot thinks the boycott is 'silly' and that people should 'accept how things are.'[1] When Wendell challenges Margot's opinion and says 'Dis country belong to alla us' she doesn't disagree, but her use of the words 'accommodated' and 'tolerating' suggests that Bristolians are putting up with West Indians rather than welcoming them and including them – she also emphasises the word 'us'. The effect that Odimba wants to create is a separation between Margot and people like her, and the Jameses.[2] As Margot continues, she seems to see Wendell and Mavis as separate. She says to Wendell 'I know many of your lot' which clearly divides her from Wendell, but she says of Mavis 'Like family I am', revealing how close she feels to Mavis and how important their relationship is. This contradiction shows that Margot does not understand that the fight for equality is not Wendell's fight alone but for the whole community, including Mavis, Junior and Princess.[3]

2. Commenting clearly on the effect created by the writer.

3. Showing understanding of the wider context of the play and the theme.

Add another **point** expanding on the tension between Wendell and Margot. Use **evidence** from the play to support it and **analyse** your evidence to explain your point.

Key quotations: Race

PRINCESS. I wish my eyes were blue or green or... (page 25)	Princess wants to look more like the beauty queens in the pageants she dreams of being part of. Her wish to change how she looks highlights that she is not represented in the pageants.
JUNIOR. You think I don't know about the world. About what it means to be a man... a Black man / (page 50)	Junior is growing up in a world where there are clear expectations for young men, but here he shows that he already understands that it is not the same for him and that he will have to behave differently as a Black man.

WENDELL. Wha' kinda world put men in de same sentence as dogs? (page 54)	Wendell is angry at the injustice of his having been successful in the army and now struggling to find work at all in a country that he was invited to. Here he refers to 'No Blacks' signs put out when people were looking for work and housing.
LORNA. I'm not Black like you. (page 80)	Lorna's rejection of Princess is hurtful, especially when she highlights something that neither of them can change.
MAVIS. People looking at me a bit stranger in those houses these days. (page 81)	Mavis has created a strong reputation for herself and people like her work, but as the bus boycott begins, Mavis starts to feel alienated.

Ambition, hopes, dreams and disillusionment

Odimba presents the themes of ambition, hopes, dreams and disillusionment in a variety of ways. Princess's dreams are played out in her imagination while Junior's dream of being a photographer is shown in his commitment to his creativity.

- Princess dreams of winning the Weston-Super-Mare beauty pageant. The way her fantasy changes throughout the play is directly linked to the tension in the play.

- Wendell Junior wants to be a photographer and dreams of being an apprentice in a photography studio.

- Mavis's dreams are for her children, that England will welcome them and offer them opportunities. She also hopes that Wendell will show Junior how to be a good man.

- Mavis tells Wendell the importance of him understanding Princess's dreams.

- Mavis and Wendell's community hope that the bus boycott will be a success and the colour bar will be lifted.

- Mavis and Wendell arrive in the UK with hopes, dreams and ambitions for their future, but they are disillusioned by their treatment and the barriers that surround them because of their race.

Writing about ambition, hopes, dreams and disillusionment

Princess and Junior's hopes and dreams are for themselves. The play begins with the audience fully immersed in Princess's dream of winning a beauty pageant. Odimba's use of the verb 'explodes' and the adjective 'booming' in the stage directions suggest that Princess's fantasy is big and immersive, with Princess firmly in the middle of it. The fact that 'Mavis's voice can be heard shouting above the noise –' highlights how caught up in her dream Princess is and how important it is to her.[1] In her acceptance speech in Act One, Scene One, we see the people that are important to Princess: 'I want to thank my mummy, my friends, Margot and Junior…' The reference to friends shows that Princess feels included by other children at the start of the play. We also see that Princess is kind and thoughtful: 'I will use this money to help the poor… After I have bought my mummy a new coat.'[2]

> 1. Commenting clearly on the effect created by the writer.

> 2. Linking theme to character.

> Add another **point** examining how Princess's dream changes. Use **evidence** from the play to support it and **analyse** that evidence to help explain your point.

Key quotations: Ambition, hopes, dreams and disillusionment

VOICE-OVER. *Ladies and gentlemen, I present to you the winner of the year's Weston-Super-Mare Beauties of the West Contest –* (*Voice booming.*) *Princess James.* (page 6)	Princess dreams of winning the beauty pageant, and the stage directions clearly show that her fantasy is detailed and well-practised, highlighting that this dream is important to Princess and she imagines this often.
JUNIOR. Leon and some other guys wanted to take photographs by the docks. And you know I'm trying to learn everything I can… I'll be an apprentice one day in one of them studios. (page 9)	For Junior it was worth the risk of making Mavis angry by sneaking out on Christmas Day to try to learn from other photographers. Junior's ambition to be an apprentice is clearly important to him.

WENDELL. When mi come to dis country I was ar god man. Ar soldier. Fight far King an' country. (page 53) MAVIS. [...] They tell him to start as a junior clerk. He was a second lieutenant back home [...] He didn't understand why they invite him to come here if all they want to do is make him feel invisible. (page 83)	When Wendell was invited to come to England he had hopes of a good job that meant he could provide for his family. When he arrived, things were different; he was treated badly and made to feel unwelcome. Instead of being offered the good job that he was capable of, he was offered a low-paid junior job.
MAVIS. I feel so lucky Margot. A husband with a job, a baby and this new land of Hope and Glory. 'Cept you see when we move here to Hingland we didn't find no hope that for sure. (page 83)	Alongside Wendell, Mavis hoped for a new life in England. She was excited about what life held for them but the way they were treated left them feeling disillusioned, unwanted and hopeless.

Family and parenting

Odimba presents family as important throughout the play, and the theme of parenting is examined through Mavis and Wendell's parenting of the three children.

- At the start of the play we see very clear expectations from Mavis with Junior and Princess. They are both expected to help, and when Junior challenges Mavis, the threat of physical punishment comes quickly.

- Mavis is a single mother and there is no mention of family to support her, so she carries her responsibilities alone.

- Wendell arriving with Lorna is difficult for Mavis; she has struggled alone with Wendell's other children.

- The different way that Lorna has been brought up is highlighted in a variety of ways at the dinner table and after she has been invited to Barbara's party.

- Wendell leaving the girls unattended at the docks shows his lack of responsibility for them.

- Lorna slots into family life easily but as the tension rises she misses her mum and wants to go home.

- Junior cannot accept Wendell back into the family; he remembers how much damage was done when he left.

- Margot sees Mavis like family and has a close relationship to Mavis and her children.

- Margot refers to herself as a widow and mentions 'my Fred' in the past tense (page 92). She seems to have a strained relationship with her own family.

- It doesn't take Princess long to accept Wendell into her life, highlighting her adaptability.

- Wendell agreeing to dress up as a beauty queen in Princess's game shows that he is prioritising Princess's wishes over his own.

Writing about family and parenting

Family is presented in a variety of ways in the play, reflecting how complex family life can be. Margot returns early from visiting her family for Christmas and we learn she had been involved in an argument. Margot's description of her sister-in-law as 'nothing more than one of the witches from that play' shows us how upset she is. When Mavis responds that 'you can't talk like that about family' we see that Mavis feels surprised that Margot would feel like this about her family, suggesting that Mavis had close family relationships of her own.[1] Margot elaborates on the argument: 'If only the silly cow dinned start throwing all my stuff out the door first. Dinned have much choice. Asking me to keep my filthy language to myself.' and Odimba's use of the verb 'throwing' and the adjective 'filthy' highlight that the argument was heated.[2] In contrast to Margot's feelings about her own family, she feels closely connected to Mavis: 'like family I am'.

> 1. Linking theme to characters.

> 2. Commenting clearly on the effect created by the writer.

> Add another **point** examining how family is important. Use **evidence** from the play to support it and **analyse** the evidence to explain your point.

Key quotations: Family and parenting

MAVIS. You turn the handle of that door and it will be the last thing you do on this God-given earth. (page 8)	Mavis's parenting is strict and we immediately see her high expectations of Junior's behaviour. We have no doubt that she is not making an empty threat.
Wendell is standing at the door holding the hand of a girl barely younger than Princess. (page 20)	Wendell's choice to introduce Lorna to his family like this tells us a lot about him. He knows that Mavis will be angry when he arrives, but he also knows how she feels about her children and that she would not be able to turn Lorna away.
Lorna picks a fork up – WENDELL. No Lorna! *Wendell puts a hand on Lorna's arm before the first mouthful goes in.* (pages 26–27)	This interaction between Wendell and Lorna tells us that Lorna has been brought up differently to Princess and Junior. She is not used to waiting to say grace before eating, and Wendell's strong reaction tells us that he knows that Mavis will disapprove of this because saying grace is an important part of the meal for her.
JUNIOR. You've come back just so you can leave again. That's what you want isn't it? To break us all over again. (page 46)	Junior cannot accept Wendell back into the family. He clearly remembers how sad and broken Mavis was after Wendell left and he is angry at the idea that this could happen again.
FAMILY. Di hotta di battle, di sweeta di victory! (page 106)	This line said in unison to celebrate the lifting of the colour bar is significant because the whole family is united, giving us hope that things might work out.

Bristol bus boycott, and the colour bar

The theme of the colour bar and the bus boycott runs alongside the family tensions. While things are strained and difficult inside the James household, life is also difficult in the outside world. While it is only the characters that are affected by the action inside the flat, the wider community is affected by the bus boycott.

- Leon has to help his dad set up for a meeting. It is implied that it is where people will discuss the colour bar.

- Junior mentions the protests when he is telling Wendell what a good man Leon's father is.

- Junior tells Mavis and Wendell about a press conference and the start of the bus boycott. Wendell is keen to support it.

- Margot expresses her opinion that the bus boycott is 'silly' and we see that she doesn't support it.

- Wendell is enthusiastic about the bus boycott and plans to give out leaflets and get involved with telling the community about the situation.

- Junior gets involved in a march with students to protest about the colour bar but is attacked by a group of white boys.

- Margot tries to talk to Mavis about the protests and it is clear that she sees Mavis as unconnected to the community that is trying to fight for equality.

- Wendell returns after two days missing and Mavis's anger soon vanishes when he tells the family that it looks like the colour bar will be lifted.

- The radio announces that the colour bar is over.

Writing about the Bristol bus boycott and the colour bar

> 1. Showing understanding of Junior's character.

> 2. Showing understanding of the wider context of the play.

Junior is very involved in the protests against the colour bar and when he announces 'The bus boycott!' to Mavis and Wendell it is clear that he wants to be a part of a change in society.[1] Wendell matches Junior's enthusiasm and he is energetic when he tells Mavis 'mi kyaant leave dis alone. Now dem man Roy Hackett an' Paul Stephenson announce de bus boycott it all going to get very interesting.' Roy Hackett and Paul Stephenson were very important in the protests, and Wendell's reference to them highlights this.[2] Wendell's enthusiasm for the cause matches Junior's and despite

Junior pushing against his father we see a noticeable similarity between them. Junior's enthusiasm is ruined by the attack that happens. His initial description of the protest is positive: 'So many people. Walking proud.' and 'It felt good. No trouble really.' Odimba uses the adjectives 'proud' and 'good' to show how Junior felt in the crowd. This is then contrasted with 'We see four white boys. Big. Ugly.' The use of the adjectives 'big' and 'ugly' shows how the good feelings were destroyed. Junior speaks in short simple sentences, which also emphasises his feelings of shock and upset at what has happened.[3]

> 3. Commenting clearly on the effect created by the writer.

> Add another **point** showing the importance of the bus boycott and the colour bar. Use **evidence** from the play to support it and **analyse** the evidence to explain your point.

Key quotations: Bristol bus boycott and colour bar

JUNIOR. The bus boycott! They've officially called for a boycott. Today May 1st. Today it has happened. We can't ride the buses no more until they win. (page 65)	Junior is enthusiastic as the bus boycott begins and people take action against the colour bar. Junior's passion for the cause emphasises that he willing to stand up and fight for what's right.
WENDELL. Tomorra mi knocking on every door an' church of every Black person inna Bristol telling dem 'bout dis situation. (page 75)	Wendell's enthusiasm for the cause shows a different side to his character and the audience can see the motivated, passionate man that Wendell can be.
MARGOT. You mean that silly bus-boycott lot? (page 71)	Margot is dismissive of the bus boycott, emphasising her lack of understanding of the reality of life for the Jameses.
VOICE-OVER. *Bristol coloured immigrants are grateful to the many Bristolians who gave support and sympathy in their struggle against racial discrimination.* (page 107)	A radio announcement that the colour bar has been lifted, highlighting that it was a community effort between immigrants and Bristolians, emphasising that many people did not support the colour bar, and coming together to take action was effective.

Motifs

A motif is a dominant recurring idea – like a mini-theme. A few motifs pop up repeatedly throughout the play:

Poverty

The theme of being poor underpins much of the Jameses' family life, and the family's economic circumstances are made clear from the beginning. The family don't have much but they manage; Mavis and Junior both work hard but it is clear that there isn't anything to spare, e.g. the 'sad and withering' Christmas tree, the lack of presents, the modest dinner. Despite this, Mavis doesn't hesitate to take Lorna in and provide for another mouth to feed, highlighting that Mavis is a caring and nurturing person.

Mavis has been in England for around seventeen years and is still just scraping by, emphasising that despite her hard work and skill, progression was not easy and she was still taking what she could find rather than being able to settle into a job.

The lack of work opportunities for Wendell means he can't earn any money and remains poor. He has skills and the potential to earn, but society is not giving him a chance.

Margot's small bedsit room suggest that she is in a similar position.

Religion

Odimba presents religion as something that is important to Mavis and her family life. Religion is often very important to people, and many immigrants found comfort in keeping up their traditional ways of life, including religious rituals.

Both Princess and Junior use religious references to try to get each other into trouble.

Mavis refers to God when she is angry at Junior, she uses a religious reference when she is shocked at Wendell's arrival, and when she raises the knife to Wendell she asks for God's forgiveness.

Saying grace before dinner is an important part of the meal, especially for Mavis.

Later, Wendell refers to Mavis as a creation of God, and when Mavis tells Wendell about her dreams, she tells him that she prays they will come true.

Beauty standards

Princess's fascination with beauty queens highlights ideas about beauty standards both then and now. Throughout history there has been an 'ideal shape' for women to aspire to and, although this shape has changed and evolved, the idea of a definite beauty aesthetic hasn't changed very much at all.

The children at Princess's school would have clear idea about what beauty queens should look like according to beauty standards of the time, and Princess would not have fitted into this idea, which would have been difficult for her.

One of the ways in which this theme recurs is through hair. Princess describes the beauty queens as having 'perfect straight shiny hair all down to their waist' and we later learn that Princess's hair is one of the reasons the children say she can't win the pageant. Barbara tells Lorna that she can wear her hair like hers at the party, suggesting that this is a way that Lorna fits in with the girls and Princess doesn't. Later in Margot's flat when Princess has cut her hair, we learn that Margot wears a wig over her 'limp and lacklustre hair'.

Pioneers

Odimba presents both Mavis and Junior as **pioneers**. Mavis represents a group of people who arrived in the UK and started a new life, bringing elements of their own life and culture while **assimilating** into a new culture. We can see through Mavis's use of language and her friendship with Margot that she is settling into a new life while continuing to remember her old life.

> *Keyword:* A **pioneer** is a person who is among the first to explore or settle a new country or area, or to do an activity.

Junior represents a first generation of people who were born in the UK to parents who were immigrants. Junior and his friends are ambitious and creative, wanting to pursue their photography dreams. They represent a generation who were growing up feeling like they could chase their dreams despite the difficulties they faced being Black in the UK.

> 🖉 **Playwright insight:** This idea about her play's characters being pioneers us a theme that is particularly important to Odimba.

Structure, Form and Language

Structure

The structure of a play is the way it is organised. Books are often written in chapters, and plays are commonly written in acts, divided into scenes. *Princess & The Hustler* is written in three acts: Act One has seven scenes, Act Two has five scenes and Act Three has six scenes.

Timeline

Act One, Scene One: 25th December – Christmas Day 1962 –
 Cupboard room and front room
Act One, Scene Two: 25th December, ten minutes later – Front room
Act One, Scene Three: 25th December, a few minutes later – Front room
Act One, Scene Four: 25th December, 'meanwhile' (at the same time) –
 Bedroom
Act One, Scene Five: Half an hour later – Front room
Act One, Scene Six: Three days later (28th December) – The docks
Act One, Scene Seven: January 1963 – Front room

Act Two, Scene One: May 1963 – Front room
Act Two, Scene Two: June 1963 – Cupboard room and front room
Act Two, Scene Three: June 1963 – Front room
Act Two, Scene Four: July 1963 – Front room
Act Two, Scene Five: 24th August 1963 – Front room

Act Three, Scene One: 24th August 1963, evening – Front room
Act Three, Scene Two: 24th August 1963, even later that evening –
 Margot's bedsit
Act Three, Scene Three: 25th August 1963 – Front room
Act Three, Scene Four: 28th August 1963 – Front room

Act Three, Scene Five: 28th August 1963 – Front room
Act Three, Scene Six: September 1963 – Front room and cupboard room

The three-act structure has a beginning, middle and end, and follows a specific pattern.

- Act One is the set-up or **exposition**, and the **inciting action** happens. The inciting action is the thing that happens to the **protagonist** (main character) that sets them on a particular path. The inciting action in Act One is the unexpected arrival of Wendell. We also hear about the idea of the bus boycott, and the first act ends with Mavis agreeing to let Wendell move in.

> *Keyword:* **Exposition** is the background information about the characters and the setting that is explained at the start of a story. The exposition will usually contain information about things that have happened before the story begins.

- Act Two is the confrontation, where we see the **rising action** in the play. The rising action is where the tension starts to build. In *Princess & The Hustler*, Act Two begins with Princess not being invited to Barbara's party. The action builds to a climax and we see tensions rise between Margot and Wendell, leading to the breakdown in Mavis's friendship with Margot, Lorna's rejection of Princess, Junior offering Wendell money to leave and Princess cutting her hair and destroying her cupboard room.

- Act Three is the resolution, categorised by the **falling action**. The falling action is what happens after the climax and where conflict starts to be resolved. In *Princess & The Hustler*, Mavis discovers Princess's hair and they realise she is missing, as well as Wendell. Junior admits to offering Wendell money to leave but Margot returns Princess to much relief. Wendell returns to a frosty reception which soon thaws with the return of Junior's money and the news that the bus boycott has been successful.

Passage of time

The structure of *Princess & The Hustler* is **linear**, meaning the action runs in a straight line from 25th December 1962 until September 1963.

Foreshadowing

Foreshadowing is when something happens that hints to the audience about what is to come. In Act One, Scene One, Mavis *'walks to the door and opens it – She shuts the door quickly and goes back to clearing the table.'* (page 14) Mavis's actions tell the audience a lot. It is Christmas Day and the mood in the James family is festive and cheerful as they get ready for lunch. Mavis is expecting it to be a neighbour with undercooked mince pies at the door and she is still laughing from her joke with the children when she opens the door. Her abrupt change in mood immediately tells the audience that something is wrong. This continues into Scene Two when *'ten minutes have passed'* and *'the knocking at the door is persistent now.'* (page 15)

Repetition

An example of repetition in *Princess & The Hustler* is Princess's cupboard room.

In Act One, Scene One, the cupboard room *'explodes into a world of pageantry – scenes of people jumping into a swimming pool, Union Jacks, music and fireworks – fill the stage.'* (page 6) We feel the full excitement of Princess's fantasy and this tells the audience a lot about her imagination and her character.

We see the cupboard room repeated in Act Two, Scene Two, after Barbara has not invited Princess to her party. Here the room *'explodes into a world of pageantry – seems less alive... still there... but somehow subdued.'* (page 66) This change in Princess's fantasy world reflects her inner feelings: she feels less like herself now because of her rejection at school. She tries to play her game, but we see that her confidence has been affected by what the children have said, 'I want to be the prettiest girl in the whole of Weston-Super-Mare and Bristol... But everyone in school says I can't be...'

At the end of Act Two, when the tension reaches its climax, we see the cupboard room repeated again but this time *'we see it for just what it is. A dark room, strewn with mop and bucket, brooms and other rejected items from the household.'* (page 88) Princess's destruction of her safe space indicates her struggle with the family tension and the impact it has had on her.

The final time the audience see the cupboard room is when the conflict in the play has been resolved. Mavis has built Princess's self-esteem back up and Wendell has allowed Princes to dress him up and bring him into her fantasy world. To reflect Princess's increased confidence and happiness, when the cupboard room comes alive, *'for the first time she imagines a pageant where all the beauty queens look like her'* and we see *'a line of the most beautiful Black women of all sizes and nations.'* (page 109)

Dramatic irony

Dramatic irony is when the audience know something that the characters don't. An example of this is when Lorna is pushed into the bedroom with Princess and Junior. When Lorna at first refuses the lollipop from Junior, saying 'Daddy says I can't take things from strangers' (page 23), it is dramatic irony because Lorna sees Junior and Princess as strangers but the audience know that they are all siblings.

Tension

Tension moves the dramatic action forwards in a play. In *Princess & The Hustler* there is a lot of tension for different reasons, and it rises and falls as the story unfolds. The tension in the play begins quickly and builds in a number of ways.

Moments of high tension:

- Mavis opens and shuts the door.
- Princess opens the door and Wendell comes in.
- Mavis slaps Princess.
- Mavis slaps Wendell.
- Princess is not invited to Barbara's party.
- Wendell challenges Margot's behaviour at the club and Margot disagrees with the bus boycott.
- Junior returns from the protest and has been attacked.
- Lorna tells Princess she doesn't want a sister.
- Margot confronts Mavis about Wendell.
- Junior offers Wendell money to leave.
- Princess destroys her cupboard room.
- Princess is missing.

Form

A play's form is its dramatic style. *Princess & The Hustler* follows some quite traditional conventions from a style referred to as the 'well-made play':

- It has a three-act structure (see page 123).

- The play is plot-driven, which means the story focuses on the things the characters have to deal with. (In a character-driven play the story would focus more on why the characters deal with things the way they do.)

- It has a plot based on facts that the audience know but not all of the characters are aware of. At the beginning of the play, Princess does not know that Wendell is her father and Princess and Junior do not know that Lorna is their sister.

- There is a strong central plot, and the action is connected by cause and effect, e.g. when a character does something this affects how the story progresses.

- The action is increasingly tense.

- There is usually a revelation or a misunderstanding. The revelation in *Princess & The Hustler* comes quite quickly, with the identity of Wendell and Lorna being revealed.

- It has a logical and believable conclusion, usually depicting an ending that the audience want. In *Princess & The Hustler* the audience want the bus boycott to be successful and for Princess to return to herself.

✐ **Playwright insight:** Odimba often experiments with form in her work, but *Princess & The Hustler* uses a traditional form. Odimba felt that it was so important that the story was the main focus for the audience that a traditional form best suited this play.

Princess & The Hustler is a play, not a novel – it is written to be performed, which means there are certain conventions that we would expect to find:

Stage directions

The most detailed stage directions are for Princess's cupboard room. They give quite exact instructions for what Odimba wants to create. Many of the stage directions also give important information about the characters.

Mavis gives him the coldest stare imaginable. (page 58)	Mavis does not want Wendell to stay and has only agreed to please Princess, so when Wendell makes a joke about Mavis being tempted by him, she is not impressed.
Wendell sits back down at the table and smiles wryly to himself – (page 58)	Mavis has just agreed to let Wendell stay and given him her rules. Wendell's wry smile suggest that he has got exactly what he wanted and his plan is coming together. It is also important that Mavis has exited before this, so the audience see the smile but Mavis doesn't.
Margot pours herself another large glass of rum – which she downs in one mouthful – (page 72)	Margot helping herself to another drink tells the audience that she is comfortable and familiar in Mavis's home and company. Margot downing the drink in one mouthful clearly indicates her mood.

Set

The action takes place in five locations, which are described on page 4 of the playtext:

1. Memories of home.

2. The flat isn't really big enough for the family.

3. Family meals are important.

4. Important sign of Mavis's work.

5. Mavis has created a comfortable home for the children.

The front room – A small front room with an even smaller kitchenette in the corner of the room. It is decorated sparsely with pictures of the **Caribbean and family members**[1] on the walls. There is a **small sofa**[2] and a **dining table**,[3] where a **sewing machine**[4] sits occasionally. A wireless radio sits on a small mantelpiece. The walls are decorated with a bold vibrant green pattern and the carpet is brown and white, colours that were popular at the time. **The flat is clean, neat and tidy.**[5]

Cupboard room – A large cupboard big enough to stand and walk in – not big enough for a bed. The room stores household items such as a **mop, bucket and brooms**,[1] as well as Princess's **costumes and her artwork and decorations**[2] on the walls and ceiling. The cupboard is behind a curtain positioned **upstage left**.[3] When Princess is in it, the room is brightly lit in pinks and purples.

The other room – This is the bedroom that Princess and Junior share at first, and later Junior shares with Wendell.

The docks – The play is set in Bristol in the 1960s when the docks would have been a place of work and industry.[4]

Margot's bedsit – A small bedsit room with a dresser and mirror.

1. A functional space that is transformed by Princess's imagination.

2. The things that help transform the room into the world of pageantry.

3. Turn to the Glossary on page 151 to see a diagram of how a stage is described.

4. *Context:* To read more about this setting, turn to page 23.

Costume

The play is set in the 1960s, so costumes would have reflected the fashion at the time. Mavis is a seamstress so it's likely that she would be wearing handmade clothes, as would Princess. Although this wasn't unusual at the time, buying fashionable clothes from shops was becoming more popular. As teenagers, Junior and Leon would be likely to be wearing clothes that were fashionable.

How do you think Mavis and Margot dress? Are there similarities or are they very different?

Do you think there would be differences between how Princess and Lorna are dressed?

Sound

The play uses a voice-over which booms out that Princess is the winner in her fantasy, as well as to announce the news that the colour bar has been lifted.

> ✏ **Playwright insight:** The music used in the original production of the play was all music from the 1960s, with the exception of the final beauty queen parade, when a Beyoncé song was used. Odimba says that the use of a contemporary song at the end of the play was to connect a story from the past with today. The struggles that Princess faces are still happening now and it was important to highlight that.

Dialogue

Odimba uses dialogue that portrays realistic speech in many ways. In the text, characters trail off at the end of sentences at times (indicted by '…'), and characters also overlap each other (indicated by '/') when they are speaking, which makes the speech more realistic.

Language

You will be expected to write about how Odimba uses different literary techniques in the play, and the effect of these techniques.

Use of language

Mavis uses a mix of Standard English and Jamaican Patois: 'Yuh two children fool fool fram mawnin' till night! […] You watch yourselves and don't bring no mess to my house you hear me.' (page 14). The phrase 'fool fool', meaning silly, and the pronunciation of 'morning' emphasises Mavis's Jamaican accent. This mix of language shows that Mavis is used to speaking a more standard version of English with the children, but lapses into patois when she is joking with them.

Mavis uses patois more when she is angry. 'Mi nuh *vex* Wendell. Mi beyon' vex. Mi angry. Mi angry nuff to kill yuh right 'ere an' den go tell yuh modder why.' (page 19) Mavis's use of only patois when she is shocked and angry shows us that when she is emotional she is more likely to use language that comes more naturally to her, suggesting that Mavis's use of Standard English in her everyday speech is more of an effort.

> Why do you think Mavis chooses to use a more standard form of English most of the time?

Wendell uses Jamaican patois all of the time, regardless of who he is speaking to. 'De bwoy gon' broke 'im voice.' (page 17)

> What does Wendell's consistent use of Jamaican patois tell us about him?

Princess, **Junior**, **Lorna** and **Leon** all mainly use Standard English and occasionally youth slang: Junior says 'I split from those guys...' (page 9), and 'That is so uncool.' (page 10); Leon says 'Cool it Junior. You dig?' (page 53). There is also a hint of Lorna's northern dialect when she says 'She said she's going to do them into ringlets for me. Nice like t' other girls at school.' (page 78)

Margot uses a more non-standard form of English with her Bristolian dialect. 'If only the silly cow dinned start throwing all my stuff out the door first. Dinned have much choice.' (page 35)

> ✏ **Playwright insight:** Odimba wanted the way the characters speak to reflect their relationship with England. Wendell doesn't feel welcomed or settled here and his use of only Jamaican patois reflects this. Mavis has made a great effort to **assimilate** (fit in) and her use of mainly Standard English indicates this. Junior and Leon use language that puts them into a group with teenagers of the time.

Symbolism

There is symbolism throughout the play, in that each of the characters is symbolic of a particular example of life experience for people in 1960s England. For example, Wendell is symbolic of the way in which the poor treatment of immigrants when they arrived in the UK could lead to wider problems; and the fact that he chooses to continue to speak in Jamaican patois rather than **assimilating** in the way that Mavis has done is symbolic of his pushing against his poor treatment. Meanwhile Margot is symbolic of British people who were inclusive and not openly racist up to a point, but who were ultimately most concerned about their own and their families' jobs rather than ending discrimination.

There are also symbolic moments, for example:

- Princess cutting her hair is symbolic of her disillusionment and her broken dream of becoming a beauty queen.

- Princess's cupboard world losing its lustre is symbolic of the same thing.

- When Junior takes a picture of the whole family together, and then the family speaks in unison, it is symbolic of the new connection that has been forged between them all.

Can you think of other examples of symbolism in the play?

Imagery

Odimba uses metaphor to create strong images. One of the most powerful metaphors is when Wendell says 'An' I never plan to be nuh strange fruit.' (page 55) The image of bodies hanging from trees is striking, and the audience are left in no doubt about how scared Wendell would have been to think that this might happen to him.

Essay Questions and How to Answer Them

Understanding the question

In the exam you will be required to answer a question based on the whole play. The first thing to do is break down the question so you understand exactly what it is asking.

> **Question: How does Odimba present ideas about prejudice in _Princess & The Hustler_?**
>
> Write about:
>
> - How Odimba presents prejudice.
>
> - The impact of prejudice on the characters.

The first thing to identify is the key word **prejudice**. Next, the use of the word '**present**' tells you that you need to write about the techniques Odimba uses to show prejudice.

Planning

You need to plan quickly and efficiently, so briefly list your main ideas:

- Wendell experiences prejudice when he first arrives in England.

- Princess doesn't get invited to Barbara's party.

- Junior is attacked after the protests.

Try to add useful quotations:

- Wendell experiences prejudice when he first arrives in England. ('When mi come to dis country I was ar good man', 'but it never make far respect'.)
- Princess doesn't get invited to Barbara's party. ('Barbara says she can't invite Phyllis!')
- Junior is attacked after the protests. ('They jumped us in town.')

Plan each point:

Introduction

Introduce the argument you are making: Odimba presents prejudice as an important theme in the play which has a negative impact on many of the characters and their lives.

Point 1

How prejudice is presented? Wendell experiences prejudice when he first arrives in England. He was a lieutenant in the army, but when he arrives he is told to take a low-paid office job.

The impact? Wendell struggles to find work and this affects his behaviour.

Evidence? Use a quotation and explain how it supports your point.

Point 2

How prejudice is presented? Princess experiences prejudice when she doesn't get invited to Barbara's party.

The impact? This hurts her more because Lorna is invited. Lorna says Barbara can't invite Princess. Princess starts to become sad and quiet after this.

Evidence? Use a quotation and explain how it supports your point.

Point 3

How prejudice is presented? Junior experiences prejudice when he is attacked after the protest.

The impact? Wendell is really angry that this has happened to his son, and he rushes out. This links to Wendell feeling afraid when he lived with Lorna's mother.

Evidence? Use a quotation and explain how it supports your point.

Conclusion

Sum up what you have said: Prejudice is presented as a key theme in this play. It affects both the children and the adults and the way they live their lives. Odimba suggests that prejudice will continue to be a significant part of the characters' lives.

Assessment Objectives 1 and 2

Most of the marks in the exam come from Assessment Objectives 1 and 2:

AO1

Read, understand and respond to texts. You should be able to:

- maintain a critical style and develop an informed personal response.
- use textual references, including quotations, to support and illustrate interpretations.

This means that you need to write in a formal manner, showing that you have your own ideas. You need to accurately use some of the literary terms you have learned, and support what you say with evidence.

AO2

Analyse the language, form and structure used by a writer to create meanings and effects, using relevant subject terminology where appropriate.

- Analyse – write in detail about particular parts of the text or language used.
- Language – words/vocabulary, imagery, dialogue, type of sentence used.
- Form – the style of the play and how it is told.
- Structure – the way the play is organised, the order in which things happen.
- Create meanings – what conclusions can you make from what Odimba tells us

in the play? What can you infer (conclude) from what is implied (indirectly said) in the text?

- Subject terminology – the language you should use when you are writing about a play, e.g. character, audience, stage directions, scenes; and words that refer to literary techniques used by the playwright, e.g. metaphor, tone, dramatic irony, foreshadowing.

Inference phrases

Throughout your answer you will need to be **inferring**. This means that you will be interpreting meaning from the play, e.g. Princess destroys her cupboard room. From Princess' actions you can **infer** that she is upset. She doesn't say she is upset, but we know that she is from how she behaves. To vary your writing you can use a range of inference phrases:

Instead of 'shows'	Instead of 'suggests'	Instead of 'draws attention to'
Explains	Symbolises	Reveals
Portrays	Signifies	Emphasises
Depicts	Represents	Underlines
Illustrates	Implies	Highlights
Expresses	Indicates	Clarifies
Demonstrates		

You will be marked on your spelling, punctuation and grammar, so aim to be accurate.

- Make a list of key spellings and learn them before the exam.

- Try to use a range of punctuation and avoid using either very short or very long wordy sentences.

- Always use the present tense to discuss the text and the writer's techniques. e.g. 'Princess *is* an imaginative child who *uses* her pageant world to explore her dreams of becoming a beauty queen.'

Sample essays

Character-focused

Question: How does Junior respond to the return of Wendell?

Write about:

- How Odimba presents the character of Junior.

- Why he responds in the way he does.

Mid-level response

Odimba presents Junior as a teenager who is protective of his mother and sister. He wants to take care of them and therefore is concerned when Wendell returns.[1]

In Act One, when Wendell first arrives, Junior and the rest of the family are surprised by his visit.[2] Mavis tells the children to go into the bedroom but Junior says, 'You want me to stay?' This shows that he wants to make sure that his mother is all right being alone with Wendell.[3]

Junior makes it clear that he does not think Wendell is part of their family, he does this when Mavis allows Wendell to stay for Christmas lunch. This can be seen in the stage directions when it says, 'He scrapes the chair noisily away from the table and sits as far away from Wendell as possible'. Doing this, Junior is showing a lack of respect for his father, this is particularly important as showing a lack of respect for an adult or parent in those days could result in physical punishment.[4] Risking this type of punishment shows that Junior's feelings about his father are so strong that he is willing to accept this if necessary. Junior continues to show that he does not want Wendell to stay when he repeatedly asks when Wendell and Lorna are leaving, 'How long are they staying for?' This shows that he is happy to question why his father is there as he has no respect for him.[5]

> 1. Introduces the main basic characteristics of Junior to clearly link to the question.

> 2. A new point is clearly signalled in a new paragraph. This point clearly links to the question.

> 3. The point is linked to a quotation and then explained.

> 4. Referring to the context in which the play is set.

> 5. Explaining the significance of the quotation, but closer analysis needed. Consider Odimba's use of the pronoun 'they', and include terminology.

6. Unnecessary description. The first sentence in this paragraph is all that is needed to make a clear point.

Junior shows that he thinks Wendell is irresponsible when he finds that he has left Princess and Lorna on the side of the docks. Wendell took them to the docks as he was playing cards there and hoping to win some money. He does not tell them what he is doing but says that he will be back soon.[6] Junior says to Wendell, 'you left them here waiting in this place on their own'. Junior's comment shows that he thinks Wendell cannot be trusted as a father to look after his daughters.

Later in the play, Junior shows that he still wants his father to leave because he is concerned about Mavis. We can see this when he says, 'I remember hearing her crying'. This shows us that he understands how much Wendell hurt Mavis when he left and he does not want her to be hurt again.

7. Draw ideas together at the end to reach a conclusion. Try to come up with an interesting final way to address the question.

At the end of the play Junior has accepted Wendell into the family, he shows this by taking a picture of them all on his camera.[7]

Good-level response

1. Introduction that clearly addresses the question and shows understanding of the character of Junior.

Odimba presents Junior as a teenager who is protective of his mother and sister, he has undertaken the role of father figure since Wendell left and therefore the return of his father is of great concern to Junior, as he feels both that his role is threatened and that Wendell cannot be trusted.[1]

2. A new point that clearly signals a new paragraph. This point distinctly links to the question.

In Act One, when Wendell first arrives, Junior and the rest of the family are surprised by his visit.[2] Mavis tells the children to go into the bedroom but Junior asks his mother if she wants him to 'stay'[3] so that she does not have to be alone with Wendell who is not welcome in their home. The use of the word 'stay' and the question that Junior is putting to his mother shows that he is not intimidated by the arrival of his father and that he still sees his mother as the one who is in charge.[4]

3. A quotation that is embedded fluently in the sentence.

4. Zooming in on the quotation and clearly explaining its effect.

Junior makes it clear that he does not think Wendell is part of their family, he does this when Mavis allows Wendell to stay for Christmas lunch. This can be seen in the stage directions when it says, 'He scrapes the chair noisily away from the table and sits as far away from Wendell as possible'. Doing this, Junior is showing a lack of respect for his father, this is particularly important as showing a lack of respect for an adult or parent in those days could result in physical punishment. The reality of this threat of physical punishment has already been shown in the play when Mavis 'turns and slaps Princess across the face' when she does not leave the room as she has been told to do.[5] Risking this type of punishment shows that Junior's feelings for his father are so strong that he is willing to accept this if necessary. Junior continues to show that he does not want Wendell to stay when he asks repeatedly when Wendell and Lorna are leaving, 'How long are they staying for?' This shows that he is happy to question why his father is there as he has no respect for him. Junior's use of the pronoun 'they' shows that he is unwilling to call Wendell his father or use names at this point, which highlights a lack of closeness in their relationship.[6]

Junior also shows that he thinks Wendell is irresponsible when he finds that he has left Princess and Lorna on the side of the docks.[7] Junior says to Wendell, 'you left them here waiting in this place on their own'. Junior's comment shows that he thinks Wendell cannot be trusted as a father to look after his daughters.

Later in the play, Junior shows that he still wants his father to leave because he is concerned about Mavis. We can see this when he says, 'I remember hearing her crying'. This shows us that he understands how much Wendell hurt Mavis when he left and he does not want her to be hurt again. Junior's comment here can be linked to his earlier question to his mother, 'You want me to stay?', as this shows that Junior sees his mother as vulnerable to Wendell because of the effect he had on her in the past, and therefore Junior does not want to hear 'her crying' again.[8]

> 5. Reference to the context of the play and a clear link to the rest of the play.

> 6. Using terminology and explaining its relevance.

> 7. Uses a **discourse marker** to make a clear link to the previous paragraph.

> *Keyword:* **Discourse markers** are words and phrases used to connect ideas together, e.g. 'also', 'alternatively', 'in addition', 'on the other hand'.

> 8. Detailed analysis that comments on structure as well as language.

9. A clear conclusion that shows an understanding of the development in the relationship between Junior and Wendell.

At the end of the play Junior has accepted Wendell into the family, and he shows this by taking a picture of them all on his camera. This action from Junior highlights a change in his attitude towards Wendell. The hostility and lack of trust that was shown at the beginning of the play has now changed into an acceptance of his father and his role within their family.[9]

High-level response

1. Excellent, cogent opening that clearly understands the relationship between Junior and Wendell.

Junior's hostile and antagonistic reaction to the reappearance of his father in the family home springs from a desire to protect his mother and sister and is clearly linked to the unanticipated return of Wendell.[1] This hostility symbolises Junior's awareness of the hardships that Mavis has been forced to suffer as a single mother and Black woman in 1960s Bristol.[2]

2. Follows on using a literary device linking the text with the context in which it is set.

Wendell's first introduction to the audience, and indeed Junior and Princess, in Act One builds tension on the stage. The reaction to this entrance is one of 'shock' and Junior, the audience is told in the stage directions, 'remain[s] still – frozen', reinforcing his complete lack of readiness for this meeting and his lack of control over it.[3] Although this stage direction describes the physical reaction of Junior, it can also be seen to symbolise his emotional response to this event.[4]

3. Quotations clearly and seamlessly embedded in the text.

4. Clear consideration of form and inclusion of an alternative interpretation.

Junior makes it clear that he does not think Wendell is part of their family, he does this when Mavis allows Wendell to stay for Christmas lunch. This can be seen in the stage directions, 'He scrapes the chair noisily away from the table and sits as far away from Wendell as possible'. Odimba's utilisation of onomatopoeia by means of the verb 'scrape' displays the disharmony that Junior feels Wendell is introducing into their family home,[5] which is further reinforced as he undertakes this action 'noisily' to ensure that Wendell is completely aware of his feelings towards his father, thus immediately creating conflict between the two of them.[6] Junior continues to show that he does not want Wendell to stay by asking repeatedly when Wendell and Lorna are leaving: 'How long are they staying for?' This shows that he is happy to question why his father is there as he has no respect for him. Junior's use of the pronoun 'they' shows that he is unwilling to call Wendell father or use names at this point, which highlights a lack of closeness in their relationship.

5. Literary device and its effect highlighted through close analysis of language.

6. Further close analysis to make a point more sophisticated.

Junior also shows that he thinks Wendell is irresponsible when he finds that he has left Princess and Lorna on the side of the docks. Junior says to Wendell, 'you left them here waiting in this place on their own'. Junior's comment shows that he thinks Wendell cannot be trusted as a father to look after his daughters. The lack of trust that Junior feels towards his father is a significant aspect of the failure in their relationship, and the audience could interpret this incident as a metaphor for Wendell leaving his son, the docks here being symbolic of the family home and Princess and Lorna representing Mavis and the children.[7]

> 7. Sophisticated alternative reading to consider the incident metaphorically.

Later in the play, Junior shows that he still wants his father to leave because he is concerned about Mavis. We can see this when he says, 'I remember hearing her crying'. This shows us that he understands how much Wendell hurt Mavis when he left and he does not want her to be hurt again. Junior's comment here can be linked to his earlier question to his mother, 'You want me to stay?', as this shows that Junior sees his mother as vulnerable to Wendell because of the effect he had on her in the past and therefore Junior does not want to hear 'her crying' again. Odimba's use of an interrogative sentence also highlights his indecision caused by Wendell's arrival and his appeal to his mother as the adult whom he can trust.[8]

> 8. Uses terminology and considers sentence function.

At the end of the play, Junior has accepted Wendell into the family, and he shows this by taking a picture of them all on his camera. This action from Junior highlights a change in his attitude towards Wendell. The hostility and lack of trust that was shown at the beginning of the play has now changed into an acceptance of his father and his role within their family. This gesture can also be interpreted symbolically, as the audience are aware of how significant Junior's camera is to him. Furthermore, a photograph creates a permanent image, therefore highlighting to the audience that Junior has begun to accept Wendell as a permanent father figure in his life.[9]

> 9. A sophisticated conclusion that considers the relationship between Junior and Wendell both structurally and symbolically.

Theme-focused

Question: How does Odimba present ideas about prejudice in *Princess & The Hustler*?

Write about:

- How Odimba presents prejudice.

- The impact of prejudice on the characters.

Mid-level response

1. Focuses the essay on the question, with a clear point that shows an understanding of the significance of prejudice to the play as a whole.	Odimba presents prejudice as an important theme in the play which has a negative impact on many of the characters and their lives.[1]

In Act One, Wendell explains how he first encountered prejudice when he came to England and how, even now, he is still experiencing the same racial prejudice.[2] Wendell tells Junior and Leon about his experiences, 'Wha' kinda world put men in de same sentence as dogs?' This shows that Wendell is seen as more like an animal than a human being.[3]

2. A new point is clearly signalled in a new paragraph. This point clearly links to the question.

3. The point is linked to a quotation and then explained.

4. Referring to the context in which the play is set.

5. Explaining the significance of the quotation, but closer analysis needed. Consider the use of the noun 'things' and include terminology.

Princess is another character within the play who experiences prejudice, this can be seen when Lorna is invited to the party of one of their classmates and Princess is not. Lorna says, 'Barbara says she can't invite Phyllis!' Barbara's comment suggests that she is not able to ask Princess to her party, this is significant as it suggests that her parents are not allowing her to invite a classmate based on the colour of her skin. This form of prejudice in 1960s England was common, often non-white people were treated differently and this was seen as socially acceptable.[4] Wendell and Mavis both agree that Lorna should not go to the party but Wendell does not think he needs to tell her why, he says to Mavis, 'Where she come fram dese things nuh spoken 'bout Mavis'. This shows that Wendell is so used to this type of prejudice that he accepts it rather than fights against it.[5]

Prejudice is presented through other characters in the play and their response to it. The audience see this when Margot gives her opinions regarding the bus boycott. She does this when she is drinking with Mavis and Wendell, she talks about her brother Dan who she thinks might lose his job because of what is happening and she is unhappy about this.[6] Margot says to Wendell, 'You just have to accept how things are'. Her comment shows that she does not recognise the prejudice that the Black bus drivers are experiencing is a particular problem, it is something that they have to put up with.

Later in the play, prejudice is also presented as something that is displayed through physical violence. This is shown when Junior is attacked whilst involved in the bus-boycott protest. We are told by Junior that, 'They jumped us in town'. Here the protestors are attacked in order to prevent them from demonstrating.

Prejudice is presented as a key theme in this play. It affects both the children and the adults and the way in which they are forced to live their lives.[7]

Good-level response

Odimba presents prejudice as having a significant impact on the narrative of the play. Many of the characters experience the harsh realities of prejudice and the influence and control it has over their lives and the decisions that they are forced to make.[1]

In Act One, Wendell explains how he first encountered prejudice when he came to England and how, even now, he is still experiencing the same racial prejudice.[2] When describing his experiences to Junior and Leon, Wendell uses the word 'dogs' in the same sentence as he uses 'men'.[3] The use of the word 'dogs' presents Black people as being seen by society as not only inferior to white people but subhuman.[4]

---

6. Unnecessary description. The first two sentences in this paragraph are all that are needed to make a clear point.

7. Draw ideas together at the end to reach a conclusion. Try to come up with an interesting final way to address the question.

1. Introduction that clearly addresses the question and shows understanding of the impact of prejudice on the narrative and the characters.

2. A new point that clearly signals a new paragraph. This point distinctly links to the question.

3. A quotation that is embedded fluently in the sentence.

4. Zooming in on the quotation and clearly explaining its effect.

Princess is another character within the play who experiences prejudice, this can be seen when Lorna is invited to the party of one of their classmates and Princess is not. Lorna says, 'Barbara says she can't invite Phyllis!' Barbara's comment suggests that she is not able to ask Princess to her party, this is significant as it suggests that her parents are not allowing her to invite a classmate based on the colour of her skin. This form of prejudice in 1960s England was common, often non-white people were treated differently and this was seen as socially acceptable. This racial prejudice has already been shown to the audience at the beginning of the play when Princess tells Mavis that she was 'the best in the class' which impressed her teacher, 'considering [her] ability', an obvious reference to the notion that Black people were less intelligent than white.[5] Wendell and Mavis both agree that Lorna should not go to the party but Wendell does not think he needs to tell her why, he says to Mavis, 'Where she come fram dese things nuh spoken 'bout Mavis'. This shows that Wendell is so used to this type of prejudice that he accepts it rather than fights against it. Wendell's use of the common noun 'things' rather than the terms 'prejudice' or 'racism', suggests that he has no control over preventing them or changing attitudes towards him or his daughter, therefore his language is the only way in which he can distance himself from them.[6]

Prejudice is also presented through other characters in the play and their response to it.[7] The audience see this when Margot gives her opinions regarding the bus boycott. Margot says to Wendell, 'You just have to accept how things are'. Her comment shows that she does not recognise the prejudice that the Black bus drivers are experiencing is a particular problem, it is something that they have to put up with.

Later in the play, prejudice is also presented as something that is displayed through physical violence. This is shown when Junior is attacked whilst involved in the bus-boycott protest. We are told by Junior that, 'They jumped us in town'. Here the protestors are attacked in order to prevent them from demonstrating. Junior's description here of the violence enacted against him can be linked to Wendell's comments earlier in the play regarding lynching, when he describes to Junior how he came back to Lorna's mother's house 'to find ar rope hanging fram de tree', showing the audience that Wendell has also experienced the threat of physical violence.[8]

5. Reference to the context of the play and a clear link to the rest of the play.

6. Using terminology and explaining its relevance.

7. Shifts successfully to a new paragraph. Uses discourse markers to make a clear link to the previous paragraph.

8. Detailed analysis that comments on structure as well as language.

Prejudice is presented as a key theme in this play. It affects both the children and the adults and the way in which they are forced to live their lives. By the end of the play, Odimba suggests that prejudice will continue to be a significant part of the characters' lives in 1960s England, but the overturning of the bus boycott reinforces the idea that this prejudice should not simply be accepted.[9]

> 9. A clear conclusion that shows an understanding of the significance of prejudice to the play and its impact on the narrative and the characters.

High-level response

Odimba presents prejudice in many aspects of the narrative. Its centrality highlights to the audience the situation of many of the characters in the play, and the perception of them as outsiders.[1]

> 1. Excellent, cogent opening that clearly understands the significance of prejudice within the setting of the play.

In Act One, Wendell explains to Junior (and thereby the audience) how he first encountered prejudice when he came to England and how, even now, he is still experiencing the same racial prejudice. He tells of how although he was a 'good man', 'it never make far respec'', reinforcing his complete lack of control over the situation.[2] When describing his experiences to Junior and Leon, Wendell uses the noun 'dogs' in the same sentence as he uses 'men'. Although the use of the word 'dogs' presents society's perception of Black people as inferior to white people, almost subhuman, it can also be seen to reinforce the lack of power that Wendell had in that situation, placing him firmly at the bottom of the hierarchy.[3]

> 2. Quotations clearly and seamlessly embedded in the text.

> 3. Clear consideration of an alternative interpretation.

Princess is another character within the play who also experiences prejudice, this can be seen when Lorna is invited to the party of one of their classmates and Princess is not. Lorna says, 'Barbara says she can't invite Phyllis!' Odimba's utilisation of the contraction 'can't' suggests that this is not a decision made by Barbara and that society's prejudices, symbolised by her parents, have prevented Princess being given an invitation.[4] This separation is reinforced through Lorna's previous comment, 'But she asked *me*'. Splitting these utterances, Odimba reinforces the gap between Princess and Lorna's treatment by society.[5] This form of prejudice in 1960s England was common, often non-white people were treated differently and this was seen as socially acceptable. This racial prejudice has already been shown to the audience at the beginning of the play when Princess tells

> 4. Literary device and its effect highlighted through close analysis of language.

> 5. Further close analysis of structure to make a point more sophisticated.

Mavis that she was 'the best in the class' which impressed her teacher, 'considering [her] ability', an obvious reference to the notion that Black people were less intelligent than white. Wendell and Mavis both agree that Lorna should not go to the party but Wendell does not think he needs to tell her why, he says to Mavis, 'Where she come fram dese things nuh spoken 'bout Mavis'. This shows that Wendell is so used to this type of prejudice that he accepts it rather than fights against it. Wendell's use of the common noun 'things' rather than the terms 'prejudice' or 'racism' suggests that as he has no control over preventing them or changing attitudes towards him or his daughter, therefore his language is the only way in which he can distance himself from them.

Prejudice is also presented through other characters in the play and their response to it. The audience see this when Margot gives her opinions regarding the bus boycott. Margot says to Wendell, 'You just have to accept how things are'. Her comment shows that she does not recognise the prejudice that the Black bus drivers are experiencing is a particular problem, it is something that they have to put up with. Her comment here could also be seen to symbolise England's attitude to race relations in the 1960s, the notion that 'You', the Black members of the community, should simply accept their inferior position in society.[6]

Later in the play, prejudice is also presented as something that is displayed through physical violence. This is shown when Junior is attacked whilst involved in the bus-boycott protest. We are told by Junior that, 'They jumped us in town'. Here the protestors are attacked in order to prevent them from demonstrating. Junior's description here of the violence enacted against him can be linked to Wendell's comments earlier in the play regarding lynching, when he describes to Junior how he came back to Lorna's mother's house 'to find ar rope hanging fram de tree', showing to the audience that Wendell has also experienced the threat of physical violence. Wendell's use of the verb 'find' highlights that physical violence can be intimated as well as carried out. The 'rope' being a powerful expression of racial prejudice.[7]

6. Sophisticated alternative reading to consider the incident metaphorically.

7. Uses terminology and links close reading to historical context.

By the end of the play, the audience have clearly been shown that prejudice has permeated the lives of all the characters, whether it be via their treatment due to the colour of their skin or through their attitudes created by a bigoted society. The overturning though of the bus boycott can be seen to reinforce the idea that this prejudice should not simply be accepted. This is further supported by the very final image that the audience is left with, of Princess in the middle of 'a line of the most beautiful Black women' – suggesting that prejudice can be overcome.[8]

> 8. A sophisticated conclusion that considers the significance of prejudice across the whole play and the intended impact of this on the audience.

More practice essay questions

Question: How does Odimba present Mavis as a strong female character in *Princess & The Hustler*?

Write about:

- What Mavis says and does.

- How far Odimba presents Mavis as a strong female character.

Question: How does Odimba use the character of Wendell to explore ideas about fatherhood?

Write about:

- What Wendell says and does.

- How Odimba uses Wendell to explore ideas about fatherhood.

Question: How does Odimba present the importance of family in *Princess & The Hustler*?

Write about:

- The importance of family to characters in the play.

- How Odimba presents the importance of family.

Question: How are the themes of hopes, dreams and ambitions presented in *Princess & The Hustler*?

Write about:

- How Odimba presents hopes, dreams and ambitions as important.

- The impact and effect of the characters' hopes, dreams and ambitions.

Question: How far does Odimba present Princess as a character who changes in *Princess & The Hustler*?

Write about:

- What Princess says and does.

- How far Odimba presents Princess as a character who changes.

Glossary

Accent – the way you pronounce words.

An **adverb** is a describing word for a verb.

To **assimilate** means to fit in by doing things in a similar way.

Catalyst – a person or thing that causes an event.

Contrast, which highlights a point of difference, is often used to emphasise ideas in literature.

Creolisation – when two or more languages and cultures blend together to create a new one.

Dialect – the words that you use, usually influenced by location.

Discourse markers are words and phrases used to connect ideas together, e.g. 'also', 'alternatively', 'in addition', 'on the other hand'.

Dramatic irony – a literary technique where the readers or audience know something that the character(s) in a scene do not.

Ellipsis is the literary term for the symbol '…'

Emphasis is sometimes indicated using italics or bold fonts in written text. It is when the speaker or writer wants to highlight something important.

Euphemism – an indirect word or expression which is substituted for one which is considered rude or embarrassing.

Exaggeration and **hyperbole** are English and Greek words meaning almost the same thing – but 'hyperbole' is particularly used when writing about literary technique: it means 'exaggeration used for effect'.

Exposition is the background information about the characters and the setting that is explained at the start of a story. The exposition will usually contain information about things that have happened before the story begins.

The **falling action** is what happens after the climax and where conflict starts to be resolved.

Hustler – a person skilled at aggressive selling or illegal dealings. Somebody who gains money from another person using deceit.

Hyperbole and exaggeration are English and Greek words meaning almost the same thing – but 'hyperbole' is particularly used when writing about literary technique: it means 'exaggeration used for effect'.

The **inciting action** is the thing that happens to the **protagonist** (main character) that sets them on a particular path.

Irony expresses meaning that is deliberately the opposite of what is meant or what is true.

Linear means that the action in a story runs in a straight line through time.

Lynching is when a mob illegally carry out the execution of someone accused of a crime, without giving them a trial.

A **metaphor** is a form of imagery where a thing is described indirectly by referring to something it resembles, without using 'like'. 'Strange fruit' is a good example from the play.

A **noun** is the type of word used for a person, place or thing.

Pejorative – a word expressing contempt or disapproval.

Personification is a type of **metaphor**, where something which is not a person is described as if it is.

Philanthropist – a person who wants to encourage the wellbeing of others, especially by the generous donation of money to good causes.

A **pioneer** is person who is among the first to explore or settle a new country or area, or to do an activity.

Possessive pronouns are words which refer to things that belong to people, such as 'my', 'your' and 'their'.

The **protagonist** is the main character in a story.

Proxemics is the use of space on stage and the distance between characters. Proxemics can tell us a lot about how characters feel about each other.

The **rising action** in a story refers to the things that happen that build to the climax of the story. This includes the development of the characters and things that create suspense.

A **simile** is a form of imagery where something is described as resembling something else. It is usually signalled with the word 'like' or 'as'. 'Because my hair is as pretty as a doll's she said' is a good example from the play.

Stage directions are written into playtexts to tell the director and actors what should happen physically on stage. Where on the stage things should happen are indicated by specific locations, which you can see in this diagram:

Upstage Right	**Upstage Centre**	**Upstage Left**
Stage Right	**Centre Stage**	**Stage Left**
Downstage Right	**Downstage Centre**	**Downstage Left**

Audience

Subtext means information which is *suggested* by the words on the page, without being said directly.

Symbolism is when symbols are used to represent ideas.

A **verb** is a word which expresses an action.

Further Reading and Research

Clickable links can be found at this book's dedicated webpage:
www.nickhernbooks.co.uk/princess-and-the-hustler-study-guide-further-resources

Books

Black and British: A short, essential history by David Olusoga

Voices of the Windrush Generation: The real story told by the people themselves by David Matthews

Homecoming: Voices of the Windrush Generation by Colin Grant

Mother Country: Real Stories of the Windrush Children by Charlie Brinkhurst-Cuff

Online material about the Windrush generation

The Bristol Museums website is full of useful information:
collections.bristolmuseums.org.uk/stories/bristols-black-history

Read about the Windrush Generation on the British Library website:

www.bl.uk/windrush/articles/windrush-and-the-making-of-post-imperial-britain

www.bl.uk/windrush/articles/how-caribbean-migrants-rebuilt-britain

A short video about the experience of Rosemarie, who migrated to the UK as a child in the 1960s as part of the Windrush generation: youtu.be/3sATGOklv2I

Videos, podcasts and articles about the play

Trailer for the play. The voice-over is Princess and you can hear her Bristolian accent: youtu.be/B81fJKoYDXU

Playwright Chinonyerem Odimba on why she wrote the play: youtu.be/iS2WgUZ7uIs

A Q&A podcast with Chinonyerem Odimba about writing the play, recorded in June 2020: www.nickhernbooks.co.uk/playgroup

The play's director Dawn Walton on the history in the play and its plot: youtu.be/ =eTtbkz2Nee8

An interview with Chinonyerem Odimba about her research process and writing the play: www.bristol247.com/culture/theatre/preview-princess-and-the-hustler-bristol-old-vic

Reviews of the original production

www.theguardian.com/stage/2019/feb/24/princess-and-the-hustler-bristol-old-vic-review

www.whatsonstage.com/news/review-the-princess-and-the-hustler-bristol-old-vic_48517

Exam board information: AQA

Assessment resources: www.aqa.org.uk/subjects/english/gcse/english-literature-8702/assessment-resources

Schemes of assessment: www.aqa.org.uk/subjects/english/gcse/english-literature-8702/scheme-of-assessment

www.nickhernbooks.co.uk

facebook.com/nickhernbooks

twitter.com/nickhernbooks